These Beans Have Too Much Salt

Barbara Bonneau

These Beans Have Too Much Salt

These Beans Have Too Much Salt

These Beans Have Too Much Salt

And I, looking more closely, saw a banner that, as it wheeled about, raced on-so quick that any respite seemed unsuited to it.

Behind that banner trailed so long a file of people-I should never have believed that death could have unmade so many souls.

Dante Alighieri
The Inferno

These Beans Have Too Much Salt

Petticoats and Preaching

The children were running around barefoot the day it happened. Mérite-Lajoie Dufrene-Robichaux had put her horses out to pasture on the small lot beside her home. A few days before, I flipped the Girl Scout calendar page over to the month of March. As I wrote over the first Tuesday with my red pencil, its point broke, and Mardi Gras was on us like a flame.

Like me, spring had stumbled on its pile of laundry lying at its porch door. The whole room smelled of impatience. The Callery pears had all shrugged their petticoats and their T-shirts. Someone had to start the wash.

Emmy Robichaux knocked on our front door and opened it before I came back through the house and into the living room. "Bee Leblanc are you in there?" My best friend swirled through the screen-door and stood before me. "Hey, wanna come with us? What do you think of my outfit?" Her black patent leather *ballerines* twirled her around again. I looked at her. Did she have glitter in her hair? When I think of it today, I tell myself that I had some, but in my eyes. My heart was telling me what to see.

Catching my breath, I countered, teasing, "I don't know. Where ya headed dressed up like that? A weddin'?" Her white ruffled skirt, all in chiffon and taffetas, was making eyes at me with its *moiré* motifs. A deep desire to feel it, to crush its stuff in my fist, overcame me. Emmy stood there--magic, cloud-like even. So much

6

more than her skirt. Even if Cajun, she wasn't at all from a family like ours. Had she been dressed like me; she was still different. She looked like she didn't belong here. Not a regular Cajun, not a girl from Louisiana, not even like one of the travelers who came to town from somewhere else, looking for the birth of the Blues in bars where they could not find entry. She resembled an illustration in a tale for Christmas. Enchanted. Impalpable.

In spite of her appearance, Emmy was a kid, like the rest of us. And lately, I thought she was overdoing it. Overdoing what? I didn't know yet how to say. But sometime, I wanted to--not exactly hurt her... Sometime I just wanted to make her wallow in dirt. There. I said it.

"We're goin' over to the Five and Dime in Natchez this afternoon," she replied.

How many times had she sworn she was my best-friend-for-life? Seeing her there all in silk-floating-skirt, I thought again about this declaration of friendship, and asked myself: deep down, what did she want? She didn't come as often as before to our house and when she did show up, she seemed like she was always looking for something. And that something seemed to escape us both. So, she just stood there...again.

Oh no! I wasn't inclined to be suspicious. It's just that...It's just that for some months now, Emmy was acting strange. "Who's we?" I asked, but I pretty much knew whom she was talking about. I knew where she got a skirt that no Cajun girl could obtain in any honest way. Mérite-Lajoie would have never bought it for her. Not even her father, Deux Ours, while he was alive, would have stood for it, had he had the money. So, why was she showing off? There was no need for it in order to invite me to go somewhere with her. To tell the truth, knowing what I knew, and thinking what I was thinking, didn't keep me from wanting what I wanted. I then started using all of the cunning I could muster, not because what I was saying was true or fair, not because I wanted to her to remember our friendship, but because I wanted to wear her skirt.

From happiness or just plain cupidity, after a few minutes, and feigning a complaining voice, I cried out, "Oh! Come on! I'll give you five cents. I never wore anything fluffy like that before." Uncrossing my arms, I reached out to feel her skirt. Its crispiness reminded me of cool, fresh unslept-on sheets, and its softness, of cream. In my overalls' pocket, I fumbled with the nickel I had pried off the school's tar roof earlier that morning and opened my closet door. "Pick anything, anything you'd like. Just for today."

Emmy smiled. Hanging there were what before I would have proudly called my motion-picture costumes, but now as I looked, the entire wardrobe became a patchwork of old mismatched hats and dresses that my mother used to wear on special occasions. Would Mérite-Lajoie scold her if she wore one of these? She was probably tending a colt in the side yard and wouldn't have seen Emmy when she went out the front door, on her way to our house. Perhaps she wouldn't have allowed Emmy to go to the Five-and-

These Beans Have Too Much Salt

Dime dressed as a princess, but what would she think of us exchanging our clothes?

Emmy let me stew a minute, pretending not to be interested. Then she pointed to a homemade blue poplin skirt, one of my first sewing attempts, and not the best. She would have picked anything just to flatter me and convince me to come with her. As it was, I thought that she was just trying to be generous. I still ignored that she had a mission.

At the time, being only eleven, I can't say that I understood all the ins and outs of our exchange. One minute, I was doubting our friendship, and the next, it seemed like it was bolstered by sharing something new. I felt confused again when she justified herself, "Uncle Harper says we should be generous with sharing. Like in *The New Testament*. He won't mind us trading, as long as we both go to Natchez and ride in his pickup, up front with him."

I can't say that I disagreed, this time, with her uncle. I don't think I asked myself that question. The ease with which she talked about her uncle and her new religion no longer surprised me. The unease that I sensed at the time, dismissed itself beyond my calculations. Then, I didn't much like crossing the Mississippi River bridge, especially in the bed of a pickup. I wasn't afraid of much, but I often had a nightmare where my sister and two brothers were dumped out like Cornflakes in a bowl, while crossing the river in my grandfather's pickup. This time, sitting up front with Harper, seemed like it would be the best option, especially as an exchange for the skirt with just a tarry old nickel.

Grinning, I tried on her new skirt. It was just my size. The idea that I was winning with this exchange may have entered my mind. No one grows up in a large family without developing some form of ingenuity to better his or her lot. If this question became conscient, it was quickly relieved by other pretenses. I reckoned I could share her feelings, if I wore her clothes, and even told myself, I'd only be better for it. Emmy took the nickel. Noticing the tarry edges, she frowned a little, putting it in her pocket. "I can buy a Coke or popsicle with it." She had lots of skirts and other gifts given to her by Harper. I had not yet imagined what these gifts could have cost her.

That is when we heard Skizzum come in, slamming the front door. Our younger brothers were there, squabbling as usual, waiting for Mama to come home for lunch. An opaque cloud covered my older sister's usual sunny face as she stormed into the bedroom. She found Emmy and I, exchanging our clothes. "We're fixin' to go to Natchez with Harper this afternoon. He wants to buy some children's Bibles and he wants us to help choose 'em." Skizzum's eyes flashed. She threw a bag on the bed from which tiny clothes peeked. "Y'all better come in here first. I have some parables to tell ya."

Even then, my sister was not what we would call desperate. At that instant, it still seemed like she had a plan. If only we had understood, the disorder on the back porch seemed to say something else. However, as with the dirty clothes piled up on the porch floor, Skizzum let the mystery ferment. Her morning chores would wait as much as we did.

"Sit down in *Holy Corner* and hear my words." And so, she began with a preachy voice, similar to Emmy's when she was explaining her generosity. Was she going to use a riddle this time to make a thunder revelation? Practically everyone in Ferriday, Louisiana was talking. The subject wasn't of what was going on in the small neighborhood church, not really. As with all rumors, the subject of these conversations was something closer to home. In small towns, the inhabitants are more likely to be interested in who is sleeping with whom, than the strategies of their elected officials.

They thought they knew that the father of her baby was a man of cloth. Gossiping about it behind her back wasn't nice, but she couldn't expect to keep us guessing forever. Spending all of her free time at church only made things worse. Here she was, pointing to a corner in the next room. Emmy and I got ready to listen to her confession, along with the rest of her nonsense.

We followed her as she began to preach, as if a girl of her age could have a bearing, imposing enough to preach. We were only children, after all, and this could have been a game like any other. "As soon as I entered this room, I saw the need. A girl was sittin' in the dinin' room smokin' with the boys." T-Pierre and T-Beaux both chuckled. We had heard enough preachers on street corners when our family

11

visited New Orleans to recognize this sort of sermon. These preachers were all adult men, and because they spoke of Jesus, even our grandfather, who scrutinized soap at the bottom of its dish, considered them to be incorruptible. Yet the evidence was against her. This sermon went sideways. This was no avowal. This was no comedy or play. Skizzum was evangelizing.

As a child, I didn't yet know this word and even now, I don't mean that my sister was delivering a true religious, or even benevolent teaching. Our brothers were too young to smoke, and her moralizing words missed their targets as soon as she aimed them; these couldn't offend anyone. For my sister, it was as if the hunter and the hunted were one.

She was poaching, trying to capture us. In some way, she was trying to catch hold of herself. Her words brushed up against, and twisted, a biblical story where a man claimed the same wealth as his brother, and where Jesus responded that he would be the judge of the inheritance. My belly froze. A fear that I had known when a bear near the river had seen me, gripped me once again. Skizzum had not been there during the discussion with Emmy. How was it that she was aware of it? Was this coincidental? I only knew much later that my ambivalence had become my shield at the same time that it gave me a sword. Not ready to admit my envy, not understanding the stakes, I attacked my accuser. The only other thing I could think of was to camouflage the game, and give it time to sense the danger, in case the boys, like myself, had begun to take her seriously.

Skizzum continued, using a tone we had all heard with Harper. Thinking of what Papou had said concerning him, I began to feel uncomfortable. Our grandfather didn't like this Harper fellow, and I began to understand his hostility went beyond the pregnancy of my sister. "Oh! For pity's sake! I've had enough of hearing all that! We want to be movie stars! " I cried, still envious, but now, envious to have my friend to myself.

"Quieten down! Y'all s'pposed to pretend I'm the preacher." This wasn't the real Skizzum. This wasn't some pretend voodoo; my eye-rolling, or even now strong, very real complaints, weren't enough to get through to her. There was no use getting upset about her words. I asked myself if she didn't have a grain or two in the attic. She talked louder and louder. Emmy's eyes widened. I had to resign myself to listening until the end.

"I'm obliged to preach. Our Savior called me to do so. I can't disappoint him by not followin'. Ok. I'm only tellin' y'all this for your own good. I honestly believes if you listen, y'all will have a chance to be saved. I also believes what the first chapter of John says: 'No one has ever seen God. But if we love each other, God abides in us, and his love is perfected in us. Listen, now, and don't laugh. God dwells in his creation and I'm part of that. So y'all might as well listen up and be saved by me, as good as anyone else."

Skizzum glared out at the snickering boys, pointed her finger, and deepened her voice an octave lower. "I took up the newspapers and I saw Bingo parties and dances advertised in connection with some of the local churches. This was a wicked thing. Card parties, dances, movies, the Sandwich Bar, all represent agencies of the Devil to distract de attention of boys and girls away from spirituality... And I say unto you the Anti-Christ is amongst us. He tempts us away from our Savior."

"I was down near the lake, and I caught a crawfish," Skizzum chanted. My already tried method of sending my mind reeling elsewhere started to kick in, but she continued, unperturbed. And now, the boys were captivated. Emmy sat, watching. "No sooner said than done, a white, wood ibis swept down and speared it with its beak. These are mysterious things. I turned my eyes to the Lord, and the bird returned. The repenting pirate flew over to me and returned my catch. The popchocks, and the poule d'eaus even brought their treasures to me. And the fishes jumped fresh out of the water onto the pier." Skizzum's eyebrows moved up and down as she unfolded her tale. Our brothers' eyes and mouths opened like the frogs gigged by the ibis in her story. I watched her watching them, until I imagined pieces of the sermon breaking off and slipping away on other words that were not hers at all. They joined a river of words, and there, they were diluted like drops of water in an ocean. This was a swindled story she got from Harper, one that he probably got second-hand. It was meaningless, this tale of an ibis offering its catch. I told myself. Yet, somehow, her list of Louisiana's fowl and her encounter with them, seemed to dazzle us.

Then, my resentment, my jealousy, gulped down like a tadpole from a bad joke, and still secret from myself, began to grow and was metamorphosing into its clown. The sarcasm, which I knew how to use even before junior high, made ready to jump out of water. Dirty words kept swimming up from the deep, splashing about, and making me bob about a few more minutes more, while I found myself in a duel with a fish made of my own questions. Fast and slippery.

Harper's sermons were wacky; there was no other way to describe them. Coming from my pregnant sister, these didn't make rhyme or reason. "Emmy…" I figured. "Did she come over here on a fishing expedition? Did she know what Skizzum would do with her there for support? The trip to Natchez, only about twelve miles from Ferriday, and the skirt, are pretexts." Somewhere in the back of my mind, I was trying to untangle the ambiguous relationships Harper had with my sister and my friend. "So…" I thought, "it all started like this, with a story, a hook. It's really a kind of lie made to seem like friendship or love." Without knowing it, I was realizing that I didn't win anything at all with my nickel and the skirt. And I felt overcome with anxiety.

"If you confess your sins, abandon your treachery, and put faith in the Lord Jesus Christ, the Spirit of God shall be given you."

"Sins? Hell, and damnation!" Nervous, feigning as best I could a minstrel voice, I joined in, bursting out laughing. I couldn't hold back any longer. Playing the fool seemed like the best way to get to my brothers, and even distract my sister. But she…she didn't get it. She was still serious.

These Beans Have Too Much Salt

By now our younger brothers were suspecting something odd and began giggling again. Emmy tried to make us sit still. She shared Skizzum's beliefs. Both were again bent on converting us. Their being children themselves never entered out minds. And me? From this furtive instant where I knew I had to do something; I no longer took them seriously. Why? I would only later understand. But my growing cynicism wasn't caused by the lack of maturity of the preachers.

Not wanting to reprimand the boys, but wanting to stop this carnival, I spoke to my sister instead. "Ok Sista. We'll go along wit tcha for now." I winked at her, almost sorry for trying to be funny. I did pity her, in a way, although she was unappreciative of my attempt to be complicit, as I almost knew she would be. I must have had my own reasons for trying to do one better over her. She flustered. An awakening call had to be bellowing out from somewhere. It had to be, or else, she was brain deaf.

Raising the bathroom plunger over us she continued to pretend, not pretending at all, her stance losing ground and making her hesitate: "I'll …I'll flush any of y'all sinners out with the Devil, just like our Lord Jesus Christ. Let him…let him change your individual lives and save you from your misery. Later this afternoon we'll go to the lake and wash away your sins. Let your spirit be saved if you can't help your mouths. Remember… remember these words. Praise the Lord. Hallelujah."

These Beans Have Too Much Salt

Skizzum stopped, the plunger suspended in midair, moving up and down like a pogo stick: "Tryin' to do anything wit tch'all kids is like herdin' cats. Don't y'all wanna be saved?" She glared at us through slanted eyes, as we scrunched our faces, smirked and giggled.

"Well, if y'all's too childish to realize what your doin' to yourselves, I'm gonna give up. Jest wait 'til the Lord comes. He'll look right past tcha." She was furious now. Perhaps her rage wasn't against the boys, but against her situation, which we hardly understood. "Jest wait 'til there's a hurricane. Come on girls, let's git out of here." She put up with my mockery better than she did the frank laughs of our brothers. She flung the plunger in the direction of our brothers, who by now were laughing out loud. The boys dodged it.

"If you are so worked up, put your butt in the air," yelled T-Pierre. "Catholics ain't no holy rollers anyway! Eat your tart. Release your fart. That'll cure your achin' heart," they repeated with a small boy's childish vulgarity, one echoing the other.

"I'm gonna kill you T-Pierre, you too T-Beaux." Trembling with anger, she picked up a brick holding up a shelf, making the picture frames fall on the floor. Clack-clack-clack. When Skizzum was angry, a certain rhythm followed. Papou came out of nowhere and grabbed Skizzum's hand. "You ain't killin' nobody. Not in my house. Not anywhere. When you're finished calmin' down, you can take care of the wash."

17

Down-to-earth and reassuring, our grandfather meant it. Skizzum handed him the brick. Afterall, no one wanted to see our brothers transformed into ghosts. Emmy and I followed her to the back porch, leaving the boys on the floor. I agreed this time with my brothers and grandfather; this saving business was starting wildfires in the middle of town. She picked up the pile of under-garments and stuffed them into the washing machine. "Leave me alone," she wailed.

"Why don't we just pretend to be someone else? Why not? We could be Mardi Gras queens, or movie stars? All we have to do is puff up our hair and put on our lips." I mimed putting on lipstick, kissed the air, and held up my hair with my hands.

"No!" Forgetting to start the machine, she slammed the trap and tore through the house, towards our bedroom. Emmy and I followed. "Stop followin' me!" She still wanted to get back at someone. Fighting back her tears, she shrieked: "I ain't gonna be no queen, not even for Mardi Gras, and I ain't gonna be no movie star either. Leave me alone! " Her eyes were red with anger and tears waltzed on the edges of their lids. "Besides, I just read *The Second Sex* book in the library about girls doin' anything they want," she proffered. "Why won't you listen to me?" Perhaps my sister believed that if she became a preacher, at least someone would.

The Tattoo

And there, without enquiring on the sex book that normally would have caught my attention, I suggested, in my quietest, and most mischievous voice, the player in me not having yet given up the game: "Why don't we draw tattoos on each other then?"

"Hmff, she grumbled. "I'm an abolitionist. I don't know what I would do with a tattoo. Why, with my big belly?"

"Oh, come on Skizzum, like the one we saw on the circus truck in Natchez." While I pleaded for a design that had its own will power, I imagined life as a sailor or a sort of Monté Cristo, alone in my prison, with my name carved into my flesh.

Skizzum glared again. Her anger and determination indicated that she realized the injustice of her predicament. Her eyes sparkled with tears. She had gotten in way over her head. As an unmarried pregnant teenage girl, she knew her condition left her open to attacks. These moments of so much more than pretense may have helped to alleviate the advancing doubts in her mind, but couldn't hold off the truth for long. Anyone could offend her. Worse, our slander had some legitimacy. She probably meant to say *feminist*, but the word didn't seem like it made sense any more. Her problem wasn't her baby, but in a town like Ferriday; it had no name and circulated on suspicions.

Then, her moment of uncertainty seemed to melt. All traces of struggle dissipated as they had appeared and Skizzum announced her new plan, as if she were playing a role in a movie after all. "I'm gonna be an artist if I cain't be a preacher…God will settle with it." Her change in perspective delighted me and I hurried on with my idea before she decided to renounce. This new project seemed to have brought her some appeasement.

"Well, why not draw tattoos then?"

"Ok, ok, let me tattoo you both then. Who wants to go first? Let me just say this: I might draw now, but later on, I'll be an artist, but an artist-musician…Who wants to go first? Let me tattoo you."

"Let me be first." Emmy held out her arm.

"Silly, there's not enough room on your skinny arm. We have to let her do our backs." Emmy raised her shirt. She was always a good sport, unless she was conjuring up other schemes to please Harper. This thought crossed my mind. What did she know about tattoos?

Skizzum took a ballpoint pen and drew a slightly inclined face looking out to the world. I watched as a naked woman, with full up-turned breasts, took shape and found her body wrapped up with a dark thick blue snake encircling her waist, sliding between her legs, and positioning its head on her shoulder, before at last, sticking out its forked tongue beside her ear, obviously whispering something.

These Beans Have Too Much Salt

Skizzum wanted to devil Emmy a bit too. At once, she seemed to be enjoying herself.

I almost laughed out loud when I realized that she had taken my suggestion seriously, putting my hand over my mouth, to prevent the sound from bursting forth. Skizzum was a true artist. The drawing was both beautiful and poisonous. Having my fill of envy and unfathomable vengefulness, enjoying the concept of the project, I didn't tell my unsuspecting friend what I saw. As soon as Skizzum progressed with a similar figure on my back, Emmy gasped. Her baby-like features twisted and contorted; her cheeks blushed.

"That's fornication!" Overwhelmed with horror, she ran out of the house and down the street wearing my blue skirt and forgetting hers.

A smile flooded Skizzum's face. "She gulps down anything he puts out there! I could see it in her eyes. She sits there, pretendin' to be holier than thou and on our side. Then, she will jest go off straight and tell him everything we do. Well…now she has something to say."

Later I understood that Skizzum's view was that of a rejected teenage girl. Her heart filled with tears. She hadn't realized that the ballpoint pen tattoo bullied and sliced Emmy's already black and white world in half. What girls shouldn't know about sex fluttered and spun about her like a moth lost in lamplight, its virginal flight gravitating between two opposing celestial bodies, one promising life and the other, death.

As soon as she got home, Emmy showed her mother the tattoo. They went straight across the Lake Road to the trailer lot to seek Harper's guidance. With tools of fear, he sucked the color out of their minds, substituting it with an artificial enhancement. Not long after this, we were told he began to show signs of fearing the outside world himself. He would yell: "White Light! White Light!" Everyone was supposed to flee into the woods and hide. And for Emmy? Even the word, sex, was supposed to remain gray. The tattoo may have reinforced the idea that evil was lurking about and could come in the form of a person or an authority, and even a child. Mérite-Lajoie, a widow, was by that time a full-fledged member of the First Evangelist Church. Neither recognizing art nor a childish prank, she only saw what Harper wanted her to see on her daughter's back: "She bears the mark of the Anti-Christ and risks eternal death".

I liked Emmy's mother better before she got saved. She had been one of those people who could squeeze a story out of an acorn and serve you the juice with all its pulp and, its bitterness. Our thoughtlessness was seen for the meanness it only partially was.

On my back, I had a drawing of a naked woman too, but I didn't feel threatened by it. Other than having lost the opportunity to go to Natchez, what I wasn't sure I wanted to do anyway; I figured the chances of being struck down by lightning were rare, unless I told on Skizzum. After all, I had suggested the tattoos and we had both asked her to draw them. Papou also punished us for tattling. Besides the circus wagon, Skizzum and I had seen a tattoo kind of like the drawing, on the arm of a man in the Piggly Wiggly. We weren't aware they were both copies of the late nineteenth century Austrian, Franz von Stuck's, *Sensualité*. We were not only intrigued by the snake-woman duo at the age where flesh and time begin to slither silently with its stench of sweat and tobacco and startle a girl with a nudge or pinch that leave a fingerprint on the panties. The face of the woman was finely developed and her expression undecipherable by us.

Had the man with the tattoo seen in the painting of Eve as an allegory of a *femme fatale*, a perfect alliance of Eros and Thanatos? I knew by Emmy's reaction we had gone too far. If Emmy had wanted to frighten her mother, she could not have found a better way. Nudity was practically forbidden now in the Robichaux household except when one was alone in the bathroom.

Our family was not obsessed with the same modesty. Skizzum and I had seen a lot of naked women at the funeral home where we went sometimes with our mother while she worked. One would hold the clothes for our mother as she struggled to put them on the stiff bodies. Sometimes when the adults were busy with other business, we would look under the sheets and make sketches in notebooks we kept secret. It wasn't the fantasy of life that might continue that encouraged us. Taking experience where we could find it, we even drew victims of accidents and other bad luck.

These Beans Have Too Much Salt

I promised to myself to never end up like Connie Taylor. I hadn't seen her body, but Skizzum, and everyone at the funeral home, had said that the mortician called to do the makeup at the Black funeral home said it was a real mess. The blood, the broken fingernails, the arm jerked out of the socket, the ruptured femur tearing through the skin, the face, swollen, *meconnaissable*, the jaw jutting past the nose, more like a portrait painted by Francis Bacon, than a blossoming woman in her twenties. Other than the portrayal of perhaps some sort of mortifying satisfaction, the body bared no resemblance at all with the woman in the drawing. Even I knew that unless you are one of the living-dead, enjoyment goes out with death.

The tattoo on my back was not a real one either. Nevertheless, it was soldered with guilt. When I think about what happened to Emmy and her family, I still feel its stinger, red-hot with fiery blame, underneath my skin. I have come back again and again to this day for the last thirty years and wondered how I contributed to putting Emmy in harm's way, and her mother behind bars.

Mérite-Lajoie's Nightmare

Years later, on a day when summer was *louisianaing* through the small windows at St. Gabriel's Correctional Institute for Women, the lines I had not drawn for myself as a child began to condense and darken all around me. The air was heavy with the odor of confinement and I almost fainted when I went into the small cell.

"I woke up on the floor," rasped Mérite-Lajoie, rubbing her face with her large hand. "My cellmate was laughin' at me. She was laughin' so hard, she almost choked. I said somethin' in my sleep again. Awake, I couldn't talk. My chest hurt too much. I climbed back into my bunk. Then I started coughin' up the rogue's velvet lining. Fanny stopped laughin' then and called for the warden." These were Mérite-Lajoie's first words to me when we met again years after her incarceration for a crime many would have committed in her place, or not; if only had they had the presence of mind.

"He's after my lungs now! I mean the possum." Mérite-Lajoie stopped to catch her breath before continuing. "You see, Bee, it's my nightmare. There's this demon. He's been comin' back for years. It's only a dream; I know that. Though, most of it happened for real, and I still cain't get it figured. Do you remember that year, Bee? You were eleven. I guess you'd be about forty-two now, like my Emmy. Do you remember the possum? Do you remember what Harper did?"

Hearing Mérite-Lajoie name that animal, the possum, I can't help but ask myself: "Has she gone nuts? Why is she talking about a possum?" Then my mind spins away from itself like it tends to do when I meet with memories that oppress me from the inside. By the time I am half way through consternation's revolving door, I am reminded that in Louisiana, this is how we say and write, *Opossum.* The word opossum is from the Powhatan, but I never knew what happened to the *O* in our use of the word.

Maybe when we get a glimpse of the creature; we swallow the first letter in a reversed exclamation. Could gulping down this initial vowel be the local version of the New Yorkers', "What the fuck is that!" or like Simeon gasped when he recognized *in extremis* the Messiah, "Now I can die in peace!"

So, did I remember any possums? Mérite-Lajoie's question stirs up memories of those ugly creatures that wandered over our porch through the years and of talking about the possum's genitalia with the boys in school. Because of the girl I was, I was sure they were pulling my leg with their story of a double-dicked beast. Having one was enough when it came to being one. Their joking embarrassed me and I hated them for their treachery. Although I had tried to raise my share of orphaned possums, I had never noticed their odd genitalia, but I didn't want to let on. One year, a male possum lost its way and got into trouble with our pet raccoon. We then had to close them both up in a shed, separately of course, to make sure neither had rabies. Yes, I'd had many opportunities to learn about possums, but Mérite-Lajoie's Possum was another story. His misdeeds did not go unnoticed, but he was never quarantined. Did I remember this possum, *that* Possum? Exiting my mind's eye, I ask myself: "Who could possibly forget?"

My patient coughed up more blood, wheezing noisily. Her jail pajamas were wet with sweat. "Was she speaking of a garment like this one? I couldn't imagine her acting like Bill Grogan's goat, swallowing pieces of red shirts or any other type of fabric; but some inmates will do about anything to go to the infirmary. Who or what is this *rogue*? I'll have to look and see if she has mentioned it before." I put my stethoscope to her chest and listened. T-thup, t-thup, t-thup, t-thup. Her heart, was beating faster than I could write. "Settle down Mrs. Robichaux or you'll hemorrhage. An ambulance is going to take you to the hospital for X-rays and some tests. I'm going to give you something to help calm the cough."

It was obvious to me then that she had a serious problem and was already hemorrhaging. I tried to sooth her; speaking to her as I would to a child, making sure that my intervention would cut short any mention of my childhood again. Of course, I remembered that year, 1963, every American did. It is also the year the word *envy* hit a major road-block, changed its course, and left a gap in its meaning for the child I was.

In the infirmary ledger, there are notes about inmates who wake up at night. I knew this wasn't the first time Mérite-Lajoie had woken up with a nightmare. One warden likes to jot down what they say when they talk in their sleep. It helps him to stay focused. Prison nights are long and eerie. His disrespect for the inmates bothers me; but when I heard my old neighbor cry out over the monitor, I wrote down her words for myself. I heard her cellmate guffaw, "Mérite-Lajoie cough", then, the cry for help. I was on duty at the Infirmary for L.C.I.W. where I was one of six doctors, and the only woman. I was alone on duty, making rounds in the West yard, when I heard: "The possum! The whiskey possum! Get him off! Get him off!" What's that about? I wrote. Of course, I remembered before Mérite-Lajoie reminded me, but I hadn't thought about all that in years. Sometimes I even convinced myself that every other version of memory was still possible.

Suddenly I was back on the banks of November 22, 1963, flooded with emotion, my mind had gone fishing without me. When my grandfather drove me back to school after lunch that day (something he only did on rare occasions), I reckoned I-didn't-know-what had gone awry, or my piece of the world was about to fall apart, again. His face wore the same floppy expression as it did when he told us our father had left. Papou leaned over, put his hand on my knee, and I braced myself for the worst. "Bee, this is gonna be hard for me to explain so I'll just say it outright. A judgment's been rendered." "They're gonna let Mrs. Robichaux go?" I questioned and answered excitedly with my guilt-ridden expectations. "No." Papou shook his head and peered at me with wilted eyes. "She's been condemned to the chair." I was shattered.

Although she wasn't exactly a hero, I never believed that the state of Louisiana would execute Mérite-Lajoie. In a child's world of right and wrong, how had she ended up on the side of the evildoers, those facing capital punishment? We had just read *To Kill a Mockingbird* in Mrs. Adams' class, and I wondered where Atticus Finch, the defense lawyer of just causes, was keeping himself locked up. Why couldn't he have defended her? How could Justice put to death a beloved mother and friend? How could that happen? Was she the guilty one? I didn't cry, not right away, but felt myself sinking. I wanted to grab ahold of my friend Emmy, but she had not come back to school since the shooting, and my older sister, Skizzum, had already left home. Instead, I ran off to class and left my grandfather sitting in his pickup alone.

At school, I managed, not without difficulty, to turn the dials of my combination lock, fumble through my locker, and find my English notebook. I made it to my desk somehow because I remember hearing the principal come over on the crackly loudspeaker announcing, all in a blur with my anger, something about President Kennedy. Several girls burst out crying, providing me with an alibi to let myself go. I said then, it wasn't fair. I was talking about Mérite-Lajoie. Mrs. Adams tried to explain to the class that we were not speaking of poetic justice at the moment, and to suggest we all say a prayer for President Kennedy.

It was not until a second announcement by the principal, stating that the President was pronounced dead, that I realized that John F. Kennedy had been assassinated, engraving this date forever in my mind along with my grievances about Mérite-Lajoie's judgment. We were all dismissed for the afternoon. In most homes, like ours, families were glued to the television with tearful, worried faces for the next three days. But we were mourning more than the loss of our president.

Two days later, although we felt that the assassin got what he deserved, we sat in horror watching the broadcast as Ruby shot Oswald live on national television. Kennedy's killer had torn order from the world. Its flesh was ripped to pieces and thrown out into the universe to Chaos' dogs.

Once dead, Mérite-Lajoie's Possum was like one of those dogs whining and scratching around for scraps under Justice's table. He was dead, but he was hardly a victim. He loaded the gun and pulled the trigger on the weapon that'd kill him. The irony of it all was a perplexing maze for the adolescent I was becoming.

"You know Bee, a caged bird never dreams peacefully." Mérite-Lajoie pulled herself up to talk. "When it ain't singin' for survival, it sings its death, even in its sleep. If I'm gonna die, I'm gonna die," she told me the next time I was on duty. "As a dyin' woman, I have some last requests. Would it be too much to ask you a favor? I don't wanna take nothin' with me to the grave. I jest want you to take down a verse or two, and tell Emmy. I don't want her to receive a letter from the Chief Warden about my passin' without me havin' given her my side of the story. She's old enough now. If I've learned somethin', I've learned there won't be Justice until she hears and understands what happened."

These Beans Have Too Much Salt

Mérite-Lajoie Robichaux's Blues had an ever-changing hue. She was no longer awaiting execution. Her sentence had been reduced following changes in the law. Back from the hospital, she knew she was condemned. The cancer had spread. Fear sweated out from the listening prison pores. These transpired with truth until the walls were wet, and salty water trickled onto the floors. In her not so best moments, Mérite-Lajoie murmured, and talked on.

As it was, now she was whispering a song of her own making, reflecting her state of mind.

"The Whiskey possum looks at me; he looks at me and grins.
He is always happy, tryin' to make me sin.
The game he plays, I know it and know that it ain't right.
He comes to me and haunts me, in the middle of the night.
The Whiskey possum's tryin', is tryin' to make me sin.
I can smell it in his eyes, and I can taste it in his grin.
Now that he is on me, he wants to make me fight.
He comes to me a-hungry, in the middle of the night."

She made her rhymes in English rather than in French. I wondered if this was another Harper effect or if the years of incarceration had taken her Cajun language away from her too.

"I ain't finished dyin' yet." Mérite-Lajoie looked at me questioningly when I dragged my feet on the doorpost. I wanted to help ease her pain if that was at all possible, but more than that, I wanted to erase the past. Mérite-Lajoie knew. She had to know because she knew as much as Sitting Bull, who had had the power to see beyond appearances and cure the sick or heal the injured. Seeing her now, I guess that is an overstatement; if she had had the venerated Native American's clairvoyance, she would not be in prison.

Another day, standing nude with the drip in her arm in the prison infirmary, she called out to me again by my nickname, "Bee, Dr. Bee". The orderly, another prisoner, put a sheet around her shoulders and led her back to bed. Being naked if front of me, or anyone else, was no longer a concern of hers, if it ever was. A few years before she had been one of the inmates refusing to wear clothes, refusing to wash her prison trousers again and again in the cold stopped up shower, protesting the lack of decent hygiene and laundry facilities. I sat in a chair next to a woman who seemed so old she could have been my grandmother, yet she was a generation younger, in her early seventies. I wanted to reach through the distance and hold on to her, remembering what I had tried so hard to forget, looking to her for comfort instead of the contrary. Her thinning head was splotched, and her face was gray with the greenish tint smokers all seem to acquire. Her frail hands trembled as she clutched the glass I held to her lips. It was hard to remember the woman she had been, sitting tall in her saddle, riding through the woods near the swamp, and harder still to imagine her as a criminal.

"Mrs. Robichaux, who is this rogue and his velvet lining you were talking about the other day?"

She smiled. "I think I probably meant red. You know the color of blood, *rouge*, but there was a rogue; more of a monster and you know who I was talkin' about." She was suddenly impatient.

By then, Mérite-Lajoie had more than once told me of that first morning she had had this recurring dream. "That mornin', I jumped out of bed nearly draggin' my husband with me, tryin' to get to the dressin' table and see my face in the mirror." At first, I supposed her to be like a Dorian Gray in a tale of self-infatuation. Had she feared her fault had floated up from her guts during her sleep and changed her appearance forever? Touching the lines of her face, one after another, as she did now in her bed, did she wonder if it showed? Now as she examined her hairless chest and felt the skin under her collarbone, I realized that there was much more going on with her, but I couldn't yet say what it was.

"Is my heart still there?" She seemed delusional. It was beating, if only too fast. "Was it only a dream? My parents told me sleepin' alone caused nightmares. They warned me before I married." The incubus was there, nevertheless. I wiped the sweat from Mérite-Lajoie's forehead. Again, she found herself back in the woods on the Louisiana side of the Mississippi River near Natchez, holding her shotgun, with the reddish-brown briars of destiny entangling her feet.

"What happened to my gun?" Mérite-Lajoie sat straight up in the bed and looked at me angrily. "Overnight, have I become one of these disarmed people qui *se couche* without a thought?" In a state of panic, she looked around the infirmary, as if it were her room. "It isn't in the corner. Why isn't it hangin' on its rack? Have I left it somewhere? I don't want my husband to notice how upset I am. But I see now. No. It's as clear as day; a missin' gun could never alone explain such a state of fright."

The events she spoke of were as muddled as her dream. The day it appeared the first time, her husband got up and moved about the room. "Have a bad dream? You yelled at someone in your sleep and cried real tears." She remembered his face as he contemplated her expression, disfigured by her wrinkled forehead and wild, nightmare filled eyes.

"I was runnin' through the woods, my clothes covered in blood. I got into my pickup," she stuttered. "It seemed unreal."

"Was it a dream?" I asked.

"I dunno. My head hurts. I was huntin' and killed an animal, or, at least, that's what I thought. Maybe I did drink too much."

Medicated heavily, she mumbled under her breath, repeating what could have been her husband's words, "Honey, don't let it give you a spot of bother. We've killed a ton of animals. What was so special about this one?" Did Mérite-Lajoie remember him kissing her and pulling her towards him, holding on to her thick dark hair? I remember how it hung over her shoulders, almost to her waist until she started wearing it in a bun, then cropped it short.

My former neighbor couldn't shake off her nightmare. Bits of it came back to her as her mind cleared and she awoke to find me next to her bed. She tried piecing them together, repeating the dream once again. "There was the soul of a man in it too. He kept starin' at me; it looked like a possum, but it had a man's dick and was tryin' to tell me somethin'. He had a gunshot wound right there." Mérite-Lajoie turned towards me and pointed at her own bosom.

"I bent over to look at his wound. He talked about death then took out a knife. He jumped on my chest, then cut me open and took out my lungs and heart. He only left my spleen and liver. I jest gave up the struggle right away. He then helped me up and walked with me to the father of rivers. There was a girl there. He picked up stones and threw them at her. He said she was a demon. Then he disappeared."

Mérite-Lajoie looked at me with frightened eyes, as if she wondered if I could have been that girl, and then she recognized me again. "Another one of the Possum's tricks; it won't let me be."

"Well, I looked on the ground for some stones to throw at the girl but saw my biscuits instead. An elder came out of these, and his soul stood beside me. He whispered in my ear, tellin' me to kill the child who looked like an animal now too, or to drive it into the river. He was talkin' a lot and I learned his doctrine by heart. The animal answered, sayin' somethin' I don't remember now. It upset me, but I dunno why. I wanted to shut it up. I think I killed it! Then I woke up fearin' somethin' terrible had happened!"

Her watery eyes floated around the room as if they were following someone. She spoke of how her husband moved about in the bedroom that morning. "I can almost see him as he moves about and with his back turned, getting' dressed. He was still handsome after his first heart attack, but couldn't see well enough to hunt anymore. He never could find his way in the forest alone without getting' lost, so he stopped huntin' all together. Some Indian, huh? I don't know if he was listenin'."

Was it so hard to listen to a bewildered grown woman as she questioned her dreams? Her husband, who disregarded his tribe's beliefs in cosmologies and even totemic animals, probably teased her gently, the way he always did, even in public. "There is one word. It's the word of God. Ain't no animal got a soul. A talkin' animal, now, that would be somethin'." Usually, his laughter helped her overcome obstacles. "The situation was absurd this time, and I knew it without him sayin' so and without him movin' about, tellin' me how ridiculous I was. Deux Ours was not a weak man. He didn't have a lot of friends here in Ferriday and spent most of his time with Emmy and I, but he had his beliefs, and I had mine."

My resistance came from another source, something almost visceral, poorly digested, that pinched and pulled the walls of my belly until I couldn't ignore it and yet, it was impossible to let it go.

Some parts of her dream, she repeated, over and over, like a leitmotiv. Not knowing the truth felt almost as bad as being certain of it. The scene with her husband, along with the rest, was painted on memory's canvas. More than thirty years later its details were as intimate as in Audubon's watercolors, but the background was as blurry as the *aquarelles* of a Sunday artist.

Like the painter, Mérite-Lajoie had often spent hours alone in the woods, or in the swamp. Hunkered down against a tree, or in her boat, hunting to supplement her family's diet, she often observed two sparring parties challenge each other. This predicament could have been as dangerous for her as for the weaker opponent, had she shown a pressing interest. She watched without moving, as the dominant male proved its worth and disappeared with the female. Once the bout had finished, the hunter contributed as best as she could to the preservation of the species, killing the lower-ranking animal. On the morning of the dream, there the Cajun was, as walleyed and as pitiful as both animals had been facing each other in the standoff.

She complained to her husband, terrorized, and worried she had killed a man. Her embarrassment lingered a moment, maybe only a few seconds. "Do you remember what my husband's real name was? People in Ferriday called him Frenchy, but his Houma name was Two Bears. My father always said I was one of 'em." Mérite-Lajoie laughed and coughed some more. "His people called him *Deux Ours*, in French, and so did we."

These Beans Have Too Much Salt

"I recall then jumpin' into my pants and puttin' on my boots before hurryin' out to my pickup. And there it was on its rack where it had spent the night…Somethin' had happened. I would never leave a weapon in my truck outside my home. Next to the driver's seat was my shirt, covered in blood. But there was no animal in the box on the truck's bed."

Although she found it hard to shake the nightmare-induced stupor, the events of the day before, and those of the years still before, came back to her, and into our conversation. The accident, the man with the wound, the spring, the dead, salt covered possum, her knife sterilized with a lighter. She recalled trying to get the bullet out and to stop the bleeding, trying to lift the man up onto to her back, falling, dragging him to the gravel road, running to find help, then to get her truck; throwing rocks at an animal in the shadows before leaving it, poised in the weeds; heaving the man into the passenger side, and finally, driving him to the hospital, unconscious and she thought, probably dead.

"Wasn't the creature speakin' to me, just before I saw the man? There was somethin' religious about it." Mérite-Lajoie tried to separate her dream from the real world. Feeling she had been changed forever; she had wondered then if she would be charged with murder. She told me how she got into her pickup that morning, and drove back to the Louisiana hospital, leaving her daughter to have breakfast alone.

The Wheel of Fortune

Mérite-Lajoie had long since broken enough rules so that her husband's family and half the people in Ferriday thought she was as crazy as a Bessie Bug. In those days, not many women set out with rifles to go on hunting or fishing trips alone. Mérite-Lajoie did, and pretty much looked like she fit the role. I learned to use a gun too, but I wasn't supposed to make use of it alone. We all knew Louisiana was a man's state. There are no exceptions made in a court of law for self-defense or protecting one's friends or family, at least not for us Cajuns. However, it didn't seem right to me that Mérite-Lajoie was convicted. It was against everything I was taught, everything I believed.

When we were children, Mérite-Lajoie lived down the street from us. Although at first, she did not ask me to contact Emmy or deliver this story to her (seeking Emmy out was not my idea), keeping track of Mérite-Lajoie's words became my official purpose when I met her again and again. She had had visits from her brothers, and her mother, while they were still alive, but she had not seen her daughter all these years since the shooting and could not attend her mother's funeral. Once she was off death row, she hadn't allowed her daughter to visit her in prison like some of the other children did with their mothers. A second heart attack took her husband well before the shooting. Her daughter had grown up and moved far away in her mind. Perhaps even to this day, Emmy felt bound by secrecy. Yet, in all truth, with each scrawled word, our memories seemed to pull away from a shadowy oblivion.

"When Emmy was a child, I felt it best to protect her from the prison environment and best not to stir up thoughts or feelins that should remain buried." Mérite-Lajoie cringed as if in pain. "My mother told me she had fits and screamed enough as it was. We feared comin' here would make things worse."

Even the few times I had seen her as an adult, Emmy became so accustomed to her days without vicissitude; she couldn't step out of the cocoon of safety her grandmother had built around her, too late. Over and over, I asked myself as a child; why didn't a moth's instinct teach it that it wouldn't ever reach the moon without a rocket? Why did its disappointments continually lead it to a light bulb's flare? Returning to these questions has helped me to put them in their place. I'm inscribing them along with these memories for Emmy, to use, as she is able.

Like Mérite-Lajoie, I left home early, driven by something more urgent than a need for independence. I was trying to lose myself, to find a part of me that had gone missing, looking for a father who I had grown up without. Strangely enough, the D-day Museum, in Normandy, seemed closer to my research than Louisiana's bayous, for many Cajuns used their language skills in wartime France. My father was one.

Thus, my first adult encounters with my absent father were on the other side of the Atlantic. There my French improved, but as life is all but a museum, my purpose became wrapped up in the adventure itself. I recently returned, fifteen years after having stumbled on the letter that took me to Colleville-sur-Mer, my experience in my pocket, and not much else.

When I ran into Mérite-Lajoie again, tattoo or not, my boat was adrift. The rudder was broken and turned inward. I had not become much of a boats-woman. While I was trying to locate my father and grasp why he left us, what happened that terrible year in Ferriday overtook me. All the details were there, but most remained out of reach, just on the other side of the mirror, where I'd put them.

My pirogue keeps turning around and around, around and around, under the same cypress trees, in the same swamp, Mérite-Lajoie has practically never left. Here silence is damp with the sounds of many revenants; I can decipher their words and adopt some of these. In certain ways, Mérite-Lajoie's confessional is as much mine as it is hers. But I was a mere child, and for that reason, will never be judged for my misdeeds, my hesitations, or my inability to act.

I came to St. Gabriel as part of the maximum-security prison plan, which allows for improvement of medical care within the penitentiary. Ironically, the location of Louisiana's Correctional Institute for Women near the Mississippi River, adds almost a home-like atmosphere.

Mérite-Lajoie has been here now since 1964. "My sentence for first-degree murder was commuted in 1972 followin' the *Furman versus Georgia* Supreme Court decision, which said capital punishment was unconstitutional, and also decided it was cruel and unusual," she added, keeping with the terminology of the law. "Did you know they shaved your head and legs and made you wear a diaper?" Mérite-Lajoie knew what happened to a human body submitted to two thousand four hundred volts. The wardens made sure that all the prisoners were aware. She had no illusions about what would remain of human dignity. "More than that, here, I missed out on raisin' Emmy. I tried to forgive Harper. But there are some things you just can't get past."

"What do you feel about it, Bee? Do you think some murders are justified?" I couldn't answer, and for a while, she couldn't speak.

Mérite-Lajoie jerked away when my hand approached her shoulder. "I'm not used to bein' touched anymore. We ain't even s'pposed to shake hands here now."

"You know I have some of my own demons. I'm not sure where I should begin to tell you about them." When I admitted that, which wasn't much after all, she went on with her story and at the same time, her search for rest without nightmares.

"My death sentence was suspended along with those of six hundred and twenty-nine other inmates across the United States. Then they brought it back in some places. This is one of those states, which reinstated the right to decide who lives or dies, and gave this authority to one of those Furies disguised as the governor. Justice comes back to its birthplace to be buried where crime digs its grave and calls it: revenge. My name was on the executioner's list again."

"While we were awaitin' Gruesome Gertie, we were officially restored to the margins of humanity when a 1977 decision held that crime and character had a hand in the game. The exactions just got worse, but I began to make plans for a future reunitin' with my family. These were short-lived." Mérite-Lajoie was repeating elements of law and its changes I had learned about during my internship.

I didn't want to think about what balances in the seats when the wheel of fortune momentarily stops turning. I told myself I didn't want to know about the system of deprivation or substitutions in prison life; how these negotiations figure in with the decisions of justice, or how medicine and religion can contribute to repression. Under a 1926 law, a Louisiana lifer could be released for good behavior after ten years and six months of incarceration. For victims and their families, ten years no longer seem like much of a punishment when weighed against the offenses of murder or rape. I never thought about how, in prison, each day had its sanctions until I tended to these women and realized how the hope of parole carried each one through daily trials of pure hell. How could they be seen by some as monsters? Not wanting to know, I came to the right place to dig up old skeletons and to learn their names.

"I thought I would get out then." Mérite-Lajoie bowed her head. "I started to believe I'd get a second chance. I served my ten six, but

43

shortly before the federal conversion of mandatory death sentences, the Louisiana lawmakers changed the rules again. They eliminated the precedin' considerations for early release. A *life means life* law was instated which murdered all my hopes. I then knew I would die at St. Gabriel's, whatever I did. Did we riot when we figured we were pawns of a changin' game?"

"Most of us became what my friend, Fanny, calls the livin'-dead. She's a prisoner who ghostwrites for *The Angolite*, the prison newspaper published from the men's prison. We'd heard that nine of the men from Angola had been put to death in just nine days, and we couldn't stomach any more. But bein' a livin'-dead among other inmates who still had other options ain't such a good idea. Many of the women who come here are very young and use their strength to make the weaker women their domestic slaves. Only, their force is made more of fear than anything else."

"Some inmates are lucky to have trustee jobs; they earn four cents an hour. It keeps 'em from bein' bored all the time. The work used to be a kind of slavery, in particular for the Black prisoners when the women were still kept at the men's prison until 1961. They became like the men: violent with each other. When I got here, they had it in their papers I had been a postal employee. They put me to sortin' mail. It wadn't hard. All I had to do was read the cell numbers, put them in order and clean up the place. They wouldn't let me do much of the out-mail. The work was easier than the fieldwork I did as punishment for participatin' in a prison protest. But it added insult to injury. Had I not been in trouble enough, I would've refused to do it on account of my experience in that domain."

"After a while, my skills as a horsewoman and a *traiteur*--uh, that's Cajun for healers--found me in good grace. At St. Gabriel's, there's a cryin' need for animal caretakers, almost as great as the need for medical care for inmates, because there are a pack of horses to tend to; with guards on horseback watchin' over the cotton and sugarcane plantation farmed by prisoners. So, I got the opportunity to take care of the most livin' beings doin' time at St. Gabriel, and I was almost happy until the wheel stopped again. With the new chief warden, takin' care of horses became a privilege to be given or to be removed by his authority. Same with playin' a guitar."

Mérite-Lajoie talked between naps now. "A lifer's sentence can still be converted to a capital one, and many times, I felt I found myself, in a kill or be killed situation. I've had loads of fear. Fanny's been here longer than I have. She was sentenced for vagrancy when she was only just nineteen. When she got to Angola, before the transfer, one stud-broad claimed her, and she found herself turned into her old lady for a while. She'd seen what happened to another inmate when four or five beat her, because she refused the protection of one. That girl wound up in the nut house."

"Fanny figured since she was a small woman, she'd better deal with only one jock, a trustee guard, thinkin' she'd get out on parole in a few months. She's what we call an Oreo. Black on the outside but acts White, like on the inside, calculatin' all the time like what she s'pposed to do. Fanny did 'bout everythin' a wife could do for a husband, washin' clothes, straightenin' the beds, all the menial things, and even more, if you see what I mean. But in prison, you gotta live, and her stud-broad had a heroin problem and wound up sellin' Fanny in exchange for drugs. Fanny decided she didn't wanna be a canteen whore no more and found herself set up for life for defendin' her own. I managed to avoid compoundin' my term without bein' killed or without becomin' a wife. You believe me don't you, Bee?"

"One onion-eater from Vidalia told me that my mother didn't bring Emmy because she resented my bein' in prison and her havin' to take care of her, with her bein' sick and all. She kept on and on until I'd had enough. I jumped her and she threw scaldin' soup on me. I wished I was dead. The guards said it was an accident. But since the altercation didn't cause the total loss of any vital organ, once I got out of the hospital, they put me in the cell for eighteen months and took away my job with the horses. Since then, I worry most of the time that they'll get after me again, but I ain't as friendly as I used to be. It's different now, but worse in some ways. It's hard because, because you remember the past and what it could've been."

"Some of the women here are lookin' for temporary comfort. That's okay with me, but I didn't want to get forced into anything. I used to feel guilty most of the time about fights, and especially about leavin' Emmy. But here, they've got no use for guilt. Guilt only slows you down and makes you lazy. Instead, you's s'pposed to say, 'bless you,' all the time, and read the Bible. These words are magic here. And with them pills they give you; you got the key to a successful sentence. The new chief warden thinks belief transformation is more fundamental than medical attention. There's nothin' that can't be healed by divine intervention. 'It is all up to our Lord. God never makes mistakes,' he says every day. He says that God is goin' to use us, and our situations, to make way for the Gospel. I still don't know how he figures that."

"You think they's become authentic penitents?" Mérite-Lajoie sarcastically added, indicating her fellow inmates as much as the guards. "It's a power thing when you don't have money."

"It's not my temperament to find a wife. Sex is forbidden here, not only for the guards. But they made fun of my name, sayin' I must be a whore with a name like Mérite-Lajoie. I don't think that's what my parents had in mind for me when I was born. Lajoie was my grandmother's maiden name. Most people just call me Merit here. Anyhow, there must've been near ten or fifteen fights over a three-month period durin' the first years I was off death row. All this wore me out and I smoked too much. Since a lot of those women from the Angola prison are gone, things have calmed down somewhat with the new wardens. Now, I'm dyin', but worried about this conversion shit." Mérite-Lajoie shook her head as she confided her new anxiety. "All that talk about bein' saved and healed by the Holy Spirit hasn't helped me figure out what needs to be done."

These Beans Have Too Much Salt

The inmates spoke of one matter, and I, as well as the rest of the prison employees, spoke of another. At that rate it was hard to come close enough to make a leap in Mérite-Lajoie's direction. Her train was moving fast, and I doubted anti-depressants or religion could do greater harm than good.

Working nights when the radio is off, I hadn't heard what she calls the Gospel drills. I tried hard not to build one prisoner's complaint up into a generality covering the entire prison population. My patient spoke of the other inmates as if many could be represented by one, and found it difficult sometimes to single herself out of the group. The chief warden told all of us that the whole country was watching us and we had to set an example. He said we had to let our lights shine and that we couldn't allow them to dim.

I admit that even when I was first hired, his words did sound a little religious to me. His idea of implicating each of us as part of a symbol of universal light made me think of other lessons. However, Mérite-Lajoie's theory of how hearing preaching over the radio could make a prison sentence worse seemed at first, farfetched. I came in with a desire to help others, and I thought that a little prayer wouldn't hurt anyone, myself included. Everyone has faults to amend. I had put aside my childhood memories for years and had no desire to stir these up. I couldn't see how bringing these back to life could help anyone else in any way either at this point. Then I realized what was considered as religion at St. Gabriel, and I remembered how a well-meaning teacher had swept the emotional haze of a class of seventh graders under the rug by insisting that we pray instead of talk about our fears or our anger. Had I woken up to find that the entire state of Louisiana had become an expeditious place?

"I'm gonna tell you why I think this prison religious transformation does more harm than good. You can be sure of one thing, and I'm glad my husband ain't around to hear me say it; God ain't nowhere to be found in the picture. If he is, he has some twisted sense of humor."

"Maybe some of us need God, but no one 'spects us to return to society and live in a civilized manner with our families. We have a punishment to bear, and we'll carry it alone, closed up here 'til we die. We don't hope for any kind of real life here. We are beyond the pardon of the families we've torn apart. Our flags will forever wear our stains. Sometimes we want to die. Death means freedom from sufferin' not only on our bodies but also on our souls. In the meantime, hearin' that damned savin' and healin' by the Holy Spirit business preached on the radio all day long, don't give anyone hope. I wish they would just leave us be. We need music more than their blabla."

Mérite-Lajoie is not the only inmate who demonstrates unappeased moral strife. I'm often called late at night (or early in the morning), before finishing my treatment notes for maladies and skin infections, to tend to one isolated prisoner, or another, who has burst her head open on her cell wall because she is distressed and cannot sleep. As I hurry to the cell where a guard is waiting for me, blood explodes onto the sheets piled up on the floor. "Bless you for comin', Dr. Leblanc. I just cain't sleep. I got a migraine. Maude down there is snorin' too loud, keepin' me awake, night after night." I turn to the guard to ask him to open the cell.

"Don't come in here. You cain't help me unless you call my mom first. If you don't, my head is gonna bust open like a watermelon hit with a sledge hammer." At first, she tries to stop me, but when she realizes the guard is telling her to back away from the door, she continues to talk to me. "I won't try anythin'. I got religion now. The Lord Jesus Christ has saved me; so, you got nothin' to worry 'bout. I just need to talk to my Mama and cain't do it with the others around. Just call her, will ya? I'll say a prayer for you." Obviously, this inmate's beliefs about the salvation in the formula, if they are genuine, do not calm her nerves.

Many of them seem to think key religious words are supposed to provide me with some guarantee or satisfaction. These women thus justify their medical care along with their so-called religious redemption, as if they thought they could bribe God with their ready-made conversions.

When I treat them, one guard explains why only an older woman could risk getting close to them, as if expressing these raw statements about inhibited desires would prove his worthiness. "Dr. Leblanc, if you was younger, you couldn't be in there with that woman. Only now, the Lord keeps me from actin' on my own instincts. You know there is a closet off the guard's post. If you wanted, I could show you a thing or two you won't find with these women, or any woman for that matter." My thoughts are sent off reeling in the direction of my childhood while my body stands here wondering what I'm doing dealing with a convicted murderer and a male prison guard who is talking to me about his instincts.

All the sudden, a familiar flutter of apprehension's wings has stirred in my chest and salvation seems of little importance to me. The prison neon reality, along with the inmate's head banging, forces my mind back to the present. My potential patient's head has doubled in volume. I try to negotiate with her for her care. Acting in for one mother or another, I convince her to take a tranquilizer, before sending her with two armed guards to the nearby hospital for a head X-ray. I can't forget where I am. Some of these women have committed violent crimes, but the guards are undereducated and exposed to complex human situations. With their fantasies they might become just as dangerous. Prayer won't help either.

"At night, loneliness creeps in bringin' depression and suicide. Many of the inmates have had their brains fried doin' fieldwork. We badly need medical care. This prison was built for nine hundred. There are over a thousand of us now. Some women here have lost their minds waitin'. Water and prayer ain't enough to cure 'em. They will cut their veins open on their head, neck, face, arms or legs until someone stops the one-woman massacre. I used to crush raw onions and smear 'em on my chest to bring down my body temperature. You can drink the juice too, but the women they got here today don't trust my secret foul-smellin' cures…and they told me so."

"It isn't easy for us either. There are nights when I I'm so covered with blood, I'm worried that I may have been injured while tending to a distressed patient. This is part of my usual job; doctors are bound by *Hippocrates Sermon* and need no other belief or conviction to care for the sick or the injured."

"That ain't true for the prison authority. Some of the guards wouldn't intervene if the new prison rules didn't oblige them to insure order. Others feel inmates must live out their terms, and if at all possible, with their mouths shut. With AIDS, there are now some who are afraid they'll get sick if they prevent suicides. The world has become a mighty poor place if people can't take care of each other no more." She continued talking with her ragged voice, wiping her mouth with the back of her hand whenever she had a coughing spell.

"Inmates now toss in those religious formulas for goodwill, for good luck, or for good measure," says Mérite-Lajoie cynically, the next time we talk. "What they really believe in is a soft bed and a good hot meal washed down with a cold beer. Salvation is the way the administration gets control over your body now, unless you get a ton of meds. Instead of prison pimps, religious macs do the hustlin'; get up your ass, and in your brain. You can't have your own ideas, and without ideas, we's left without a clue 'bout how to survive here."

These Beans Have Too Much Salt

As Mérite-Lajoie tells me this, I'm unwilling to let go of my feelings about how men and women get through their lives in prison. She almost sounds like she thinks there is a prison conspiracy to turn her into some sort of religious prostitute or whoremonger, and abduct her thoughts. With a newcomer's pride tinted with a self-righteousness only the guilty share, I respond, "Living without hope is the worst part of any prison sentence; without redemption, you need to find something to give you hope."

Having probably heard this line before, she isn't at all satisfied, and answers, first with a question: "What do you know about hope? The hope they say they's givin' us is really an excuse for an *Inquisition*. They ask us all kind of things, but all they wanna know is how to control us. They ask us if we have found peace and healin' from the Holy Spirit. If we've have been saved. Saved from what? I wanna know, 'cause they don't save us from nothin'. When you been around here long enough, you figure God has other stuff to tend to. Hope through religion is an after-death affair. If God sees us as humans anymore, he don't need to get permission from us, or from the chief warden. This new one thinks he hands out the truth like favors, but he ain't the one decidin' bout me. He ain't got no right. Hope here is just like another sentence, only it hasn't yet been pronounced." I wondered if Mérite-Lajoie was making play on words. In addition to *sentence*, as in a string of words with a meaning, in Cajun French, *to hope* also means *to wait*.

"The women ain't all complainin' 'bout the salvation. There's less violence here with more guards, but they ain't figured out what the warden is after. He wants to turn us into zombies", Mérite-Lajoie explained. "They ain't satisfied with an *eye for an eye*, they ain't worried about the taxpayer's burden, and they don't even think capital punishment works. Here they use another kind of cruelty. They destroy all earthly hope all right; then they put religion out there like bait for us fish to grab. But can they give us back that hope like they could save our lives? Nope. They might take away both. The hope offered here is no more than a carrot sword they hang in front of us mules to make us think about the metal kind danglin' by a single horsehair, over our heads. One day you're gonna mess up. They'll take the carrot away, kick you in the ass, and stick the sword in your face to keep you goin' all the same."

"They's playin' a kind of tedious and revengeful game; I'm tellin' you. You call that justice? It's easier to fight meanness than this sneaky business. Here you cain't ever leave nor do nothin' 'bout it. They think if you repeat somethin' enough, you gonna absorb that mumbo jumbo like paper on a runny poop. And if you ain't nibblin' that shit; you're stuck here all the same, while they try to force down more than you can swallow, or spit out, until you gag on it. Here, I learned to be scared of not just one man. I learned to be 'fraid of men and women alike. Not because they might kill or rape me, but because bein' a prison zombie means we ain't got our wits about us. Hell, we's so stuck on prayin' and forgiveness; we cain't even think or feel. We hardly know our names anymore. We ain't much different than slaves, but satisfied slaves, if you see what I mean." I didn't know what she meant, but then, at the time, I didn't give much thought to what she was saying. I hadn't even considered that repentance required more effort than just memorizing prayers and *Bible* verses. It only seemed to me then that she was rejecting religion, as I had, after having had it shoved down our throats, before putting some of us to sleep.

That summer before I worked at St. Gabriel when I showed up for the job interview, it was short of a miracle that I ran into Mérite-Lajoie for the first time since I was a child. She had a family visitor, and I, a visit to the penitentiary. In spite of the years of confinement, and her burn-scars, I recognized her, as well as her brother. She smiled at me with a slow glance of recognition.

Perhaps my arrival at St. Gabriel could be likened to when a Ferris wheel comes abruptly to a halt. When this one stopped, the gondola jolted, bumped, and before I had time to climb out, the rotation began again, scraping into its capsule a piece of memory from the softened soil, and dumping us both on my fairground without giving me a chance to tighten my grip on the brake.

As I look around the prison, familiarly called St. Gabriel's, after the town, I realize it is not a model of sanitation even though it is relatively recent. Overcrowding makes a uniform odor of stale cabbage, mixed with tobacco, dirty feet, and the stench of drains. It is overwhelming, even sickening, especially in the heat of the summer months when the new air conditioning is down. Roaches run rampant, chased by fat mice and rats in cells where Mérite-

Lajoie was once obliged to live after leaving the solitude of death row. I wonder how this once gentle woman had survived confinement there. The paint on the walls there is chipped, and humid spots are covered with lichen and mildew. Cracks run through the floors and the walls. "That cell block is no different today than when I lived there. The chief warden maintains the building in its original state as a reminder of the improvements he has made since his arrival at St. Gabriel. Now, he forbids withholding sanitary napkins to punish us like they did at first. But I tell you, Bee, even that ain't the worst."

Convinced I didn't come to this penitentiary to learn of prison life, or of its history; I am beginning to shift through her anecdotes and get a glimpse of what is at the bottom of Mérite-Lajoie's lasting quarrel with the religion offered here at St. Gabriel.

"What they call rebirth is just another name for returnin' to childhood." Mérite-Lajoie nodded her head. "Eh huh. Do you think we're children here? I don't think so, but they like to make out like we are."

Mérite-Lajoie reminds me. "The permanent residents here are made-to-order enemies confrontin' a blank space for a would-be hero. The wardens are always tempted to occupy that slot, even now, in an all-women's prison. But bein' a martyr is the final act of any play that starts off like that. The last one alive rarely steps into a hero's shoes for long. They might get away with it here; but one day, maybe on the outside, somebody else is keepin' score, and it ain't Destiny. Pardonin' someone you have killed, and asking for their pardon, in return, requires a lot more gut-wrenching meditation than we demand of children when they have wronged. And nobody can be forced to do that."

Beyond the haloed promise of hope and religious salvation, I thought that there were only two alternatives from which inmates may choose. My patient asked to be buried in Evergreen, Louisiana alongside some other family members and especially not at the Point Watch Cemetery within the prison boundaries. She had never wanted to be a hero, and she'd had more than enough of surveillance.

Hero for the Day

On that regretted morning, Mérite-Lajoie directed her pickup through the pecan grove and turned towards the Clayton highway, and back to Ferriday, where she found the wounded man in a hospital bed. "'He doesn't remember a thing.' The sheriff leaned in the room to see if the man was awake, 'but one thing is certain,' he said, 'the wound wasn't caused by a shotgun. It bled a lot before you got him here, but had it been a shotgun at close range, he wouldn't be here at all. I can tell you that. We have a witness. And soft ground tells a heap of tales. You can go in, but don't be too long. He's comin' along slow and sure, but is still very weak. I'm sure he'd like to see the man who saved his life. Uh..Er.. Well, you know what I mean.' The sheriff shook his head. He sounded like my in-laws. They could never get used to me huntin' and fishin' and drivin' a pickup. But after *Deux Ours* had his heart attack, I had to step up. He sure didn't mind. I don't know why anyone else would."

Mérite-Lajoie felt both relieved and more worried than before. According to *The Concordia Poste*, the shot came from out of town, and as usual, from organized crime, from New Orleans or Baton Rouge, where politicians were soaked in all kinds of goo: "It seems some of our representatives have been bathing again in corruption. They are weakening our state, handing out bids like they were bonbons. One politician was recently arrested and questioned about a slush fund. Only yesterday, a shooting took place near Ferriday. According to an official who preferred to remain anonymous, the crime is linked to cronyism and left one man seriously injured. He suffers from amnesia as well other injuries."

Of course, everyone in Ferriday knew Mérite-Lajoie had brought the man designated by the article to the hospital. "I was fortunate *The Daily-Picayune* connected the whole incident to the Cuban communist ring instead." She snickered. "This put the shooter practically out of reach, and thus forever remainin' the absent, though suspected party, but far away from me!"

Little imagination is needed to work up emotions and get tongues wagging all the way down to the feet in Ferriday. Communism was on everyone's minds in small-town America, and hence, accused for many incidents. Once one explanation wore thin, another took its place. Local Baptists were the first to doubt the accusation. They pointed at oriented partnerships, noting an eccentric gambler who happened to be a perennial gubernatorial candidate. This idea was without consequence either. Since the last governor had been constitutionally barred from the election, the outcome was determined by a segregation platform, no matter what sort of payments went on under the table.

And off they were, talking about the Governor election instead of the shooting. The men in white, as well as their wizard, came up with the ultimate punch line, but, in the long run, they didn't weigh much against a country music singer who used his popularity to stomp out those candidates and steal their words. He declared his opponent was supported by the NAACP, wrapping up all the fears of Louisiana's White population in five letters. Of course, Louisiana's citizens knew what went down, and most of the voters recalled their reasons when pressed. They voted for him for his jingle, forgetting his lightheartedness as he wrote off a large part of the population. It was easier to remember a happy dog, just as with a happy song. Both will hang in your mind ever so long, sweeping away ideological constipation along with constitutional headaches and chronic disorders.

Sometimes it seems people, myself included, remember whatever suits them, preferring to put their illnesses, and their guilt, in a safe place so they can be nurtured privately. As for the turncoat Republican candidate, there wasn't a chance of his winning. "Did his life-riskin' efforts to rid the state of racketeers have somethin' to do with that shootin'? Ha. In Louisiana, you could never tell which communist-mafia-politician was involved in the murders or assassinations you heard about. But all I worried about was how I got involved in all this." Mérite-Lajoie retained a bewildered look as she spoke in spite of the passing of time. "Conversations about lustful women weren't the only ones that hung around bars. On any night from Shreveport to New Orleans, from Vidalia to Lake Charles, you could chase remarks about conspiracy until you were drunk on theory, and that leaves out a good part of the boot. At least you knew the next day why your head hurt." And barely in the front door of the hospital, Mérite-Lajoie had a migraine.

"Was the sheriff referring to footprints on soft ground, or to the man, being softened up enough to render the truth about the incidents leading up to the shooting? Had he interfered with government projects as was suggested? Was he a member of the Cosa Nostra?" Mérite-Lajoie felt she hadn't saved anyone. Such an idea was unsettling enough in itself, even without suggesting involvement on the part of that Marcello fellow. Mérite-Lajoie's father had run across him in Metairie during the 1920's, left with a blackened eye, and vowed to steer clear of his gang of bootleggers and thieves. Perhaps the same wasn't true of her uncle. Yet, here she was, barely one generation later, finding more to worry about than she had bargained for by tidying up their botched deals if she had not thwarted them. "Either way, I thought it would probably be better to decamp, go undercover, and forget about the whole thing. Wasn't that what the victim was doin'? At least the visit brought me some relief; the sheriff said nothin' about the hemorrhagin' being worsened by my intervention. Neither had the doctor. Perhaps this much of my part had gone unnoticed."

The man motioned for her to sit on the edge of his bed. There was something flurried and unsettled about him. As soon as she had done so, he grabbed Mérite-Lajoie's arm and looked at her almost desperately, yet with feisty eyes warmed over by Mérite-Lajoie's arrival, "'You saved my life,' he told me, 'And now I'll be eternally indebted to you. If it weren't for you, I'd be dead. The Devil run roughshod on me in that possum patch. There wadn't anyone else round to save me and low and behold you was there and gave me hope and new life. I couldn't walk a single step. You didn't give up on me. The world's greatest, a hero, I'll say you are, even if you is a girl, and I'll see to it you is generously rewarded.'"

"I thought the man was exaggerating somewhat." Mérite-Lajoie sat up in the bed and adjusted a blanket she used as a pillow. "Not only I wasn't a hero; I didn't feel like I was the greatest at anything, and figured I was in trouble enough as it was. 'Don't let it bother you none,' I said. 'Anyone else would've done the same thing. It is jest natural to try and help.'"

"'You ain't from round here are ya?' said the man. 'That gives us something else in common. I got cousins here, but I'm from farther south. You a Cajun ain't ya? I ain't got no more use for my cousins, but I ain't got nothin' 'gainst Cajuns.'"

The man we came to know as Harper had a vainglorious way of delivering an encomium. From his standpoint, to say he had been saved by a hero raised his personal level of esteem; adding the superlative accentuated in some way his control over the domain of revere. The rescue, thus became spectacular, the danger, eminent, the recovery, miraculous. It was as if though he imagined he was a character of an adventure novel that revolved around excessive passions and in particular, those that concerned him in the first degree. Thus, his admiration for the Good Samaritan was disoriented, aimed at applauding himself instead of his hero. His compliments then turned sour; what remained of the provocative solicitations that burned the ear would suddenly cool off the listener with its following billowy praise. Instead of relaxing Mérite-Lajoie, these ovations confused her. She could never figure out how to respond or if she were called upon to do so. For years, Harper maintained in this way a sordid victory over his many fictitious adversaries, pretending to vehemently address a crowd, inhibiting barely the angry gests, starting a fire only to throw water on it. He spoke of multiple threats that surrounded the community. If you asked too many questions, you would quickly become one of his many scapegoats. In this way, he cast aside doubts, solicited worry, and even fear. From this perspective, mortal enemies were all around them. You never knew who to watch out for, where the danger was coming from, or who had brought the munitions. Neither realized that in naming Mérite-Lajoie as a hero, the injured man was also indicating an enemy in their midst.

"I didn't care much for effusion and hoped to leave the Ferriday hospital room as soon as it was decent. 'Promise me you'll come back,' the wounded man begged. 'You'll come and see me and take me somewhere else. Anywhere. I don't remember where I came from or even who I am. I was only jokin' about the cousins. I'm issuing warnins only to protect myself. I don't wanna stay here! I'm worried 'bout my life. Somebody wants me dead, but I don't know who it is. The sheriff is watchin' over me now, but that ain't gonna last. I can see your ring. You gotta a husband somewhere? He wouldn't mind helpin' a solid citizen, I suppose?' He wouldn't let me leave until I promised I would come back, pick him up, and take him to Natchez."

Mérite-Lajoie sighed, looked around the room, and then continued with her story. Perhaps in the short interview, Harper's pleading had invested her with enough aplomb to attempt an extraordinary feat, unprecedented at least for someone of her means, background, and upbringing.

"Later that day, after seeing to it that Harper was resting comfortably, and after having chatted with the doctor, I drove back to the town of Ferriday, then back to the area where the events had occurred."

Ferriday Louisiana's center looks like it was laid out according to some surveyor's plan if you limit your driving only through the first few streets. After meeting with Harper, Mérite-Lajoie drove through the town; as if driving up and down ordered streets could help her to assimilate the bedlam invading her soul. "Who is this man who wants me to believe I am the only person on earth who can save him? But as I turned my pickup, at the end of one street, out came another; making these seem more like a vine of kudzu, fallen from the Mississippi side of the river, than anything an engineer would draw, except in his spare time. These streets seem to have doodled out through all the gutters! I tried to calm myself through driving, but my panic began to grow out of control. It was my truck that did the driving, and I held on to the wheel, while it conducted me up one street and down another, as if I ignored most of what I had already discovered the day before. 'Cain't never could find much,' I remember sayin' to myself, to settle my guts".

She wasn't sure what she was looking for then, but thought it had to be near, "if only my pickup would've thought to take me back home." She laughed at herself half-heartedly. "Ah…I'll find answers somewhere." She shook her head, her features slightly distorted. "In those days I still believed in God, but today, I don't take him as a witness anymore."

"The man at the Esso station was eying the partially dried blood in the cab as he filled my gas tank. 'I'll tell you what," he said, 'if you leave your truck here 'til this afternoon, I'll clean that seat and floor for you for a dollar. You were axin' 'bout who owned those lots for sale out by the lake? All this part of town, all this,' he pointed with his index, holding the rag he used to wipe the windshield out like a signal, 'from here to the end of the cotton field, including the gin, and the farm equipment store, all belong to the same family, the Ferriday's. There are at least three hundred acres. If you go far enough back, they once owned everything from Ferriday to St. Francisville. Do you want me to check under your hood?'"

"'Nah' I replied, handing him three dollars and twenty cents for the full tank, tryin' to put the different plantations into perspective, wondering if the attendant was a distant cousin of this once rich family, tryin' to figure out why he was swaggerin' about like a wealthy landowner." She had realized the man was curious about her truck, but Mérite-Lajoie usually took care of these things herself, and she wasn't much of a talker. "'What kind of animal did you kill?' the man finally asked, shiftin' from one foot to the other, pullin' up his pants on one hip, then the other, actin' as if he had suddenly grasped some wisdom, which placed him above others. I looked at him hard, readin' him and replied, 'a possum.' The man laughed, expectin' perhaps another response, 'you thought he was dead huh? They pretend like that. Looks like he surprised you, didn't he?' I forced a laugh, imaginin' a scene where the bleedin' animal stopped *playin' possum* and decided to escape out my window, leavin' a bloody mess. 'Sure did,' I told him.

"'I guess next time, you'll put it in the back?' questioned and answered the man still holdin' the rag, this time next to his head, like a mail box flag pickup signal, stickin' out from under his hat." I thought of the rag flying up and down according to the gossip waiting to be picked up or delivered.

"'I reckon I will,' I told that troublemaker." Jittery, now, as then, Mérite-Lajoie unfolded her story, telling me that she didn't drive off right away. Talking with the nosy service station attendant had helped her move a little closer to life, or at least further away from her distress. Not wanting to lie, she had changed the subject back to the Ferriday's. 'I know some Ferriday's, at least the name. They're over in Natchez, where they have a Greek revival mansion. I seen the name on a mailbox.' The gas jockey tipped his hat and moved away from the truck when he saw another customer driving up to the pump."

Forgetting to ask about a Ferriday address as she drove off from the station, Mérite-Lajoie turned her head hard on the left to see if there was an antebellum home among the trees in the curve of the road. She had been disappointed, finding only new wooden or brick homes, wondering where she should go to find the answers that she felt she needed, juggling a kind of undetermined bitterness in her soul, as though to prevent it from settling or taking hold.

"I didn't know how I was goin' to find out about that spring or well, if they didn't live there no more. Surely there had been a house; there had always been a house, where once before there were as many slaves tendin' to the cotton crops, they had there in Ferriday. What kind of people they was, was hard for me to judge. Some do more than accumulate wealth. Some hate everyone so much they try to wipe everything clean off the earth as if they wanted to start over fresh. Had one such of that kind struck a match to that house and left nothin' but tears in his wake, I had no idea. Had those people got past those backward years? The foundin' families were like their kin in Mississippi, two generations later they still was rememberin' what they never themselves owned, no matter who they was in their hearts. I was thinkin' they probably built a copy of the house in the same place, wherever that was. I figured it was for some kinda retribution. Maybe nostalgia. Who knows where they found the money to reconstruct. Rich people's always prayin' for it. Probably get it at interest. Seems like these people always livin' on somethin' they got somewhere else. And they call that independent livin'. They hold on to too much stuff, and got too many debts ever to be free."

While she wanted to explain to herself why her own ambitious scheme would be different, how she could have money without becoming someone she mistrusted and even despised, Mérite-Lajoie had tried to imagine the family who once owned property enough to cover the size of the town and up to a hundred square miles, and what had become of them. She pictured them now wandering about, like the Cajuns they had forced into battle and despised for desertion. "Well, you can't squeeze blood out of a turnip." She spoke under her breath, gathering up many thoughts about the Civil War and past debts on all sides into one phrase. "My mind went from the Ferriday's to the possum, and then to the man with the gunshot, or Harper, as he called himself. The panic returned. I shrank into myself again, my lungs like a crushed tomato. I had trouble gettin' enough air."

"I stabled myself behind the wheel, and drove north again that day, towards the woods where I'd been huntin' the day before. There, from a bird's eye-view, I think you could probably still imagine the old plantation, its former, as well as its later, economy. Not ready to go home, I turned right, across from the cotton gin, which flanked the northern side of town. Maybe it still does?"

As Mérite-Lajoie spoke, I found myself for an instant in the abandoned gin, thirty years before. She didn't take notice of my absence, and chattered on, probably happy to find someone to talk to that knew the town where her drama had unfolded.

"My heart began to beat fiercely as I approached the place where I had parked my pickup. I noticed some partially cleared land that looked as if it bordered the lake. Seein' the half fallen *For Sale* sign, I parked; got out and walked towards the place I thought I'd been the day before. I must have lost my sense of direction as well as its butt, enough to follow the lake and miss the road. I must've plunged deeper into the other side of the woods before I came back to my truck. The path seemed simple the second time around."

Mérite-Lajoie had been wary of her growing disorientation, swelling with the emotional awareness of Deux Ours' lifelong struggle with direction, amplified by the anticipation of finding the spring. She had thought about attributing this confusion to an outside force. Unlike her husband, it was so unlike her to feel uneasy in the woods alone. "What could happen to me? I noted the phone number on the sign as if the series represented the winning numbers on a lottery ticket."

"That fear kept rolling over my skin, up my nose, and into my heart. The smell of it was all around me. I was afraid, not afraid like when you find yourself face to face with an alligator or even a feral dog, and you say to yourself: 'It's either him or me', but afraid of the thought of the gator or somethin' just as frightenin' that I couldn't see."

"I called it a gator (because it helped to call it out) but I felt it all around me. Cold waves went up and down all through my body. These even went all the way to the soles of my feet. I could then feel the thing comin' up from the ground. But it didn't come out of hidin'. I waited for it, but you don't know how to prepare for what you cain't name or see." It had murmured to her in the breeze; now, it growled at her in her dreams.

"Wanderin' through the briars, I found some flies and dried blood, nothin' as spectacular as I remembered, not half as bad as my nightmare. But just there, next to the remainin' evidence, the ground was still wet, and tastin' the wet grass, I found it was salty. That was proof enough of the existence of a spring. I thought it must be underground. I walked about for at least a half an hour, frantically at first, then more and more purposefully. Unable to shake off a strange feelin' of excitement, not quite as panicky as before, I didn't find the saltwater spring, nor did I find the remains of the animal I thought I had killed."

"Anything could have happened. I thought I always shot true, but it might have been pretendin' to be dead after all. 'Nah. A buzzard probably got it', I thought. But I needed a shovel to find the spring. So, I gave up on findin' answers and returned to my pickup. I drove to the Lake Road, still feelin' queasy."

The morning sky had lost some of its remaining fuzziness. The white veil had followed its nocturnal beasts back to the water, leaving behind an air heavy and stale with their breath. "The humidity made my face clammy." She reached for her handkerchief and wiped her brow. "I looked out over the cotton field, thinkin' it would probably rain in the afternoon. John Deere's two-row pickers were busy even though in some places farmers with small plots still handpicked the cotton bolls and put it into long bags."

"I drove near the brick red vacated elementary school, behind the gin. Thinkin' it was a big school for such a small town, I wondered if Emmy would be happy there come fall. I saw some children jumpin' off the roof and runnin' around the side. But, no matter how hard I looked over the surroundin' area; I still didn't find the rebuilt mansion." Her eyes turned on me as if she wanted to question me about some part of Ferriday's history she could have ignored.

I never thought about a plantation having been the point of departure for Ferriday. The truth was, it hadn't burned. It had rotted and its location was finally sold and converted to a railway terminal long before we came there. Its residents had at first fled, then come back, too poor to make repairs, and lived in the decaying house until it finally sunk, collapsing under the weight of saltpeter and time, like an abandoned ship in an ocean of weeds. However, the cotton plantation survived, and so did the name. Thus, a neighborhood was born, on the unplanted part of the plantation, behind the school now. It was a lower portion, there where everything else returned to decompose, except the name of the former owners. And this name would surely disappear one day as well.

"Now, what are those chillens up too?" had she asked, seeing two barefoot girls run across the empty playground towards the houses.

One of them, Skizzum, was wearing a dress and had long legs, the other, me, wore overalls and had braids. The playground was our territory in the long hot summer months when the building was vacant, and the grass was high.

As Fickle as the Weather

"They say folks on rich bottomland quit braggin' when the river rises. But at least they have someone watchin' over their kids," Mérite-Lajoie sighed as she recalled looking out over the cotton field. "Suddenly I felt very small like someone might when looking out from his ship at a starry night's sky, realizin' the sun was only one of billions of stars, and me, such a tiny dot on the ocean waves. The opportunity of operatin' a Salt Spring Resort offered such large perspectives, I felt dizzy."

"In fact, whenever I get one of these disproportionate ideas, I get some kind of vertigo. As a child, on the point of frazzled panic after hearin' Orson Welles' radio show, *The War of the Worlds*, I thought I would go out to defend the planet from any intruders. As soon as I got my ammunition gathered (I probably didn't have more than a three or four rounds) I started off for my treehouse. Somehow, I couldn't make it higher than the third rung of the ladder. I don't think it was fear of Martians, but rather the idea of bein' some kind of superhero that bothered me. I didn't want to end up alone. Instead, I wound up stirrin' up ant beds and watchin' the little insects run frantically this way and that. I put obstacles in their way until they found me in the grass, silently ran up my legs, and stung me all at once. Once my head stopped spinnin', all the ants in a fury, and my legs swollen; I tired of that."

Fire ants were indomitable. Later, Mérite-Lajoie tried pairing herself with an equivalent force. "When a boy talked to me, I was too embarrassed to answer. I walked around after church with my hands behind my back, tryin' to find places people gathered on Sunday before returnin' home for dinner. On the way, I threw rocks at old empty houses and once broke a window and had to pay for it by cleanin' out pig sties for a month."

"My discomfort let up only when I was with my horses and later, when I followed Deux Ours off to the war, and wound up as a nurse in France. There I watched out for bullets like I kept an eye out for fire ants. You could negotiate with neither. I pulled over that day after I had visited the land, and stopped the pickup again. 'How could anyone want all this?' I thought. Again, this staggering feeling of insignificance couldn't be explained by any peripheral cause. Only now, I understand that this feeling comes from the realization of what being alone really means."

"It wasn't that I found livin' among other communities or ownership distasteful, but my people had almost always been immigrants of one sort of another and never owned much in the way of land. They stuck together, but no longer had the same sense of property, or of propriety, for that matter. We all thought we were capable of complete self-sustenance, but without each other, we were like isolated circus acrobats bitin' the dust, and it wasn't a figure of speech." She forced a wooden laugh before continuing, "I couldn't imagine remainin' somehow faithful to a defeated flag or tryin' to keep a disappointment alive at such costs the way these people did with their little Confederate banners flutterin' from their dashboards, forgettin' again a large part of the population who wasn't interested in those symbols. Wasn't goin' to war too steep a price to pay for one's sole values? Why hold on to somethin' that only stirred up painful memories? There had to be other reasons." I could almost see a farmer wave at Mérite-Lajoie as he turned his huge machine around on the road in front of her, adjusting it and descending again with it into the surging cotton stalks, almost five feet high, with mice jumping out of the furrows, as the machine charged.

"I finally got out of my pickup. Whatever the southerner felt about his land, the Cajun loved Louisiana even more. Like me, we all like the way our feet sink into the rich earth and the perfume of the overturned humid soil. I walked around for a dozen yards or so, enjoyin' the mornin' sun on my face. For a minute, I could almost see myself on the cotton-pickin' machine, listenin' to a transistor, and allowin' the dust to stick to my sweaty skin and run down my cheek. I remember wonderin' about all that DTT they put on the crops of cotton since the war. Did that stuff turn out to be dangerous? It stuck to the crop and didn't wash away with the rain. It smelled like chemicals when they sprayed it into the air. It was a chemical, but everyone said since cotton wasn't a food crop, farmers should use it to keep the boll weevils down. I bet it cost a bunch nowadays, keepin' the pests out. The salesman rang even those days at your door boastin' about *Miracle Kill* and you'd wind up buyin' their products to spread on your garden or in your house. But do you need them all that much? Do these chemicals work as well as they say? Does killin' everything make you the strongest? The two-legged variety is the worst kind anyway. More than once,

I bought the stuff to get rid of the salesman. I don't think a woman would have ever invented such a thing. Maybe farmers here could plant something else here for a while until the damn boll weevils go away? How did farmers get along without usin' them at all?" she asked. "I picked up a dirt clot and smelled it to see if I could smell the chemicals. I put it on my tongue and spat. The ground mostly tasted like good Louisiana dirt to me that day. Knowin' its origins made it seem more digestible. Knowin' I will never taste dirt again makes me lose all appetite."

Many of Mérite-Lajoie's family members had been migrant workers. Like the farmer who found freedom in mechanization and the itinerate worker who had become a sharecropper, she had wanted to become self-reliant and stop working as a postal employee. As a disoriented construction worker, her husband had trouble keeping any job at all. "We had to invest to get ahead, but buyin' things on credit was sellin' your soul to the Devil as far as we was concerned. I once tried makin' a catalog to sell herbal cures, but didn't have enough money to get my project started right."

"In spite of my burdens and my worries about buildin' a project on my own, my eyes looked beyond the farmers that day on their shinin' machines."

"The watchman from the temporary buildin' next to the gin waved as I rolled away, studyin' the surroundin' area. I wondered where the man was the day before when I needed him. I'd knocked on the watch-house door, almost kickin' it in. I thought he was probably off fishin', thinkin', 'that's some job; you just have to wake up in the morning and walk around the place a couple of times, look busy and call it a day'. But to be fair, the watchman had three shifts on weeknights. You could see his flashlight move about inside and outside the gin at night. There was another guardian there on weekends and the other nights. He was nearly always drunk and kept to his cot, which was the case when I beat on his door that Sunday morning. Jim Taylor was there the morning after to pick up his check and ask his boss if he could have some more hours. He wanted to buy a house with his wife. None of us yet knew he would lose her in what was called an accident later that day when he went to pick her up from her job as a housemaid. A nasty epoch had begun in Ferriday that week."

"Luck is about as fickle as the weather, especially in Louisiana. You can't ever count on it to get you through, even on a daily basis. This much is true even if you avoid lookin' at the new moon over your left shoulder or go to church every Sunday. People who say storms are worse in Haiti because of the revolt of the slaves are pushin' punishment theory a little hard. It don't take no prophet or Toussaint Louverture to predict what'll come of an ill wind."

"Hurricanes are sufficient enough exactions to prove that sin of paradisiacal proportions exists even among White God-fearin' Christians. Once I saw eighty-eight Black and White bodies stripped of every last thread, laid out side by side like piano keys. But in places of retribution like Angola or St. Gabriel, where everyone, includin' the preacher, been washed out more than once with floodwaters, the unleashin' of biblical storms ain't the first cause of death."

Mérite-Lajoie recalled noticing a graveyard in Ferriday behind the gin she hadn't seen the day before. "Not many headstones there, maybe bout as much underground? It looked old, all the same." There, on this deserted plot, lay many other cotton pickers, all remains of people who had been reduced to enslavement. Their tombs, and their inscriptions (if there had ever been any) no longer divulged the names of the people who finally had been set free. Most of the people who had remembered them and had set the tombstones were either dead or had moved away. Most of the ones who had desecrated the epitaphs had left as well. "I bet that place'll cause hair to raise on the back of your neck if you hang round at night."

Enslaved people were buried, as anyone else from the plantation, but not in the same cemetery. If there were such a thing as *post mortem* equality, you could find no trace of it there. No caretaker cleared the weeds that covered the tombs; no one set the sunken headstones straight; the place was left neglected, and remained unnamed and overlooked by the town officials. As a child I remember staring at this desolation and thinking it looked like a craving mouth with half rotted broken teeth. Then, for the first time, I thought of death. Perhaps from the teeth, I contemplated skeletons in a bone yard. It was not so far-fetched an idea. I had played dominos many times with my great-grandmother who sent me to the *bone yard* with toothless glee before she went there herself. And

I was frightened, not of the tombs, not of the idea of an inert human body having ceased to function, not even of having lost a loved one, but of the sickening awareness that we all will one day sink into oblivion. I comforted myself for a while with the illusion that I might somehow avoid this abandonment, telling myself that this was the sort only reserved for slaves in the south, then for the unlucky, for the callous, or for those who were simply too foolish to be loved and to be remembered. However, the more I observed, the more I calculated my escape from my catalog of disregard, the more complete it became, extending its categories among all walks of life, excluding no one, even if in Ferriday there were separate entrances.

There were many adults in town who adopted this two-door attitude. They lived as though death did not exist for them. They went on about their lives, not concerned with the strife of people living just across the road, behind the tracks and the trees. They did not care about the descendants of the once glorious Helena (Ferriday) Plantation's enslaved people. Most pretended not to know the men in the white sheets who carried burning crosses, threatening, when they did not kill.

Mérite-Lajoie disregarded this part of Ferriday history when she moved there, and especially its gossip. She had lived in Natchez with Deux Ours since the end of the war and only came on this side of the Mississippi to visit family further south, in St. Martinville, or to hunt in the swamps. Her comments to herself that day, took no more heed of the graves abandoned to nature, or to other forces, than they had of the gin's watchman. This internal gibberish was solely designed to keep herself company and ward off her anxiety. Had she thought about it, she would have figured the graves had gone the way of the house. Only now did she share with me her fears about the void.

Had Jim watched as Mérite-Lajoie drove by, bending over slightly and spitting out some of the tobacco juice on the ground in front of him, like I'd seen him do? "What's a gal with an out-of-state plate drivin' round here? Probably got lost," I could almost hear him say. Such were the reflections of people who had little time on their hands and about as much conversation with others as time. They were left to imagine what a bystander, a passer-by, or even a neighbor was doing, and they were bothered more by their internal acuity than by actual events. As a woman, Mérite-Lajoie's ears burned with more than her share of unwelcome comments.

A Visit to the Neighborhood

Our neighborhood ran from the railroad track along on the other side of the elementary school to the new Farm Outlet Store on the Lake Road. A small bayou, the last trace of a muddy horseshoe, meandered along under a bridge and between two rows of houses. This once surging inlet dried up leaving only small souring puddles in the summer. There, mosquitoes found refuge and my friends and I played, in spite of my grandfather's warnings of typhoid fever, boils, or even spirits from the bog. None of us paid much mind to these so-called dangers. Besides, we wore devil's shoestring in a red mojo bag around our necks to fend off bad luck (especially gossip), but after all, we agreed we only did it to spook off one of the tattletales, the only enemy we had in those days.

Off the main road, a smaller road led to a series of empty neglected patches bordering the oxbow lake. Another led to a neighborhood, called Chocolate Quarters, a sensual and aromatic name. More than a neighborhood, this community formed a small town itself, segregated from the other, with protocoled exchanges between the two. A forest grew on three sides and separated it from the lake lots. Overhead, you could still see these homes were once part of the plantation, and they were following the same course as the big house. Most had not been modernized in the late sixties, had no electricity or running water, and were slowly, and even more assuredly, collapsing and rotting away. These sparse buildings were once the homes of enslaved people, but as a child, I never grasped what living there could mean for its inhabitants. In Ferriday, memory went to sleep like death.

On the side of the Lake Road with the waning bayou, the homes were more recent, and in better shape. These houses were built on each side of the street and, right before the curve, instead of a mansion lawn lined with oaks, there was a large brick house with useless white columns decorating the front, in a simulation of a former plantation home, but much closer to the street. In order not to reduce the pretentious *façade*, no trees were planted in the yard.

"The nouveau rich like to show off their wealth," resumed Mérite-Lajoie, "but they forget to plant trees, and they cut the ones they have." Here, no decoration or swimming pool indicated to the passer-by the house had been occupied for at least ten years, yet a fence closed off the yard from the neighboring properties. The families were all middle class, but for Mérite-Lajoie, they each seemed to enjoy a cozy life, much easier than her own.

"As I drove by, a thick disheveled green curtain, decorated with lush tropical vines and flowers, reminded me that the only thing without impediments in Central Louisiana was the gossip. A fence sometimes gives people an incentive to lean on for chattin' with their neighbors without invadin' their yards or their privacy, but movements behind curtains are a sure sign of less than cordial commerce. A word intended for one over the fence would wind up in the ear of another, on the other side of the window coverins. In those days, the late fifties, most of the talk was about who they thought was cheatin' on their wives, or who was pregnant without a husband, but with the Evangelists, the rumor-mongers turned their interests to homosexuality or to what they were startin' to call women libbers. People couldn't stand to have nothin' talked about them. That's why there were so many fights. 'Probably sick from eatin' too many jungle toads,' I thought, noticin' a painted monkey on one curtain. A painted monkey! Can you just see it?"

"For some reason not clear to me then, I despised people who lived behind their curtains, lookin' out on the world and never getting' their hands dirty. Bunch of shit-blabbin' prudes. Those people cover their ears and pretend to hear no evil, and be shocked 'bout anything. But they spread injustice around like fire on a hayfield." Mérite-Lajoie recalled thinking, laughing again. "Too bad the Plymouth Rock didn't fall on those Puritan heads before they spread out over the rest of the country."

People often suppose others to be much different from themselves, especially in small towns, although they persist in loaning violent intentions or pleasures to those they hardly know. Granting a lender's confidence to perfect strangers is all the more surprising because of the passion, which accompanies the loan. Before they are of age to suppose much about anything, children listen to their parents, their neighbors, their friends, and grow up adopting their expressions of hatred without thinking, repeating these without experimenting, until one day, if nothing intervenes, they believe them, and surpassing their beliefs, their parent's expertise becomes unquestioned certitudes in their children's minds. If prejudices were golden gifts, outsiders would be rich.

These beliefs concerning inconnus, the opposite of awareness about visitors, remained suspended at the stage of repetition for Mérite-Lajoie. She wondered why Harper clutched on to her like he had. "He probably didn't know much about Louisiana's French. He's like a loose oyster; if he cain't find a rock, he'll incrust on another's shell. I felt as sorry for what happened to Harper that day as if I'd shot him myself. I never could figure out why. Maybe I thought I should've been happy to let him ride on my back. At least for a while. Maybe he was surprised a woman had brought him to the hospital? It's funny I didn't think he was hittin' up on me though. I was much younger then. Can you feel guilty a long time in advance for something you don't even know you're gonna do?"

Even though the Cajuns were often cited as vagrants or thieves, the people who lived in the Quarters were not considered at all by most of the inhabitants of Ferriday. Prejudice is an imprecise term, and the discretion of the Community Service Club was about what could be considered as the least contained in town, meaning that if the news of Mérite-Lajoie's visit had been bourbon in a barrel; it would be bottom dry before the week had passed. Mérite-Lajoie decided soiled hands were proof of a well-kept if however not spotless, mind. The only people she suspected of proclivities were people who were always without a job; in this way, she resembled almost everyone else in Louisiana, and even those who were unfortunate enough to be without a job. She made an exception for her husband, whose health problems, along with his lifelong apprehensions and his racial difference, made it difficult to find anything.

Still further down the street the houses were modest. Saint Patrick Green for a fervent Irish household, but the other neighborhood houses were simply painted white. Many had trees or shrubbery. Some looked bare on empty lots. Our house was one of these. Pierre Gautier, my grandfather, who we called Papou, had bought land in this part of Louisiana in the late twenties and had built the house with the help of his cousins. Since my father's disappearance, I lived here with him, my mother, Elizabeth, who we called Skizzum, and our two younger brothers, T-Beaux, and T-Pierre. My father left after the birth of my brothers, never to be seen in these parts again. Until I went to France, I thought having sons was more complicated for him than having daughters. But in France he unknowingly had a son before any of us came into the world. There was nothing simple about any of us, although my grandfather would never mix with most of our neighbors. After Papa left, I was sometimes worried my mother would disappear as well, and I never permitted myself to love her much. At home with Papou, Skizzum and I had to do most of the chores Mama did before she had to work two jobs.

My sister, Skizzum, used to be a brazen girl. Until that summer, I cannot remember her being worried or afraid of much, but it was hard to make her laugh. She would keep on a poker face forever so long. When we went swimming, she would be the up the tree and yell "Snake bait" before swinging on the rope and dropping off first in the bayou. Although Black kids often played the *Dirty Dozens*, and sometimes even the White boys of Helena Addition squared off at school, girls never did, except Skizzum. She would pick up after a boy's "Yo mama is a slut," and respond: "Yo witless fuckin' buttrumpet" or "yo ma is a skunk-wearing gin-lickin' degenerate," continue developing insults that would win their applause and admiration until the teacher came over to see why there was a crowd. For her, she wasn't insulting anyone or their mother; she was showing off her skills of intimidation. I never heard these expressions elsewhere, even in an integrated high school later. Sometimes I think she made some of them up and spread them all the way to Canada. Why she never used them with Harper, I will never explain to myself.

I was proud of what seemed to me to be her freedom. A talented musician, Skizzum could play the piano for hours. It wasn't a Cajun instrument, but the local radio station had given it to our grandfather in exchange for repairing someone's accordion, and she learned how to play it by herself. Before that summer began, she was the best of us all. Afterward, she left home without telling us where she was going. No one thought much about her leaving like that. She was seventeen and through her pregnancy had attained adult status. She was expected to go to work, with or without a high-school diploma, but our mother never thought she would leave Ferriday. No one did. A family friend told my grandfather later that year he had seen her in playing guitar in a New Orleans bar. I could tell by the look on Papou's face that he wasn't reassured.

These Beans Have Too Much Salt

In 1969, she wrote to me to ask me to go with her to the music festival with all the hippies at Woodstock. She had changed her name to Bobby McGee, sang swamp blues songs or scats she made up in her spare time and was headed up there with a girl she had met hitchhiking from Port Arthur to New Orleans. I'm almost sorry to say I didn't go with them, but who knows what I would have gotten into. Her girlfriend died only about a year later from an overdose, and Skizzum was off somewhere else. College was around the corner for me. I had a Louisiana State University scholarship, but I still wasn't ready for the world five years after the tragedy that rolled over our lives. Skizzum certainly wasn't either. Although she didn't brood much over her own heroism, she wrote songs about the pain of others and drank too much.

Defining what happened is as difficult now as it was then. Crimes have strict definitions, but this one was off the books. The people the closest to me were gone. Skizzum never came back to Louisiana. I won't say here much about my brothers, as they don't appear much in the story. They both grew up to be fine men with good jobs and families, but they left Ferriday as well. As for Emmy, it is hard to judge her life, but what happened created a vacancy in my heart where there once had been a close friendship. A couple of years ago one of my brothers met Skizzum, still going by the name of Bobby, in Nashville, Tennessee, where she was pushing an upright piano on wheels down the street. She said she'd even composed for Katie Webster and played with Lightinin' Slim, Bonnie Raitt and Robert Cray. He almost didn't recognize her, and probably wouldn't have, if she hadn't called out to him. Music is the only thing that has never abandoned us.

That summer when Mérite-Lajoie showed up at our door, we were all still very much children in our hearts and minds. We played out the long summers at the lake, or at the school grounds behind our house. There were no limits for our games. We could try anything, as long as it was fun and no one got hurt. That our neighborhood, our town, perhaps as well as the entire state of Louisiana was a place of corruption, ruled by a particular form of innocence, meaning no one wanted to know; we would not have learned in school. But what we learned in the neighborhood changed our lives forever. Who lived there, what they did, and what they would become; to us that was all that seemed to matter. And it did. When Mérite-Lajoie came to into our lives, she brought us something. I'm still weighing the negative against the positive for each of us. Sometimes I feel without her, we would not have come face to face with the Devil, but we might not have come face to face with ourselves either. So, Mérite-Lajoie came, bringing gifts of unmistakable ambivalence.

Mérite-Lajoie knew that the man at the station was erroneous about the ownership of the property, but she let him talk to avoid conversation about the shooting. It was bad enough an outsider had noticed the blood in the truck cab and she was still worried that she might have some trouble with the law. Harper's doctor knew the land for sale across the Lake Road belonged to Papou, and not the founding family; making him, a Cajun like herself, the man to see.

These Beans Have Too Much Salt

Such meetings take a nick out of any keg and spice up the most tasteless plates. Cajuns are known for their hospitality, especially towards other Cajuns, and for their food. Like most of the people in Helena Addition, the service station attendant couldn't imagine a Cajun owning any land; but before anyone else could beat him to it and full of useless knowledge, the flag next to his hat flipped up. He bragged to his next two clients about having seen the fool who was going to purchase the lowest part of bottomland that could almost be called dry and continue with the second best known inconspicuous peddling that money could buy. He was referring to bootlegging of course, as that is what had been going on the leased land for more than thirty years. He imagined that its new owners would take up the *tchouflangue* (small, cheap business) where the others had left it.

Now, my grandfather was not responsible for what went on over on those lake lots he had bought with plans for his own thwarted money-making projects. Since then, he got along with most people by not running across information he wasn't supposed to meet up with on less formal occasions, and never visited the land he had leased. Whatever the occasion, gossip is only a tool used by envious people whose only purpose is to humiliate. Perhaps in the long run, this incontinence serves to spice up their otherwise prosaic lives, but in short, it is hateful to all those concerned.

A Louisiana Purchase

It didn't take long for Mérite-Lajoie to find Papou and discuss buying the lots. So unsure of business dealings, and in particular, this one, she began by stammering, introducing herself and telling him why she had come. Papou brought her a glass of ice tea, and both sat in rocking chairs on the porch. It was a large covered screened porch with a ceiling fan and enough room for more than the two rockers. These were close enough to each other for conversation, yet separated by a pedestal table, and far enough for reverie. "I had not planned on speakin' of the events of the day before, but I didn't get very far with that idea."

"I explained why my husband couldn't buy the land here. He being a Houma Indian and as such, was considered by most as a free person of color. Hell, they were barely considered as American citizens at all! He would've had a hard time gettin' the papers notarized or filin' the deed. I understand times have changed, but in those days, it was worse bein' a colored person than a woman."

"I had a hard time stayin' on track. What I kept referrin' to as an accident was takin' up so much room in my mind that even if I had not felt I owed it to one of my fellow Cajuns to tell him about it, I couldn't see any way around it. I couldn't stop myself from mentionin' the facts. They came tumblin' out all at once like groceries out of a wet paper bag. Of course, your grandfather knew most about the incident already, or thought he did. He listened attentively, as much as a sign of respect as of confusion over my excitement and surprise to find a woman there on his porch talkin' 'bout buyin' land that had been for sale for years. I thought your family was hard up for cash and hopin' for a quick transaction, and the incident in itself would not hinder the sale. I imagined that day that someone else would beat me to the natural spring I thought was there, if I didn't act fast."

Mérite-Lajoie's natural reticence encumbered her as she spoke of her meeting with Papou. It made her slip as she shifted into gear and plowed through the circumstances surrounding the proposed acquisition. "'J'étais en train de chasser là-bas', I said to your grandfather in French with my Cajun accent. 'I was huntin' over there when I shot a possum covered with salt.'" Mérite-Lajoie's face, which had been almost as white as a fish belly when she started spreading her tale, recovered a healthier glow as she set forth the details of her misadventure. "'The creature uttered some powerful words,' I told him. What I understood was this, 'Par mon extinction, ton tribu continuerai à vivre. (By my death, your tribe will continue to live.)' I swallowed hard, pretendin' to gulp my tea, before continuin'. 'I dunno what the possum meant, but somethin' good has to come out of it.' It sounded mystic, religious, kinda like it knew the truth. That's what I thought and I accorded it unlimited credence. Talkin' critters are rare today. I thought it had to be the right time for me to leave the civil service anyway. I jest couldn't sit back and watch things happen. I thought this was the opportunity I was waitin' for. The clouds got much thicker all of the sudden and Pierre Gautier looked up and said, 'A gully washer's headed this way.'"

That was Papou's way of saying he had heard enough about the incident for the time being. The talker had better get on with his or her request before the rain. However, Mérite-Lajoie, not versed in my grandfather's ways, missed the cue and kept right on talking.

"Of course, the animal spoke neither English nor French. I thought the creature repeated words from the Bible. If I only knew these better, I could verify."

"'Let me get somethin' will you?' Your grandfather said, goin' inside for just a second and bringin' out a small book a few minutes later called *The Good News*. He said it was bound to have some enlightenin' lesson that would help me."

I remember my brothers squabbling in the house. I was sitting on the couch in the living room with the window open, trying to hear their conversation as it turned to something about possums and the Bible and got so mad, I wanted to sock them. Papou sat down and opened the short version of the *Gospels*, given to him by some people who came to the door, probably Jehovah Witnesses'. I don't know why he kept it. I suppose he didn't have another copy of the *New Testament*, but he may have been afraid to throw away anything that he thought might be sacred. He looked around in the book, and read a passage of the *Apocalypse* (called *Revelations* in the small copy): "Although, the days'll come, dat Heaven and earth shall pass away; yet my words shall not pass away, but all shall be fulfilled. By my death, you an' your tribe will thrive." Although a little tangled and with uncertain presage, Mérite-Lajoie's translation of the possum's prodigious speech satisfied both, and they began to discuss the price of the property.

"Talkin' about what had happened made me feel better than when I kept it secret. My nightmare seemed farther from me then, but my heart tightened again while discussin' the sale. All throughout the negotiation, I made no allusion to the fact I had stumbled upon what I thought to be a natural salt well and a real miracle. To me, it was so spectacular and mysterious I had a hard time suppressin' the jubilation and abashment that filled my heart that I accidentally mentioned the salt on the animal. Your grandfather didn't ask me about the salt's origins. Maybe he hadn't taken into account all I said. I didn't want to put another lie on myself, especially not about what I thought to be proof of a salt spring. My wantin' to tell the truth confronted my powerful desire to acquire the land at a good price. In the end, when I spread the facts thin, the stronger will, prevailed."

"Both of us knew most Louisiana inland water is remainin' seepage water from floodin' or rain, but I had heard about *Ocala National Forest and Salt Springs* in Florida." Mérite-Lajoie frowned, shaking her head. "Some salt-water springs could be used for cures. With a moneymaking scheme like that, I imagined myself for an instant getting richer than the foundin' families." Thus, she also avoided making any allusions concerning her hesitations, about the presence of a creature from the shadows or about a possible error of syntax. "My translations sometimes left room for interpretation.

Perhaps the animal babbled about someone else's death in its last dyin' rant? Maybe he was speakin' 'bout someone else's tribe? I didn't tell Gautier about the man's injuries. It was best not to bring up my dream or that other thing under the trees either. Mystical developments left me more often than not without a clue. Later I came to believe that the possum was exorcised by my shot and the demon had left its body for Harper's, kinda like in the Gospel accordin' to Saint Luke, but in a backward sort of way. At the time, I felt so many unfortunate things had happened to my clan throughout the years we was due for a portion of better luck, as if someone kept these accounts somewhere, and each person was allotted equal shares of both good and bad portions."

By Mérite-Lajoie's estimation, this division had nothing to do with sin. This time, she had forgotten to negotiate the taking of her prey with the spirits of the forest the way Deux Ours had taught her to do, and she had a fear, not quite a fear, but an uneasiness about the entire situation. Even with her new brainchild, and her discrete victory in the bargain, Mérite-Lajoie had apprehensions she could not explain. "I began to develop a grudge against your grandfather, but couldn't figure out where I got it. I figured he had a hard time listenin' to me because I was a woman. But he had been nothin' but hospitable and even helpful, not forcin' the sale in any way, conversin' with me for more than an hour, tellin' me where I needed to go to file the deed. Instead of lookin' inside myself and boldly examinin' this hint of avarice, instead of understandin' my mistrust of any landowner as inherent to the operation, instead of acceptin' my skepticism, I turned my vision towards supernatural explanations or at least sexist ones."

"That day, I began to wonder why I was palaverin' so long." She smiled shyly at Papou, who nodded his head, smiling back, knowing the smile did not say everything, yet knowing from other arbitrations what could be behind a smile. Mérite-Lajoie moved along now with her doubts, seeking reassurance within her beliefs, "I didn't wanna give him any concrete evidence of foul play on the part of outer world offenders or otherworld beings, even if partial. I didn't want him to think I somehow brought unfortunate circumstances with me or think I'm some sort of Calamity Jane. That might have been just reason enough to toss out the owner financin' deal and I didn't want to start any rumors about my projects or my family. That wouldn't be right. He seemed like a laid-back community man. He trusted me to transmit any important observations about the property I visited." And true enough, had either been aware that that part of Louisiana ground had once also been consecrated by Indians until they were deported to Oklahoma or moved further south, neither would have risked confronting the wrath of an unleashed supernatural custodian. But no one alive remembered the ossuary, and there weren't any signs left they knew how to read. Papou was a shrewd enough when it came to business. "Your grandfather wouldn't let any dead Indians, or even ferocious beasts, get in the way of a sale, yet I watched as he rubbed his eyes, reddened I thought, from lookin' too far back in the past. He said to himself under his breath as he sighed, 'as in life, not much is spread evenly.' I thought about his words a long time. They didn't quite fit in with my reckonins."

"It wasn't a dream, I decided then, sippin' my tea, still deep in speculation, watchin' as T-Pierre pulled a wagon full of rocks out onto the street, then rememberin' the girl in my dream. Gautier sat still too for several minutes before yellin', 'get out of de street, boy. How many times do I have to tell you?' He knew your brother was spoilin' for a fight. That's the way it is with boys. I had two brothers."

"It was more like a vision, a revelation, although part of it was real as the biscuits and cane syrup I missed having for breakfast." In a short second, Mérite-Lajoie ran the scene by her mind again. "'Was this a foreshadowin' of the events to come?' I asked myself, and ask myself even today." Mérite-Lajoie repeated her questions to me as I adjusted her drip. She said she should have known it doesn't do any good to ignore such signs. "What struck me wadn't so much the possum's words; next to the possum, I also found Harper, then a poor gaunt, unshaven fellow with half of Louisiana sticking out the end of his boot. The man was slouched over, sittin' on the ground with a gunshot wound in his chest and bleedin' slowly to death." Mérite-Lajoie reconstructed the events. She had tried to stop the bleeding and to extract the bullet with her pocketknife.

By the time she got Harper to a hospital, she was not sure he had not shot the man herself. "Did I shoot him when I shot the wise possum?" she had asked the sheriff. "As soon as I saw the man, I wondered if the possum was talkin' about something religious. Part of what Harper whispered had come from *The Holy Bible* as well. I'm pretty sure of that. With these theories of talkin' creatures flitted in another, even wilder idea: 'Could this man be Jesus, mumblin' words about our Heavenly Father? Nah, no Jesus Christ would be half-dazed, gazin' around like that with those gold-flecked eyes', I decided. 'Only God understands such things.' But there was somethin' about him I jest couldn't make out, like with priests who listen to confession. Your grandfather then left the porch for several minutes and came back with some more iced tea."

"I remember contemplatin' a wheel bug killin' a caterpillar on a watermelon leaf, as I thought about what happened the day before, wonderin' how it got there; thinkin' someone had spit out a seed and it just growed up there as well as anywhere. Life is sort of like that, just sproutin' up anywhere, for better or worse. I needed to hang my vision on somethin' solid while I wondered about the possum, wondered about the man."

"About Harper, on the Sheriff's account, the chest wound came from another source. This fact should have served as a warnin', or at as least a second presage, and, a bad one. However, as I had first tried gettin' the bullet out usin' only my sterilized pocketknife, and in my distress had left a terrible mess, I was never sure if I could be blamed for Harper's loss of essence. I was nailed to the event. The elements of the scene stacked up in my mind and blurred like a pirogue in a fog. It was there on the bayou one minute and faded out of the scene, the next."

These Beans Have Too Much Salt

"I tried itemizin' the details, assignin' each one a *word*, pronouncin' each syllable out loud, repeatin' them in my mind, composin' them with punctuation, presentin' them with the word "the", extractin' them one by one from the world of specters. '*Briarsspringpossumblood*, briars, spring, possum, blood, the briars, the spring, the possum, the blood.' The man was losin' his mind, as well as his reserves, and was in such a weird entanglement with the brambles. How did this happen to him? How did I happen on him? His silhouette was so close to the animal, right next to the spring; so close he couldn't miss starin' me in the face. But he wasn't makin' a sound. It was almost an image from a magazine, cut out and put there for me to stumble upon, like an outside hand placed him on my path."

"The discovery of the salt spring, so wondrous, I could hardly get past the edges. I must have stared at the trees, the animal, the spring, and those briars, for at least ten minutes before I realized I could walk in and out of the scene. Then I saw the man. The logical explanation for the freakish rescue out in the middle of nowhere is pure hazard, excludin' of course, references to marvels of nature or to powers above. But since then, I thought of all kinds of wild things, even Jesus drivin' the demons out of a man and into the swine, wonderin' if he didn't put one in that possum there before me, or later, into the man."

Mérite-Lajoie had a hard time defining her sideration. She was reminded of the photos she took during the war as part of her mission. She would look at the scenes of horror, the mangled bodies, through the aperture of her Zeiss Ikon Contax IIa 35 mm rangefinder. *Clickclickclickclick*. Click. Click. Click. Click…Click. It was difficult for her to put her camera down and get past the frames to go help with the living. The injured lay on the ground in front of her and she was first and foremost an army nurse, but she remained paralyzed behind her device focusing several minutes on the scene, freezing images for the future, moving the one last part of her body that could still respond, the tip of her forefinger, before realizing that the flattened image in front of her was not flat at all. It was the theater of the living, and the soldiers, bleeding to death. Sometimes, she had to help with the transportation of the injured.

Perhaps she should have continued with her methodical treatment of her encounter with Harper, committing the photograph to words rather than simply watching reruns of a silent horror movie she imagined now in Technicolor. It wasn't that she lacked the science. Her beliefs were not certitudes. The sort of reasoning that took her in a straight line from a dead animal to a supernatural or religious sign was cursory. She knew that was short cut thinking. Had she thought about it enough, she would have seen the glitch.

She was stunned. "I began to feel embarrassed, for no one other than me because he was unconscious by that time. I was not able to stop the bleeding. Worse, I nearly killed the man by removin' the bullet." In short, she lacked the humility to admit her incapacity, regardless of her wartime training. And her pride, her *mens sibi conscia recti*, her feeling that she could do no wrong, was about to lead her down an obscure path, the only path she could find in the forest of bleeding trees.

Farther away from her moneymaking scheme was Mérite-Lajoie's respect for all creatures in the animal kingdom and their omens. Thus, she was drawn into the decision-making process sooner than she might have been. She could not escape the possum's words. She found herself wishing to move with Deux Ours and Emmy, right away, to what she imagined was a hospitable Louisiana town, in spite of the shooting. She also thought perhaps Harper had somewhat of a claim to the salt-water spring, although Harper (perhaps named Swaily on account of his whisperings during the transport) had told the officer in charge he didn't remember anything other than waking up in the hospital. Neither vouched for the exact place the accident happened. (It was in the interest of all parties to keep the spring secret). After all, Mérite-Lajoie was tired of working for the Federal Government, and a move would bring her back to Louisiana. Perhaps, in the long run, the desire to let spill more than invisible ink blotted out the rest.

Genealogy

I remember Papou calling us out on the porch on a hot day in August, a short while before a storm broke lose. "I wantcha to meet somebody." Mérite-Lajoie tells me now that she recognized my sister and I immediately as being the ones she had seen run away from the school. She smiled, shaking our hands. Papou on a talking streak continued: "Mrs. Robichaux 'ere was born on The Island at Parrioc just like me. She grew up on the water. She's a Frenchie too. Mrs. Robichaux is a traiteur, like 'er father, but don' go confusin' 'em with trait-ors, which they ain't by a long shot. Dey's healers and do a good job wit' people just like wit animals. She's got a daughter about your age, Bee. So, when dey get settled over in der new home, you can go over and meet 'er." Although he wanted us to continue to speak French, he realized the 1921 ban on French in schools meant we would all would have to speak English at home if we were to learn. His generation had not done so with their children and our mother had suffered in school. He thus adopted the language, if with considerable difficulty, acquiring a language from speakers in bed with a heavy southern accent. Mérite-Lajoie, on the other hand, improved her English as an army nurse. She still missed a lick once in a while, but made conscientious efforts to improve each time she spoke.

That day I measured Mérite-Lajoie with curiosity. She was the first other Cajun I remembered meeting: "Can traiteur's heal baby animals? I found a baby possum and he don't look so good. He keeps sneezin' and faintin'."

Papou told us to go back inside. He had gone back to speaking French. "Plus tard, plus tard! There'll be plenty of time later. Bring some more ice tea for Mrs. Robichaux. Dat possum is just too little to be away from 'is ma and'll probably die. I toldja to leave it alone. Maybe another possum would've adopted it. You just can't take creatures out of der natural 'omes." Skizzum left the porch, but I tried to hang around. I had to be reminded more than once to go back inside. I liked listening to adult conversations and would drag my feet and try to hear more whenever I got the chance. I decided I would go to my place under the porch and lay back in the cool dirt so I could hear the rest. Perhaps from my perspective, I believed they were going to speak of caring for sick or injured people or animals. I was interested in all things that could contribute to my still unconscious, but budding vocation, and was never bored or squeamish, no matter how the subject varied. What I learned that day didn't teach me a bit about treating a dehydrated baby possum, but taught me more about waterlogged and isolated people than I think I have ever learned since, until I came to St. Gabriel.

"I thought then, if I knew myself, I knew other people with lives similar to mine, better. I imagined how hard it was for your grandfather to move you all to Central Louisiana and what it meant to him to meet another displaced Cajun and speak in his dialect. We both thought of the livin', as well as the dead left behind. 'It just wasn't the same', I told him sadly, 'with mon Papere (my grandfather) alone in Evergreen with the baby. Most of our people are buried in New Orleans.'"

"'Yeah,' agreed your grandfather, 'when you move far away from your burial grounds like dat, it feels like you're betrayin' 'em. Worse, it's kinda like leavin' a piece of yourself wit' 'em. Maybe all Americans 'ave to abandon der folks somewhere. But it don't seem right. We already was forced to forsaken our tombs in Acadia.' Your Papou's eyes seemed to cloud over then."

"Our conversation then went completely off subject and rambled off to *Perpetuity Swamp,*" admitted Mérite-Lajoie.

As a child, I had a hard time following the conversation in French from my secret place under the house, but as I listened now to Mérite-Lajoie, the expression *Perpetuity Swamp* sent me out on a boat ride in my undeleted memory of bayous with cypress trees and low hanging moss. However, the pain of generations separating the elderly from the sacred grounds of their ancestors was an abstract idea for any child. That day I heard in his voice, what Mérite-Lajoie saw in his eyes, as Papou slobbered and drizzled, speaking of old desecrated blood, deserted on ground hacked out of the forest under extreme, nearly freezing conditions; toiled over, bled over, nourished, cared for, to finally abandon in the hands of hoodlums; and wondered if he was all there. Part of him was not.

It was as if the killing and thievery that he spoke of had happened to him, and not to several generations of people before us; as if the cold of the Nova Scotia coast, as well as the weight of the indifference of the British settlers, had followed the Acadians all the way to Louisiana, penetrated this coat, on this man, and had settled down on these shoulders. Other than as a soldier, Papou had never been out of Louisiana. I had never heard him tell this story. But memories do get made even as they get lost, and my grandfather must have been bent on fabricating some with bits and pieces of frozen grief he had picked up on his own, perhaps in France in yet another war, mixing them with a veritable account that someone else had forgotten along the way. Regrets were good for that; scattering them about for others to claim. "Compassion for others is perhaps built on regrets." Mérite-Lajoie was obviously thinking of her father. I was looking for mine in St. Gabriel's secrets.

Although I was only six, my mother had explained, when I pressed her for answers, "It's easier for him to explain the tears picked up somewhere else than let loose those made in his heart." I learned later that he was only twenty years old when Papou volunteered to drive ambulances in World War I, before the United States got involved in the war. Stationed in Mollau, Alsace, with the American Field service Number 3, he and fifty other people, mostly students from Harvard, evacuated injured French soldiers in the black of the night with the lights of the Model T Ford ambulances turned off. It was dangerous. On Christmas night of 1915, a bomb hit his ambulance, killing his companion, Richard Hall, and crushing his leg in the metal jaws of the wreckage.

Papou had not talked so much since we had moved in with him. Most of the time he pointed at things, and you had to guess at the missing words. "What?" you would say, "you want a glass? The bottle of milk?" He would shake his finger until you found what he wanted. Some days he would holler out excitedly, "Y'all come here, quick!" You would show up, looking as he did, out the window. He would vaguely point at something. He didn't say, "A squirrel." "An owl." "A star." Or, "a newly painted car." You would have to guess until the thing would dart off before you had time to adjust your vision to the right place and then, you would only see a blur. Next, he would grumble and fall in his chair.

As he spoke that day, he cleared his voice and covered his eyes with his hand, complaining of the sun. He continued to speak of deportation and ruin; painting history as though retelling his ancestors' fate would filter and ease the dolor of a memory yet unborn when the events took place but, doomed to live in the hearts of the expatriated descendants. "We took the same route as de slaves," he spoke out loud enough, now for my benefit, who he discovered was listening from under the porch. "But, de swamp has a way of seein' things all of its own. It depends on which side you were on when you woke up. Some was on de dry side and went on about der business; and some was stuck in de mud, yellin', tryin' to find a way out of de trouble." He went on, having dredged through a trauma, as much as through a swamp, but not the one that they were referring to on the porch and not the one I had in mind that day. He stomped his foot on the porch, making dust fall between the boards and made funny grunting sounds with his throat.

These Beans Have Too Much Salt

I remember watching as a locust hornet came out of its hole, wiping its antenna, before flying off. I had been keeping an eye on the hole, worried about a possible sting. Once I had been stung on the butt when I peed under the house. Skizzum laughed until her giggles grinned. I suppose the humor she found in this scene is linked to some intimate desire or jealousy, but I couldn't help laughing either, although the sting hurt and my rump was swollen up on one side twice its size and looked like a lopsided peach; one you would never find in the supermarket. My thoughts had gone off long enough to miss the other rhythms they were stomping. I crawled out and stared at them. Papou no longer noticed me, but Mérite-Lajoie leaned over and told me a little secret about possums. She made my day when she said that the young sneeze to call their mothers, faint involuntarily and that the one I found appeared to be in perfect health.

Louisiana Nostalgia

While telling this saga misted Papou's eyes as he spoke, Mérite-Lajoie meandered back to her interior geopolitical landscape. Maybe after having seen so many dead, so much ruin, Fortuna sung by others brings you out of the desert and back to the swamp of your own sorrowful beginnings, and to the one shared by others with the same inglorious ancestry. Mérite-Lajoie began rowing through hers with the paddle passed down from one generation to another, yet at once more detached and more implicated than my grandfather. She sounded almost as if she was singing, and like my grandfather, told a tale of previous generations. "Even if the Confederates called my great-grandfather a deserter, he'd been called so many other things he didn't take no account. My grandfather said his Pa lost a leg, bitten off by an alligator while hidin' in those boggy bottoms. He carved himself a new one out of a cypress knee. We still have the cypress knee and thigh, all in one piece, but the foot got burned off in a fire. A new factory leg was made for him before he died, but he didn't find much use for it and would hobble around with his crutches and the footless cypress leg with a shoe nailed on it. Yep, those alligators can be ornery critters if you get too close to their nests. He fared better than the gator though."

Mérite-Lajoie laughed as she chanted, perhaps unconsciously thinking these distant relatives were gone long enough for her to make jokes about them without disturbing anyone. She realized when she did, by the look on Papou's face, that there had been a painful precedent somewhere in his lineage too. She hesitated. Should she go backward now, or forward full speed to abort this new thread, growing longer each instant? "After the war, the Vieux started foolin' 'roun with a few canailles. Not carpetbaggers, but almost jest as bad. There wasn't much competition in Louisiana. He found he could invent medicines, first to cure his ailments contracted in the swamp. Then he made them to sell. In fact, he found he had a real knack for it, and he could even make an almost honest livin' out of it and that's what he did. Then one of the sons, my grandfather, settled back at Grand Isle with his wife and two sons. They lost their home in a hurricane too in 1915 and resumed a long migration, somewhat similar to a piece of driftwood. Churnin' debris-filled waters, bloated headless bodies, collapsed gutted homes…" Mérite-Lajoie's balmy voice trailed off telling the tale of hundreds of Cajuns. She too had seen this saturnalia of the heavens that left behind death and ruin and spoke of it as if describing a painting, but in fact, it was closer to her life.

Before landfall, a storm starts off with a heavy, humid atmosphere. Laughing breezes develop, their gentle gusts sweeping idle leaves or paper off the streets like animated toys. The same wind sharpens, and comes in hard thrusts. Soon, it will be all you can do to shove back or hold your weight against them. Then street signs bend against the gale, and rain begins to fall heavily. You can run from porch to porch to try to stay dry, but you will wound up soaked whatever you do because the gust of wind blows the water under all open shelters, seeking those who stay outside to play. The drops become larger until they are almost like a river, falling from the clouds. Tree branches or traffic lights spin around and sometimes fly out, tearing through a building, or a man. By now, everything not tied down has left its place, soaring about like boomerangs in rotation and ready to kill. If you are too close to the coast, the waves will carry you out to sea.

It is easier to speak of the hardships of your ancestors, and even cry over them, like you might when you read a poem and shed a tear, all the while keeping the water damned up when it comes to narrating your own biography. In a hurricane, as in a deportation, people lose all sense of time. In such circumstances, it is all you can do to keep from losing your mind. Years later, you might still be looking for it. There between the notes is where Papou and Mérite-Lajoie were finding something that sounded more like their tribal soul than anything I've yet come across. They were partisans separated by only a decade of memories, a few songs, and perhaps fewer cousins. As they united in tears, I imagined them contributing to the Blues of future generations of both Cajun and Folk composers from Slim Harpo to Lonesome Sundown.

"We remember the night, weeks after the hurricane; the festivities and the crawfish boils, and we never stopped saying: 'Let the good times roll'." Mérite-Lajoie managed to laugh again, but all the while, in both their hearts, both Cajuns added: "instead of the thunder". Their *complaints* were in fact story-songs, said in a singsong voice without instruments and much stomping. I had never heard this part of our heritage, until the day Mérite-Lajoie came to our porch.

These Beans Have Too Much Salt

"The sky over Ferriday was covered that day with low cumulus movin' along slowly from the river." Mérite-Lajoie sighed. "The air was like a sponge, ready to unleash a stream if pressed. Your grandfather shook hands with me. He agreed to finance the loan at twenty dollars a month for fifteen years. That was quite a price, but I considered it a good deal. I finished my ice tea. My memory restored; I rambled back privately to stories about how my family was again left homeless again during the *Eau Haute* of 1927 when I was only two." She reminisced also as she talked to me, her thoughts traveling back, not realizing her memory was colored with a child's hand, not knowing the umbrage of the faces of her parents and her grandparents held more than the anguish of the forsaken. They too had been among the artists of their misfortunes.

"Deux Ours and I had been wantin' to put down roots for a while. Off the Lake Road in Ferriday, Louisiana was as good a place as any. I thought I'd have time to set up a new business before leavin' the old and Deux Ours would be enthusiastic about gettin' back to Louisiana." The Robichauxs, like many Cajuns, had traveled all the waters in South Louisiana on pirogues, and rafts, up the Atchafalaya, through the Plaquemine Locks and even navigated the Mississippi. It was as though makin' round trips on a body of water, or even several bodies of water, after seein' its torso dressed or undressed like a wife and layin' with her on uncountable nights would make one a husband, and possessory manager of its flow. Several times we went ahead like sleepwalkers, plungin' ahead in the dark, puttin' a flood behind us. On such nights, guided only by a sort of reverse homin' instinct that steered us away from home to a more benevolent site, we journeyed as far north as Natchez, pitchin' camp where we could, many times near other migrant peoples, and even a few times, not far from a Circus with a Gypsy style quartet. As a child, I was told my mother was fathered on one of these unchartered maneuvers Up-the-Bayou, leaving her for a time without a patronymic and later, without a mother's love."

Mérite-Lajoie conjured up exotic images of these past encounters for my grandfather as well, forgetting to offer him the first installment as she got into her pickup. Her mind waded back, or rather, back paddled, as in her boat, the water whooshing past the aft, as if you could remember, see the past or even the present, as the current turned your vessel against your will. Still, the wandering eye snatched up a rare event, a souvenir, as the eagle catches a fish leaping from the stream, or the fish, a buzzing fly. "I remember an exceptional musical combo, and once, a run in with an elephant. At that time, my clan picked up on some distinctive musical ornamentation they added to our Zydeco and Cajun styles. We called these French, whether they be Creole, Atakapa, or Houma, without regard to what epoch or with what instruments they were composed, or how the added faster tempo, played now by an accordion or at least a *frottoir*, changed them. I attribute an exaggerated splendor to these chance meetins. As long as I can remember, music and food were shared with other travelin' people around a campsite."

These Beans Have Too Much Salt

"That afternoon, with the zephyr flowin' off the windshield, the raindrops beginnin' to fall, my wipers slappin' time, and my window rolled halfway down, I could almost hear the music fricassee and the different communities still tellin' stories from the animal and spiritual world. *T-thump, T-thump, T-thump, ping, ping, ping, whoosh, whoosh, whoosh...* Each one offered a word of wisdom, a recipe or an herbal cure. 'The Exodus (as mon Vieux referred to the long migration) brought us things other than trouble. And I'm not referrin' to my wife. We lost a bunch of good people, though, includin' mon Vieux (my old man).'" Mérite-Lajoie didn't realize the remedy she had concocted against tragic recollection, with its a-capala blending (*carry on, carry on*), was not enough to counter the consequences of what she would do that day.

"On the way back to Natchez, the rain had slowed to a drizzle. I glanced at myself in the rearview mirror for a second, just long enough to run over something on the road. I looked behind me to see a rattlesnake coilin' about the place where the wheels had run over it. I stopped the truck and backed up. I watched as the viper's life dwindled until he lay stretched out in the road, its smooth belly exposed and bent like a measurin' tape extended too far from its chamber. I wondered what brother *ventrambulons* was doin' up on the highway? I should have seen it was a sign."

Mérite-Lajoie appreciated reading Ambrose Bierce's *Latin Dictionary* on occasion and impressed herself with the Latin words or Latin-sounding words, mixing them with what she memorized from Sunday Mass, whenever she could. She continued, "for a rattlesnake to be there, somebody probably threw it out of his or her vehicle. I don't know why people are always playin' with animals in this country. Possums and snakes! Why don't they just leave 'em where they be?" She disliked killing snakes for fun. She had a loathing for foolish teenagers capturing poisonous snakes to frighten someone, usually a Black Creole. "Don't those kids know what they're doin'? Why don't the sheriff stop 'em before they hurt someone?" Mérite-Lajoie had spent her adolescence hunting, fishing or trapping with her brothers, when she wasn't taking care of the horses. Like most Cajun's before her, she never had the leisure of playing with animals for fun and often interpreted their encounters as participating in a larger, more omniscient project.

"That day I jest got ahead of myself on so many things." Mérite-Lajoie shook her head, telling me how almost to Natchez, she could have called the whole deal off by simply continuing on her way. The snake had stopped her, but her vision, troubled by nostalgic realism had not taken in to account what she felt she should have seen as a bad omen. What was bothering her was the fact that as a woman, she was making a deal that was ordinarily made between men. How could she know if Gautier was not somehow cheating her? What would her husband say? Would Deux Ours know better? Would a man try to cheat on him? Would he do it, knowing an Indian would have a hard time defending himself in a White man's court of justice? Realizing she had not completed the deal, she drove back to Ferriday, without another thought.

These Beans Have Too Much Salt

My grandfather laughed as his new acquaintance handed him a twenty-dollar bill, a small package of chamomile, for conjunctivitis (that he didn't have). "I just figured your mind wasn't made up yet." Papou laughed. He offered her a drink of whiskey this time. Mérite-Lajoie laughed too, correcting him. "My paternal grandparents, who were also known to have made some authentic brews and various medications, were never able to cure an absent mind, although most of their clients were satisfied. I guess you'd have to say these were inflicted with impediments different than that of their doctor. But I did inherit the gift of layin' on hands from my father, who got it from his father, as I mentioned earlier. My uncle had it too, but it didn't do him much good. He got into trouble before he made much use."

She recalled, telling me how both her father and her uncle, were bon riens, bons à rien, good for nothings, depending who you asked, although, if such were possible, of varying degrees. "My father had a talent for leaving a labyrinth of absurdities, bouts, and scuffles behind him. Of course, I made no mention of this to your grandfather. And I didn't bring up the details about my uncle either." These memories were among those she would have preferred to remove from her local treasury. She didn't yet realize that these possessions were prized because they held the key to her cure. She would keep coming back, forgetting, preferring to forget, remembering, fighting memory's hysterical grimace, its meaningless laughter, its probing glare, and deal with her absentmindedness in a way similar to the one Papou used with his trauma: accepting these symptoms as part of nature's peculiarities and moving on as if they were a gnat that you would brush aside, minute after minute until you got up and found something to do. But the gnat was always there, and if you thought about it, it was living proof that all was alive, if not well. Enough of them were buzzing about both of our heads by now.

"Times were rough. Uncle Landry was accused of stealin' horses from the Houma Indians and was hung by other Cajuns after a quick trial. I remember my father stumblin' into the house one afternoon, cryin' out about his lynched brother in drunken fury, and, demandin' that the tribe restitute his gun (some years later). But Bienvenu Dufrene (mon Vieux) managed to do little better than his brother. He bottled too many remedies, good for everything from ingrown toenails to dog mange; thinkin, not realizin', hopin', not wantin' to think, adoptin', not rejectin', the idea that any means of makin' a livin' were as good as the next. One day, a cat was found lickin' a bottle of a cure for warts. After realizin' the animal appreciated the freshly bottled medication, the cat's mistress emptied out the whole bottle. She determined it contained milk only (as only a cat could do) and decided to file a complaint with the sheriff. Other plaintiffs found their cures for ulcers or garden mildew interested their cats as well. They felt they were indeed founded in their complaint, even though the medication sometimes cured their ailments, and their cats were well fed. We had no cows or other large mammals from which we could draw milk (though my father pretended he could milk his mule). We were run out of town short of bein' tarred and feathered (not for charlatanism this time, but for milk theft). Hard times were to be blamed. There are some things that can't be forgiven. Although, in an odd way, being run out of Metairie was not such a bad thing. It was indeed better than fallin' in with Marcello's gang and kept the family out of trouble for some time. But as I mentioned, crumbs swept under the table have a way of attracting vermin. Before you know it, you'll find yourself overridden with varmints of the kind you'd hoped to avoid."

Mérite-Lajoie wiped the sweat from her forehead with her handkerchief as she recollected for my grandfather what she had heard of her father's rehabilitation. Bienvenu (later known as Papere), like Papou and many other Cajuns, had been an interpreter for the Great War in France. He resisted provocation rather poorly. Although Mérite-Lajoie had quite a few memories, her mother spoke often enough about her husband and how he was regularly involved in snits and sometimes in open fights. Remembering how, even in Louisiana, the English-speaking population continued to persecute the Cajun families, calling them coonasses, vagabonds, and other even more ungracious names. In spite of their wartime sacrifice and assistance, she said Bienvenu couldn't quite get over his lie about stealing milk. Part of him revolted and washed away the bitter, the unpalatable, the repugnant element of truth. "'How could you demand such of a man,' my old man had asked, swearin', not waitin' for a response, 'knowin' he would commit a forfeit, knowin' ownin' up to such a fact could only jeopardize him? Is it because you own up to somethin' or you spit it out, the ownership or the spittle tells the whole truth about you?' The other part of him

115

sought to justify his blunder by sayin' his lie was a small one because he only stole discarded whey."

In the end, Bienvenu made a compromise with himself; stealing it was a concession to his morality, rationalizing the theft brought him back on the valorous side of his philosophy. "Hadn't he stolen to feed his family? Hadn't he transformed diluted muck for the good of his fellowman?" asked Mérite-Lajoie.

I wondered if these minute arrangements people make with themselves weren't pieces of evidence that they require to be able to go on living without relocating their minds.

In spite of these relinquishments, they had established themselves in the New World, and for better or worse (and mostly it got worse), in Louisiana.

The downpour was intense now. Mérite-Lajoie swallowed the rest of her whiskey and ran out to her pickup.

Personal History

Her thoughts rambled back to her days in wartime Europe. She had done some interpretation in World War II, like her father. "I was kinda good lookin' when I was young, especially in my uniform, though I wasn't much of a charmer. For a Cajun I was tall, and for a Cajun woman, even taller, but my accent and poor English made me the subject of mockery in the Tent Hospital."

Mérite-Lajoie reconsidered her service and her self-worth. The young surgeons were curious and always asked her questions about her life in Louisiana. They enjoyed her non-solicitous manner, her smooth voice, and her careful explications about river lore, boating or hunting in the swamp. However, their affection made the other nurses wary. She was not from a military family, quite the contrary, and any back-rubbing with the doctors was considered foul play. "I don't know what they suspected me of doin'? I was jest tryin' to be of service when they was worn out from work. If they'd been horses it was all the same to me."

"We landed in southern France just behind the troops. There were eighty-eight-millimeter artillery shells going on over our heads while we unloaded. We moved many times through the mud, slipping and sliding, following the troops, not far from the fighting. We were pretty much in a cow patch half the time with an open latrine. The city girls had a hard time. This made me laugh. They avoided some of us country folks. They didn't care how gifted a horsewoman I was. They wasn't interested in my ability to shoot a gun or hunt for food. They couldn't even see the importance of speakin' French in a war in France. When the action let up and the boys went to England, the inexperienced nurses competed for recognition from the White officers and probably hoped to find husbands. I guess if they had had somethin' to say about me, it wouldn't have been very nice. So mostly, I guess they just kept it to themselves. But I still think they druther sent me off to Japan."

Other than the misguided scandals, her usefulness as an interpreter did not override the fact that she was benefitting from privileges they felt belonged to themselves. In their eyes, Mérite-Lajoie was not only an adversary, but also a factor of risk to be avoided at all costs. They had all heard about New Orleans and its wild nightlife. "Had I won the Vivien Leigh look-a-like contest I might have understood. These stiff ramrods thought I was tryin' to hit up on their boys and marry their Laurence Oliviers. I remember lookin' at myself in the mirror and findin' I did sort of look like the actress who starred in *A Street Car named Desire* after having won an Oscar alongside Clark Gable in *Gone with the Wind*: the same raised right eyebrow and cat-like smile, the same black hair, and soft green eyes. Some people are afraid of everyone except themselves. Now I'm not sure we are much different here in Louisiana, but at least I don't look like the actress anymore."

In spite of other's judgments, Deux Ours had seen Mérite-Lajoie as a woman of character and fell in love with her, not only for her beauty or her soothing voice.

Mérite-Lajoie smiled a little, and began telling me more about her defunct husband and how they had met. "Before comin' to Natchez, Deux Ours had been with his tribe who live near Lafitte. Independent people, they are mostly fishermen and hunters, and travel between their settlements by pirogue. Most of them continue to speak their own language, which today is French with a few Houma words that we employ as well. As with us Cajuns, as long as they are near their camps, they choose their affiliations with care. They have their tradesmen, their tinkers, from blacksmiths to net weavers. However, emergencies do happen."

Mérite-Lajoie explained how the Houma crossed their family plots near Belle Chasse by the simplest route when one of their horses was injured there. She already had a great deal of experience caring for animals as well as people; she cared for them whether they were a person or an animal, a friend or an enemy. The Houma's healer having remained at large, Mérite-Lajoie patched up the wound and sent the creature, and its owners, on their way. At the moment, no one ever had thought they should beware of an injured horse, even if Destiny were its name. Nevertheless, Deux Ours managed to entrust the young woman with a leather seashell-beads bracelet, in spite of his parent's warnings, and subsequently, Mérite-Lajoie could never get him out of her mind. "When you marry someone." Mérite-Lajoie stared sadly out into the infirmary, as if she were hoping to find support from her husband. "They become a member of your family, and you become one of theirs."

"Deux Ours already had French ancestry somewhere, but in the early forties, before the war, the Houma were very wary of strangers. My mother has Redbone ancestry and told me the Indians of Barataria were once invited to special feasts. As for Bienvenu, he had mixed feelings about all this. He wasn't quite ready to marry off his only daughter and in spite of our already mixed family; he had hesitations of lettin' me marry an Indian. On the other hand, he said I was too big and too strong for any White man." She laughed.

After the war, when she was discharged from the army, as a veteran, Mérite-Lajoie easily found a job with the United States Postal Service and was appointed as a postal worker to the town of Natchez, Mississippi. She did not wish to continue working under doctors in a hospital setting where there were too many people, as far as she was concerned. American Indians were mostly sent off to the Pacific, but Deux Ours found her there after the war, married her and came to live Up the River.

It was in this post office where she began to print out her catalog for herbal cures and sell them for two cents a copy a few years later. Shortly after, she received a letter from the government that said: "You cannot operate a business on federal property." One day she went to work and found the FBI confiscating her remaining catalogs along with her hand press and letter drawers. She then had to wait for an administrative decision and thought it might be better to quit, especially after finding Harper and the spring.

Vocations

No one came to visit Harper at the hospital other than the sheriff and Mérite-Lajoie. This lack of visitors did not surprise the medical staff. He had lost his driver's license and wasn't sure about his name. No one had been called.

"Harper said, 'I sort of think I was born on October twenty-fourth nineteen twenty-nine, but why don't you just write down March seventeenth in the same year? It seems like a better day for me.' I had no idea why anyone would want to change a birthday he wasn't sure of in the first place. Ain't there somethin' fraudulent about that? I was tryin' to be of service to an injured man. I felt somehow responsible for what he was goin' through. Harper kept on, 'my angel has abandoned me three times already and told me I must now defend the church at the doors of Hell.' I didn't pursue my questions, took down the date, and sent it to Vital Statistics, vouchin' for the name of the injured to be 'Patrick Harper' and his date of birth as 'March 17, 1929', on account of it bein' the Irish Patron Saint's day. In that day and age, people could get a birth certificate if someone said they knew their family and knew when and where the person was born. So, I lied. I figured Harper had seen enough, and I wanted to give him a hand, although it was impossible to determine his real age. It was like the man went into one season and out the next, changin' his skin, takin the few existin' lines and scars with him, just enough to be recognizable and give him character, but all in all, unchanged."

These Beans Have Too Much Salt

"A few weeks later, Harper was out of the hospital and in my pickup. As soon as I was behind the wheel, my passenger started talking about one of his past vocations. He said he had been sent to explain the adjustment of economic views. 'Soon there will be worldwide upheaval. I read particular signs in the moon. In the *Gospels*, there is a moral code explainin' sex education, commerce, and religious rites. I'm in relation with men of good faith, and they tell me of the wicked ones. The Babylonian Ambassador don't use any kind of ordinary procedure to influence people. He never read the Gospels and don't hesitate to cast spells or use voodoo to make his transfers. He did some trials on me. I saw the magic screen in front of me through the flames. That's why I ran. I wanted to get away from his butcher.'"

"He didn't seem to be talkin' to anyone in particular, even though I was sittin' next to him, drivin' the truck. I scratched my chin and tried not to show my surprise. I'd seen many things around these parts, and I no longer trusted my sentiments. I wondered if Harper had suffered a brain injury. I thought about all I'd heard, about money, magic screens and such. Finally, I asked him if he used to be a professional poker player? I'd been to Arabi's Le Beau's Casino with my father some years before and knew they had a fancy set up there. I wondered if Harper wasn't confusin' *smoke screens* with magic screens and gamblin', with teachin' economics in Louisiana and makin' bank transfers in a particular way." Mérite-Lajoie never put any stock in Wall Street and in consequence ignored the possible significance of the October 1929 birthdate, or even if this date was somehow fraudulent as well. Harper, on the other hand, had his beginnings on an infamous day preceding the depression, a day that left scars on many Americans and had thus been branded on his heart in a nearly invisible manner.

"Harper looked around as though he could see something of that day among the rusted parts of machinery as we passed near the gin and abandoned cemetery. He had hidden his camper near there, but as he said he didn't remember anything, he didn't reclaim it just yet. He was contented with blurting out Bible verses from time to time for the rest of the ride to Natchez. I felt it best to hold off on showing him the property until he regained more completely his self-control."

"His religious knowledge seemed a little cracked. I attributed this too, to his loss of blood. 'It's in the *Bible, King James Version*,' he cried out, as if in answer to someone. 'First book of *Corinthians*, chapter six, verse nine: 'Know ye not that the unrighteousness shall not inherit the Kingdom of God? Be not deceived: neither the sexually immortal, nor idolaters, nor adulterers, nor effeminate, nor abusers of themselves with mankind.' He actually translated the words he thought I didn't know, and called the fornicators *sexually immortal*." Mérite-Lajoie shook her head. She would have laughed had she not felt responsible for allowing a predator into her community; but that day, she couldn't make out what Harper's swagger or appeal to immortality in such terms could mean.

"When we got back to Natchez, Deux Ours and I talked and decided Harper could settle in a room in the old barn behind our rented house until he was on his feet. It was more of a shack than a barn, but it satisfied the tenant. He helped with chores until he was ready to go back to work, doin' whatever job he could find. I settled down at my desk in the main house, not much more than a shanty either. I was glad to get my mind back on my catalog."

While still in the military, the catalog of ailments Mérite-Lajoie had begun to create included not only a questionnaire useful for diagnosis, but also incorporated original research for some herbal cures for animals, with their Latin names, translated into both Cajun French and English. She had handwritten it from her notes, and had already made several copies with her postal based press. "Why don't you ask Emmy if you're ever up that way? She might still have that last copy. I'd been so proud of it as I turned the pages. It had useful diagrams of many plants and a few animals. I managed to earn some royalties from the sale to local farmers who bought their copies displayed in Kings' Feed and Seed." Mérite-Lajoie told me how she carefully subtracted her costs and noted the benefits in her journal on the right side. The idea that her setup of making profits as an author while on government payroll may have triggered her downfall never entered her mind. The publishers of the *Farmer's Almanac* apparently had not found any interest.

"I got tired of waitin' for a response from them and bought the press from a local printer who had found it too small for his business. Had I sold the copies from the U. S. Post Office without givin' them a percentage, I would have understood. But I hadn't allowed myself such extravagance and put two percent right away in their cash register. Besides, I only printed the copies in my spare time. In those days, you wouldn't have called my undoin' a conspiracy, even if my descriptive was better than the one the pharmaceutical companies called the *Diagnosis Statistical Manuel* later on, and one of their representatives had asked me for a copy. The Gods (unless it were the odds?) were against women, had always been against us, and were even against my family from very early on."

I almost agreed; it was as if some of the Cajuns had been followed all the way from Acadia to Louisiana by some archaic creature from a foreign monarchy, which instead of looking for food at large for itself and its offspring, wreaked havoc among us and harvested the fruit of our misfortunes. For women it was worse.

Mérite-Lajoie sighed. The confiscation of her press had been a setback and a shock. I could imagine her carefully putting away her original and her last copy printed on her press as she began to think of the future. "My parents were by then gettin' old. I thought I could get them to come to this part of Louisiana and settle them in the trailer park I intended to establish on the land we bought from your grandfather."

North of Alexandria, some of the displaced Cajun families already lived in trailer parks. There, they implanted groups among others known as White Trash. These were poor, mostly White, Southern families caught up in the whirl of life, having lost bits and pieces of their identity to the wind. The Cajuns had tried living on solid ground, but the water would come up so often under their beds they would have to leave. They would come back, clean out the gunk, and set up house again. Mérite-Lajoie imagined they could move the trailers if the Mississippi started getting too swollen in the spring, overspilling into the lake, which would in turn spread out over the land. The families would come back once the water receded. She had even visited some trailer homes with a system of flotation devices. When the water rose, the numerous empty barrels attached under the wooden caravans would lift them off the ground. This trick worked all right except when the house was too big, and it would sometimes break up under the force of the river currents. She talked to her parents about it before talking to her new friend. Her parents had been happy with the plans to move next door to their daughter and granddaughter. It went without saying that they would be among other Cajuns. Mérite-Lajoie had made neither mention of how she found the land nor how her American scheme had pushed itself inside her dreams.

Friends

"When he heard of my trailer park project, Harper got so enthusiastic he forgot to turn off the water hose and left it runnin' all night. He suddenly became an expert in homesteadin', and you couldn't shut him up without offerin' him a drink of whiskey or at least a beer. The next day, the horses' trough overflowed, the cistern was empty, and the garden was flooded out. Even the carrots were washed downhill and formed a small dam in front of a homemade creek. None of this would have happened in Louisiana. As I was of a forgivin' nature about material things, I pardoned my friend, and we settled up with another bottle of Harper's siphoned whiskey, from a barrel dug up from who knows where. Harper got on to tellin' us about the reservoir on the parcel of land we bought, dispellin' any ideas about a natural salt spring, but openin' up the new prospects of distillation. Even though I then realized Gautier had not told me everything about the property prior to its purchase, I was happy I didn't outwardly mention the salt, because as it turned out, I was mistaken about its provenance as well. I didn't much like makin' a fool of myself, especially in front of a newcomer."

"Harper, on the other hand, had the gift of runnin' his mouth off about anything and didn't seem to mind how foolish he appeared. On many occasions, he was noisy about subjects you couldn't figure out. On these days, it wasn't as if he was speakin' another language; one minute you might hear him cry out: 'Life, death, Hell, eternity', and the next, "Economy, prices, credit, books." He would end up with 'May the Lord *circumscrible* you in the circle of purity.' He didn't seem to care if he used words that weren't in the dictionary. He didn't seem to notice if people listened to him or not. However, most of the time they did." An ingenious rabble-rouser, Harper had a talent for transforming simple subjects in such a way; his street congregation thought he was more intelligent than they were. "He would pick up a newspaper and, low and behold, he seemed to have written to the journalist, providin' the details himself. On these days, he rallied everyone around ideas even a Cajun could back. He would cry out: 'freedom, truth, justice, God,' before getting on to his particular way of seein' the world." Mérite-Lajoie, closed her eyes and winced, remembering Harper's talents with ambiguous feelings. "It wasn't so much his ideas. These could be found anywhere and sometimes weren't so easy for us to get behind. I can't say it was his appearance or his manner either. It was almost like he told us that what he had to offer we wouldn't be able to find anywhere else and this was our last chance, forever, and that was enough. Last chance to leave, I wish I'd had thought."

Thus, Harper's captivated audience would come to think in terms they would have rejected if these had been presented in a more natural way, and if they had had the opportunity to see beyond the ornamentation. Some of them received the predicator's sermons as if they were in a trance and peering through a golden veil. Mérite-Lajoie started again, sitting straight up in her bed. "If one ventured so far as to have doubts and ask, 'what do you mean?' Harper would respond with a quick phrase, such as: 'Nonbelievers will be punished in the fiery Kingdom of Hell.'" All the while he peered at the guilty party, Harper would swallow up many as if they were one, casting to the soles of their feet any further objections to his litany. The adepts would then find themselves tramping on their prior faith with their soon worn-out shoes; feeling uplifted by their convictions, they were flying over the infernal void.

One day, in the presence of Mérite-Lajoie, Harper opted for a particular string of sounds, if ever there was a choice in the matter, because if having a quick spirit was a blessing of nature, some people blurted out whatever prevailed at the end of their tongue. "He chirped: 'Christ-and-some, Chrysanthemum, Vade mecum, o-possum, um-um-um.' I was startled by the curious hodgepodge of words that ended up in rhymin' syllables only. I told him, 'I can't make heads or tails out of it. What are you talkin' about?' I thought to myself, 'How did he concoct that? Could this be a coded message for me? I never told him about the talkin' possum. Maybe it was chattin' with him when I shot it? I thought maybe there was a link between the two, before I figured otherwise. Harper's a musician. He just liked makin' rhythms with words.' Not receivin' any answer from him, or from my inner-self, I added, addressin' my friend, 'But really, for Christ's sake and cemetery flowers! What're you getting' at?' Harper frowned and started up again, gesticulatin', making nonsense out of words that ordinarily had a meanin'. He didn't seem to appreciate my interruption, not even as a joke."

There was something peculiar about this newcomer in Mérite-Lajoie's life, although much of what she felt about her associate came from her illusions. "Maybe he was under a spell of some sort? Maybe he could communicate with the animals?" she questioned.

These Beans Have Too Much Salt

Mérite-Lajoie had no knowledge of those afflictions, which crowd the mind into its darkest corners, torturing its buried inhabitants, scaffolding monuments to their memory, and lending fear, clairvoyance, and certitude to ordinary concerns. Nor could she understand these outbursts as cries from a troubled soul's grave. In the beginning she thought of them as riddles, but in the end, what she thought was fused with the terms of her own making.

Clever at hooking people who barely glanced at him or showed any interest, Harper seemed to be like Tom Sawyer, possessing another rare quality: that of getting you to dig his ditch for him, or convincing you to do whatever else he needed to have done, while he chatted freely and drank your liquor. And sure enough, that day he was supposed to make fence posts for his lodger, but as it turned out, Mérite-Lajoie and Deux Ours were the ones doing all the sweating, bankrupt on all accounts. "Instead of thinkin' Harper was lazy, I thought he was enterprisin'."

Instead of concluding their renter had a nervous affliction, they suspected he had an uncanny sense of the natural world. Had they reflected upon these ideas for very long, they might have concluded that one does not exclude the other. You could be indolent, and creative. You could be insane, and possess a remarkable perception of the real world, at least most of it.

"In some ways, maybe Harper had some sort of sensory problem." Mérite-Lajoie paused for an instant. "There was a fellow with anosmia in the army. He couldn't smell or taste anything but salt.

He contrived some remarkable ways of getting around that defect to allow himself to carry out mess duty and the food was still edible." Only with Harper, Mérite-Lajoie couldn't quite figure out just what was being compensated or how. While, she made exceptions and excuses for her friend's cuisine, in the back of her mind a question had been turned over, "Would it be edible at all?"

"'Let me expose my idea to you, Two Bears', Harper said as he opened another bottle, touching his arm, and addressing him by his English name. By this time, I had locked myself into the house with Emmy and told Deux Ours, 'you can sleep in the barn with *Delirium Furor* if you want, but I ain't gonna let him in my bed.'"

"Harper went on to explain that evenin' his plans for a church. He spoke of the dimensions, the need for materials, (and our money) and what benefits could be ours to have. Deux Ours concluded Harper was speakin' of a Catholic Church. Wasn't he of Irish descent?" As if hearing a person's accent, knowing what foods he enjoyed or where he was born were enough to tell you enough about his character, Mérite-Lajoie told me how they gathered that Harper was born in circumstances and in a family much like their own, and had similar values. "Aside from any past excursions away from our personal standards on the part of my ancestors, I come from a decent group of people. I figured I could trust this other Louisiana man with almost anything." Mérite-Lajoie expressed herself as if she thought class values and morals were the same thing. She related Harper's words as follows.

"I saw the power creationist of God in the form of a light beam that touched me as it descended through the leaves as if they formed a stained-glass window. I saw images that weren't from earth. The Lord put them there. The light was meant for a stone that had been set there for early believers. We know life is the light of God's intelligence, and I felt it stir within me, as if I were with child. I made a personal opinion about it and the power of God then moved his grace to my loins. I asked myself if the Lord had not put the birds here as angels to give counsel to man and to make a paradise on earth. I heard this advice coming through one: take care of the children. I mean to do just that. I'm in relation with some men of good faith. As long as I can remember (he mentioned this point, forgetting he had already forgotten everything), I have been a servant of the Lord. At my first communion, I saw these people around the table who were only about an inch high. This was a visual phenomenon due to a magnetic accumulator set there by the Lord for the men of good faith. I have been atoned to create the conditions for the same in the area of Louisiana where you have acquired a piece of land."

"Deux Ours was again surprised, this time with alcoholic laughter. He slapped Harper on the back and told him, 'Whatever you say, my friend, it's okay with me. We're no specialists when it comes to religious matters, but there is enough room for a church and a very fine one too. We even know a girl you can marry, if marriage suits you. Mérite-Lajoie has a younger cousin. Pretty girl too.' Harper suddenly stopped talkin' and twitched his nose before wipin' it off with his handkerchief. 'How old is she?'"

These Beans Have Too Much Salt

"He told him she was almost eighteen years old and *ripe for pickin'*, before he realized the whiskey had gone to his head. Both Mississippi and Louisiana laws allowed girls to marry before they had the right to vote. In general, he never spoke of women in this way, much less, girls in the family. He didn't know how then to interpret Harper's jerkin' around when he said it and found himself laughin' with him. Men are such weak characters when it comes to whiskey and women, no matter what they'll tell you."

"Leona, my young cousin, soon joined us in Natchez. She would've done most anything to go somewhere else. As soon as we got in touch with her, she packed her suitcase full of a bunch of old clothes and childish keepsakes and fled her home near St. Martinville. She walked all the way to town and took the first Continental Trailways bus to meet her future husband."

For Leona, making these changes in her life seemed no more difficult than changing her clothes at the time. She was like many ordinary girls from other small American towns sitting on their front steps, watching the cars (or the pirogues) roll by, waiting for the first handsome, or not so handsome, young, or not so young, man to smile and wave at them, before coming to their homes and proposing to take them into the chartered kingdom of ill-founded marriage. Unsealed from their base, for a short while they became permeable to outside influences. That was long enough for them to change their beliefs and engage in creating a family project. And it all seemed for the better. But the participation of time, buzzing by like an insect, is not the only thing to blame for what happened. We all have about as a hard time admitting our mistakes, as we do accepting change. No one ever admits what he is charged with. The condemned almost never do. "There is somethin' about what they say about you that you jest can't get used to. No matter how many times you hear it said; it is still hurtful to your ears." Mérite-Lajoie's eyes glittered. "But the ax, the sword, or the can, is held ready, and might fall at any time."

Alliance

Although she had only been in Natchez for five weeks, Harper proposed to Leona, and she accepted. She didn't bother asking him why he didn't use his given name. She didn't even hear Mérite-Lajoie's mention of her future husband's hesitations about his identity. She would have fallen in love with him whatever his name. At the time, these considerations seemed secondary. "She was not much different from a mail-order bride and Leona took all her new obligations with a stride. She felt her life would be much better than that of her parents. The couple set up house in town. Harper's big mouth seemed to serve him well. His audiences seemed to like it when he yelled out: 'Lust. Sin. Chastity. Purity.' To me these sermons didn't amount to anything more than foolishness, but a nearby radio station engaged him to preach and to direct a group of gospel musicians. For Leona, Harper was a celebrity. It wasn't long before their first son was on his way."

"Durin' this time, both our families drove over to Louisiana on weekends and began to set the foundations for our church. When we both had enough money, we bought some used trailers and moved them to the lots near the lake. I sent for my parents who moved from along Bayou Teche at St. Martinville to Ferriday. I didn't have to keep on helpin' Harper, but once I started, it was like finding my way home again. I know now that is what happened with Deux Ours. Harper provided direction like a North Star."

These Beans Have Too Much Salt

"My husband had this flag he was proud of flyin'. After having flown the banderol at the crawfish festival in Beaux Bridge, where it reinforced Bishop Schexnayder's blessing in holdin' off a thunderstorm, Deux Ours got out his banner and started to hoist it over the trailers. It was a bold creation with a crawfish raisin' its claws, drawn with fine lines in red thread over a white silk background. The crawfish was a Houma war symbol before becomin' a Cajun one. Houma comes from *saktce-ho'ma*, meaning red crawfish. My Mama, Esperanza, had embroidered, with green capitals, our motto below: AUSSI INÉNEBRANLABLE QUE L'ÉCREVISSE (As steadfast as the crawfish). Our family didn't think much about havin' this motto wavin' over our park, but with the lastin' banishment of French in Louisiana, the whole town of Ferriday soon decided they were dealin' with brazenfaced communists."

Mérite-Lajoie had presented Harper to her cousin's family on Mardi Gras in Saint Martinville at an epoch when the *courirs* in small towns were still the great thing. "Harper was no longer an adolescent who could go from house-to-house beggin' for a chicken. The men all dressed up in costumes, rode horses, and drank heavily. Harper took a whip away from the *Capitaine* and began to flog himself cryin' out: 'I'm a penitent, I'm a penitent.' We presented him as our friend, and durin' the drunken revelry, no one thought much about it."

"My parents were polite and allowed Harper to stay at the home they still maintained in town, but my father began to oppose allowin' Harper and Leona set up house in our community. 'It's one thing to run with him during the festival, but another to live next door,' he said. 'I don't know why you keep draggin' him round like some old dog. He might be smart, but he ain't that smart. He might have conversation, but he's even missin' a notch or too, ain't he? *Il vaut pas la merde.* Ah, I guess that's what it is? You figure you are the one who knocked it out of him? Don't you know the world is full of nincompoops? If leather were brains, he wouldn't have enough to saddle a Junebug.' I thought he was just pitchin' a fit because of me bein' a girl and because of that, accordin' to him, not bein' able to judge about such things. I wanted to prove him wrong. He went on about it for days, but in the end, my mother's wheedlin' won over. I'm sorry to say I wish it hadn't. I wish I could even say it was her fault. It was like bein' a lawyer for Harper pleaded for me at the same time."

"Harper began to show another facet of himself as well, by whinin' and sort of beggin' us to do his will. 'Do you realize how uncomfortable your family makes me?' he asked us one day. 'Jest think how I feel. I'm alone with my wife, we need people, and I can tell, they don't want me hangin' round you. Merit, your Paw makes me feel like a dog. It's a hollow world that can't let two individuals who love each other to thrive amongst them.' Again, Harper held onto my arm. He looked into my face with a sad dog's expression, like he almost always did with people when he wanted something. I hadn't figured this out yet."

"I began to feel uneasy 'bout the whole thing. I tried talking to Deux Ours 'bout it. He asked, 'well did your Vieux say they couldn't come?'"

"'No, but it is almost the same thing. He doesn't want anyone who ain't Cajun with us." Mérite-Lajoie explained she thought her father's idea was to hold on to the French cultural identity, and in his small way, reinforce it by forming a close and a closed community.

"'I'm not a Cajun. Do I have to go?' Like my mother had done with my father, Deux Ours reduced my hesitations to dust, reassurin' me of my father's good, but short-sited views. 'In time, he'll come around. Besides, how do you want to be included with other Americans if you don't even mix with them in your own neighborhood?'"

"My mother, known by now as Mamere, took my less reluctant side and argued for allowin' Harper to park his trailer under the Robichaux-Dufrene flag on the new property. She figured his knack with languages (even French) and musical ability justified this exception. 'I put more stock in the Tarot than in the local gossip. What you cain't say to my face, is like squeeters over the swamp.' And by this time, *maringouins* were buzzin' in our ears."

As for Mérite-Lajoie, although she had begun to have some doubts about Harper's character, she felt a sense of responsibility for his wellbeing, and now in more than one way. On one hand, she felt a conflict of loyalty with her father and on the other, as a cousin-in-law who now lived in her clan; Harper's financial stability was becoming a sobering reality. Even though he always found some moneymaking scheme, his job at the radio had amounted to short sessions. He did not obtain an official salary, although he held in expectation a listening congregation for more than an hour. Finally, Mérite-Lajoie, who had acquired a non-mitigated feeling of her father's past professions and past-times, as with her own, bided by now by a scrupulous morality, and convinced him to look for better-paying work.

Deux Ours found a newspaper ad and shoved it one day into Harper's hand. With much coaxing, he again served as the driver and escorted his cousin-in-law to the door. Harper was hired the same day and soon began to earn his living selling cars. He was an exemplary salesperson and quickly earned the esteem of his employer. Always a roving eye, ready to pounce on a distracted customer, Harper had bookkeeping skills, and his boss trusted him enough to take care of the register and the accounts. The trailer payments seemed secure, and the church continued to be built.

"A few new families moved their trailers to the new lots durin' this period. They weren't all Cajun, but Bienvenu and Deux Ours had already accepted to change the banner, and the newcomers paid a small rent, which helped with the land payments. The flag had been modified to accommodate Harper's family. Now instead of a crawfish with its claws raised showing a faithful creature true to its post, there were two reddish hands painted over the embroidered claws, which passed from prayer to the Devil's rhythm when the wind went wicked and a storm was brewin'. Of course, there were some who didn't always put faith where others did, holdin' that the flag only celebrated all that the Harper-Dufrene-Robichauxs found to be sacred: honor, justice, and God."

"One weekend while Deux Ours and I were in a South Louisiana swamp, lookin' for herbs for our horses, and my parents and Emmy were visitin' members of the family in Saint Martinville, we came home to find Harper had moved his trailer, puttin' it not only on the unique spot with a full view of the lake, but right between our trailer and the church."

"'I'll be closer to the church now. And when it rains, my sermon won't get wet as I cross the yard. We can adjust your trailer and move it over there a little.' I was dumbfounded. I couldn't find the words, but my father began to spit his out without chewin'. My fists hardened. I could see myself jumpin' on Harper like a mad woman. Deux Ours pulled me back before the idea came to fully to fruition. To keep the peace he explained, 'This is jest a misunderstandin' and it's all my fault. I told Harper he could put his trailer where he felt the most comfortable. I'll jest move ours over about twenty-five or thirty feet, and it'll be alright.' Harper stood there with a smirk on his face."

"Before, I enjoyed the lake view each mornin'; with the swamp irises and the dark green cypresses framing the yellow sun-streaked water. I could see the bass jump and the birds dive, and almost pick the possum grapes from my kitchen window. Now I could only have a view of the parking lot and the other trailers. 'You could've said no,' I told Deux Ours. 'He wasn't that far from the church. He finagles to get what he wants. He takes advantage of your good will. Doesn't that bother you?' Deux Ours didn't have much to say. All at once, Harper's words about my husband came to my mind: 'When you try to tell him somethin', he looks like a big cow starin' at a water hole,' he had said. Then I found myself chasin' that idea and defendin' Harper instead of holdin' my ground. Worse, I convinced myself Harper meant no wrong. 'He's only tryin' to arrange things for the best of all of us,' I told my father. 'Leona can't even see that view from her kitchen. We'll build a houseboat and attach it there on the pier.'"

"After nearly a year on the job, Harper came to work one day to find the Internal Revenue Service inspectors roundin' up the records. His boss frowned. He hadn't appreciated being inspected. However, as a law-abidin' citizen, the boss handed everythin' over. A few weeks later, the IRS was back; declarin' there had been some serious doctorin' of the books. Both men were arrested. As it turned out, the cash register was missin' well over a thousand dollars, which was a lot of money durin' that era. Harper was condemned of embezzlement. He was fined and was to serve a small prison term in the Parish Jail. Before he left the home, he assured his future in the family. A second child was on his way. This birth gauged somewhat for forthcomin' generations, but Harper's past weighed heavily on the scale. Little did our community know at the time, he had been indicted on charges of carnal knowledge of a sixteen-year-old girl in the past and had jumped bail before he stood trial. Now that the judge had caught up with him, he was lookin' at a longer prison term, and this time, in the State Penitentiary."

The Penitentiary

Again Mérite-Lajoie felt somewhat responsible for what had happened. The fact was the verdict on Harper's account was not what she had expected. She had no knowledge of his former crimes. Mérite-Lajoie earned her living as a horse specialist of sorts, bringing in money by small allotments, enough to get by, but in an honest way. She had resigned from her postal service and had in this way avoided being laid off. She figured accepting to pay a fine was the best way to stay out of the government's eye, even if she did not think the outcome was balanced in her favor.

There had been convictions in her family. A local veterinarian heard about Harper's gunshot wound and Mérite-Lajoie was fined for operating without a license. Most of the time, the court decisions acknowledged a rich counterpart, usually a man. Mérite-Lajoie harbored the furtive idea that Harper had made simple mistakes, as she had done, as we all do. However, when Mérite-Lajoie sent one of her brothers to visit him in prison, these notions about legal inequality culminated with a new discovery.

After a short time in the parish jail, Harper had been convicted to *Angola*, but there was no Patrick Harper to be found on the premises. The sentence was not for embezzlement, but for leaving town while on bail for a more serious accusation. There, her brother found him under the name of Tyrone Swaily, Ty for short, in a section of the prison where he already had quite a reputation and no one had forgotten him or his slippery name. Mérite-Lajoie had

143

noted the name Swaily when Harper was injured and about half out of his mind, but had not yet come to the realization her future cousin-in-law might be a criminal evading justice, and that his gunshot wound was not at all accidental. Mérite-Lajoie had an unsuspicious mind. She had a hard time imagining people who would want to take advantage of her, and even had more difficulty believing that some people brought trouble upon themselves.

While in confinement Harper (Swaily for sure) managed to beat his jailers out of their paychecks and to burn it all up on indemnities for his fellow inmates. He was quite a flamer all right. He knew how to make friends wherever he was. He also made enemies.

Though Mérite-Lajoie's brother, Thibodaux, brought news of the birth of another son, Harper seemed little interested in how the labor went or even giving the child a name. He laughed and passed cigarettes around, using obscene gestures, intended to impress the other prisoners in the room. He put on this inappropriate display in front of the families who had come to visit someone else: "Hey Y'all hear that? My wife's done dropped a sprog. I'll have to stick it to her good when I git out for permission in a couple of months. I'll give her the time of her life. She's only twenty years old and is probably yearnin' for it right now. She's finally got a bit of meat on her tits. They'll be just right for suckin' if that brat don't get it all. I'll whup his ass and put him in the drawer if he starts bawlin'." The prisoners all sneered. His crude speech was cause for much blushing, whispering, and head bowing.

These Beans Have Too Much Salt

Perhaps the women understood their husbands used the same language in confinement somewhat, but being confronted with hot words in a cold prison annex added humiliation to disgust. The guard told them all to cut it out, or the visits would be interrupted. Harper was pleased with himself and smiled at everyone, even winking at one of the younger women. Thibodaux wondered just how much the prison had worn off on him in such a short period. There didn't seem to be much room for the pastoral talk of before. He wasn't interested in the well-being of his wife or that of anyone else in the family, further than his needs for them. The construction of the church was far from his latest project: "Next month when you come, buddy, bring me a *Playboy*. I get bored here without a belly-warmer and most of these white-collar idiots are just too flabby-assed to be worth a fuck." He winked again at his inmate's wife who had heard everything Harper wanted her to hear.

Mérite-Lajoie listened as her brother explained how Harper complained of the conditions of prison life, and in particular, the food, before he shifted to other subjects, closer to home, which she related to me along with the rest: "'That fella, Leblanc, or is it Gautier, the one who sold ya'll the property', said Harper. He's a friend of yours ain't he? Don't you think he is a little stupid? Besides acceptin' that that no-good son-of-a-bitch called a son-in-law run off to France with some foreign slut, he's takin' in his daughter and her four brats, and they live at home, free of charge. Besides, I hear from one of the town talkers that his daughter has put that deal by many men and even got turned away from her church for trying to move in with more than one. I don't know what

145

will come of those young'uns without their father. I don't even think they go to church either.'" Harper seemed to know a considerable amount about the goings-on in Ferriday, but I will say this is the first time I had ever heard these tales about my parents. Had I not known the personage better, I might have worried, although, I'm not quite sure why. Both of my parents are now beyond rumor's grip, and none of us live in Ferriday anymore. Nonetheless, he had had other visits, and long ago, there had been talk.

Once he got on the subject of women, there was no stopping him. Again, upon hearing this, Mérite-Lajoie responded in favor of the besieged, attempting to prevent a calamity by refuting his slanderous remarks. Flummoxed by the energetic assertions that my grandfather was foolish and shortsighted, Thibodaux spoke of how he began to laugh with Harper about his fellow Cajun, agreeing my mother was now dressed "like a whore" and would soon be working at the King Hotel. "The girls", meaning my sister and I, "wouldn't amount to much else." Nevertheless, Mérite-Lajoie tells me that as he snorted and slung mud with the prisoner, Thibodaux had almost swallowed his tongue. He did not enjoy speaking ill of anyone, much less another Cajun. He became aware of the other prisoners and visitors listening as well.

"When I got home, I headed straight for the shower. I felt I had to wash off the prison talk itself. It wasn't so much the hardship of prison life. I had seen or heard many things in my thirty-two years. For days, I couldn't distil the images conjured up by Harper's language." That man had no discernment about manners. His uninhibited gestures and tentative to flirt with the other prisoners' wives could have disappeared with the next wind. However, as colorful remnants of a war documentary, the words remained engraved in Mérite-Lajoie's mind. And even these she didn't wish to repeat. Nevertheless, the calumny in which Thibodaux found himself enrolled filtered out of prison and found itself on the town square of Ferriday, precipitating the end of almost all relations between my grandfather and the trailer park clan.

"As predicted, Harper got out of prison for a short permission two months later. He was to appear at the courthouse to settle a few questions about his employer's potential role in the embezzlement. His other judgment had not yet been set. Contented to be home, he did as he promised, shuttin' his children off from their mother and spendin' much of the day with her in bed. As a young woman, Leona was glad to see her husband but found it difficult lettin' her two babies alone in their bedroom. They cried for their dinner, after having cried for their lunch, and having cried because of their dirty diapers. Harper would not let her take care of them. He yelled, 'If you get up from this bed before I'm ready, I'll leave and go to town to get what I need. You're spoilin' them. You got up in the middle of the night and gave the little one a snack. He can wait awhile. I've waited nearly nine months. I want you do stop this breast feedin'' shit too. You ain't no cow. I don't want no saggy tits. You might as well stop right now while I'm still home.'"

"What could she respond to that?" asked Mérite-Lajoie. "While Harper dozed off, she got up, dressed silently and brought her children to me. 'You got to help me now. He's some kinda hungry. He won't let me even feed them,' Leona cried."

"I was happy to help my cousin with the little ones. Emmy was in the first grade, and the circumstances were more favorable for takin care of her boys. They both had diaper rashes, and the baby was inconsolable. Leona left, however. She was certain Harper would do what he said if he woke up and found her gone, but at this point, she almost didn't care. At least she did not put any anticipation of his infidelity in front of her children's needs."

Later, Leona described the scene with Harper to Mérite-Lajoie, who was now telling me. Leona had silently undressed, not daring even to shower. He watched her through narrow topaz eyes and grabbed her arm yanking her down, as soon as she put her hand on the bed. "'Where have you been? He wanted to know. 'I told you not to get up.' He sat up and slapped her hard on the side of her head. 'Am I gonna to have to get rough with you so you'll mind me? I've been gone for months now, and this is all the respect you have for me?'"

"Tears formed in Leona's eyes as she spoke of this with me. She had tried to explain to her husband that the children needed to be fed and cleaned. She told me later how he had put his hand over her mouth and straddled her saying, 'you shut up now. What kind of wife are you anyway? I bet you been off flirtin' with Deux-Ours or some other skunk while I've been gone?'

"'No, why would I do that?' Leona was shocked at her husband's suggestion. She had barely a relationship of any sort with him, and none with any other man. She didn't drive, and her youngest baby was only two months old."

"Harper just kept on sayin', 'bitch. I'll show you. I'll make sure only the virtue of continence remains in your loins.' His anger made him more lustful than before. Had they not been married; his violent attack would have been called a rape."

"When he had felt he had given his wife a lesson, and proven his manhood to an invisible spectator, he granted in terms such as I already had heard from him: 'The Lord has a preference for me. He wants me to have numerous children. I have only been translatin' the Gospels in prison; I'm goin' to act on them soon. If everyone followed the Gospel, everythin' would be all right. You got to act accordin' to the Bible and submit to your husband. If you don't, you'll be prey for the Devil, then what kinda Ma would you be? You'd be a whore, right? What kinda Ma is that? I ain't gonna let you pervert my sons. You should let the Lord encircle you with Purity. Now I'm gonna ask God what to do. I know some men of good faith. It is time. It is almost time for the Second Coming. Accordin' to the Gospels, we gotta get ready. I'm not talkin' about a reform; it's for the accomplishment of the Time, which will come accordin' to the Gospels. I'm not ready. Before I didn't have faith. Belief came to me all the sudden one day like a cut in the sky. Before, I didn't see, but it was a revelation, a huge upheaval in my soul. God is Goodness. We are obliged to die for love. It is the belief of ancestral transmission. Do you perceive what your part in this is?'"

"Again, Leona was uncertain what to make of her husband or understand what he said was her part other than being a wife and mother. She thought prison had changed him, but she didn't dare discuss it. She was only a woman of twenty, even if she had two children. Harper again added, puttin' on his belt. 'Now these men of good faith are goin' to keep an eye on you while I go back and finish my prison term. I've got six months to go, and I don't want to hear about any more goin-ons. Let the Lord silence your libido. The men of good faith measure the thermodynamics of fidelity. They can tell what intentions you have. You better straighten up and start gettin' the church ready with the others. You'll have to be on my staff when I get out. The kids can come and see you, of course, but you got to do the work right. I'll send you some letters to post for me from here. I'll mop the floor with you and whup your ass for forgettin' to do the corners if you don't get it right. And in the meantime, stop puttin' sweetener in your tea. Sugar multiplies the aphrodisiac effect caused by the liberation of libidinal gases in women when hot water is added. So, if you get gassy while I'm gone, I'll know. You know what I'm talkin about don't you? I don't have to spell it out to you, do I? They will send me a report.'"

"You might laugh at what I'm repeatin' here and think I'm makin' it up. We never knew who was he talkin' about or what? Leona didn't dare ask for explanations and answered only, 'yes'. No one had seen these men of good faith or their instruments." It was clear Harper had not been speaking of the other men in the clan, or any kind of contraption available in any store, not even in New Orleans, but he said there were accessible men, ready to assist him with their paraphernalia for measuring fidelity and feminine libidinal gases when the Time would come. Leona believed then she should keep an eye out for them too. Where he came up with some of his other ideas remain a mystery.

Time

"Time came and passed. Harper got out of prison and fathered yet another two sons, identical twins. With each birth, there was a new wave of excitement, merriment, and preparations that fell upon the clan. Harper made a bonfire and played the guitar with some of the men until finally he was the only one around the dead fire. He went to the new church office and began to write. It was a wild dithyramb about the thermo-dynamical gases in women, about the transmission of a new religious and economical order, and about his being chosen as God's look-a-like. After havin' kept his desk at least twelve hours, he explained his project again to Deux Ours, sayin' he perfected the one he had worked on in prison."

"My brother, Thibodaux, found some of Harper's writings after the fire. They repeated much what I'm sayin' to you. He even explained his ideas to my face, 'Before, I didn't see,' he said one day. 'Then I had a revelation. It was a great upheaval in me. I noted the gaseous productions of my wife and their effect on my libido. God is goodness, don't you see. There is belief by ancestral transmission. Every time I have a newborn legitimate son, there is a transmission of his spirit. Even if I was in prison for a spell, we can't say that perfection didn't already exist in my blood. It's God. I can get close because I'm the image of God. We don't know everything. We don't know the future. Sometimes the men of good faith have prevented me from speakin'. To hear their voices, one must believe in God. God spoke to me. The Devil doesn't know men of good faith. I'm a believer. I went to church when I was a child. When I grew up, for a while I didn't go. But in prison, all that changed. Why? It is hard to explain, but I had a revelation, a direct light, suddenly, like when you find the answer to a problem. There is goin' to be a new order of the universe. There will be harmony between finances and religion. I will create a new economy. I stayed awake for nights and wrote the foundations of my manifest. The other prisoners listened to me. They knew I had found the truth.'

"Harper rambled on like this sometimes for hours about the Glory of God, about sin, about repentance, about thermodynamic fidelity and a new world order, without expressin' much interest in his newborn boys outside their part in his revelation. Once I ventured as far as makin' fun of Harper's excessive religiosity. 'Sin,' I said, 'you've got to be jokin'! We haven't seen it around these parts since the crawfish said his prayers!' Choked on his own emotion, he stopped talkin' to me. He threw his crawfish pole down and tromped back to his trailer without sayin' a word."

"The next day, Deux Ours came upon Harper discussin' somethin' with my brother, Thibodaux. He didn't hear the entire interview but thought he heard something somber concernin' me. Harper quickly changed the subject, so expeditiously that Deux Ours had a hard time graspin' when Harper asked him: "In your opinion, what purpose does your work have for the community as a whole?" Deux Ours had begun to feel wary of Harper's attacks. He wasn't ready to reveal his innermost thoughts about his métier. He disclosed his feelin' in one short phrase: 'Like Mérite-Lajoie, I'm a healer, but especially a horse trainer.' Harper responded vigorously: "Well, you know most of your clients are stupid rednecks that don't know their dicks from a doornail. Now I'm not gonna let the public sue me for malpractice done on your part. I found a few problems with the way you both are goin' about your business. I'm gonna to explain them to you. First of all, you ain't makin' money off those clowns. That's where you come in."

Deux Ours looked at the ground. Thibodaux made up some excuse and hurried off to his trailer. "Let me tell you how to do. Jest listen to me and those other traitors, or whatever you call them will jest have to commit suicide 'cause they won't have any more business. But if you want me to help you, you're gonna have to make yerself a little more available. When I come over to your office or home, your gonna have to listen up. I'll be bringin' information you can't do without. Second of all, I've got ideas, ideas, tons of ideas about how you can be more efficient in your work." Deux Ours started to object, arguing that his friend knew nothin' of medicinal plants or taking care of a patient, but Harper interrupted him. "Nonsense. I'm talkin' about makin' money here, not carin' for a bunch of good-for-nothin' jerks who might as well croak over and die."

"I worried more and more. Since I met Harper, much happened in my family, and not much on the lines of any divine settlement for the ill fate of my forefathers, two or even three hundred years before, but, consequences of my own impulsive knee-jerk decisions. My father had mocked me, saying I paid far too much for the mosquito-infested acres. Thibodaux had discovered the spring was only a local water collector for moonshiners, and the salt, a block of salt lick set out for deer. Our relationship with other Cajuns degenerated. But I got over most of these frustrations. If these upset Deux Ours, he never mentioned it. We never spoke about not convincin' the Sheriff of the talkin' possum. I never dreamed anyone outside our clan would believe me. My whole family had seen enough trouble and complaints filed against them for sellin' false remedies and moonshine. But that didn't feign to bother any of us at all. Prohibition was over, and, the decade's end was bringin' many changes. We had become accustomed to the aromas and the low fire from the distillery; having cheap whiskey was a compensation, however small."

Even without that benefit, for the most part, the pitfalls of her new life all seemed trivial to Mérite-Lajoie. One or two began to emerge as something more perilous. "The mistake beginnin' to write a letter of blame on my heart was the one I made when I insisted that Swaily (still called Harper) marry my cousin and accept him as the preacher of the church we had built."

Thoughts of these disasters began to invade her zydeco, the Creole music that was already forming salty discordant melodies whenever she hummed a tune. This music, along with some others, came from her mother's side of the family. On each occasion, when the recollection of a shared event with Harper was called to her mind, the incident hung there for several seconds, suspending the naturel rhythms of the movements at hand. Maybe even several minutes would pass before Mérite-Lajoie could get past the memory. She would try to think how she should have handled the past to avoid falling victim of it at the prevailing moment, or in the future.

The clock would not slow down, but the Cajun's activities would halt. The music would fade. She would discontinue her hammering on the fence post, and the goat would jump through the gap in the wire. She would stop digging for fish bait, and the earthworms would wiggle away. She would interrupt the hornet nest burning before she had finished, and the irritated wasps would fly out at her. The raucous music played against its own harmony, enjoining her motions to a jolt. Without a doubt, if a simple desire could kill, Harper would long since be dead. Fortunately for both, as soon as this last idea clearly emerged it would be interrupted by the task at hand. There was always a goat to grab, a fish to bait, or a sting to attend to. These absences of resolve crippled her efforts, dampened her jazz, and Mérite-Lajoie feared they would make her resemble Harper (or whatever his name was). Her mother, now conscious of a problem, but remembering how Bienvenu usually handled them, reminded her daughter: "if you fight with *hogoramus intolerabilis,* you both end up covered in shit, but only the hog enjoys it. Do you really want to give this man his just desserts? As with the hog, he will have it and eat it too." She too spiced up her pot using Latin-like arrangements with French, Spanish, or English expressions, and especially salted the beans about unbearable human creatures. Even Deux Ours was at a loss about what to do. Harper had a way with stirring up problems in the couple. Only, they didn't realize he was to blame.

Changes

Instead of acting on her deepest feelings, Mérite-Lajoie convinced her husband to build a house on the other side of Lake Road, in Helena Addition, to get a new start, so to speak. They had acquired the other lots near the entrance of Helena Addition from my grandfather and organized their family to move their trailer. Later this became an office for the *traiteurs*, and the brick house became their home. Deux Ours and Emmy moved in with her on the new lot.

The Harpers, now six of them, remained across Lake Road only a few feet from the First Evangelist Church where Harper was now minister of the cult.

"Harper didn't see these transitions with a clement eye. He began to harass me, 'I'll be damned if it ain't old Merit...The JOY...' He laughed as he slapped me on the rear and drew out my name with a saccharin sound. Harper realized that my name meant something and was makin' fun of it, coinin' up ideas intolerable for any woman. 'I haven't seen you in church lately, darlin', said Harper. 'These other folks, it don't matter to me if they come or not. They bring their money, and I'm content with that. It could be them or someone else fillin' the pews. But you, Happy Ass? You are my girl, kinda although I know you are already betrothed, but I'm talkin' about in a spiritual sort of way. If I was a priest, you'd call me Father and you'd be my daughter, spiritually speakin'.'"

"'You and me have the same objectives,' he continued while I felt a kinda rage buildin' in me. 'We speak the same language,' he said. 'I'm not talkin' about real languages like French or English; I'm talkin' about the language of the heart. You know I'm the only one who listens to you. Is it your husband? Jest tell me what's wrong?'"

"'I know why you must be holdin' up on your own', Harper just kept on. 'Let me help you with your words. It's The Bear's fault. You've been cheated on. Now he has driven you away from church so he can enjoy his social life. Let me let you in on a secret.' Harper began to unroll one of his cynical theories about Indians cheatin' on their wives. Then he would do the same thing with Deux Ours when I wasn't around. Workin' one's anger up to a frenzy was one of his specialties."

"As he worked on Deux Ours, Harper scratched his nose with his dried purplish hands. 'Hell, if we weren't there to explain it to them, how would they uncover the truth? None of them think in terms of compassion.' He said to Deux Ours one day. 'They only care about themselves, tryin' to cover their natural body odor with deodorant or perfume. Just see how they get all dolled up. I bet your Merit spends an hour a day in front of that mirror, tryin' to get ready for all that Joy she's wantin'. You should restrain her. Get rid of the mirror, the frills and that bottled junk. What do you think she is doin' it for?'"

"'Look', Harper said. 'No one else thinks of these diabolic creatures as people. They are like n.i.g.g.e.r.s. That's right." Deux

Ours got up to leave. He didn't tolerate racism. We didn't use that word. He couldn't find anything to say that would set things right. I was in the kitchen stirrin' a roux and couldn't leave the stove. I watched as Harper followed him and grabbed his shoulder. Deux Ours swung around, his lips curled and his gentle face all-at-once frightening with a frown that spread over his face. He looked almost like a growlin' dog, but uttered no sound before turnin' back towards the bedroom."

"'What? Harper cried, followin' Deux Ours down the hall. 'If you don't force them to do what you want, they are lazy and won't do nothin'. They know how to work the system. If you don't take a whip to them once and awhile, they won't obey. She is spendin' all those instants tryin' to look pretty, and it ain't for you. How come y'all only have one daughter? Hell, she has squelched out your libido! Just look at my family. You ain't gettin' much, my friend. No, it ain't right. Your wife has got to go from the stove to the fryin' pan sometime.' Harper continued like this for hours, draggin' Deux Ours back towards the kitchen. I was fumin' under my breath. He wouldn't give up until Deux Ours admitted some trivial argument or discordance with me. By the time he finished with him, he didn't know who to be mad at, Harper or me."

"Then Harper added other commentaries that I would have preferred not to hear. 'Weee hooo!" he explained. From my place, I get to see all them gorgeous gals. They all come up and get so close I can smell sweet nature's perfume and sometime see all the way down to their navels if they bend over enough. That friend of

Leona, Suzy, I bet she wears that tiny push-up bra just for me. I can almost see her nipples. And when they come in for meetins and start fussin' around, I can see all the way up the other side. Do you know she wears a G-string? That's what they call those French panties the New Orleans' whores wear. Both cheeks stick out like an apple or a peach hung on a string hangin' there jest for bitin'. Deux Ours didn't know what to make of all this. I couldn't find any words at the time to help him with it and started to yell."

"'Ah come on Mérite-Lajoie,' he said to me. 'It's not like you weren't aware. All pastors are in it for the goods, aren't they? I'm not sayin' we act on it, but you get my drift, dontchya? Sometimes when you listen to these women, all-suicidal, you want to comfort them, and you get these erotic feelings.' He put on his virtuous smile. 'Besides, if you don't get it, some other man of good faith will. Yep, I bet we would have a good time together, I can tell you that. You would MERIT your name.' He drawled out my name again. 'Get it? Everybody knows your husband ain't fit since his heart attack. And men on my side wouldn't pass up that ass of yours, just like little old Suzy-Q. If I'd been in school, she wouldn't have looked twice at me, but now, she never misses to come see me after church meetings on Thursday night. I've 'bout got her reformed. So, if you ain't getting' it at home, you got to get it somewhere else. That's all there is to it.' Deux Ours was in the next room and I was afraid if he heard what Harper was sayin' to me, he would kill him."

"Then, when Deux Ours came back, he continued this line with him, in front of me. 'All men do it. Don't look at me like that. You think it is immoral? Politicians do it. Governments don't care. Why should the church? Joseph Smith got somethin' on us there. Any woman can be replaced and multiplied. The same with most of the congregation; the only significance for the menfolk, as far as I'm concerned, is they can fill that plate with dollars and propel me to television.'"

By the time Harper's contemptuous mouth had unwound, Deux Ours felt more than upset. Until then, he hadn't had much criticism for Mérite-Lajoie. Suddenly, it was as if he couldn't notice anything else. Suspiciously he watched her as she dressed and brushed her hair. Ordinarily he was in a hurry to leave the bedroom. Now, as he watched, he felt aroused, and when she laughed, giving a reason for her refusal and turning back to her mirror, he enumerated these rejections in the form of a list of grievances. He ended this tally with an account of her comings and goings and wondered if Harper was telling him something of the truth. Had she been unfaithful? Would their marriage last? What would happen to Emmy? Like a pathetic Othello, Deux Ours heard the alarming words of a self-interested strategist, Iago, posing now as Brabantio: "Look at her...if thou have eyes to see. She deceived her father and may thee."

Dissonance could now be heard in the once peaceful Robichaux household. Deux Ours was already ill with diabetes and, other than the care provided by Mérite-Lajoie, he sought no treatment. He began to feel possessive. "I don't want you spendin' so much of your day at church. You can go Sunday to be with the children, but that's enough. No more meetins. And stop spendin' so many afternoons with Leona." He had not dispatched orders since the army and then, very few. Mérite-Lajoie, needless to say, did not appreciate the transformation and made matters worse by asking him to sleep on the couch. She disappeared for several days, spending nights in the treehouse they had built in the woods as a hunting camp. Deux Ours figured she was there, but didn't go looking for her on account of his disorientation in the forest.

Under the dark branches, she again had a nightmare. She recalled the possum siting on her chest, staring at her. It was no longer injured but was eating a body part. She caught a glimpse of two bears in the corner, dancing away. Jerking back the covers, she woke up sweating, her heart pounding. Light was beginning to appear through the trees. She was afraid she had been screwing with the incubus and it had consumed a part of her body like a praying mantis does with its male after mating. She examined herself, looking down at her body to make sure she was all there.

"'Chirp, chirp, chirp, chirp; chirp chirp, chirp; pew, pew pew, poo-too-eee poo-too-eee, pa-ta-cheep, pa-ta-cheep, pa-ta-cheep, cheep, cheep, cheep; pe-wey, pe-wey, pe-wey.' The mockingbird was markin' its territory, tryin' to get rid of the blue-jays, that were sky-bombin' one another, screamin' as each jumped out of the way of its relative."

These Beans Have Too Much Salt

"I sat up on the mat, my covers around me. 'This is no good, I said to myself. I can't stay here. I think I'm losin' my mind.'"

The more she thought about her dream, the more its realism resonated in her soul. The animal's effluvium hung in the air like a warm sour swamp. Her mouth was filled with a bitter tasting fluid. Mérite-Lajoie spit on the floor. Had she swallowed some strange elixir that hung about her mouth? Remembering the animal's teeth, she thought of the legend about how vampires spread their disease (not like a leech that would paralyze the skin before sinking in its teeth and drawing the stuff of life, but by hypnotizing the victim, obliging him to become leech, and to draw the substance of death and eternal damnation) and said under her breath: "Mon Dieu, superstition will take you by and by to blasphemy and then, straight to Hell." She wiped up her objection with a handkerchief and tried chasing away the hideous torments.

She wanted to laugh at herself, then as now. She knew possums were harmless animals. She told me how she fumbled about trying to find her clothes. She got up and opened the window. The limbs of the tree next to hers held its branches out and upward. It was an old oak, practically a cathedral in the forest. Through its branches, she could almost see her ancestors, watching her with worried eyes. Above and below, life was on the move, and the ears of the forest on watch. She leaned out the window looking upwards towards the sun. The old polyglot dropped a twig, hitting her nearly in the eye before flying off to bother someone else. It didn't make her laugh but did bring her momentarily back to the instant. She didn't want to pit her strength against the forces of nature, only chase the nightmare caused by her terrible chagrin. But she had to admit she was worried too. She climbed down the ladder, her face creased like tree-bark, her hair sticking up like branches; and she wandered out of the forest to the path that led to her pickup.

Secrets

All day long, Mérite-Lajoie invented errands to run. The bait store was open, so she went in to look at a rod-and-reel. Her family had been fishermen for centuries. Some of them sold the fish they caught for a living. "I used to know how to wade into the Mississippi, swim down to the bottom, where in the dark I could see only phosphorescent eyes, and put my hand, sometime my whole arm, in the gullet of a slimy catfish, forcin' my fingers through its gills. The monster, five feet long, would then struggle and try to throw me to Texas. It would calm down soon enough for me to come up for air. I knew when the *silure* was tired of fightin'. I would then bring it out to the bank, clean it and take it home to cook. Once I found a wooden foot in one's stomach, but most of the time, there were just other fish. Of course, my arms would be a bit skint up, but it was worth the fun. When the salesclerk asked me that day if he could help, if I knew what kind of bait my husband used, I shook my head. I couldn't bring myself to say anything, but, 'I reckon I jest lookin'.'"

"Jest lookin," was what Mérite-Lajoie replied to every sales person in Ferriday she met that day. "They all thought I didn't have enough money to buy whatever it was I was lookin' at and asked if I wanted to use their layaway policy. The trouble is, I was lookin', but not seein' what I was lookin' at. From Mr. Melton at the Dairy Queen, I had to buy a milkshake because there was nothin' I could look at other than the menu, and people were waitin' in both lines, one 'for coloreds' and one, 'for whites only'. I went into the Baptist Church to find a bathroom and found two doors, one was marked 'Ladies', and the other, 'Men'. I hesitated. It's like I couldn't read the sign and I sat down in the chair to recollect my thoughts."

"I was in a wretched situation; havin' gottin' into a bad way with my husband, bein' from out of town, havin' lost connections with my friends and family outside the trailer park, and I was bein' faced with a dilemma the size only a politician could entertain."

Mérite-Lajoie carried on her forehead, from that day, forth, the omega of those who venture too far inward, forgetting to open up their hearts to a willing ear. Instead of confiding in a trusted friend, she then drove around town, out of town, out to Waterproof and back, and was about to head to Natchez when she noticed the open doors of the King Hotel. The manager, Doug Knight, a Klansman, was sitting in a plush armchair in the tired showplace lobby where anyone could see him, talking to Harper who had his back to the door. "I drove past, then stopped at a bar where I heard a blues band starting to warm up. A Black-Creole at the door blocked my way: 'Are you shore ya wanna come in hea?' he asked. 'There's fried chittlins and muscadine wine in da ally, and ya can hear da music good from der.' Smoke hung thick around the bars on both sides of the room. People were already clingin' to each other in the back part of the bar. I got back in my pickup and rode down Fourth Street around about a half-block, passin' again the King Hotel, and found Big George's in the raw and littered ally next to Haney's Big House."

"Harper saw my pickup, I guess, as it passed and was sure to have converted me to his idea. He was sure that I had been spendin' my nights with another man, in the King Hotel, and was now sneakin' away. I would never have gone there. Besides bein' faithful, we had been told that the Klan had secret meetins there, even before the *Civil Rights Act*. Now, what would a Cajun, part Redbone, and probably Creole, be doin' with folks like that? Instead, Harper found me behind the Negro bar, drinkin' the local wine and listenin' to some blues comin' from next door. He started up with his rigmarole, harassin' me even more vigorously than before, and even threatenin' me."

"'Don't you know you will fall victim to Satan?' He questioned. 'Did you see your husband go in Haney's Bighouse? As a colored man they let him in.' I shook my head in disbelief before he went in the bar himself. He came out sayin' he had seen Deux Ours run out the front door. I didn't believe him, but I did have some doubts. Later he told me that Harper had seen him in Haney's before the doorman threw him out. Deux Ours told me on his death bed that Harper had said some terrible things."

"Harper said, 'You can fuck one of these wayward women if ya snif 'em out, but you need to come home and stop hangin' out around here all night. Buddy Bear, you got to snap out of it. You don't know what you're liable to fall a victim to, hangin' around with night-lifers like these. Like all Indians, your father was a drunkard and weak man. He let your Ma turn him around her little finger. He hung out in places like this where he picked fights with the coloreds. He was probably, you know what I mean even when I don't say the name, like when you speak of something no one wants to talk about, but everyone knows what it is? That's right, a latent one. How do you think you got your name? Two Bears, come on. One on the other. I'm sorry I have to be the one to tell this to you, but my observations are always right. People wind up comin' out with everythang you want to know or not. And if you don't want what has already rubbed off on you to take effect, you'd best follow my example and keep your nose and ass clean.' All this nauseated Deux Ours half to death. I think that is what finally brought about the attack that killed him. Can you die of disgust?"

"When Harper told me he had seen Deux Ours, I turned away. I thought Harper took everything too much into account, word for word. Irma Thomas was singin' "It's Rainin" in Haney's Big House next door. I wished I was a Black-Creole or even only a colored Redbone man, and could go in to hear the song better. She was singin' about love, a clear and simple idea. Deux Ours and I would hold each other tight in the rain. This could have been our song. I can't tear him out of my heart I thought. He is the love of my life."

"I had heard the song before, but now I thought I wanted to buy the record as if the blues singer held the key to our love that was slippin' away. Harper had shaken me, I guess, and I was drinkin' too much, tryin' to build up my courage about somethin'. Again, Harper interrupted again the flow of the lyrics in my mind and Pee Wee Whittaker blurted out new notes on his trombone."

These Beans Have Too Much Salt

"'It is bad for you,' he said, 'bad for the church, and bad for me. Listen Mérite-Lajoie, do you want me to slap your face? Is that what it takes to reel you in? Think about my reputation. You remember what happened the last time you stopped goin' to church?'"

"By now, Harper was referrin' to the huntin' accident, or the shootin' he had been the victim of, which, as it happened, occurred on a Sunday mornin'. I didn't have to be reminded of details." Mérite-Lajoie's confusion, alcoholic or not, was that of someone who no longer knew very well who she was, nor where she stood. Even now, her nightmares floated in and out of our conversations. The past doubts came surging forth. She couldn't help but listen to this abject monolog planted in her conscious, forming images and fictions, almost as worthless as Harper's yarn.

"The next day, Harper said to Deux Ours, 'Let me tell you something else; if you are goin' to be a man of good faith, you're goin' to have to tell me if you see my wife foolin' round too. We're in this together. You know that miscarriage she had while I was in prison? That should tell you somethin'. She screamed like a Banshee sayin' she got pregnant durin' my permission and lost the baby, but it ain't my fault if her belly wadn't nothin' but a cemetery. She'd been cheatin' on me as sure as she cheated on her parents. The Lord punished her jest like he punished Bathsheba. The whole family is a bunch of liars and thieves. If you don't believe me, you're in for it worse, much worse. Now I've 'bout got my wife trained and keep her on track at the church and with my sons. She prays a lot and if she don't, well, I take a strap to her. If you don't do the same with Mérite-Lajoie, you are in for hell. She only married you for your money. She has been makin' a slave out of you.'"

"'Did she tell you that?' asked Deux Ours."

"'She might as well have. She told me you would do anythang for her. And that ridiculous necklace you made for her. You made an idiot out of yourself with those little heart carvings, you know.'"

"'She showed you, her necklace?' asked Deux Ours, raisin' his arm as if someone was about to throw something at him."

"'Well, yeah', replied Harper, 'and the bracelet,' lowering Deux Ours' arm. 'I laughed my head off when I saw it. It looks like somethin' one of my boys did at school.' Deux Ours whirled away. I can only imagine his face."

"'You're not gonna to get mad at me are you. I'm only tellin' you the truth. Hell, was she even still a virgin when you married her? If she weren't, well, you know damn well what kind she is. Just like her name, a woman of joy. That's the truth, the solid truth. Her cousin told me he seen her with some ole boy in a barn. You keep an eye on Mérite-Lajoie, but keep an eye on Leona, too. You tell me if she betrays me. You got it? You must make some denunciations if you want her to get clear with the Lord for her evil doins with them men at the King Hotel or at Orville's Lounge.

God's seen her. The mynah bird took down her name. What do you think he means when you open the door and he chirps out: 'Have fun! Have fun! Have fun! Er..ck! Right place!' And you better come with her to church and confess these sins. That is the only way you'll rein her in. Now, go on home and do what I said. If she says a word, push it right back down her throat.'"

I tried to imagine the scene. Here was one who pretended to be their preacher, going on and on with his horrible personal secrets, whispering as if in a confessional, accusing both Mérite-Lajoie and Deux Ours of wrongdoing, after having advised each one to do just what each was now being accused of, and without either having ever acted on his counsel.

Deux Ours was also listening to more of his advice, now an exhortation to a kind of duplicity he had difficulty distinguishing. It wasn't so much his desire to run that upset him, but an obscure desire to prove this man's attacks on his virility, and that of his father, in error. He knew his wife would never go near Orville's, already on account of it being somehow linked to Carlos Marcello's Cosa Nostra Mafia and the Peppermint Lounge, a cathouse in Basile, and their family's knowledge of that man. "A mynah bird sayin' my wife's name? He's got to be kiddin' me."

The attack on Deux Ours' father, suggesting in such a way he might not even be his father, was simply disgraceful. Perhaps he had done the same with Skizzum, before she came to me. Harper had a way of picking out intimate details in your life and then, later on, using them against you. He was kind of like a thief that would visit you in your home as a guest, handling your valuables, praising them, and putting them back in their place, before making off with them the next week, or month, or however long it took for you to finally trust him with the keys. Deux Ours clinched his fists in anger, then as now, trying to separate the different intrusions under his skin as if he were trying to tell the differences between scabies and poison ivy rashes. Both itched until they burned, and scratching only made them worse.

Nevertheless, whatever would be her decision, whatever would be her act; throughout her stay in the forest, she missed her husband and daughter and was tired of being mosquito-bitten every night. "My heart felt like it was ripped open. I got into my pickup and drove home feelin' tense and disoriented. It was a cloudy, dark night and you couldn't see your face in front of you. The crickets stopped chirpin' when I got to my porch and opened the screen door, hittin' myself in the nose. I was happy my glassy eyes raised no questions, and went to bed, not sufferin' to explain anything to Deux Ours. He didn't bother using his fists either. In fact, he was too sick to move." Going to bed with no explanation of where she had been for the last few days was the limit of her protest. Deux Ours somehow knew there wasn't anyone there he wanted to hit. But this knowledge was just as ineffectual in calming each one's nerves.

A New Start

"The next day, Harper came over and found Deux Ours watchin' a football game. The preacher stood square in front of the screen, before turnin' around and changin' the channel to *I love Lucy*. Emmy was lyin' back in the recliner, watchin' the game with him. 'Silly redhead,' Harper said, before turnin' off the television! 'Leona has taken the boys to Mississippi to see their grandparents. I swear', he said, 'I should've never allowed her to get her license. Now she thinks she can drive all over the country. She doesn't see how that makes me feel. I have to stay here and work.'"

"'Since she is out of town, I'll just stay over here in your extra bedroom, he added. 'That way we can freely pick up our discussion where we left off. Mérite-Lajoie can add a plate for me. It won't be any trouble. It is just for a few days.'"

"Emmy got up and left the room. She didn't much like football, but she loved bein' near her father. I guess she figured somethin' wasn't right. Harper deliberately tried to annoy me."

"'Look, Harper,' I said, 'I was plannin' on goin' huntin' this weekend. I won't be here. You can't stay.'"

"'Oh,' he said, 'you don't have to stay. I'll keep an eye on Deux Ours and Emmy. Go ahead.'"

These Beans Have Too Much Salt

"Like I would leave him in the house with my husband and child! I should have seen it comin'. I told him, 'Harper, I can't impose a visitor on Deux Ours while I'm not home. What would your wife feel like if you did that?'"

"'Oh, Leona would do like I say', he says. 'Hell Mérite-Lajoie, if you can't even trust your own husband! We ain't gonna to sleep together, are we Deux Ours?' He jerked his head around to look at my husband and winked at him. 'If my bein' here causes any problems I'll leave. But after all, what about me? Did you think about your friend here? I got my sermon to prepare and no one to fix my meals. Besides, since the accident, I'm afraid I might have a syncope while I'm alone. And do I have to remind you both what we men were taught in the army?

This is my rifle
This is my gun,
This is for shooting,
And this is for fun.'"

"Harper added gestures to his rhyme, shoving Deux Ours. Neither of us wanted to be reminded of the army, nor of Harper's accident, not even of our conversation left off the day before. I especially didn't want to consider my cousin-in-law's wanton designs. I knew by then I hadn't shot Harper, but here the man stood, in my home, accusin' my husband to confuse his gun with his dick, and wantin' to be nominated to be in charge of either of our shortcomins!"

"By this time, Deux Ours was beside himself. He was angry with me and didn't know any more if he could trust me, but he wanted Harper out of his sight: 'Why don't you take Harper with you? You can make food enough for you both.' I didn't answer. I was hopin' he would leave, too. I couldn't imagine Deux Ours seein' me off on a huntin' trip with this man. He added, 'then it's settled. Mérite-Lajoie will pick you up tomorrow.' Harper just stood there and grinned. I listened with fear and indignation."

"After Harper left, Deux Ours began to build a fence. He was determined to become less befuddled. Seekin' order in a physical way helped him to make a new start, but he had no business workin' like that with his health and wouldn't have done so if I'd stayed home. Resolvin' to keep Harper away, he began to fence in our horses on their new home lot so that they practically encircled the trailer on all sides. He felt safer with the gentle animals guardin' our front door."

"While Deux Ours was workin', Emmy came out wearin' a blue skirt he didn't recognize." Mérite-Lajoie tried to explain their deepening frustrations. "My husband remembered raisin' his head, studyin' her as she climbed up and sat on the newly installed gate. All at once he had noticed her bare legs and realized how beautiful a girl his child was becomin'. Suddenly he had been perturbed by what he felt was an improper attraction that overcame him in a sneaky way he couldn't explain. 'Don't bother me,' he yelled. 'I'm workin'. Can't you see?' He turned his back and hammered the post harder. Anger seemed to be an appropriate way to deal with confused emotions, but he couldn't stay that way long."

"Even though I wasn't happy with the situation and Deux Ours wasn't feelin' well, I decided to go ahead and go huntin', thinkin', it'd do me good. I told my husband later that all fathers went through these trials, as their girls became adolescents, but we both wondered if it was somethin' Harper did, or said, that had incited these ideas."

"The next day, I picked up Harper as Deux Ours had suggested. We had hardly been in the pickup a minute before Harper asked me to swing by the Pic Quick. He came out with several six-packs of beer and some food. 'I hope you weren't spectin' me to eat that shit, you cook. I don't know how Deux Ours can stomach that crap.' I almost backed into an ice truck. I had felt so bewildered that I was relieved when the rain started. Instead of stayin' all weekend, we left Saturday mornin'. Harper had harassed me half the night, tryin' to get me to drink his liquor, sayin' I wasn't so bad lookin' after all and that Deux Ours wouldn't mind if I comforted him in Leona's absence as he had sent us off together to keep me happy. He waved as he got out of my truck in front of his trailer, winked at me and called out, 'I'll see you at lunch.' I was exhausted from fightin' him off, but strangely all I could think of was my food. I never thought about my *tambouille* tastin' bad before then. I always had eaten it, but suddenly I was wonderin' if it was fit." Mérite-Lajoie gave me a perplexed smile.

"From then on Harper became more and more intrusive, in spite of the fence. He would open our door at any time of the day or night, help himself to a drink, flop down in Deux Ours' favorite armchair, or wake up on our couch, and complain about almost anything, and in particular about me, comparin' my decoration to that of Leona's, just to bother us. 'That green is horrible,' he'd say, as if he was some kind of judge about decoration. 'It looks like someone died and was buried here. It makes you wanna vomit, doesn't it? Leona masters *her* colors. You ought to get her to come decorate for you, Hon.' It didn't seem to be enough that he sowed discord between father and son, man and wife, now he was tryin' to stir up a fuss between us cousins. 'And she is quite a seamstress,' he continued. 'You know she makes all of our shirts? That is some woman, your cousin. She knows how to take care of the family.' His tongue flickered as he spoke."

"When I went out of the room, Deux Ours gave Harper a hard look. 'What?' he said, 'Did I say somethin' wrong? Did I say anythang 'cept the truth? Some people were born to talk, and others, well, they were born to listen.' Harper was always cheery when he thought he stumbled on some sort of truism. It was as if he couldn't do anything without these prepacked suitcase formulas."

"When I saw my cousin the next week, it was as if Leona had been the one to stir the wasp's nest. 'I don't know why you are always braggin' about how your house looks. I guess it is nice, but you have a lot of nerve sendin' your husband over to criticize me, and behind my back. Now Deux Ours is always on my butt tryin' to make me mend somethin' when I come back from the chores with the horses or huntin' in the woods. Like I didn't have 'nough to do already.'"

"And Leona answered, jumpin' in with both feet, 'well it took a lot of time to make my house look that pretty. Don't you think I have a lot to do with Harper and all our kids? I have to keep after them all day long. I forbade Harper to bring home toys. They just litter up the house with them. You've seen what they did to the yard. They dig holes everywhere and leave those bikes layin' around. I even ran over one the other day and Harper took the keys away from me.' Leona was almost as bad as her husband about running off on another subject."

"Then I asked for explanations from Leona. 'What does he want, always hangin' round the house? I like him enough, but he changes the television channels when Deux Ours is watchin' his ball games and I don't want any extra mouths over there.' I was tryin' to get back on the subject that was gnawin' at me.'

"But before I got far, Leona spouted off. 'Hah', she said, 'I don't think you have to worry 'bout that! He says your cookin' ain't good 'nough for a dog…Ah. Oh, I'm sorry, I didn't mean it! But he did say that. You don't have to run off like that.' She called out after me as I left, slammin' the trailer house door.'"

"I became nervous and depressed. I was again separated from my cousin and felt saddened by the arguments between us. These had become incessant, although I didn't give Harper's meddlin' much more thought than that. But that is all it amounted to. Meddlin'. He was tryin' to gain some sort of power over us by makin' us fight against each other. Only, in spite of my father's character, I didn't conceive before I lived in a prison that there are people who stir up shit wherever they go. And sometimes they do it for a reason."

"I stopped attendin' to our church's services and insisted that Deux Ours come with me to a Catholic church. From his point of view, the fence was to blame. He had spent his entire childhood surrounded by horses and now, he felt they should be left to roam. The First Evangelist Church was still in need of Sunday school teachers and he felt he fit the bill better than anyone else. To this day, I don't know how Harper convinced him to come back to his church and to teach the children. Makin' his way through a yard littered with horse manure in his best shoes was not the life he had hoped for when he married me and moved to this part of Louisiana. A month after I had returned home from my squeeter-filled nights in the treehouse camp, and my argument with my cousin, he crossed the Lake Road and made for the church with the determination not to allow me to interfere with his faith. If I wanted to go to St. Joseph's, that was fine with him, but he would continue to take Emmy to the First Evangelist Church with the rest of the family."

"From a particular viewpoint, as the wife of a minister, my cousin was now leadin' the more glamorous life of us two. I found myself more often than I wished, feedin' a horse or cleanin' a stall, while Leona spent her time on sewin' and decoration. What's weird is that before, before Harper that is, that wouldn't have bothered me. I had tried sewin' and all, but I was more of a huntin' and fishin' kind of gal. Suddenly, I was like, like jealous of these feminine activities, and my husband was mad about havin' muddy shoes!"

Distance

One day, when Harper and Leona drove up to the Robichaux home to drop off Emmy, Skizzum and I, Mérite-Lajoie was scooping up some mud and carrying it over to where the horses were grazing. At that time, she had oily black hair and most of the year, two large wet circles under her arms. She had become accustomed to wearing an old hat, something between a Texas Stetson and a Cajun *capuchon*. It was an ugly thing with a deep frown. Her tightened brow relaxed after the eventful day birthing two foals until she saw the truck drive up in front of her house. Her horse, Violette, had a brush wound, and she already had neglected to take care of it. It was too late to go into the forest in search of a remedy to cauterize and disinfect the injury.

Mérite-Lajoie pretended she didn't see us as we drove up, her face taking on the absent expressionless attitude it harbored more and more often. Impassive to our presence, she looked around in her reserve, hoping to give Harper the opportunity to leave. We saw her take something out of a wooden crate and pour a liquid over it that Emmy told me later was muscadine wine vinegar. This vinegar is made from *Vitas rotundifolia,* not the bitter *Vitas cinerea* or possum grapes, good only for jelly, although people often confuse the two. Then she rubbed in some salt. The mare shuddered and stamped her foot. When she was quiet again, Mérite-Lajoie tied the rag around her leg and put some mud on it to hold it in place. This cataplasm would at least reduce the swelling. Harper peered over the steering wheel, honked the horn, and drove off without making any contact

181

with his wife's cousin. Mérite-Lajoie laid her hands on Violette's back and probably repeated what I had often heard her say, "don't make her misère, cure dis here mare." Her caresses were long and tender, but her prayers were always short and to the point.

The object of most of these was always the same, she confided. With these, she chewed over again and again the rind of self-disgust, hardened after her meeting with Harper, but never fully digested. Louisiana's cuisine was a delight to feast upon, but here is one fare she preferred heretofore, to avoid. She had sat with it too long already. Another mouthful of this distasteful meal and she would have to be purged like a crawfish or a *bigarno* (a snail).

Harper and Leona let us out of the truck. Waving, they left with one of their sons. The dog jumped out and followed the vehicle, running behind, sniffing the grass, and marking its territory on the way. Heavy sighs escaped Mérite-Lajoie as she watched the animal move away. She continued brushing the mare and gave it some fresh water. Sometimes her burden was so great that she gasped, as if she were on the verge of drowning, then she wore the afflicted face of resentment.

At other moments, when she went to see her mother at her trailer, she would sit on her porch and watch Harper with his wife and think how unhappy her cousin must be. She confided in me now her doubts about the legitimacy of their marriage, under a borrowed name. "Was the woman livin' in sin? Was there a legal lien on the rest of the family?" It wasn't only Harper's insinuations, his harassments, or his dirty jokes Mérite-Lajoie found annoying. When he wasn't behind the pulpit, Harper gave the impression he was something of a ladies' man, receiving perfumed letters from women even in other parishes. Her cousin served as church secretary, and she classed these unread letters, reassuring herself of her husband's fidelity, in spite of his expenditures.

Leona sometimes complained about it. Mérite-Lajoie encouraged her husband to go over, visit with him, and try to make things right. "Why don't you give him a talk? Leona can't go on like this. Every year she has another baby, but he's gettin' worse and worse. He hangs out all evening on the porch with the other men, talkin' constantly bout girls and the skirts they now wear in town. He makes a lot of wise cracks. He smacks that girl, Suzy on the rump and even pulls her into his lap sometimes. It's hard enough on my ears, but for my cousin; what's she s'pposed to do? He doesn't stop, not even in front of the boys." Her husband looked at her with profound dejection. Before turning away, he shook his head. He couldn't see any solution to the problem.

Nevertheless, some of the other men did not despise Harper's jokes. They laughed at his puns about Old Glory, when he referred to his large family, but was meaning his virile member. They seemed to admire the fact that women were always attentive when he came around. This attention from both women and men continued to puzzle Mérite-Lajoie. Then there were the children to take care of, and somehow Harper always seemed to have money. He had kept up the bootlegging, which was soon moved off the lot, and other fringe activities.

At present, he forced upon his family new traditions, celebrating Mardi Gras with something other than a Chicken Gumbo and a King cake. *Quémander* (to beg) for food, for ingredients! Even during a festival, Harper would not hear of it! He was certain to know of other ways to promote bonding between members of the community. He knew how to inflame and to capture their allegiance. There was some discussion as to why the Dufresne-Robichaux's still celebrated at all. Harper said it was because they were still Catholics, but only on Mardi Gras, and, they did not truly honor their faith, nor did they accept the new one.

The gossip would turn into a lecture. Harper would profess about subjects such as loyalty to the King of France and extend on to explanations about illegitimate children with miniscule effigies in the cake! These suspicions outraged Mérite-Lajoie. Not so much because it was suggested that she had stopped believing in God, or even because it meant that she was associated with a band of bootleggers, religious *cooyons* (fools or idiots), and hypocrites. She was *en colère* (angry) because she felt certain her personal downfall and that of her husband's was caused by a lack of honor to their traditions. Exiled, Up-the-Bayou, their daughter hardly spoke their native language. She felt most of their headaches had come from there.

She also lived in fear of punishment, although not especially for her sins. She felt there could be no virtue found in having harbored a criminal all these years and especially by having convinced herself that this man was *un Homme de Dieu* (a Man of God). Of lately, she had to sort out her own mixed-up feelings about her relationship to her husband and daughter, and even to God. Diverting her confusion in the direction of Harper's perverted penchants seemed to relieve her conscious, then as now.

"'I suspect the man ain't got no morals', I said one day to my brother, Thibodaux. 'His wife don't know anything about him.' My brother added, 'Sure, he's so slick he could steal the sweet from sugar without touchin' a grain. He sure can play that harp though, as well as anything he gets his hands on.'"

Leona Harper (perhaps, Swaily), ignored most of her husband's past life as an Assembly of the First Church Evangelist preacher. He had also been one of Arabi's Le Beau's Casino's flamers. Harper pretended he had forgotten his name and his birthplace. He was younger than Mérite-Lajoie and had an American accent, meaning in America, he could have people from anywhere except that he had no Cajuns in his recent ancestry. But even that accent wasn't consistent. It was hard to tell just where he was from; except northerners would be quick to point out he was from the South.

Some said he was a black-sheep cousin to an already much appreciated musician from the area. Others noticed a resemblance with another Evangelist, practically famous himself. Another report had all four hanging out in the alley listening to blues behind Big George's and next to the Haney's Big House on Saturday nights. Harper repeatedly claimed he had always refused to play in a rhythm and blues group so he could spread the Word.

"Leona imagined the talk by the old folks was unjustified. He did know how to play that harp, as well as the melodeon, or any other instrument. She told me one day while I was there that his parents couldn't have named him anything else. Melody wouldn't work for a man, not even in Louisiana, neither would Harpy. 'Although' she said, and she chewed on it for several seconds, 'his principal mission of life does seem to be like harpin' or persecutin' others, blamin' them for things he done to hisself.'" For a more likely musical term, his name could have been *Agitato,* for the agitated agitator he was, I might have added.

"But Leona didn't know her husband's real given name was forged in a forgotten parent's remembrance of a strong and proud Irish county. Thibodaux found out about it and told the sheriff after the shooting. It was Tyrone, or, cut off from the very thing that made it Irish, it became a simple Ty, linked to something unavowable. Yet Ty, a family name, had never been penned down to its slithering past, yet had slipped right into a pseudonym."

"Leona ignored Ty Swaily had come to live at *Grand Isle* after a scandal in New Orleans where he spent a lot of money. No one spoke to her of accusations of lewd acts with a minor. She did not even know the gunshot wound Up-the-Bayou was a consequence of an attempted reform by the girl's father, who having learned of his daughter's pregnancy, pinned the guilt on the culprit who picked her up off the street. We found out about all this with very little research. Hell, most of it was in the newspapers! Had Leona known, would possessing this knowledge have made any difference? How many women think they can change a man? How many people negate what amounts to clear evidence? How many just don't ask questions? What went on in the mind of this woman, who married to get away from the home formed by two people and four walls she called a prison? I'd never given it a thought and I invited him to our home." Mérite-Lajoie's eyes glittered with tears. She turned her head away so I couldn't see her face.

Had Leona fantasized about a licensed-to-love truck-driver escorting her down the aisle and taking her off to blue skies in a faraway land before allowing a minted-in-Hell-Bible-driver to claim her as his sole property and sink her into a muddy trailer park in the next state? These small elements in early life make all the difference later.

"Let me tell you folks somethin'," squealed Harper one day, his shoulder jerking and his left eye batting, his voice a pitch higher than usual. "I want to disperse all doubts about the subject. Why do you think they let me out on parole so fast? I wasn't at Angola for embezzlement after all. I had been unjustly accused of corruptin' a juvenile. The thing is, I picked up that little heifer hitchin' a ride on Highway 61. She had run away from her home. How was I supposed to know her folks were regular? She told me they were mean as Hell and beat her like pancake batter. I let her sleep in my camper for one night and she was mighty grateful. I can tell you she wadn't nobody's virgin. Somebody else knocked her up and I shouldn't have to pay for that. She accused me only to get off the hook herself. Otherwise, she wouldn't have said nothin' 'bout it." An outsider could easily tell he was getting ready to lay bare a forgery when he started to twitch and grumble, but his parishioners kept in step and tried not to notice his contractions. You would have to give them at least this much credit: they were excellent dancers.

Harper's twist of the yarn was legally considered to be worthy of interest and a circumstantial reason for reconsidering the accusation of statutory rape. Insufficient proof was the reason for his early release. Whatever was the reason of the law, whatever was the reason of the moral, many of his church members then added, subdued by their difficulty to accept their own contradictions, "Even if he was a defrocked pastor from somewhere else in another life, another congregation, even if tempted by the demon he lost his way; God forgave him, and so should we." This collective clemency was all Leona heard about the episode that led up to the gunshot wound. Harper never complained of the scar the bullet hole left him, he never conveyed his pain of breathing when the weather was cold, and he never expressed anything about the trauma he had experienced in the forest near the lake. Had he spoken of it, would she have understood? Would these truths ease all doubts about his memory loss? Would she have put her husband's impairments before the condition of a young girl? Harper was a respected man in the community, in the town of Ferriday and even in the whole state of Louisiana.

He claimed not to know what kind of folks he had because he hadn't seen them long enough to judge. In fact, he was no different than a package thrown off a truck. It might have something good in it, but it might as well entertain a rattlesnake. You could never be sure.

Mérite-Lajoie was one to have more doubts than certitudes. She could not believe in forgiveness anymore either, not even for herself. She had brought Harper home, and this fact had officially driven her away from going to any church at all. In her words, she didn't trust the fellow, and wouldn't have the likes of him preaching her the good word. She argued that the conflicting ideas of the two religions (which went way beyond the language differences) had led her to feel disorganized and confused about theological matters. The nightmares she had after her first meeting with Harper followed her around in one version or another, then as now. "I sometimes wonder if Harper and the dream possum are one of the same? Maybe what he called his men of good faith are the lost souls I ran into? Maybe the animal I killed wasn't of an earthly kind either?" Mérite-Lajoie was not ready to become an animist, but so many nights had been perturbed by the malignant spirit, so much of her work stalled, she would often catch herself on a slippery road to belief. Still, she had more questions than answers, more theories than proof. And for a long time, these kept her from bogging down in a mire. With time, Mérite-Lajoie came back to the trailer park to attend the church's meetings, silently and only to satisfy Deux Ours and help keep an eye on her family. And with time, and with the Louisiana's often-extreme weather conditions, the flag began to fade, but still blew clouds over Mérite-Lajoie's head.

"I grumbled about chores now before gettin' in our car with Emmy and Deux Ours and drivin' cross the road to the First Evangelist Church. We could've walked. I said Deux Ours had become an old goat and wanted to turn me into one. My cousin was waitin' there for us, along with Harper and a young woman named Suzy. Then one Sunday, Harper kissed me on the mouth in front of them all and Deux Ours had his second heart attack. He died five days later without comin' home from the hospital. I think that somehow his profound beliefs about everything had a head-on collision right in his heart and made it explode."

Attempts at reconciliation

Sometimes I feel like Mérite-Lajoie is telling me all this so I won't blame myself any longer for what happened. Instead, I was beginning to see how much I was mixed up in the whole scheme. How many times had I witnessed Harper's harassment of Mérite-Lajoie's family? How many times had I seen him stir up a fight or get drunk on other people's emotions?

"After Deux Ours' passing, I found myself more bewildered than ever. As I was mournin', I never thought of accusin' Harper for that kiss. He made it seem so innocent after the fact. I felt guilty in a confused way and my guilt drove me to seek consolation among my family members at The First Evangelist Church. It was of course, Harper's church too. Thinkin' about it now, I have a hard time explainin' it to myself."

"One day, Harper made some pamphlets about the church and its so-called sanctified place in the community. He decided we would all go in front of the Piggly Wiggly, the Arcade Theater, the U.S. Post Office, and all of the other local establishments to recruit new members for his church. He had Leona, their friend, Suzy, and myself set up a table in front of the movie theater, as that is where most people who have their afternoons to loiter about would be on a Saturday after lunch and later. He thought the kids would be there too and he wanted them to tell all about his new Sunday school. We had all seen how the Jehovahies did it even then, but he decided the women in the congregation wouldn't go door to door like them. He just wanted us to hold a table with some information for the interested parties and to convince them, like Harper had taught them to do."

"'Remember to flatter them and say, *Jesus saves*, and tell them if they *aren't saved, the Devil will be waitin' for them round the corner.*' He wanted to invite the children to his first retreat the next weekend, hopin' the parents would come to the site, which was just a bit further down the road from the church, there, where there were never any trailers, but we had planned to put some. He promised weenie roasts and marshmallows. He promised they could camp and wouldn't have to bring anything. He planned for Baptisms to take place in the lake for those he said *were ready to leave their sinful ways behind*. Of course, all this would cost the community a lot of money, but he only thought of that later."

"I found myself servin' Harper, pouring one cup of *toyasse* (weak coffee) after another from the thermos for him. His words and manners now had a grip on me, as well as on his wife. That day, Leona twisted a mesh of her hair and put it in her mouth nervously, like she always did when she was with him in public. Harper had learned to speak our dialect, makin' us giggle like schoolgirls; but, when his eyes turned on Leona, she became like the bronze statue in front of the Courthouse. We both saw him put his hand up Suzy's dress and heard her twitter. She pushed him away while Leona pretended not to notice. Harper sat there grinnin'.'"

"I can just see Leona wipin' the twins' noses. They ran around the parked cars while Emmy tried to get them to sit down on the Post Office steps." Emmy was fascinated by Harper, but couldn't have listened to him much while keepin' track of the twins. She enjoyed bein' with her youngest cousins. I should've known it wouldn't last," sighed Mérite-Lajoie. "The two older boys were diggin' in the dirt under the bushes and didn't seem to cause much trouble."

"'Well, I do declare! How ya doin' today, Miss Emmy?' He got excited when he saw Emmy that day. 'You sure are getting' to be a right purdy little thang?' He stepped in front of her as she tried to catch the one of the boys. He bent over and touched her cheek with his scaly finger. 'You'll be comin' to the Retreat I suppose? It is 'bout time you got baptized.' I feel sick about the whole thing when I recall it. This was happenin' right in front of my eyes. It just got worse and worse, but after Deux Ours died, it's like I didn't understand anything anymore."

"Emmy's face was crimson. She wasn't used to being addressed to by another adult outside her home or school. She looked at me who prompted her for a response, 'Go ahead and answer. We talked about it. Your Dad said it was up to you to decide.' Emmy looked down at the ground, probably rememberin' us arguin' about it. Suddenly she turned her eyes back towards Harper. She knew I hadn't been enthusiastic about this second baptism, but perhaps she confused my feelings with those of her father. Had she examined the question from all sides? First of all, I hadn't wanted any baptism in the First Evangelist Church. Second, I questioned what it would mean for her godparents. Would this link my brother and sister-in-law to this faith as well? Would Emmy have to have new godparents? Third, and this part Emmy didn't perceive; I was afraid that Deux Ours' family would disown us. I was worried about other things I couldn't explain, and Emmy couldn't begin to understand. Not realizin' she was actin' on some silly, childish wish that she could move closer to her cousins, and a desire to benefit from a more privileged place in the First Evangelist Church community, she blurted out, 'Yes, I'll be there.' Perhaps bein' given the choice is what tilted the balance in favor of somethin' for which she did not choose at all."

"The followin' Sunday, Emmy had her official baptism in the Lake with the others. As a Catholic, she had already been baptized, but Harper insisted that baptism was like the other sacraments and only for those who could fully possess it. What she had experienced as a baby was only a Christenin', accordin' to him, and God wouldn't fully take it into account since she was older and she needed to make things right with him. But, you know, I think if we had been all this time regular in our own church, none of this would have happened. It's like one belief holds off the other. You just have to figure out which one works the best for you and stick with it. In a way, for safety if for nothin' else. Funny that I'm thinkin' about safety now. Safety from what? Other ideas? Livin' without beliefs? People like Harper? I jest cain't figure 'em out."

Recruitment

Skizzum and I came out of the Arcade Theater that day to find them with their table. "Well butter my butt!" Suzy yelped, dragging out the *U* with her authentic southern drawl, before she quickly put her hand over her mouth, as she saw us come out of the door. "Look who's comin'. Ain't them Gautier's girls?" Emmy was there with her mother and her mother's cousin. She looked up. She waved us over and offered us some cookies. We looked at the signs taped on the edge of the table where in capital bold-print letters was written: "THE TIME IS COMING. YOU FACE DEATH IF YOU DO NOT PUT YURSELF IN THE HANDS OF THE LORD." I looked at Emmy squarely, always joking around: "Do you think he could hold all of us, even my little brother, T-Beaux? He is pretty wiggly. Besides, there's a mistake in *yourself*. There is s'pposed to be an *O*." Emmy's eyes widened.

Harper was now standing behind us and listening. He stepped in, looking sternly, and spoke to me. "Young lady, you know the Lord can hold the whole world in his hands, like the song. I'm sure you've heard it. The panel here is copied from the *Holy Scriptures*. Make no mistake about that. You will burn in Hell if you don't change your evil ways and let some love into your heart." He corrected the sign, drawing a squashed O in front of the U. Then he passed the plate of cookies over to us.

I made a face. I suppose I pouted. I wanted to leave more than I wanted another cookie. I looked up at Harper. What I saw gazing

195

down at me was that snake-faced venom-spitting monster I had seen from time to time coiling around the girls in the choir at their church, hissing, and threatening. Now my sister was in his sites, but the lack of physical assault caused me to ignore, or almost ignore him. When he spoke to me now, I was concentrated on that tiny twisting member sticking in and out of his mouth, darting about, to see if it was forked, and thus proving one of the axioms of my theory: yes he was a snake. No, he wasn't the Devil. Without a doubt the method I had studied in my books and applied as I experimented in real life, allowed me a greater freedom of thought than a familiar ideology. Rather than succumbing to Harper's hypnotism, like Mowgli in *The Jungle Book*, under the spell of Kaa, I looked for insufficiencies: "How could a man with hair done up like Elvis', with a booger caught in his nose, be any more intelligent than Freddy Thompson who has the same haircut, is always farting and saying stupid things in Mr. Parnham's science class?" But these details made no difference to Emmy, or to my sister. Thinking about it now, both girls seemed to have a look-of–love, but I didn't know anything about being in love at the time. I had no measure of understanding about those kinds of feelings and nothing with which I could assess the starstruck-tiny-pupil-stare of these two girls who were more like myself than anyone else I had come to know. They both became unblinkingly, just as enthralled as the rest of them.

Thinking perhaps her interest made her look more grown up, Skizzum picked up a copy of the pamphlet Leona had typed out for her husband. She planned to read it later. "Young lady, would you like to help us hand those out?" Skizzum took the bait, hook, line, and sinker. What better way to bring someone over to your game than to ask him or her to play? For Skizzum, distributing the copies was not a commitment to a cause. She wasn't letting someone write into her budding adolescent compassion-for-everyone ideology. But for Harper, for the poker player, as for the house-to-house bandit, it was a foot in the front door. All he had to do now was to keep it jammed open and she would get lost in the daedal seven-card stud and soon be playing at his game, with his rules.

I looked hard at Emmy and went over to the Post Office steps and threw a pebble that ricocheted down each one. "Come on, let's play school." Skizzum shook her head. "I have other fish to fry. You gonna jest sit there and make a *bahbin* (pout)? You're gonna be lonely playing all by yourself. Who'll be your teacher? And when it's your turn to teach, who's gonna be your pupil? Emmy's here. She's helpin'. Why can't you? It's for your own good. We might even get invited to the retreat." I put my hands over my ears. No amount of coercion seemed to have an effect. I sulked, "I wanna go to the baseball game like you promised. It's no fun passin' out papers in the street witcha and talkin' about all that goodness we's s'pposed to be doin'. I go to catechism 'nough as it is." Finally, I cried out, "Why don't you both just go and find that idiot, Freddy Thompson? I'm sure he wouldn't mind."

I took the wrong route if I wanted to influence Skizzum or Emmy.

Unable to convince me, instead, Skizzum told me later, guilt turned and began to creep on its white belly to the center of her mind for leaving me alone when she had said she would spend the day with me. Anger and jealousy were already raging in my throat making me feel at fault. Papou had warned us that a predator senses fleeting feelings of fear in a potential prey. I wondered if a preacher could smell guilt. Fire flickered in Harper's eyes, now velvet with cupidity. "Let her decide for herself, she'll probably get interested later on." He put his hand gently on Skizzum's shoulder and smiled with tobacco-stained teeth. "She'll be alright. We're right here and she can come over anytime she wants to and have a cookie and lemonade." He frowned sternly again at me. Most of his tactics worked. Why they didn't with me, I still can't fully explain. However, I sometimes wish they had. I might have been able to help Emmy or at least Skizzum. Or maybe they had worked, but in an adverse way for the Evangelists.

Skizzum began passing out her copies as people came out of the movie theater. I knew her as well as I could have known anyone and as I think about it today, I can almost imagine her sentiments at the time by recalling the scene. The activity not only calmed the yellow taste of blame accumulating in her stomach and encroaching on her tongue, while I sat alone. It also chased a deeper creeping feeling; one she felt coiling around her heart simultaneously as with her feet. When they had all filed down the street, she started dragging slightly one foot behind her, putting the flyers on the windshields of the cars like the political propaganda she had picked up from under Papou's wipers once, before he snatched it away. Had she taken a hint from her foot instead of biding by Harper's encouragements, she might have dumped the whole kit and caboodle into the nearest trashcan and backpedaled within healthier limits. Perhaps she would have become another person, nicer, in a small-town sort of way, but also less worldly. Wisdom often comes with a price, sometimes a dearly paid ransom.

When she finished her pile, she came back to the table. Harper was so pleased he could not help but show it. "Now that is my kind of Angel." Skizzum was proud of herself. She looked around and no longer saw me. She began to worry. Harper caught her before she had given much thought to the subject. "Don't worry, she's sittin' in the back of the truck with my son and the dog. We'll be drivin' you girls home as soon as we get our stuff picked up."

Harper's older son and I snickered. We teased the dog with the cookies. He had been bothering us all afternoon, sniffing the snacks and taking an exceeding interest there where it was the most troublesome in a mixed company. When the truck started up, we let Skizzum in on our plans, who, barely in the truck, was obliged to push the hound away from her crotch for the second time. Instead of biting my tongue, I made a horrendous proposition; appalling not so much for what it meant to me, which was little more than a child's ventilating boast, but for what it later initiated, "why don't we tie all four paws together and attach its mouth? Then we'll put a cookie right under his nose and let it sniff that a while." I was angry, and still felt mean. Skizzum looked at us indignantly. "That's cruelty. I don't know why you wanna *tenir la dragée haute* (have the upper hand) over a dog. How would you like me to tie

199

your feet and hands up, put a rag in your mouth and a cookie under YOUR nose? Leave the dog alone or I'll tell."

"Look who is being holier than thou all the sudden", I exclaimed. Skizzum scowled and looked like she meant it. I dropped the dog-binding plan, which sounded worse now that I had announced it, but Harper's son was bored and suddenly wanted to punish the animal for gulping down his sandwich earlier that day. He especially wanted revenge for not being allowed to go *see North by Northwest* in the "best all-time double feature" with a rerun of *Rebel without a Cause*, for not being able to sneak in either, and for having his plans fouled by Miss Busy-Body.

Having been obliged to abandon my vengeful proposal, he thought of something worse. Now, he wanted to tie the animal's testicles together. "You know what?" He contemplated the relaxing hound. "I seen Uncle Robichaux castrate a cat with rubber bands once." I wrinkled my nose, scowled, and turned away, now looking out over railroad tracks as we drove past. "So, you chickenin' out? That's the way with girls. Don't you know he is gonna pollute up the whole neighborhood with his pups? Can't you just see the dogs that toothless bitch and Grits would make together? I can jest see 'em goin' at it." I laughed, imagining the dogs together. The boy snickered and threw a small rock at the hound. He figured he would end this dog's family projects as soon as he could. I was resentful at the dog for being Harper's pet and annoyed with Emmy and Skizzum for their change in loyalty. I never thought my callous announcement about tying up the dog would ever have any consequence whatsoever. Do we ever realize what we say when we say it? Skizzum interrupted, "Why don't you just shut up? Y'all done already upset that dog so much he might not ever wanna ride in the truck again." She scratched the dog behind the ear. "Poor Baby. *Pauve ti bête*" Grits leaned over towards her so she could reach the other side. Harper's son unconsciously kicked the cabin of the truck so hard the dog yelped and jumped away. Harper yelled: "Y'all settle down. I don't want the dog fallin' out on the road. He cost me a lot of money, that hound did. Yep, he's breedin' material." The rest of the trip the boy said nothing, but still didn't give him any cookies and made plans to take care of him alone if he had to.

Later, Grits became one the meanest hound dogs that Helena Addition ever saw and never sired a single puppy. Although he never roamed very far, Harper had to chain him up to prevent him from attacking even the neighbors' children. And when a stranger came along too close to the church, he began a deep yowling, at once cruel and sad. He would continue this inconsolable howl until someone from the trailer nearby threw a can at him and told him to shut up. No one ever understood how refusing a dog a cookie could turn him into such a ferocious beast. It seemed to me this incident could not have been the only explanation. Harper, being ignorant as to the root of his dog's deficiency, never put two and two together. The boy continued to develop some of his father's tendencies, and not the best ones. I'll never grow accustomed to Skizzum's voice whispering in my dreams, reminding me that our thoughts are often like flutters of a fragile yellow jacket's wings. It

These Beans Have Too Much Salt

is what we say that stings people; scorn dropping thoughtless hints on a whim in friendless flight, adding sour notes at what would be swallowed by the night. Funny how I remember the dog's name, but I have forgotten the boy's. My heart flips the pages of my mind. It was as if my ghostwriter, friendly with the animal, followed me around, erasing the movement of the letters as they curled into my ear, fanning their awful remembrance away from all sound. The way things turned out, the situation was bad enough without hatred walking away with another winning hit.

Sundays in August

Saying prayers on one's knees around a stone in a courtyard might look pretty innocent to people outside the community and even ridiculous to some. The older folks complained about their knees, but for Harper, it was serious business. As with the dark stories he often told of members of the congregation gone astray, walking around on your knees while singing religious songs and praying was a way of federating a group, and in general, steering it. It was a matter of sense; common sense, the kind of faculty that comes into action when thought dissolves and arguments are tossed out with the trash. Harper didn't bother to elaborate on this point, but it served him well. After a while, this ritual became a familiar part of their lives and they no longer had much thought above their knees or, of the dirt on the ground. The women would sweat, struggling with their shoes, their dresses, and their purses. They followed their men folk, sang *Hallelujahs* and expected their beliefs to transform the stone (the same salt lick) into life. They shelled out the precious bills they kept in the bottom of their bags and pockets as soon as the plate was passed. Dr. Harper, as the self-baptized minister soon called himself, who didn't bother with such uncomfortable praying positions, smiled down on the generous remorseful. He was happier than a two-headed cat in a fish shop.

Inside the church, talking in tongues captivated the minds of the penitent. Speaking unknown languages was a way of bedazzling unbelievers. Harper would hold all night services even sometimes for several days and during such bouts he would yell out Bible verses, or at least his translation of these. I attended a few of these services with Emmy.

"*ACT TWO versus One through Four,*" began Harper.

"Not Mercutio to Benvolio, full of new wine in a Shakespearian plot, but Paul in the *New Testament*," I said to myself as I tried to block out part of the service that already seemed silly to me. He continued in spite of my private intermissions.

"The Pentecost, Jesus's disciples were all gathered round when suddenly there came a sound from Heaven as that of a powerful hurricane blowin'. The wind filled the house where they were sittin'. And there appeared unto them cloven tongues like fire, and it sat upon each of them. They were all filled with the Holy Ghost and began to speak with other tongues, as God's messenger gave them utterance."

Harper would pray and sing out "the Lawd Almighty" and carry on until people, rocked by proverbial repetition, began to fall asleep in the pews. Then he would bring out a piano thumping, gospel playing band, and they would wake them up in rock and roll boogie Jerry Lee Lewis style on one side and rolling minstrel Liberace on the other. Before long, with the trance-like sleep-deprived state of the congregation, proof of the power of those biblical treacheries came forth.

These Beans Have Too Much Salt

One night, a heavyset man from Helena Addition got up and screamed, hammered on the pew in front of him and jittered out into the aisle. He said he felt his tongue thickening and his mouth filling up with words he couldn't understand. He broke out in a sweat and spun around before falling on the floor in a seizure, spitting out frothy sounds.

We all heard about one little girl who walked up to the altar and voiced such confusion it seemed as if she was bordering on sounds unknown to human life (at least not to the majority of the church members). The women had run about the room, gesticulating. They said they had seen moths fly from her mouth and screamed of demonic possession.

"The minister then laid hands on the little girl and prayed with renewed energy, calling for her to do as well. The congregation prayed and concentrated until the girl broke out into such gibberish Harper declared the *Most High* had touched her, and not at all the Devil. He said that you could even see a halo around her head. The same women, who a few years before were drinkin' rum and coke while organizin' beauty pageants for preteens and cake walks for carnivals, or even huntin' and fishin' in the swamp, began cryin' and huggin' one another and racin' around the room faster than before, like maniacs. Later, some claimed the child had spoken *Galilean*, but others said it was indeed the language of angels. By that time, I'd lost myself and become so much a part of it all; some sort of strange pride filled my spirit. Pride about Emmy that is."

These Beans Have Too Much Salt

I was sorry to learn that Emmy was the girl talking in tongues. My obsessive preoccupation with finding fault with the service prevented my curiosity from exercising its rights. I stopped attending the First Evangelist Church before Harper's fame became full-blown, and his demeanor, overbearing.

It wasn't until a third special service that Harper realized what kind of advantages he could obtain from these performances. News of the miracle of talking in tongues spread and seemed to assure the minister's following for many years. He probably thought he might finally surpass his cousins in his newfound trade. Harper especially eyed the pubescent girls sitting in the front pews and wanted to form a band of Angels who would help him to insure more than his congregation.

One journalist reported; the child who had come forth was aphasic after an accident and her language had indeed been affected. He deplored the exploitation of the innocent by a religious sect and bunch of fanatics led by a preacher who had already been in trouble with the law for soliciting and bootlegging. This last remark didn't dissuade any of the Evangelist's members who thought of him as their own. It took me a while to figure out; again, they were talking about Emmy. Now at every night service, women would fall out into the aisle, chattering, jabbering, and jerking their bodies into a fit. To a stranger, this ecstatic display of devotion seemed inappropriate in a church. Still, I couldn't imagine Mérite-Lajoie involved in all this. It wasn't much different than that displayed by girls at Welsh High School in Jefferson Davis Parish, upon the rumor of mandatory pregnancy tests. The crying and falling to the ground of the girls and one boy even found its way to national television. That was not the idea I had about her. These fits were appropriate to the one observed during the phase of Beatle Mania. During the local premiere of *A Hard Day's Night*, at the Arcade Theatre, enthralled groups of teenage girls would stand in their seats and faint in the aisles. The dismayed manager found this behavior to be quite unruly. No one with two cents of thought would behave as such. Nevertheless, if you think about it, the abandoned *Arcade* later seemed, without its rowdy teenagers, like a dead body emptied of its soul.

Louisiana would always be in the news. People from other regions seem to enjoy reading about the local color, but wasn't the church different? What happened to the orderly ritual of Louisiana's Catholics? Did its assembly catch some kind of contagious hiccup over the generations, sending its members out to quench their thirst among the constituents of an obscure society of Hell raising Bible drunkards?

In the eyes of the Evangelist congregation, The Lord God Almighty had saved Harper-Swaily from his bootlegging family of devil singing minstrels. The public revelation of his former (and perhaps still ongoing) activities did not harm his reputation in the least. Instead of being stabbed by some indistinct and deaf rumor, Harper found a new life. Some again were mystified and likened his arrival into the community of Cajuns on the northern side of Ferriday, as the Second Coming. Many members said, "that man can foresee the future."

"Harper would scream: 'Glory to God! Glory to Gawd! Gloray to Gawd! I am sick to death of the sinful lot of youngsters hangin' out at the Blue Hole all day, smokin' who all knows what, guzzlin' beer, honkin' horns, pinchin' whores…I am sick to death of the wayward women drivin' around the Sandwich Bar, solicitin' an honest man, deturnin' him from his spouse. I am sick to death of those teenage girls you see runnin' around town without bras. That's the Devil's flesh there under those clothes. I can tell you that. I am sick to death of the depraved son of a bitch who cheats on his sweet wife. I am sick to death of those solitary souls who don't bother to come to church. They're fixin' to become instruments of Hell!' He didn't mind using the rough language without foreplay, even in church."

"'Little chillen, it is the Last Time: and y'all have heeded the Antichrist will come, even now there are many of them. That is why we know it is the Last Time. *John, chapter two, verse eighteen.*'"

"Harper would stop to play music with the band and look out at his assembly. He thrust out his chest and strutted around the pulpit."

"'A large number of you people have fallen away from our Savior. Some of you women have been seen dressed up under the violent neon colors of the night. Some of you men have been seen in New Orleans' sex shops with women, lechin' after painted mouths!

Some have visited peep shows or even been watchin' pole dancin' strippers. Some have even fornicated with the whores of Babylon! What must be done so only Virtue and Chastity remain in you? Ours is not a congregation for the innocent! Listen up! Confess and Convert now...Repent! Re-pent! Re-pe-nt! Repent for your sins and find God's grace for your cor-rupt hearts. I ask those of you convicted of sin to now come forward to this altar and wrestle in prayer on it, in full view of the Lord God Al-mighty. You should all show your change of life and not just pretend to be one of God's children.'"

People, couples and entire families, would leave the pews and move forward on a wave of backslapping, desultory excitement. "Will you believe? Will you people believe? Will you pe-ople Be-lie-ve?"

They would not disappoint their minister and cried out in unison, "We will believe! We will be-lieve! We will be-lie-ve!"

"Harper would lay his hands on their heads or on the backs of their necks: 'Many deceivers have gone about. They are amongst us. They don't accept Jesus Christ has come in the flesh. They are liars and might be the Antichrist! Let go of your sins. Let them go! Peel back the thralldom that has enslaved you. Throw Satan out of your hearts. *Venez.* Listen to the Angels voices. Be saved by The Lord Almighty. Praise the Lord.'"

"Harper whined out the complaints with his twangin' voice we imagined like Jesus's. A few thought Cajun was the true language of Christ. Some thought the Messiah spoke in tongues or, what turned out to be an old Irish dialect. Most thought he spoke English. And when someone would speak out, Harper would not tolerate the interpretation of the Bible in any other way but his own."

For Harper, these verses became magical keys to open the doors of a theater where he could adorn many disguises. He was the magician. He was the fireman there to put out the flames of Hell. He was the hero sent to save them all (in case Jesus couldn't get through). And Harper would envelope himself in the ritual of service.

"'Our Lord is not interested in your excuses. He wants emancipation from sin. His Grace sent me here to guide you. Hallelujah! Praise the Lord," he screeched. "God's judgment is hoverin' above like a thundercloud waitin' to let tornadoes turn and hail fly. *Nimborumque facis tempestatumque potentem.* Make me the one rulin' over the Hurricanes. Praise the Lord! Be warned how you interpret his word. He gone away, but he come back. He's back among us. Jesus' gonna ask what you've done with your sinful lives. What'ave you done with the gifts that Our Father has bes-towed on to you? You'll burn with the flame eternal if you don't yield to our Lord.'"

The blackened sky, the clamoring thunder, the crackling flame, the sputtering fire, the blackened sky...the words stormed through and ignited the darkest places in Harper's mind and warmed his esprit. With his hair standing, his body curved, inclined, now straightening up, his shaking fist raised and his mouth foaming brine, he felt new vigor grow under his pulpit gown.

"One woman hunched down and began to cry, before raisin' her arms and summonin' the strength to get back up. Harper looked down on me, frownin' on me, and on the inexperienced girls on the front row, all affected, excited, emotional, quiverin', and weepin'."

Confessions

Skizzum was one of the girls on the front row. Our family was Catholic, but at our age, Mama said we had a right to experiment, to choose which church we would attend. Unsupervised experimentation was a tangled choice for Skizzum, one that was difficult to undo. Had the adults been able to admit they were submitting to the beliefs of someone so far out on a branch it would break, taking them with it, our mother might have been more cautious about letting us go over there.

It wasn't enough she would sing in the choir in the strange service concocted by Harper, Skizzum was so enthralled with his beliefs she wanted to emulate him.

The First Evangelist Church of Harper (for by now this is what I called it on a regular basis) was alive again with a young voice. Again, Emmy outpoured a monologue in one breath telling of the woman-snake-coupling-tattoo-on-her-back, tears streaming down her face. In her eyes glowed an unnatural admiration for the preacher, as much as for Christ. She gushed: 'Yes, I sinned.'"

"She bowed her head as if in prayer, 'I'm guilty of a crime,' she whimpered."

She probably felt her confession had a ring of truth—for it expressed terrible things she felt about herself. "She told of her petty lies, of the fact she appreciated the praise, of bein' tempted by the flesh. She even spoke of the money spent on popsicles that should have been used to help the poor. What else could an eleven-year-old confess?" Mérite-Lajoie's face withered.

"'Girl, you'll do…' yelled Harper, 'but you won't do right.' He shook his head coverin' his eyes with his hand like a tragic buffoon in agony of remorse. He bowed his head as if to pray before raisin' his arms outward and towards the ceilin'."

"'However, in tarnation, did you git to believe you could git to Heaven by just tryin' to git past the door of the church,' hollered Harper. He rolled his eyes and looked up towards the crucifix, then back at Emmy. 'I just can't do it alone. Please help me, Savior, I beg you. Ple..eze help me Sav..i..or. Help me to save these youngsters. Bring them to know they jest can't handle their lives alone anymore. Hallelujah! Praise the Lord.'" Mérite-Lajoie recited the service.

"'Brothers and sisters, is there anyone here who wants to be touched by our Savior tonight? Because if you do you must throw the Devil out, like our sister, the poor sinner, Emmy has done!' Harper yelled, shakin'."

"I don't know why I didn't see through all this nonsense." Mérite-Lajoie squeezed her eyes shut. "Emmy felt confused, maybe even shamed by his words that both hurt and comforted her."

"One man came forth sayin' he couldn't hear out of his right ear. 'Do you believe, brother? I hear you yearnin' for the power of the *Most High* to defend you from the evils of the Devil! Spirit of the sky and water, get out of this here body!' cried Harper, puttin' one hand over the man's right ear before drawin' it back theatrically. And suddenly, the man cried, 'Yes, broda, I can hear, I can hear! I can think with my ear!'"

According to Mérite-Lajoie, everyone in the congregation trembled, leaning to one side, then to another, again all in unison; not realizing with his *lapsus linguae* he had said something of the truth. This man's feat was not much more than that of an Andrew Jackson's African Grey, repeating what he had heard as if Harper's words were his own thoughts, and the congregation's gestures, not much different than Geppetto's marionette. With his success, Harper possibly felt the satisfaction of a creator. Nevertheless, it would have been wiser for the members of the church to view this accomplishment with modesty. The Tennessee bird, Poll, was known to repeat memorized phrases and to reiterate curse-words in two languages: Spanish and English. He even apologized for a third, and was recorded as saying: "Excuse my French!"

As for Pinocchio, the puppet did manage to free himself of his strings. This man, this assembly, whistled both bonds and mimicry like a tune they could not forget. Over and over, they repeated his words in their minds. Over and over, they repeated them to anyone who would listen. Who knows what would happen if one of these parrots, suddenly and without warning, became the sole living speaker of an extinct tribe of Louisiana Evangelists? Would these thespians then become representatives of a New World Order? Would religion be left to flocks of African Greys or Blue-Fronted Amazons?

"'Are you ready? Are you ready for Christ? He's comin' back. Are you ready? Are you read-y? Are you rea-d-y?' Harper tyrannically screamed at almost every service. 'Ask for God's forgiveness. Git yourself together and obey. Fall down on your knees and pray before it's too late! Hallelujah! Praise the Lord!'"

I had seen one service like this where he blurted, "See this little boy tremble. It's the will of God for his sins to be shaken out of his body. He is a condemned criminal. He is guilty for puttin' his hands in his pants, for the sin of masturbatin'. It's God's will he fall at the footstool of sovereign mercy. He should ask for the Lord's forgiveness and extinguish the Lust in his loins." Harper condemned the child with his harsh words and frowning face.

Mérite-Lajoie remembered. "The little boy's father tried to say his son had epilepsy, but Harper wouldn't allow interruptions. He calculated his words, swearin' and blarin' accusin' gratitude. Relyin' on the enthusiasm of his assembly, he pumped up his voice and gradually approached the most secret corners of our minds. Little by little, he nurtured the vine of fear until the poisoned belief took hold and embalmed each one's soul. He didn't mind frightenin' even the little children. He would indeed be our savior. He was also the cause of our cancer."

215

"Emmy fell to her knees before Harper, who placed his hand on her head. Her four-year-old cousin, Poochoo, did likewise. 'Oh God, can this Angel preach the Gospel? Can she pre-form your miracles?'"

"A woman, still youthful, rolled out in front with her wheelchair," continued Mérite-Lajoie.

"Emmy cried out in imitation of Harper, almost like a ventriloquist's puppet, 'Get out of that wheelchair!' The woman got up and hobbled with stiff legs and a hunched back into Emmy's open arms. Poochoo looked up, open-eyed at his cousin. Harper grinned. Of course, the woman couldn't walk that day much better than the one before, or the one after, but as with children who jump from chair to couch pretendin' they are flyin' round the room like Peter Pan, it was the belief that counted. And fervent believers we all became. I'm ashamed to say."

"Harper immediately added, that day, turnin' around to the innocent boy, 'Jest as shore as you're listenin' to me, jest as shore as you're listenin to an eleven-year-old's voice, jest as shore as you're watchin' *Superman* on TV, it's jest as shore you're gonna go to Hell if you ain't saved. And your savior ain't gonna be no hero flyin' around in his underwear with a red cape.'"

"Poochoo gasped then stared at Harper who quickly added forgiveness to his lectures, touching the children, first the little boy, then Emmy. 'Be ready! Be read-y!' he yelled, 'The Anti-Christ'll come and the Last days'll be terrible. Our Lord'll put an end to the sufferins of only the chosen ones. The others'll undergo mortification.' Harper was proud of his sermon; 'it is with this sort of show I can dominate this bunch of ignoramuses,' he bragged in a local bar. 'They know nothing of the men of good faith,' he said."

An earthy rumble of moaning began followed by a mixed musical with blood banging blues. After many hours, the walls of the church shook until man-girl-supplication formed a tragic cartoon amphigory where few set down the lines. Harper probably had not determined how to convince his audience of the foundation of his beliefs, but he had figured out how to gain their confidence, and their contributions.

"The service ended with these words, taken from the Lord's Prayer or the Benediction, but in that little known Irish language, which probably did much to explain why Emmy's jumbled trill couldn't in the least be understood by reporters, '*Diyil the sridag, taajirath an manyath gradum a gradum. Inoc,*' Mérite-Lajoie repeated, still remembering the service."

Clearly only a few people could recognize this expression in Louisiana. For these, it was as if Harper was speaking directly to them. But to the other members of the congregation, it was the jargon of a new thaumaturgy opening Up-the-Bayou each Sunday. They all waited open-eyed for signs there were changes in higher realms and none of them would miss that for all the money in the world. It was the misunderstanding, the lack of comprehension, the misinterpretation, and the ignorance that made the miracle and the mirage.

"How much would we have to *let go*?" asked Mérite-Lajoie. "When would the fog lift, when would we see through the murk? What darkness did we have to reach through to reach the truth? Had it been delivered to us, we would've only remained blind. Had Harper understood this mystery of the mind, he wouldn't have been so obsessed with makin' us afraid and cloudin' our judgments. For people to come to church, hell, all he had to do was talk mumbo jumbo and make us like him. He didn't have to be so mean."

Basically, fundamentally, and finally, what seemed to be gibberish from Babel tinged with religiosity was an onslaught of their Cajun identity, as well as that of the locals. It was even an assault on the character of the Irish Travellers from whom he had borrowed the most of it. Maybe Harper was unable to explain the method, but he was expert in achieving the purpose. The members of the First Evangelist Church would say later (had they known the name) their pastor was a Théophile de Rutebeuf, who had no more love of God than Satan himself.

"Harper would just as soon cite the Bible to you as cut your throat, although not many saw that side of him. Sometimes he would get this funny look on his face. It was a wild expression, like an animal that might go for your heart in a second and be contented with it, but at the same time, it cringed as if though you might suddenly strike it. I thought of him as a predator long before the fire, but I hadn't figured out he was preying on kids. He had stopped comin' over to the house for a while after Deux Ours died. That didn't stop the rumors. But he waited for me to come back. Oh, he knew I would. How? I don't know. You would have thought with all the accusations of affairs, I'd have stayed far away, but it was just the contrary. The more I heard them, the more I felt the need to set things right."

"Maybe Harper had a pact with the Devil. He made sure each one of the members of the congregation let go of everything that mattered with the promise of reward for the Chosen. After hearin' Emmy talkin' in tongues, so to speak, a few people even sent him their dearly departed, actually believin' that in doin' so their loved ones would be resurrected, as the Gospel promised through Harper. The arrival of the bodies did not embarrass him in the least. He said, 'God has a plan for these fine souls I have been entrusted with'. With no more formality than that, he called up Tulane Medical School in New Orleans and shipped the bodies off for science, as he said he was authorized to do, in exchange for a small donation to the church. 'Me knowin' the Bible serves the church well,' I heard him say one day, with defiance, talkin' about his ability to raise money in ways that were hardly suitable. Everyone else in Ferriday had an idea about that and was eager to share it with newcomers."

"Mamere too, had an explanation of what happened with Emmy's talkin' in tongues that day in another way, closer to a Cajun's way of seein' things: 'You can't git used to things anymore when you git too many words behind you.'"

"And she had indeed reason to believe her granddaughter would never quite get past those words, or past the community's gossip. There was something more than a passin' of time going on in the metamorphosis of Emmy. I didn't understand it. Why? I was refusin' to see too deeply in his soul. Maybe I thought he was still interested in women my age, if that was what it ever was?"

By the Lake

That day I crossed the Lake Road to try to catch Emmy before she went into the church building. It was too late. The trailer park families were already around her before I arrived. All through the ceremony I stayed hidden either behind a car or next to the church wall. Their voices mixed with the spicy wind and the ruffling water, reminding them of what they didn't know and really never would about the mysterious forces of their past. With the hot breeze, the red hands of the Harper-Robichaux-Dufrene family that floated over the park, folded and unfolded in prayer. For what seemed to be an eternity, Emmy and her clan walked around a stone that appeared to be a mere salt lick and said seven *Pater nosters* and seven *Hail Mary's* and a creed, then kneeled down at the stone alter and said fifteen *Pater nosters* and fifteen *Hail Mary's* and a creed. They continued to walk on their knees up to the door of the church, repeating most of the prayers in Cajun, and sometimes even in Cant (also known as *Shelta*).

There were others in Ferriday who spoke other languages besides English, Cajun or Cant. A few were like Deux Ours and spoke Cajun with bits of one of the Muskogean languages. The great majority of these other language speakers were the decedents of the enslaved Haitian people, forced to come to Louisiana. In the neighborhood across the woods, down the other path, off Lake Road, the many inhabitants spoke Creole, a French dialect close to Cajun. This language was close enough for us to understand. It was also enough for Skizzum to become friends with a boy who fished in the lake and tied his boat up on a landing near the trailer park's pier. One day she heard him say a swear word and call out to someone on the nearby bank. The word wasn't sour to her ears; it wasn't addressed to her. Yet its tang was enough to thrill the heart of a lonely girl with too much time on her hands. There he was, shirtless and drying the sweat off his brown body with a towel, right next to the pier from which she was swimming. Confusing jealousy with love, she laughed and threw her head back shaking her long dark hair and gloated, "If Harper sees me talkin' to this boy, he will have a conniption fit. I'll show him." She said this to herself, but all the while knew she wouldn't show the preacher anything.

Although their languages were both originally French, although segregation was the rule, hearing the weaving of French-Cajun-Creole-English-Other spiel was comforting to generations of displaced peoples who lived in the area. After exchanging not much more than a few sentences, the teens decided then they would meet secretly Sunday afternoons, on the steps of another church, next to the Quarters, and continue their conversations there. Later, he showed her how to play the guitar. He sang softly and spoke of dreams for the future. Her feelings for him deepened. Skizzum had not expected as much. Wanting to get back at Harper, she found herself in love. It wasn't safe for the boy to be caught talking to her near the trailer park. There might be some of the white-hooded blackened souls in the vicinity. Perhaps her consciousness of the dangers for them both was part of the thrill, but now she was genuinely concerned about what trouble she might have caused. The Cajuns were more or less White (at least they looked White), and this was the sixties. That was our only privilege, but it was a lot. Without going back to the main road, or directly through the woods separating the communities, there was no passage from one neighborhood to the next. As long as the families didn't mix in this part of the state, the suspicions about them didn't get much further than the skin.

Not only did the Whites not mix with the Blacks, there were the Gypsies, who operated the fair that came to town from time to time and camped with their campers on the other side of the Lake. These people were often darker than the African-Americans, but their origins were thought to be elsewhere and they spoke yet another language. There were also a few Amerindians from the Chitimacha tribe, and lighter African-Americans claiming to be kin to them. In the following years, Ferriday became the violent seat of racial crime and all these people, considered as free people of color, would find themselves threatened.

Part of the population was sure they belonged there, and the other questioned these foundations. Our spiteful designs on Emmy, and perhaps the source of strife for many Americans, plunged its roots in the soil of these hesitations. Many were looking around for certitudes, which only made matters worse. Emmy told us her grandmother said that our father was at least part Irish Traveller because he spoke Cant, like Harper, who may have encountered these people as a child. I now believe Harper was responsible for those ideas as well. I had doubts about these efforts of Emmy's to bring us closer, and within Harper's reach.

These Beans Have Too Much Salt

I had always imagined our father differently, and thought perhaps
he spoke an Amerindian language, but didn't know which one.
Papou forbade us to talk about him at home, saying that he was only
a fog weaver and a fiddler. On most occasions, we didn't much want
to speak about him either, but we wouldn't tolerate anyone else
saying what we thought were dirty lies and what might be a
reflection on us. We embellished his image, and in this light, he
seemed better to us, and so did our Cajun foundations. I always
figured my father was a man of the world with a lot of experience,
at least with enough knowledge to take him somewhere beside this
hick-town-hollow, I figured to be one of Louisiana's muskrat-
holes, and the reason he had left. I told Emmy I would go find him
in a few years in California, where he was working in the film
industry. (I told this to Emmy, but I knew it wasn't true. I had no
idea where my father was at that time, or if he was alive.) Even
without a father, I still had a Cajun accent and name. You can't
undo where you come from, and that day, I was bent on making this
truth clear to my friend.

Whatever we were missing in ancestry, whatever we were lacking
in sisterly solidarity, Emmy thought she could make up with
knowledge we didn't possess. She informed me one day that some
of the verses of *The Patterns* were useful even to get rid of snakes.
She said Saint Patrick had used them in Mississippi and Mamere
wore rattlesnake rattles around her wrists. I had concluded that their
traiteurs and other faith healers didn't have much authority Up-the-
Bayou especially since I had been bitten by a water moccasin near

their church. Emmy argued I had been bitten because my family didn't honor the traditions. Although you never knew what was behind a snakebite, I wasn't sure as I watched my friend from behind the cars. I believed in many of the things Emmy told me. What traditions was she talking about? Cajun? The Robichaux's beliefs, Harper's gallimaufry, Mamere's?

I liked to listen to these stories all the same. I enjoyed the Robichaux family even if Emmy's Grandmother was a Redbone or a Gypsy. I figured if Mérite-Lajoie could cure everyone's horses and even impetigo on the children's legs with her hands or her cataplasms, this was enough savvy for me. And yet, I would surprise myself from time to time, spouting off one of Mamere's old stories: about snakes, about ghosts, about Banshees and magical omens and how to avoid jinx, voodoo, anything to avoid talking about myself or my family, who, in fact, had their own set of superstitions I never questioned. I figured, almost talking out loud, as I watched the ceremony from afar, making a list of what I needed to do, until Skizzum showed up. I whispered to her: "God must have been young once and wouldn't be irate at kids makin' silly tattoos on each other's backs. Just to be sure, I'll do a *Rosary* as penance when I get home, usin' what I learned in advanced math to shorten the *decades*. Then I'll say the *Lord's Prayer* very fast and reduce the *Hail Marys* by half. The *Glory Be* will have to be represented by an *Amen*. That word is so often pronounced at home, it don't hardly take up much room at all, unless…" I hesitated, "unless I reckon you consider the word takes up more space for what it symbolizes once shortened to *men*. Now, that won't do. We already have enough of those." Skizzum laughed out loud and covered her mouth. I laughed too, amused at my formula, but conscious that we might be heard and chased away. "I like makin' good use of everything. That way, nothin' goes wasted." We both giggled again, bent on forgetting our earlier misconduct with our friend.

"I'm tired of waitin' on a month of Sundays. They ain't gonna let her go so soon," I told Skizzum, as we decided to go closer to the lake. I could see the tall trees hiding the church from my view. Nearby the thorn bush with its fluttering rags, tempted to intimidate the towering cypress. These colorful pieces of cloth, that looked somewhat like faded old underwear to me, would ultimately rot away, taking with them, the community's sins and afflictions, according to Emmy. If indeed these rags were old underwear, what Emmy said did have a kind of logic. The Evangelists believe some parts of the body are sinful. Until the dissipation of those sins (or the rotting of the undergarments), the sinners who had left them were, if I understood her, under protection by the Banshee thorns Emmy had said were magic guardians. I suppose I was keen on this idea because of the tattoo.

The last prayer of this strange ceremony I had come to be acquainted with on other occasions was a mixture of languages, mostly Cant (rejected in Ireland for not being Irish enough): *May Dieu be avec toi, and avec vos esprits.* The *Naderum of the Dhalum inoc* you. *Staish.*

"*Inoc* you too. " I said out loud again, with the kind of bombast and ambivalent expression you might have pertaining to religion at eleven years of age. I thought Harper was nuts and invented most of what he said out of thin air. "Whatever so-called powers Harper has, he still ain't God. *Inoc* is jest as good of a four-letter word as any and sounds better than most. And ain't the Lord's Prayer sort of wicked with its, 'Lead us not into temptation line? Jesus! What kind of a God would we have to pray to, to make him stop with the temptations? Oh, Father in Heaven please stop! You are killin' me with your temptations! I jest can't take it anymore with all these underwear flyin' around. It's a good thing you invented the thorn tree to keep us out of them drawers." I added a gesture I had seen in the movies, lifting my arm and bending it in front of my face as though protecting myself from a blow with added drama. "Blasphemy". I liked that word as well. It made Skizzum laugh again. "*Blasphemy*!" I repeated it in my mind until it became a blur; then decided maybe it wasn't such a great idea after all to play out all your cards in such a way that someone, not just anyone, peering over your shoulder might imperil your best laid game. Skizzum decided to go home. Shame began to warm its new spot on my back.

Then, having found my way again down my secret path of rationalization, I felt frustrated, feeling like God *had* forgotten after all, what it was like to be wet behind the ears (the one thing even he could have never known anyway). Hadn't he set Emmy up for punishment? Blasphemy! I again thought, as I pulled up memories of Emmy and I as we listened to Harper talk about subjects that interested me much more than religion. "Maybe that is why she is in so much trouble now?" I was too young to make the connection between the dirty jokes he had told us and the other incidents. I didn't even bother to look where I was going. However, the divinities of the forest were not asleep. The wind shook the murmuring cottonwood branches over my head, and threw the fluffy white skirt I was wearing against the briars. I jerked the skirt back, tearing it right down the front. Around me, the poison ivy, which usually enjoyed a relative esteem, seemed to disregard even its simplest imperative of making the rambler wary. The lake wardens knew they would not be disturbed again for some time. The silver cypress and the gnarled oaks could go on glaring sternly at each other and the cursing squirrels. The wind or the river would end up having their way with them too and the *maringouins* were already beginning to bite. I gave up trying to find a solution for my friend as I crushed the mosquito on my bare arm with the palm of my hand and went up the path.

"Maybe it's jest the Furies. They can't sit still for very long out here."

The gin and its watchman

It was surely going to rain. I didn't want to go home but I couldn't hope to see Emmy for hours or even for days, if ever again. What would I tell her about her skirt, if I did see her? It was grass-stained and torn. "They probably even won't let her go to school." I started up the path towards the Lake Road and crossed over near the gin. Cotton was still planted across the road, but it was nowadays shipped somewhere else to be ginned. When the gin first closed down, Jim had stayed on. "What's the use of watchin' over a decayin' industrial building?" I reflected. I didn't really think I would go in, but the guardian's car wasn't parked in front like it usually was. Getting into the yard was easy; one hard tug at the fence and a large gape opened before me. The door lock had long been broken. With precaution, I looked around before going in. In the main building, the dust from the ginned cotton swirled each time I put my foot down. In the air, there hung a bitter aroma of rank seed. One silo was still half-filled. Old machinery parts were left in solidified grease. The carder, still intact, waited for one of the rusting ladders from the catwalk to give way and to put it definitively out of order. It was not a safe place for children to play. I sat down on a forsaken bale of cotton. On the metal roof the rain thundered down.

I made up my own stories and pretended to work at the *Salvation Army* like Emmy's mother did sometimes. I looked over the bale at my dusty congregation of machine parts. I found some old crates and pulled them up to use as chairs for the crumpled rags. Looking around I saw a closed door and went to open it. The room had been the facility director's office. There was still a table in a corner. I thought the room would make a good parsonage, while the gin could be the church. I opened the shade. There was so much dust in the room. I wished Emmy were here to help me, or Skizzum. I began to open the cupboards to look for a broom. My feet were so dirty by now. What would my mother say, even worse, Papou? There was no chance of borrowing another skirt from Emmy. I briefly imagined myself going from house to house asking for a skirt, like people did on Mardi Gras Down-the-bayou, begging for a chicken.

"I can't go home like this. Papou be on me like ants on a snow cone. That would be jest like him to be sittin' in his rocker when I get there. I don't know who I can borrow another skirt from." I imagined walking down my street and saw another street in my mind's eye. It ran just short of perpendicular to Iowa Street. On one side there were the most rundown houses that were bordered by the fetid bayou. In one of them lived a girl who people said was dying. It was impossible to ask her for help, even if she did have a lot of skirts that she would never wear again. I didn't even know why I thought of it. Why did Emmy have to go and tell about the naked woman? She could have washed it off in the shower. I couldn't get my mind around Emmy's confession. Behind the tree in the schoolyard, I had let Johnny Ray kiss me on the lips and put his tongue in my mouth, and still felt I had nothing to confess. The rain lashed against the dirty window and it was very dim in the small room. Deep in my thoughts, wishing I had a transistor, and singing

"Got you on my mind" from *Cookie and his Cupcakes,* I didn't catch the sound of the guardian's car when it turned into his dirt driveway next door to the gin.

The watchman had noticed the cracked yellow shade had been drawn open. He had seen it from the Lake Road. I later imagined his approach. As he got closer to the office door, and probably taking his job too seriously, he lifted the baseball bat over his head. Inside the gin it was more dark than light. The dust swirled around his feet, sticking to his wet boots. The globules of rain dripped from his weapon and pearled on the floor. I heard him and hid in one of the cupboards. Jim Taylor came into the office and looked around. He closed the door, but waited inside the room. He had already surprised some of the neighborhood boys smoking in the rundown gin and he waited to see them pop out so he could give them a lesson.

My heart back beat like in a Chuck Berry song. Thinking the watchman had left, I slowly turned the doorknob. "Ah ha! What have we here? Git out here you little imp. You gonna be less proud when I git finished with you." Jim pulled me out by my arm. He lowered the bat. I began to struggle and pull in the opposite direction.

"You better come along easy or I'll give you a whuppin' right away." Jim wasn't a callous man. Still under thirty, he still wore mourning, as the old folks said, not even bothering to go out with other women. The Lady in White had crossed his path and he would never get married again, said the local gossip. It was suggested he had been seen at places of lost women and bad luck. The worse fate in Ferriday was that of those poor souls whose name was caught up in a web of nonsense. Jim was one of these and all the worse for it because he was Black. For that reason, we were all afraid of him, adding to his solitude.

Emmy said Jim had the evil eye on him. And some people even held for worse. The foulest scuttlebutt was started by one of the women at the Community Service meetings, Missy Dey Deed (daughter of the late Ariston Ferriday Deed and Camillia Dey Deed who went to the Southern Baptist Church), a fifty-some-odd-year-old spinster with a hair-sprayed bun, a thin figure, and tiny, almost childlike, hands. She had sold her father's plantation in return for a life's annuity, which meant when she was down with the flu or something, people were taking bets to see if Herbert Miller would finally be coming into his property. In the meantime, he ran the farm like a tenant, paying her the major portion of the profits, along with the annuities based on the total worth of the plantation, the gin, and the Farm Outlet. Needless to say, this got her family out of debt.

All her life, Missy Dey Deed had the doctor out at her place at least once every two weeks, bringing one remedy after another. She was always calling her friends on the phone, saying in a small voice that she was sure enough going to pass this time. One week she had rheumatism that bent her in half, the next, she was down and out with pneumonia and soon to be hospitalized. And still the next, she was covered with a rash no one could explain, which was all the same, eating her alive. On those weeks when she was in convalescence; she turned her maid into a mule, so to speak, making her haul her all over the house and prop her up in the room that had the most, or the least, sun, depending on the time of the day and the heat behind the window.

During one of those weeks of miraculous recovery, Missy Dey Deed had one of the ladies from the club to come over for coffee and angel cake. "I have to confess this to someone. I can't keep it to myself any longer. Y'all know that Negro, the gin watchman, don't y'all? The last time I got in my car to drive out to the plantation, I had a flat tire. I got out to look at it while my driver was off to the station to get someone to come out, and that fella stopped and asked me if I needed help. I told him right away it wasn't what he thought. I wasn't looking for a flirt, or a lift. I bent however so slightly over, showing him the nail and the hole in the tire. As I straightened up, I noticed the tops of my hose had been uncovered and even my garter belt was sticking out from under my dress. He was standing there staring, his arms hanging out by his sides and practically right on me. His mouth was open, but he didn't say a word. It was like he never saw a woman's underthings and was getting mighty hot and bothered at seein' a White woman all the sudden. I hurried into my car telling him my driver, Joe, was takin' care of it. He tipped his hat and drove off in that truck of his. Later that day when we drove by, I saw it parked out in the alley behind Big George's. Can you imagine what a fright it caused me to think of what I barely escaped?"

She said this, putting her hand just under her throat, turning one of the pearls of her necklace with a white glove, and in a voice just anxious enough to speed her drawl to a pace that it worried her interlocutor; as if she was listening to a woman who had fought off a rapist. And within a short time after the visitor had left, she called her cousin, Shirley, making her promise not to tell anyone. By early afternoon, the news had spread all the way to Natchez. At the Community Service meeting the next day, the women were all in a fuss talking about Missy Dey Deed's being accosted on the side of the road by the colored watchman at the gin, barely escaping her aggressor, thanks to her driver. They had him being held for questioning at the very moment in the town jail. It was a cruel tale.

Over the weeks it was built up in the town's imagination until it finally got to Jim Taylor's ears when a reporter from the *Concordia Poste* came out and asked him for an exclusive interview. Jim, who had not laughed since his wife's funeral, would not have remembered Missy Dey Deed's plight had it not been for her fancy car and for the fact that her tire had quite a nail in it. The tire emptied out at once when the driver had extracted the metal splinter, leaving them stranded by the roadside. What had intrigued Jim was that the same thing had happened to him earlier that same week; only he had removed the nail himself and repaired the tire at home before going on the road and getting stranded. He wondered if someone had lost his hardware somewhere. Now, he considered Missy Dey Deed with a mixture of curiosity and despondency, like one who understood the neglect and misery behind an ill-bred child, grown into a bully.

Had he realized just how far gossip could go in such a town as Ferriday, he might have not had such a benevolent view. Missy Dey Deed was known as a craftsperson of sorts. She could make a stretcher out of any bit of deed or conversation. Had it not been for her impeccable upbringing and town council influence, she might have been thought as a genuine troublemaker. But most of the time, she avoided mentioning any names directly. That would not do to bring clouds over the heads of an honest family. It was thus always hard to tell afterwards who rang up the ticket in the first place. Someone always paid the price, and you could say, they got their money's worth. And they might as well have, because there was no use in trying to return the calamity to its just place. Such talk about having a moral responsibility to turn things in the right direction is the illusion inexperienced people have when they get all disjointed about petty offenses and start heading for the courthouse (or is it the smokehouse?) thinking they'll get all they want. They should learn that if all the justice in the world was shut up inside, fattened hogs would come out lucky.

When the journalist uncovered the fact that Herbert Miller's lost bag of nails was the culprit and this was mentioned on the society page, as "gashing Missy's Day, as well as her tire", along with a Black man's name, as having "been there too", it was remembered by some to be a gash put there to cause her an accident and to end her life. Her friends then added this detail to Jim Taylor's account, as he being the suspected criminal, but for lack of evidence, "was left to roam the country looking for new victims", according to the

Ladies' Club. Shirley added another gruesome detail, mentioning that his knife had just missed the victim's heart and had plunged into her tire. Herbert Miller came out to see Missy Dey Deed when the news hit him, bringing her some flowers as an awkward apology for not tying down his toolbox on his truck bed when he had left the hardware store some days before and for not finding all the nails once the box fell off and burst open on the Lake Road. She got mad and threw the bouquet in his bewildered face, adding, "It's not time for my funeral yet." From that day on, although she was probably disappointed in the touch of reality brought forth by Herbert Miller, Missy Dey Deed's health improved somewhat. However, the bruit continued to propagate and to cause commotion in the town whenever anything suspicious happened.

I hadn't made up my mind about any of this. At that moment I wanted to get away from Jim, and his trailer, though, and this was even true according to the old folks, living on the water made girls grow up fast. "Did being ready for new experiences mean I *had* to take them where I found them?"

It's a fact this windblown fellow with light brown skin and hard arms never saw much of anyone. He had been hired by the Cotton Mercantile Company to watch over the property until the sale of the site. (Missy Dey Deed was still alive, but since the gin had stopped working, she agreed to sell it if Herbert Miller and the Cotton Mercantile Company agreed on the terms.) Jim Taylor became progressively a little rough in his appearance and in his manners. His smile was all the same broad and convivial in spite of his harsh words and gruff voice. The entire episode with Missy Dey Deed had long since been forgotten; at least it was no longer in everyone's conversations.

Jim drug me outside under the pouring rain and over to his trailer which was more of a temporary building than a house. It was the mistake he should never have made. I weighed hardly seventy pounds but fought like a wildcat, trying to kick him or bite him, anywhere I could. "You'd better settle down an' stop tryin' to bite me. He plopped me down next to the kitchen sink. "You want me to stuff ya' inside my dirty clothes basket with your ragged clothes? He held the top of my squirming body firmly against his chest. I inhaled the scent of his unease, a working man's perfume, and thought of my father.

"Hold still now and behave. I'll give you a Coke if you act civilized." He held me firmly against his body. I thought this might be my chance to escape.

Growing up fast

"You know it's dangerous in there. That's why I fetched you. There're metal pieces, rusted parts that cut. Here—jest look at yore skirt. We can even see the motor!"

I replied, embarrassed, folding my skirt under my thighs, and looking around the room to see whom *we* might mean. "I didn't tear my skirt in there. I did it near the lake. Besides, it ain't mine. And your gonna catch a cold wit dose eyes if you don't put sompin' on that stupid stare you got."

I saw Jim's hound lying under the kitchen table. I was worried he too had fallen victim to a serial dog emasculator and might try to bite me.

"It's torn all the same and somebody gonna be mad." He opened the bottle and handed it to me. I put it to my lips and swallowed so fast it burned my throat up to my nostrils. I didn't often have the occasion to drink Cokes. I had forgotten you're supposed to sip them slowly.

I looked around the room. To me, it was a man's house with guns over the door, a sofa with a television in front of it, and with empty beer cans and magazines on the nearby table. I was still in the kitchen, seated on the counter.

These Beans Have Too Much Salt

"I'll let you git down now if you want. I ain't used to havin' girls in here. You can sit over there." He indicated the couch, picking up the magazines and turning them over. Jim was conscious of the fact an unseasoned White girl had seen them, but he didn't want any problems and tried not to draw attention to them.

Jim wanted to look professional. After all, he was the gin vigil and I had penetrated the property illegally. He turned a kitchen chair around and straddled it in front of me, "Now. I'm gonna have to interrogate you. What on earth was you in there for?"

"I was jest piddlin' 'round. Y'all can't expect to keep kids out with that fence full of holes. The whole neighborhood comes over here."

"Hmpf. I suppose you is one to do what the whole neighborhood is a doin'. That's surely why I found you all alone by yoreself. Am I s'pposed to go and have a look around the gin to see if there is any other of y'all hidden in the cupboards? Maybe the wolf had done gone and eaten the other little goats? You was in there. And trespassin' is a way of lookin' for trouble. First thing you know they'll be syndicatin' ya' all over town." It was clear to me from Jim's accent and expressions that he was from the South, and he wasn't Cajun, or even Creole.

I finished my Coke and was feeling sort of torn between running for the door and hanging out to talk to him. I thought I was vaguely conscious of what might be going through his mind and retained a small feeling of triumph because he hadn't marched me right home or called my mother. "Are you gonna take me to de Sheriff's? Cuz if you gonna do it, then you better git right with it. I ain't gonna stay here all day," I threatened with incertitude.

"Listen here you little pest, if I got a mind to keep you here for an interrogation, I'm gonna keep you. Don't you git annoyed with me. Besides that, I don't know how you can go home half-dressed and covered with mud."

The rain had turned the dust into mud and I looked a bit like the homeless in the congregation that I had been playing. "Well, there ain't much I can do about that can I?"

"All depends on yore attitude. If you'll cooperate, I might have a look and see if I have a skirt that you can borrow." In fact, Jim had kept all of his late wife's clothes. She had been a small woman and her skirts might fit me. "What is your name anyway? I need it for my report."

I sealed my lips before blurting out "Beatrice". I had already thought I didn't want my name on any report.

"Beatrice my ass!" snorted Jim. "You startin' a tale as foggy as a swamp on a November morning. I know for a fact that you is one of them trailer park kids. We ain't gittin' far yet young lady. If you don't tell me the truth, what am I gonna put down? I got a mind to take my belt off and give you a good whuppin'. That's exactly what you need, you little smart ass."

Jim was trying to look angry, but I intrigued him somehow and he seemed to want the interrogation to last more than he wanted any answers for his report. "I'm gonna write you up for trespassin' and vandalism."

I glared at him. I didn't know what vandalism was but I had a quick tongue in those days and retorted, "Vandalism! Hell if I'm guilty of vandalism! You jest makin' that up to try to scare me. I ain't no blood kin to them people. My name ain't Harper, Dufrene or Robichaux."

"Ha! If it ain't, I ain't no Taylor either! Maybe that ain't your name, but you smell just as sweet." Jim was like many Southerners with a mouth-to-mouth education, a knowledge reflecting a mixture of Bible, Shakespeare and local beliefs spouted out in an English with a heavy accent that would knock the socks off the founding fathers, and make their eyes roll around in the back of their heads. I was a bit surprised at Jim saying I smelled sweet. I had never read *Romeo and Juliette* that close, and probably, neither had he. I thought he either was being sarcastic or referring to the fact that as a descendent of a slave, he had a name that didn't suit him either.

"You sayin' I stink? I hope I reek up ya whole trailer. It smelled like a *cabris* here before I came in! I gotta go home now." I didn't much believe Jim wanted to do a report and started to feel uneasy about being alone in a man's house.

"Not so fast. See here, you sit quiet fer a minute and I will see if I can find a skirt."

He had given up on the report. He was probably just lonely and wanted to keep me around for a while. He was in need of a friend; only my immaturity, his celibacy, and especially his skin color, would not allow such friendship without a chaperone. Solitude and lack of distractions might be considered the cause of the downfall of many people in the Ferriday. There wasn't much else for an unmarried Black man to do besides go to Big George's or Haney's Big House and dance all night with a woman. If Jim had been White and wanted to meet someone, he would have driven around the Sandwich Bar while some girls drove around in their car. If the scenario went this far, he might stop and roll down his window and try to start a conversation with one of them. They might get out of their cars, smoke a cigarette, and decide to meet in the drugstore for a soda. He might take her out to the Arcade, or maybe to the Paramount in Natchez, if she worked and no longer lived with her parents. However, Jim was Black. Once he got to the point of thinking about Haney's, Connie would smile back at him in his mind. The more intimate moments of the fantasy would disappear, leaving nothing, but smoke around the ceiling. Anything else would have been all over town and everyone else's business. My impromptu visit could cause the same row. It was my first genuine lesson in gossip's cuisine.

Jim got up and went into the bedroom. While he was away, I looked over at the pile of magazines and picked up one. It wasn't a

Playboy, but a kind of pornographic magazine he had probably brought home from the army. There were both naked women and men in it. I stared at the images. I had never seen anything like it. I had always been curious about the male body. I looked at art books to find photos of sculptures. At the morgue, my mother tried to prevent me from looking at the male corpses -- all dead and limp. She told me it wasn't appropriate to look under the sheet. I said I didn't think they would care. "No, perhaps not, she said, "but all the same, girls shouldn't look." Here, in this magazine, there was something different, fascinating to the eye. I reflected upon the snake woman duo Skizzum had drawn on our backs.

I was about ready to tear out one of the pages when Jim came back with the skirt. He saw me toss the magazine aside.

Suddenly, I was talking about my friend Emmy. I told Jim, Emmy had some special powers. "She can heal people. Not like her mom, with cataplasms, but jest with her hands!"

Jim probably thought to himself the Robichaux-Dufrene-Harper clan had some really outlandish beliefs. What seemed to bother him was they got their kids caught up in these superstitions at an age when they hadn't made up their own minds. They accepted these beliefs without surprise or indignity.

I went on with my apologue, "You been to the Blue Hole (not the Bar but the swimming hole)? It's off the gravel road, by the abandoned huntin' camp. There used to be a big log 'cross the creek you could walk over. The water was freezin' cold so we thought that meant there was no snakes or gators. There was this rock you could hold onto and feel the icy cold water even durin' the summer. Well right near de creek there's the *Blue Hole*. We stopped by there on the way home because we saw this ball churnin' in the water. We looked closer and saw it was a cluster of water moccasins (not the shoes but the snakes). We was throwing sticks and rocks at it when a carload of *paillard,* drunken boys, showed up from de Blue Hole (this time de Bar)."

"One jumped out of the car and ran for a swingin' rope in a tree. We started screamin' at him to stop, but he didn't pay us no mind. He swung out there yellin', *Geronimo,* and dropped right on de writhen snake nest with the snakes all woven round each other."

"We ran for the bikes, screamin' at the boys in the car that their friend had dropped on a nest of snakes. They didn't move, but stood there with their mouths open. Not Emmy. It was awful. She walked out in the water with a big branch that snagged the guy. I don't know even how she did it! I was scairt to death! He wasn't movin' and must've been completely paralyzed by this time. She pulled him out of the nest and picked off the last snake and threw it back in the nest. She put her hands on the man's still boyish forehead. When we came back, we could overhear her talkin' in Cant, sayin' the prayers that she got from an angel, (or was it the Banshees, I don't remember now)."

"The other boys came near by then. They was yellin' not to touch him. But…the paralyzed guy started to move again. He started screamin' bloody murder 'bout being bitten by a swarm of snakes, but that didn't scare off Emmy. She kept sayin' them prayers in Cant, holdin' the guy in a kind of gridlock, not movin' her hands away from his head. In 'bout ten minutes, she let go and the fella got up and walked to the shore. The guys with their mouths open weren't tryin' to catch no flies! They were lookin' at Lazarus come back to life! Even the bites was cured and nothin' left of them."

Jim started to smile. He laughed as he listened to me tell the tale and even use some of the words that only Cajuns use. But after all, he knew the words too and he had picked up on one version or another of this tale through the years. Sometimes the man was dead. Sometimes he was left snake bitten and drowned. Always, he was more or less abandoned to his own fate by his fellowmen. And now, after glancing at a pornographic magazine, I was suddenly talking to him about snakes!

"Now you best hush up and stop spreadin' those golly whoppers. They'll bring you nothin' but trouble. 'Specially if you go spoutin' off words in Cajun."

"It ain't no golly whoppa!" I screeched. "It's a well authenticated fact! You know well enough people round here talk in tongues and sometimes it gits so hot it rains snakes. Emmy said Jesus Christ is the same yesterday, today and forever, meaning if he could heal in his day, he could do the same now."

245

"I was there. He was on the rope and swingin' and screamin' *Geronimo* before his buddies got out of the car. I don't think he even got the wind of us yellin', tryin' to stop him from goin' in. It was like sompin' out of a horror movie. Snakes all movin' round in every direction dippin' down and then floatin' back to the top, makin' their way across the water. After that, we got scared for weeks and don't go swimmin' there no more, all 'cept Emmy. Some people jest don't wanna believe Emmy healed the fella. She has the Banshees with her. (Or is it de angels? I don't remember now.) And those boys who were with him jest don't want to own up. They didn't help their friend. But …when that man comes back to town, he goes to that church even still today. You can go and see for yourself! There's a lot a people come to see her. She's had the Angels with her since she was six years old. I heard her Maw say so when I took my dog to see Dr. Robichaux. It's to see her praise the Lord, the band plays, flowers flow out of that church and people go aclappin' until the air splits. That's why her Uncle Harper keeps her locked up half the time! He's 'fraid somebody gonna kidnap her and there won't be nobody at his church no more. "

Jim probably figured the guy had fainted when he realized he was falling on a ball of snakes, which is the best thing he could have done. Water moccasins will bite you even in the water, no matter what some say. And he was lucky they didn't bite him, or else, for sure, they weren't cotton mouthed water moccasins. He didn't believe in Banshees, or even angels anymore and found it hard to believe that I did either, even with my Cajun accent. The preacher was another problem, one too great for him to figure out.

"I told you, you was a Robichaux, a Dufrene, or a Harper. You gotta be one to tell an earful like that. Even if it's a good story, ain't no little girl got powers to cure snake bites. Not even any more than what y'all call the *Patterns* do to keep water moccasins away! Snakes is snakes and if they're gonna bite, they're gonna bite. No two ways about it."

Jim put some chewing tobacco under his lip. He started to act impatient with me. Nevertheless, the blood flowing into his ears was probably better than the fear that he evidently felt fifteen minutes before. He knew he had to get me out of there and faster than that before someone saw me there.

I was angry too. I was on the brink of calling Jim a bad name, thinking it was no use trying to tell him anything; but I stopped myself, realizing those words were expressions Papou forbid us to use. He said only Badjos treated other people like that. But I had heard a lot of kids use them at school, especially at election time. Papou said he didn't like Jimmie Davis very much, but I didn't say any more than that. The N-word meringue pie, thrown at me that week at school, made me wonder who I was.

Sometimes I wondered if I wasn't American, Cajun, Creole, Irish and Indian all wrapped up together. I began to wonder if Emmy's Uncle Harper, who spoke many languages, wasn't my own father.

Indeed, I looked somewhat like his kids, only they were boys. My mother had dated a few men from town after my father left. But people in small towns can be so cruel. I heard a considerable lot about what was said. In particular, it was rumored he left because she had been unfaithful, meaning we could all be from a different father, only to discover there was a woman in Natchez with a deserved reputation who had the same name (unless that was gossip too). My mother had tried to reassure me, even before she knew of the rumor. She said my whole family was Cajun, but in the North (Ferriday being Up-the-Bayou), we had to speak English (even if a large portion of the town didn't). As I wondered, I faltered, I struggled even. "I'm not one of them, I'm a Cajun, and a Catholic". But even as I formulated these thoughts, I doubted every word, and I missed my dad. It is hard for people in small towns who are unsure of their origins, and perhaps, even for those who know where they came from and whom.

"Now git that skirt on you and git out of here on the double before I change my mind." I didn't have to be told twice.

"Can I use the bathroom?" Jim nodded and pointed the way. As I slipped out of my skirt, I caught a glimpse of myself in the mirror. I had dark essentially black hair, green eyes and medium skin like practically all of Dufrenes-Robichauxs, and some of the Harpers, even though we weren't related. I was still boyish, all arms and legs, yet at that moment, I thought I noticed something different about myself that made me think of the older girls in my neighborhood.

"A-men!" I thought, dragging out the second syllable, "I'm not gonna get like Skizzum. I'm gonna leave this place." I tugged at my panties between my thighs, this time leaving no fingerprint, and walked out of the bathroom, kicking Emmy's torn skirt under a cabinet in Jim Taylor's bathroom.

When I came out of the bathroom Jim didn't throw me out right away. The door of his trailer was open, but the rain was still falling. Turning his head to look out the door and almost blocking the way, he looked like he had been on the verge of tears. His eyes glittered. Instead of rushing past him, or asking him what was wrong, I began to talk about what brought me to the gin. With a resolute step, the whole tattoo story got away from my grip. Instead of skedaddling away, the shame held fast, groping about my feet, climbing up my back, and then about my neck, almost choking me. With a whisper, I heard it confess hatred and even wishes for Harper's death.

"That ceremony sounds like a lot of hokey-pokey hogwash to me," said Jim, forgetting whatever was upsetting him and trying to comfort me. "It may be all that fire and bloom will all fizzle out like a wet firecracker and you'll have your friend back with you in no time." But I knew it wouldn't. Harper had already been around too long. I had seen what he had done to Skizzum and he was closer than ever to Emmy. Even Mérite-Lajoie now went to his church. At least Jim didn't suspect childlike jealousy. My feeling was more like that of despair, and this time there was someone to blame for it. We stood there for some time in the doorway, talking and waiting for the shower to end.

These Beans Have Too Much Salt

Although I can't say Jim found the right words to appease my anguish, I found him to be sensible. He told me not to be afraid. "People need ways to express their anger. Words are there to help you get past it, but they won't hurt nobody." I opened my heart to him and he thus became a friend I could have trusted. I was sorry for what happened afterward. My presence contributed to the suspicions about him and even made things worse. Much worse.

It was nearly three o'clock when the rain stopped. The pavement was starting to warm up and the wind over the bayou carried the sour smell of summer even though it was officially, if you went by the calendar, just barely spring in our part of the world. I walked home.

Predicament

Skizzum told me when Harper came to the end of the road, he told her to get out, adding a lot of cynical, mean remarks, "God's favor comes to those who don't deserve it. You will become righteous in his light. Don't forgit that. Now git out of the car. And don't you be comin' back to bother me about no baby. I know it ain't mine. I'm a virtuous man. The Lord wouldn't let such things happen. You got yerself into trouble and for now you are a fallen Angel to me, even, uh, uh a whore…and will suffer God's condemnation. I don't know what your Mama's gonna do, but your future is in God's hands."

Skizzum got out of the car and walked around to the window. I could almost see her tears falling on her cheeks and hear her begging him not to leave her, recalling his vow to religion, expecting some support from another realm. Sometime later, relating their conversation, she added that his abandonment, more than his cruelty, was what finally allowed her to get clear of him.

"Please don't leave me like this, Harper," she had pleaded. "I thought you would help me. I thought you had more God in you than the others. Like what you preach. I was ready to sacrifice my whole life to you and to your church. I used to think we would be together always. Didn't you?"

"You're a stupid little bitch ain't you!" he snarled. "You believe I can leave my wife and all that I have created here to take care of some teenage girl, foolish enough to git pregnant and with a baby

251

from who knows where? I never even put my biscuit in the gravy! You done let someone else put their fingers in my pie. Pretentious little heifer! You'd think it was divine intervention! Wake up hon! Wake up! Now git your vicious paws off my car and you jest git yoreself on home."

Harper drove off. Skizzum stood there a moment, perhaps realizing she had betrayed herself with her lack of dignity, before strolling back towards home, wondering what our grandfather had decided about her little one. She hadn't thought of a name for her baby just yet. She didn't want to give him up for adoption. *"The Epistle to the Romans* decreed, 'there is no one righteous.' No, not one. Not even Harper." Her vanity was eating its guts out for satisfaction.

The months she had passed with Harper had reinforced her belief in many things, including the First Evangelist Church. At first, she had felt the guilt steep through her skin as Harper touched her in the most forbidden places. In church, when his eyes crossed hers, she felt transpierced with cold, virtually feeling his loathing, though his satiety for what she felt were her darkest parts, knew no bounds. The dirt, the slime, the ordure, she was confused, helpless, and for a moment, feared annihilation. "I put stock in you Harper. I trusted you. Now, I just want to die", she was screaming when I found her, swelling with suicidal sweat, lying down on the damp ground. "Leave me alone."

I walked about ten feet away and sat on a tree stump. After a while, she began to get cold and she called out to me, "Hey, he's movin'".

The self-directed murderous restlessness gave way to another transient idea, one that left room for redemption, and even more, for compassion. The moment of benevolence was as fruitless as it was fleeting. What brought her to her feet was another motivation: her desire for revenge. The crushed grass had left wrinkled imprints on her face, making her look older, and worried enough to be a mother. But in such a moment, it is safe to say that all mothers are not of a gentle nature, preoccupied by their children. Perhaps at that brief instant, Skizzum's expression looked more like the vengeful Medea, if looking-like and being were of the same nature.

"Who does he think he is? God himself? He cheated on his wife. He used me jest like he uses everybody else. *Et il est un mauvais bougre*, a bad man. I'm tired of his meanness. I hate him. I've had enough of him. Someone should do away with that creep. I'll tell Hiram." Her footsteps were faster now, determined. I had to run to keep up with her. Even if she could draw naughty tattoos with one hand, she could wash her sins away with the other. She wondered if she told her lover about Harper, would be jealous enough to kill him. "Would that be a sin on my part?"

"That won't do no good anyhow. They'd just kill him. Both'd be gone for good and no one would make out a thing. That wouldn't be right." I was afraid she was already bent on telling Hiram.

Then, she blurted out, slowing her pace: "Well then I jest guess I'll have to count on God providin' for me an' my baby. Even if the church don't want me now, the congregation'll come round sooner or later. Just thinkin' 'bout Jesus and how helpless he was when he was born will help me get through this. Jesus had God on his side, but Mary's husband wasn't obliged to believe her. Could she have become a prophet? At least she was faithful to him 'til the end. Why didn't she spread the word of God? I wonder if they'd let a woman preach the Gospel here...There's no use ponderin' over it."

Her performance with us children had not left her with any misgivings. Reality didn't much agree with the theories she had lately formulated, neither about feminism, nor about love. Remembering the humiliating corrections Harper had inflicted upon her, she could feel the anger growing in her throat. She told me he shut her up in the church's broom closet and pulled her out by her hair. Sometimes he hit her with his alligator belt, admonishing her and calling her a wanton little bitch. Strangely, she felt proud he had chosen her, among all the Angels, for private lessons, he called them. He said they were doing nothing wrong and each opprobrium felt like a mark of interest, of love even. Not realizing her submission to his cruelty added mystery and even encouraged his fantasies; she continued to seek him out in church. She convinced herself Harper loved her because she wanted so much to be loved. Now she knew he had a dried shriveled rotten fig in place of a heart.

In truth, he went far, but never on the path she expected. He would brush his lips vaguely on her forehead, make her take her clothes off, and then without removing his own would make her lay down behind the altar. With a flashlight, he would peer inside her as she spread her legs, offering her virginity. To avoid meeting his flashing eyes, she first stared at a torn edge of one of the Bibles piled up on a pew, before concentrating on a bird building a nest outside a window. Adorning latex gloves, palpating her more like a doctor than a lover, and grumbling with disillusion, he examined her quim in the hard light. What did he expect to find there? Was she different from other girls? In an ultimate debasement, he turned her over on her belly, attached her hands then blindfolded her. Covering her horrified lamentations with her panties, he violently penetrated her most intimate cavity with a finger before removing her gag and sticking the acrid tasting thing in her mouth. As she struggled under his knee, he began panting until he swore, insulting her copiously and pouring some kind of tepid liquid that he called the Savior's unction on her backside. The memory of this indignity and abasement brought forth the nausea of self-disgust. She heaved over on the side of the road.

How depraved was she to have followed this man, again and again? How could she have believed that he could love? What kind of nefarious creature was he? What kind of vile person was she? They had committed a sin, but she wasn't sure what it was called. She was only glad she had finally found comfort and tenderness in the arms of someone else. Where he lived, in the neighborhood through the woods, was of little importance to her. All these thoughts are what drove Skizzum far away a short time later. It was as if she could not live with her former self in Ferriday, and abandoned her there as well.

These Beans Have Too Much Salt

"Sooner or later, Harper will get what he deserves." Comforted again with this thought, Skizzum hurried home with me and brought out her guitar, playing and singing a verse from "Catahoula Stomp":

"I don't want your greenback dollars
Oh, I don't want your watch and chain.
All I want is your twenty-two twenty
To shoot out your dirty brains."

Private Lessons

Both Skizzum and Emmy told me about the clan's triple harp and how Harper brought it out on occasions from behind the altar. He was still limber in spite of his thirty-some odd years on the road or behind the pulpit. Its ninety-eight brass strings sounded like tiny bells when he pinched them and stroked them with his long-tinted nails. These built-in guitar picks weren't painted like those of some women folks in town. Harper's nails were yellowish red from a combination of tobacco and henna. Mamere used the reddish-brown dye to draw lace on Emmy 's hands. She said that it was good for hardening fingernails and for keeping bugs out of their hair as well. He often questioned her advice, but seemed to abide by it for some things.

Skizzum had seen him take a trunk with personal belongings from behind the altar. He mumbled as he flipped through the pages of what appeared to be a satin covered Bible, speaking to an absent mother. Flaring up with the slightest hint of contempt, the musician lived with a perpetual disdain of others' prattle. With unmitigated ego-centrism, he despised even more their muck. Skizzum didn't dare intervene when he spoke in this distracted manner. Did he still have flashes of scenes where his mother scrubbed his skin raw with a corncob, calling him a filthy little shit? According to Mérite-Lajoie, he had said this woman rubbed him until he cried, all while citing Bible verses, exorcising what she called impure instincts. An instant later, she cried over him, stroked his hair that she let grow until it curled around his face, and called him her "little angel

257

honeychile". With piety, he venerated some parcel of her clothing that he kept secret in the trunk as well, and that was found later, after the fire, along with Harper's enflamed accounts. Bringing this relic to his nose, did he vow to himself to keep his extremities clean like so many men with this sort of habit? According to his calculations, and what he had told Mérite-Lajoie, he could transmit his doctrine only through his legitimate offspring. However, he didn't explain many other details about how the doctrine was actually transmitted, or how it included axioms concerning cleanliness and legitimate children. "Purity," he called it.

We would watch him sometimes in secret as he examined his hands. The dye made his fingers look corrupt and, this didn't settle well with him. His hands were not those of a dredger, for he was capable of the most extraordinary dexterity, especially when he touched a musical instrument. The harp was part of Mamere's dowry and had become one of the community's most treasured possessions. How she came about acquiring the instrument was a horse of a different color. Some said it was a present from the Gypsy king who wanted to marry her. Her people, as much Spanish as French, had maintained relations with the Romani over the past decades. Harper had learned to replace the strings from them and taught himself how to play. Now he preferred this instrument to the lighter harps built in the tradition of his forefathers (who he said he didn't know or had forgotten).

Earning money was the only way, according to him, for a man to gain respect in this country. The best way to make one's living was to either become a politician or to start a wandering minstrel church. Since he had had some problems with a congregation in Tennessee, and with a girl's family in New Orleans, he now seemed to have lesser ambitions for himself. Caring for his Angels was what had become his foremost mission. Founding a small church was the simplest way to get close to the nascent girls and not draw attention his way. He felt no culpability about promising to follow Catholic traditions and inventing a cult based on fear and on deploying his performances. He had no qualms about dumping Skizzum, no guilt about luring an adolescent girl into his bed.

Between the rounds and the festival, there was still at least an hour where he could practice his instrument. His hands sculpted the sound as his fingers moved up the strings. He concentrated on producing each note until Emmy came in. I had again tried to catch her before she got to the church and followed her through the back door. Harper was already there, so I hid behind the curtain in the choir. Sitting near the altar, Harper called out to his favorite choirgirl who was on her knees, desperately praying, "Emmy, come over with the stool will you'". His request was so out of tune with her feelings she was caught off guard. Cautious of her uncle's surly ways, ready to amend for the tattoo, she ran over with the humble chair. "Do you remember the last time you played the harp sweetie? I know it's been a while, but do you think you could call up that tune?"

Why did she go in there? She wasn't always so religious. What had he done to her? What had I done to her? I couldn't swallow any explanation. The words were like mush in my mouth. They all made me want to vomit.

Emmy sat down on the stool before the carved instrument and placed her head on the left side with part of the weight of the harp on her right shoulder, like her uncle had showed her. In the beginning, she played the chords cautiously, swirling, like the sands of the Mississippi near the start of a whirlpool. Then slowly, she tempted a glissando, where she could imagine herself gliding into the eddy, being swept away, with only the harp strings to hold her back. She quickly strummed the bass row and the outside row in unison as part of the *prise en main*. Harper leaned over and brushed her hair away from her bowed face. He kissed her cheek.

"You know if you gonna keep talkin' with the Angels, you gonna have to mind yoreself. That Bee and her sister will git you in trouble. Her family has lost the Traditions. Her parents can't teach them to her. Don't you know there is even talk she gave a classroom report on Darwin's evolution? You know evolutionism is Satan's workins. He's been battlin' the Hosts of Heaven to impose his law. It's poisonin' the minds of the little children. The Bible ain't jest some theory among others. You can't even trust schools anymore. And those girls go too near that fellow at the gin, too. Some say he is the Devil. You know about his wife, don't you?"

Harper scowled pressing his lips as he spoke, letting his self-assured hubris take hold of him. He frowned as his thoughts ran past him. Sitting down on a chair beside Emmy, he moved in closer and put one hand on her knee. From the choir I heard his tongue clicking and saw him move his hand upwards, as far as he dared, squeezing Emmy's thigh. I couldn't move, or wouldn't. I just stared, hypnotized by what seemed like a film I was watching.

"Sweet Angel, my own Angel, you know the *Patterns* love you and don't want you to git into trouble." Harper spoke as if the *Patterns,* the Redeemer, and the Angels were the same entity and indeed someone he was rather intimate with himself. Unable to calm his ardor, a kind of agitation took a hold of him. He was speaking of trouble. Emmy knew that, even without thinking or having to be told. We all knew. I could tell it without even seeing it in his eyes. Besides, the one thing you couldn't see in their gaze was shame.

"If Skizzum hadn't gotten *mal pris* with some man she could still be an Angel. She won't say who tempted her away from God. She has become the most beautiful girl over these last months and still tried to preach the Gospel the last time I saw her. I just cain't figure out how she could have fallen. I know the evidence is 'gainst her now; she's 'spected to deliver in a month or so. Do you think Jim Taylor is the father? They could get married if he is. and live here. Could we do somethin' to help her?" Emmy questioned Harper with the sincerity of the child she was.

Harper mentioned the *Lonesome Jim Taylor and his ill-fated wife* whenever he could, and in the same sentence when it came to talking about Skizzum's fate. It sounded like the verse of a teen tragedy sixties song; similar to the ones I listened to on the radio. It didn't surprise me to hear Jim mentioned again in the conversation. Sometimes Harper forged words and names from an unknown realm. Once I heard him speak in church of someone, he called *Ginwatchraper*. I used to think he coined this expression, and his accusations like this, to deflect blame from himself, to our neighbor Jim. Now, I'm not so sure he spoke with the self-possession of a criminal. I'm not sure he knew who Jim was either.

"Honeychile, don't worry so much about Skizzum. She'll be alright". Harper groped around like he wanted to pick up Emmy in his arms. Her skin was soft and fine grained, like a baby's. I knew that. Even then I thought it was weird, but I wondered if, after the *Pattern* rounds, her body gave off a light scent of child flesh like it did when we played together? I could see him sniffing the air as if he was trying to smell her. He pulled his chair around behind Emmy's, his knees on each side of her body. He took her hands in his, placing them on the harp. Emmy fumbled after the instrument. I recognized the melody from the song Skizzum sang, "Catahoula Stomp"; only, Emmy sang a private version.

Once I loved a darlin' seaman
Oh, and he thought the world of me,
Until another girl persuaded,
And then he cared no more for me.

I don't want your greenback dollars
Oh, I don't want your watch and chain.
It's all I want is your heart darlin'

These Beans Have Too Much Salt

Oh, Won't you take me home again.

Oh, I have prayed to you my Lord, in vain
That Your precious Blood can clean my stains,
Until each one is in your sea, oh
And no longer held a-gainst me, oh."

The harp's ample twang could be heard outside and mingled with
the splattering of the grease from meat roasting on the campfire and
the exuberant *bel canto* of Emmy's promising voice. She was a
bright star. Somewhere over the treetops and across the lake,
another fire might breathe its secret spark had it not been for
Harper's vigil. The song probably sounded to him like a
sentimental, teenage view of love, mixed with some Gospel
overtones and perhaps a New Orleans funeral tune. He frowned.
The words were not those he remembered. Songs aren't something
you keep in a jar, like aged whiskey. When you tap into a whiskey
jug, the same spirits are almost always stirred. But when you open
up a vessel for a song, the vital spark burns each time differently. I
almost laughed out loud. He didn't comprehend Cajun ways well
enough, I thought.

Emmy's slender fingers climbed once again the long, taut strings
as she started to weave a refrain into her tale. But Harper held her
now tightly against him, so tightly she could no longer reach them
all.

These Beans Have Too Much Salt

"That's it, my pretty Angel, let us ask for God's forgiveness, " Whispered Harper as he gently kissed Emmy's hair. He demanded redemption even as he sinned.

"Honeychile, maybe we could try to save your friend. But you'll have to stay away from boys and older girls outside the clan. I haven't decided what to do about her, since she and Skizzum came up with that tattoo idea. That was a sinful thing to do. We can work on your prayers together."

Emmy nodded her head. At school, she would see all of her classmates, but in the afternoons and weekends, she could stay at the church.

"Bee's Mom doesn't want her to become an Angel. She says her mom has reasons. It's a shame because Bee has a lovely voice and could sing with us at church."

The muscles in Harper's face tensed and he made a smacking sound with his tongue again. He sounded more and more like a rattlesnake, or a possum. Not slowing down to listen to the explanations for my mom's refusal, Harper attempted to steer the conversation, trying to convince Emmy not to meet with any boys on the outside. She was far from thinking about them at the time, but Harper was working on her. I watched his performance without saying a word. Without demonstrating outright guilt feelings, himself, more than anything else, this man with so few scruples

264

seemed somewhat disturbed by the thought Emmy might doubt his virtue (whatever that idea could represent for a snake).

Skizzum wasn't in the clan and she could have met with any man. He always managed to stop any criticism about the time he spent with his Angels. According to the sheriff, he had stopped Harper once for speeding with Skizzum in his car. After writing out the ticket, the sheriff, meaning well, casually asked, "Where are you and the young lady headed in such a hurry in this afternoon heat?" Harper prided himself in quick replies, and Skizzum told me he had a fast one ready for the sheriff. "Sheriff, I have lived in this town for some years now. You surely know me, and you've seen what I've been through. For my sins, I've asked God that none be remembered against me anymore. The Lord answered my prayers and told me to call on him whenever I felt the need...I have summoned him, and he has done well responded. He said it is flat none of your business where we's headed. And when was the last time you was in church? You sure as hell don't come to mine."

That was pretty much the end of the sheriff's questions (at least that day.) Harper's sharp reply probably caused him to reflect upon his religious affairs.

Harper had other things on his mind. He didn't seem to think like the sheriff. He believed he, and his Angels enjoyed some sort of privileged relation with the divinities. He kept an eye open for Mamere who might show up smoking a pipe at any moment.

These Beans Have Too Much Salt

I hurried outside as soon as I heard a door slam. The edge of the woods seemed close around me, and I could smell the heavy perfume of the not so far off magnolia trees. The waxwings had settled in the pyracantha bushes. Nearby in the clearing, the briars grew in an enthusiastic way, forming, for the greatest part, a safe place for the coons to forage for their nighttime meals.

Harper finally released his anger; I could hear him yelling at his wife, who had come to the church door, perhaps worried that he was spending too much time with her cousin's daughter. "Leona, what are you doin' here interrumptin' my lessons? Well, since you're in the door already, git your fat ass over here with somethin' dry to wipe my face on. You know I cain't play if sweat is rollin' down my neck. I'm drippin' wet from playin'. Ain't you got other chores to tend to instead of botherin' me all afternoon? How many times to I have to tell you? You'd think you's lost your wits or somethin'."

Leona had already given birth to four living children at the age of twenty-two. "I'm only twenty-seven now, pregnant again, and already with a passel of young'uns. I gotta do the wash for more than six people. If they keep makin' that whiskey out there, I'm gonna have still another shirt to wash. A shirt to me, but for him, we might as well number them and name the next one *Etcetera,* for all his sweat. Hell, look at him! He is happier than a pig in shit heaven and don't give beans 'bout me." Leona wavered over to the caravan, appearing to be talking to herself.

These Beans Have Too Much Salt

Harper followed her with eyes like slits in a window shade. Did he suspect his wife had been plotting with his cousin-in-law concerning what to do about Skizzum? They couldn't allow her to come to their church any more. Leona, obsequious, was in fact relieved her husband had given her yet another chore to do that sent her away from them all. She knew well enough his forehead would be soon wet again with transpiration. He would then need a new sweatband. These small discomforts would not hinder his fiddle playing in the least. She accepted, however, these constraints from her husband as well as from her sons. That was how things were. She couldn't imagine them being otherwise. "Honest to God," Leona said one day. "My husband is a prophet. I would do anything for him and his church, even if I had to destroy everything that we have built to save his name." She would go on mumbling to herself and thinking of the esteem she figured their marriage allowed her, all the while being jealous of the adolescent girls, but doing nothing to prevent her husband's actions.

Getting Ready for Mardi Gras

Mamere heard Leona and turned toward the church, creasing the line between her eyebrows, seeing both the past and the future. Although the women would often sing with the men, she regarded with a pointed eye Emmy's playing that harp. As far as she was concerned the inclusion of Harper in the Robichaux-Dufrene clan was turning out to be as hazardous as inviting a Badjo. If he didn't prove to be a spy for some other congregation, his inclinations towards the young girls were to say the least without reverence. More than once she had found him in the church behind the altar with a mere child, in search of *qui sait quoi*, pretending to be looking for a Bible. And there he was again, and again, with her granddaughter. If Leona could be accused of neglect, Harper's hands were never idle enough, she told Mérite-Lajoie much later, regretting she had not said anything before the fire.

Mamere was relieved that Papere was gone, and glad enough he took his shaming voice with him. He would not have stood for these changing ways. Then there was the Misbegotten, as she sometimes called the unborn child of Skizzum. None of her grown children had done anything about that (arguing Skizzum was not in the clan). Now, everyone knew and was talking. She figured the child had a father who wasn't likely to claim his paternal rights, even though she suspected everyone knew who he was, too. She sighed and returned to her trailer.

These Beans Have Too Much Salt

Turning the leaves in the water, Esperanza summoned the spirits. "With the wind, *vient les espirits* (comes the spirits). Indeed, it is an ill wind that doesn't bring somebody some good."

"How could it have been otherwise?" Mérite-Lajoie asked. "Too many dead were behind us already. The Mardi Gras festival made my mother nostalgic about the past days in New Iberia with her grandparents before she and her *Defan* Bienvenu were engaged."

The bewitching sound of Emmy's voice, now beside the fire, began to fill the air again. Did Emmy turn her eyes towards the trailer? "She quickly stopped singin' when she saw the shadow that was on the point of coverin' her grandmother's face." Mérite-Lajoie sighed. "Once again, future aspirations were dismissed. Once again Mamere's severe look left us all with the impression that the Mighty Arranger was discontented. Papere had momentarily fooled himself into believin' his vigor was not quite yet extinct. He stirred up some leaves. Thibodaux stopped pinin' for his wife. Harper ignored her. And Emmy, had she known what she was feelin', wouldn't have been less bothered. Mamere shook her headful of hair, and laid down the Tarot."

At crepuscule, a couple of possums had been caught in the live animal trap. I was watching from the woods when Papere's old dog, Caillou, not as old for his race as his master had been for his own, flared the *radbwah (rat de bois* or woodrat or possum) and alerted his mistress to their near-bouts. Mamere brought Papere's old cane out, ready to use as a hook and debunked the animals from their

269

cage, barely hidden by some branches, scraping them into a gunnysack.

"Although these creatures did not make up a favorite culinary dish for much of our family in the past, none of us would make any spite about it now. Some of us even craved for it from time to time. My father had even eaten muskrats at the Segura's table, way back when he met my mother's family in Opelousas. The meat was tough and better fit for pelts and pelages than for human consumption. Both communities were accustomed to hard times and prepared this recipe with the same ritual, in autumn or winter and, since those Hard Days, even in the impure season of summer. Those smelly animals were naturally replaced, even sometimes by name, by the possums here, Up-the-Bayou." Mérite-Lajoie motioned to me for a glass of water. She wiped her wet mouth on a corner of her sheet.

I watched as Mamere put the not so defenseless critters in a crate along with a few more of their congeners, all ignorant of the destiny reserved for them. The *chaoui* they had trapped the night before was another can of worms. Even before they built the fire, the creature, staring at her with sorrowful eyes through its mask, seemed to understand its captivity. Hadn't it tried to sacrifice its foot to get loose of the snag? "*Pauve ti bête*" (Poor little thing). The old woman seemed saddened that the raccoon had suffered for her family. She sighed perhaps in remembrance of an era when her clan would have rejected a man for matrimonial purposes for much less than his family's failure to honor the dressed animal. All the same

270

she had to assent; she must have come to like these wild dishes even if they were for outsiders, a little disgusting.

She began to sing an old song we all know in in the south, adding Cajun flavor.

"Jambon am sweet,
Chicken am good
Possum meat am very, very fine and so,
Mais donne-moi, oh give me,
I really wish you would
The watermelon a-hangin on the vine"

Melon season was a few months away, but I suppose the smell of possum musk, made her think of the song. Dufrene Dufrene, her oldest grandson, now an experienced hunter, lifted the cover and peered through the dusk, admiring his latest prizes. Despite the late hour, and the time needed for preparation, this game was to be part of the Mardi Gras meal. They didn't run the *courir* much in the North and didn't have many chickens. Crawfish would become the main dish during Lent, as it was in our house. With a large wooden hook carved for the purpose, he scooped out one of the furry balls, which was starting to smell like rotten meat. He began to rub its back vigorously as soon as it hit the ground to stop it from playing dead. The animal unrolled, showed its teeth, and tried to scramble off, when a sharp strike of a bat came down upon its head, killing it instantly. A trickle of blood spread out from its fat nose. Dufrene Dufrene suspended it from its hind legs on a branch, assuring that

271

the animal would be emptied of its spirits and would reserve its delicate taste.

I came out of the woods to ask him about Emmy, and to watch how he dressed the possum. He mostly ignored me. He seemed content enough to skin the first animal, but kept angrily looking towards the church, complaining, "why am I dressin' game while Emmy's singin' with Harper?" It ordinarily took two to do the job. One held the creature's hind legs and the other held the front and after making a small incision, pulled its skin down as if it were a stocking, before turning it to the opposite side. "Here I am, as gripped as I feel, gettin' ready to pull with all my might." He rolled his dark eyes, before telling me, "I'll soon be off to Norman Land's Kingsland Talent Agency in Monroe with my fiddle and move out of this swamp. Don't know how they'll do without me. I can skin these critters better than anyone else."

He bragged to Poochoo who approached, allowing his anger and his newly acquired distaste for girls to show through. Like Mamere, he had begun to feel that Harper's Angels were a pernicious innovation if there ever was one, although his prejudice was neither formulated for the same reasons, nor was it aimed at the same person.

"I'm skinnin' these possums like this 'cause you have to hold 'em tight, huh, and cut through all this fur with a razor. Girls ain't natural born trappers and don't do it right. If you cut inside elsewhere, it's all over. *C'est terminé.* If you cut inside the skin there, those beasties in the fur touch the flesh, it's dirty, and it's all over and lost. *Mais tu peux le couper* (But you can cut it) real deep and avoid the pollution, but if you do, you'll lose all that fat there, right under the skin. That would be a downright shame... Now once you git the biggest part of the fur out of the way, you can pass them over a hot flame then scratch off the rest as you do when you gits a chicken or *un cochon*. We's gonna bake 'em in clay that jerks the last hairs out when ya breaks it off. If the animal *est vieux*, you have to parboil it first...Now, as with horses, you can tell their age by looking at its teeth or its paws. These are youngsters. You have to be real thorough when you clean even them. They already has scent glands high on the inside of the forelegs and in the small of the back, kinda like muskrats. You have to cut the hide, so you don't touch the glands. It's gotta be done right. It's a serious thing. *Les filles*, girls, jest don't do it right. Afterward, you cut off the ears and the nose, then the fingers and the toes."

I thought, seeing as to how he had an older sister that could not only hunt and fish, but could also perform surgery on animals, Dufrene Dufrene was stretching his prejudices a bit.

Poochoo was frightened at seeing his uncle strike the creatures. I wondered too how he managed to catch them alive in the first place. They weren't juveniles and had so many teeth and had a wicked look about them. Poochoo may have realized Dufrene Dufrene was griping about Emmy, still playing music with Harper. He was not old enough to have followed his grandfather explanations about why dressing an animal had its importance beyond the hygienic aspects. He would not yet have understood why the ritual of having one's hands full of blood would make them ponder about taking the life of another creature. One generation later, fathers would have forgotten to explain the reasons for these customs to their sons. Soon these would be lost. "What's the use of a senseless ceremonial?" thought Dufrene Dufrene, although deep in his soul, he knew this was why his niece could not dress the animal. She was too innocent to have blood on her hands. Poochoo would go on being afraid unless his father, or someone else, told him the reason for all rites and sacraments, in default of being able to justify killing. His rodomontade didn't fool me. I saw Mérite-Lajoie heading slowly in our direction and slipped off into the woods again.

"And that's about what's goin' to happen to you, my little *Radbwah,* if you don't stop messin' under our feet," playfully threatened Mérite-Lajoie, looking around, perhaps having had a glimpse of me flitting in and out, and surprising Poochoo from behind. The little boy, having acquired an all but instinctive caginess, blissfully jerked away and fell back onto the soft ground. He was old enough to know the Cajuns' tales about muskrats were true, but he wasn't sure about the possums. "*Radbwah*", as Mérite-Lajoie called them, "are familiar with the order of all livin' things and are quite like the Cajuns themselves. Once they're weaned, they're off for the journey of life, carryin' their unique means with them. When the time comes, they find a campsite. They pull up some dried straw and hide out under the leaves of a bush or tree until it's time to go, unless, of course, somethin' bothers them before. Muskrats live in holes. And who knows what is at the bottom of those!" She mimed a possum's movement as she went along with her story.

Totems

Poochoo lay back on the ground where he had fallen. Dense mossy aromas arose from the thick forest humus, reminding Poochoo perhaps of the fumier he was still fresh enough to remember. He turned over, face down in the moss. He reckoned he was like the furry animal: He forgot his birthplace but not the bittersweet fragrance of his infancy. Did he believe Dufrene Dufrene's remark that little boys grew out of the forest's fungus and his penis was the proof? He began to worry that someone might pull his little mushroom if it grew any larger and throw it in the pot to cook with the meat. Off over the green and gray lichens that marbled the fallen trees, close to the trailer, he became aware of his cousin improvising a song. Forgetting his plight, he lifted his head, wiped his tears, and moved his attention towards the sound.

"'Love is a child of the wind so free,' Emmy whined. Mamere watched Poochoo run towards Emmy now sitting on Harper's porch playing a guitar. She hoped she would find some way to keep the Angels from being alone with Harper, even if it meant sendin' little Poochoo over to interrupt. I guess I didn't have eyes to see. Emmy strummed the guitar strings again. But, Papere wouldn't have it." Mérite-Lajoie coughed and shook her head again trying to hold on to words surging forth like a lynch mob on a wave of truth.

"'Voila Sin, coilin round Joy's hands and feet,' the apparition said. 'Now, she's showin' off, pretendin' to be inconsolable in her song, and that reptile has come to feast.' Was he talkin' 'bout me? I

276

thought he was talkin' to me 'bout Emmy, usin' the word joy, and not my English nickname."

"While Bienvenu was still alive, he was often annoyed by what seemed to him to be gleeful insolence that attracted nuisances of all sorts. And child's play was to him just that. Now he whirled around like the song Emmy was singin' and kicked over the pans with a blast of wind. Before he could get to Emmy, Mamere stepped in his path."

"'*Tu ne peux pas l'arrêter comme ça!*' I heard my mother cry out to the air. 'You can't stop him like that! Your wild recklessness still won't do no good. She is singin' another version of a Cajun song; our song, about our lost loved ones, even you...old *Defan*. A funeral song for you, I'm sure of it', hazarded Mamere, 'to praise the one who carries our banner, the one who represents freedom, love, and Heaven most of all. If you breathe a dog's breath of it, you'll lose her.'"

Out front, these words addressed to the revenant, carried the promise of the future, of descendants but also a complaint from the past, mourning a lost love one. "Had he caught somethin' else, somethin'' that stirred his tempest from the grave, well beyond the wakeup call of his widow?" Mérite-Lajoie rolled her eyes. She was conscious that I might not believe in spirits, but she was bent on telling the story like she saw it. "Esperanza was sensitive when it came to other's concerns, especially celestial beins. She was determined not to let my father become conscious of what his

277

whiskey perceived. She could grasp what Harper had been fantasizin' about, but thought she could convince Bienvenu's spirit that Emmy was indeed invokin' the love of God, singin' of the deceased, and not talkin' about elopin' with some stranger. My mother hoped she was wrong about Harper, as we all did. Perhaps she thought, or wished, my father could still help. She realized if she criticized the culprit, Emmy's love for him would grow, as it had with Skizzum, and she didn't want her old *Defan* roamin' around forever. Papere kept walkin' around and knockin' things over, causin' a row between us, now near the fire, tunin' our instruments. It was always the same rundown, even if the trigger diverged."

"'He started it,' declared Dufrene Dufrene, firing up, abusing everyone in general and Thibodaux in particular."

"'No! I didn't! You are the one who stirred up the dirt, knockin' your damn guitar case around like that. It hit the bench. I had to hold on to my glass to keep it from spillin',' scoffed Thibodaux."

"'You did dump it out, and on my foot. You're such a slob. You always spill your drinks. A fuckin' *tafiateur* (drunk).' Dufrene Dufrene insulted Thibodaux. It wasn't the first time he said something about the quantities of alcohol our brother had been drinkin'."

"'Hey don't take it out on him, one of those kids ran through here and stirred up a bunch on leaves, makin' them stick to the *chaoui*

278

roastin' there, too. He probably accidently dumped the guitar case, but I was busy tuning my guitar and I don't know which one did it.' I said, tryin' to calm my brothers down. I knew the things life could throw at a man, and my brother Thibodaux had seen a lot. Not that it stopped him from jumpin' into the fire. He was like our father, always answerin' when someone accused him, respondin' present whenever someone called him a name."

"'Yeah, accuse a kid. Just shut up and get those screws for me will you.'"

Mérite-Lajoie raised her eyes to the heavens. "I thought they'd drive me nuts. I passed the box with the accordion screws to Thibodaux all the same."

"'You bastard, you're ignorin' everythin' I just said.' Dufrene Dufrene, steadied his drink again. He was tunin' his guitar."

"'Be careful not to bring shame on our mother.' I took on a hard, dry tone with my younger brother. Dufrene Dufrene had a short fuse too. He thought a lot of himself; a real bawcock and drinkin' made him pot-valiant. What ticked him off were remarks about his age, or his place in the clan. This was never what he thought it should be, but he could be almost a despot about a small breach of discipline from anyone else."

These Beans Have Too Much Salt

"'And you're in my place. You know I have to sit next to the other fiddle, so I can pick up after him,' Thibodaux came back with more nonsense."

"'You both calm down now,' I told them. 'You'd think you didn't believe in brotherhood or nothin' else! We ain't even goin' to play 'til after dinner. You got time to rest and to change places."

"Thibodaux scowled. He felt repugnance about his own lack of sobriety, but resented anyone sayin' the slightest thing about it, especially me. He took the invitation to take a nap as if it had been a letter with a personal address."

"'Now look.' Thibodaux pointed his finger at Dufrene Dufrene. 'Shouldn't he be the one to be ashamed? He started it. He is such a punk, always thinkin' all this is jest for him.'"

"'Yeah, well, I'm goin' to finish it too, just wait 'til I get ahold of you.' Dufrene Dufrene jumped up, knockin' off the glass for good and breakin it as he stepped on it while he grabbed Thibodaux's shirt. Dufrene Dufrene still acted like a young rooster, gettin' his feathers up if anyone said somethin' that sounded like he was inexperienced or tractable. He didn't take it well either if he was pooled in with his brother's generation, he considered as old-timers since our father had passed on. He preferred to think of himself as belongin' to Emmy's generation, except for the war that was brewin' in Southeast Asia. So far, his number had not come up. Whether he acted the same as a hot-blooded youngster by choice or by succumbin' to an unmanageable drive is another affaire and one, which is not easy to get around, as it seemed there were arguments for each case, and even for a mixture of the two."

Mérite-Lajoie tried to separate her brothers. Every weekend, every holiday, it was the same thing. Those two would get into a fight, and Mérite-Lajoie would try to pull them apart. However, next to the Mardi Gras fire, before dinner, the brothers could feel the growing tension between them. They felt something was about to happen, the way brothers feel it first. It was eating at them from both inside and out. Of late, there was a lot of scandal mongering going on in the town and even inside the clan. You couldn't tell where it came from, but it was there around the campfire, just like the small children playing tag, weaving in and out between the adults. They sat there a minute, maybe two, with their jaws tightly clamped shut, their fists closed, and staring at each other like a snake and a hawk. Dufrene Dufrene finally mumbled another remark, about Emmy not being in her place, now unconsciously trying to provoke Mérite-Lajoie. It was a vague remark and didn't seem to ring a bell until much later, like when you forget where you put something and much later, you find it and remember as having put it there in the first place. Mérite-Lajoie dispelled Dufrene Dufrene's remark even as abruptly. Concentrated on the brewing thunderstorm she didn't see the hurricane sneaking up behind it.

Harper stopped playing and came over near the others, pretending to do his job as the tribal minister.

These Beans Have Too Much Salt

The Mardi Gras festival, (Harper called it *The Patterns)* began early that mornin' and continued to near dawn the next day. Even the night was exceptionally warm for early spring. "Although we couldn't spend much time at the well (the new word for the moonshine reserve), the meal was the most elaborate we'd feasted upon since New Year's Day."

I remembered a dense steam loaded with the fleshy aroma of the *filé* gumbo escaping from the three-legged Dutch oven. "Mamere cut up a small fern rhizome. Mérite-Lajoie smiled an instant almost with delight. "'To give it a little licorice taste', she said, while grinin' at me. She had already mixed in the Tabasco sauce and was keen on addin' yet another mysterious ingredient."

A look of disgust clouded Mérite-Lajoie's face. "Harper, gussied up in his royal attire, said the blessin' with the sign of the cross." She relaxed a second later. "The hardened crockery armors were cracked open before the flickering eyes, delivering the dark meat from its last fervent escort. At one end of the table, Mérite-Lajoie proudly placed on a colored cloth an assembly of boiled eggs of all colors and sizes that would have delighted even today's Easter baskets. The filé, the roasted coons, some *ail des ours* (wild garlic), red beans and rice, a pot of pickled onions, and another, of marinated goat cheese, accompanied this dish. The rose jelly shimmered in the candle light and the skillet of cornbread revealed its delicate hazelnut perfume as soon as Mérite-Lajoie's knife penetrated its golden crust. Mamere brought out her marshmallows, confectioned with cane sugar and egg whites. No matter how colorful, the commercial varieties are a far cry from these treasures to which she added a little bit of whiskey to round out the flavor. These billowy deserts melted in your mouth and left you feeling lighter than a cloud's fleece. I had had some of these treats a time or two before, and now seeing the children grab them, and stick them on whittled green stems before roasting them over the fire made my mouth water from where I was sitting, in the shadows, under a cypress tree.

No one wanted to pay any attention to the pompous display of Harper's wealth. In addition to his crown, he wore several gold necklaces, bracelets and rings on every finger. This time, he was the only one playing masquerade. Although they might have felt uncomfortable, they preferred to pretend they hadn't noticed. He passed a jug of whiskey to Dufrene Dufrene, winking his blackened eye through his mask: "Here, it'll make hair grow on your chest." Dufrene Dufrene swallowed hard. The alcohol burned his throat, but helped him get past the fears about his virility that have a tendency to sprout in a young man's mind. Harper bent over towards Mérite-Lajoie, pointing, "Your shirt is stained." When Mérite-Lajoie looked down at her shirt, then back up, Harper raised his finger, poking her right up under the nose, irritating her once again. This childish game might have provoked a fight with Dufrene Dufrene, but Mérite-Lajoie didn't know what to think of Harper's gestures. Were they a part of some kind of playful innocence? Wasn't he aware of the exasperation he caused? I hated him. I hated the food in his mouth and the plate in front of him. I almost even hated Emmy for not moving away.

These Beans Have Too Much Salt

One by one, Harper shook their foundations, and at the same time, stretched out his net, where they would sooner or later fall. Had he planned it that way or not, he could count on his royal apparel, as well as his mask, to serve as reminders of his character in another way. The very singular style of this disguise was unforgettable, especially given the chosen menu. Under his crown was the large face of a fat gray possum, with a shiny flat, almost pig-like nose, and sporting a wide, pointed-toothy grin and hairy lycanthrope face. He had bought it in New Orleans before coming to Ferriday, before his run in with the runaway girl's father. This was the second time he had worn it. Even though he had to take it off to eat, years later, each of them would recall, as did the girl, its foreboding nature as he said the blessing over the victuals.

Doubts about possums having human souls, or even being possessed by alien spirits, seeped into Mérite-Lajoie's mind as she remembered how she stared at her plate. She stopped teasing her nephew. She then thought of the slave, Aesop, and his fables and how the animals were in fact messengers representing people. "He only presented them as animals to avoid bein' censored. There was nothing religious about them. La Fontaine's tales either. Nah, all that was a coincidence. Why does this idea keep comin' back to me? Why won't it leave me in peace?"

Although ordinarily she enjoyed the dark meat, that evening she turned it over and over with a fork in her plate until finally, when she did put a small bite in her mouth it seemed to expand and swell, filling the insides of her cheeks with an indigestible molten putty. She felt culpable for not enjoying a meal prepared with love and attention, but when no one was watching, she spit it out and gave it to Caillou, who in turn, buried it under the table. No one else did much with his or her possum-favorite either. Had Harper wanted to discourage them from enjoying Mardi Gras by disguising as the Possum King and by creating a new commandment, he could not have been more successful. "Thou shalt not consume a totemic animal" was a first food ban among these Cajuns, who ate just about everything comestible by human beings, up until that day.

Mardi Gras Traditions

"Mamere remembered the last Mardi Gras Day Festival where Papere presided. Mon Vieux rattled on; punctuatin' his tale with a vaguely tubercular cough, 'Laugh at death…sure…but not at those who die needlessly and before their time. What did Jesus, what did Jesus say?'" Mérite-Lajoie, remembered, talking now about her parents.

"His voice became gruff and half smothered. He had become susceptible to any hint you might make of his failin' health. Mamere had tried to sooth him, by choosin' subjects that annoyed him less, smoothin' out the wrinkles before handing him the shirt. The truth is, it was far sweeter to accuse her of his anger than it was to ponder over a too near passin'. Suddenly, Bienvenu seized Esperanza's arm, knockin' her pipe out of her hand, and countered, 'You're the one that dreamt up the match between Thibodaux and that Zingaro girl. You didn't want to wait to find one of our folks. Now he's without a woman. He's drinkin' too much. It ain't fit.'"

"It didn't seem so important to him that Poochoo no longer had a mother although he had written many verses about the separation with his own. That romances might turn sour, whatever the culture, never occurred to him. All the same, he had come to scorn Mamere, practically as much as the Badjos, and the Zingaro (the name my father reserved for Spanish Cajuns, Romani, Gypsies, or Tziganes) who had become part of the family through the years, addressin' both from time to time with more characters than a printer has in his drawer. It wasn't they deserved these invective criticisms. Had he been able to give reasons for these admonishments, these would have come close to expressin' his own regrets. He thought these other people, as well as my mother, were as incapable as he was to adaptin' to livin' Up-the-Bayou, as inadequate as any of them at acceptin' his dependence, and especially because he felt that he had left a part of himself buried in a cemetery miles away from where they should have been."

"At the last meal we had together, my father sat at one end of the table and brought a bowl to his lips attemptin' to absorb the broth without openin' his eyes. He had lost all appetite, but his fondness for us and for his grandchildren, aided by the diluted whiskey, encouraged a better disposition. He managed a growlin' sound for Poochoo's benefit provokin' a wave of admiration and giggles from the other children."

"Mamere untied the homespun *tignon* covering her thick, *sel et poivre* hair. Dressed in a blue skirt and muslin blouse with a flowered shawl for the occasion, she had regained some of her former elegance. Seated at the other end of the table, she distributed the tin plates filled with the all the specialties."

The Mardi Gras meal I watched from my hiding place, where Harper tried to impose himself as master of ceremonies, was much different. Poochoo and the other little boys began to get rambunctious before the meal. One even spit on one of the little girls, calling for Mamere to scold them and putting an end to the

287

meal, except for the digestive. Most of the time the children were well behaved, only giggling when the adults started to drink too much or when they perceived something puzzling, like innuendos or a conversation about sex, or both. Their bellies were full and they meant no ill will, but boys for some unknown reason like teasing girls until they get snitched on for going too far. They moved their chairs around the fire and Mamere filled the whiskey glasses once again. Soon Mérite-Lajoie began to reveal her fable, another *complaint* with no more than foot stomping and a few chords played on the guitar.

"Vanity of vanities, all is vanity! What was, will be, what's done, will be done. There is nothin' new under the sun. Thus said the great King Salomon." Mérite-Lajoie rolled her eyes and moved her gaze from one to the next of the adults and the children, as her father had done, beginning her adventure in the same tradition. Since the passing of Deux Ours, most of the time Mérite-Lajoie kept to herself, like a crawfish barricaded in its tiny fortress, except for church or family events.

"Listen *Petiots* (little ones). There was once a *Badjo*, who thought he'd know it all. He had the finest horses and the best dressed wagon in the region."

"An' a big house", added Mamere.

Mérite-Lajoie continued as uninterrupted, "he reckoned he'd also git the Acadians' know how. So, he went off through the country, prancin' bout all the towns, a smile on his face, but like a scoundrel, rotten to the core. As chance would have it, soon he met an honest Cajun woman. He tried to find out how to read fortunes, how to go bout layin' on hands, and all that could be uncovered bout medicine and such things. He offered her fine clothes and jewelry, and she looked deep into him. She was 'bout to tell his fortune, but he wanted to know how she went bout to know it. He offered her pieces of silver, but she druther continue empty handed than to show how these things got to be done to a Badjo who had no Merit (Lajoie)." Everyone laughed.

"Then he met with a fiddler. He acted like he knows what instrument was the most pleasin'. But the musician was made wary by the man's ignorance and made like he didn't himself know any songs. Then he met a trapper and pretended to be dazzled by his furs. And so on. *But*, far from being interested in what each one could prophesize or trade, he wanted to out fox 'em. He reckoned that way he'd discover all their secrets for jest his pretty manners. But genteel he was yet to be. He didn't even know how to mark his respect."

Mérite-Lajoie punctuated her tale with a cough, as her father had done, and began the sequel, eying them all one after the other, "Listen *Petiots*. One day he met a community of Cajuns who had rested in a campsite near here. He strolled from one family to the next, carrying with him his bag."

"You all knows every family had a lovely girl", added Thibodaux, scratching himself inappropriately as he was accustomed to do, even in public, itching to put in his two cents.

As I listened, I could almost see Dufrene Dufrene's mind leaving Ferriday on the Continental Trailways. He told me how he saw himself in Monroe, where Norman would meet him at the bus station. In his dream, Norman would be his manager and would show him all the tricks. First, he would show him around the town, before his successful audition.

"But the rich man was unable to convince one of the *paperes* (the grandfathers)," Mérite-Lajoie continued, stretching out her finger as if to show where the man was headed.

Harper yawned; disappointed that no one had paid much attention to his attire, keeping his eye on Emmy seated only one seat away. He kept teasing one of his younger sons until the little boy got up and left to find his mother. Harper slid over closer to Emmy. Dufrene Dufrene listened again to see where Mérite-Lajoie was in her saga. He followed along for a while, before drifting off again to the Monroe Musical Paradise. Maybe Mérite-Lajoie's youngest brother decided then he would go to Memphis or even Nashville one day. Skizzum had mentioned him to our brother, T-Pierre, when he ran into her many years later.

"Each valued highly their *petiots*. First the Badjo went to one wagon. The *Vieux* told him how he should purify himself in order to receive grace from the Almighty before he could know fortunes. So, the man changes his shirt and washes his face. Then he goes to the next wagon. There, the family laughed at him and told him to know their fortunes he should memorize their songs. But the next family *rigolait* and told him to sing their songs he'd have to tan their hides. He took out a knife, pretending to be of good faith, but even a youngster made fun of him because to tan their hides (not their skin, but their furs), he had to know their fortunes. The man got so put out at tryin' to please the Vieux, changin' his clothes and his stories, that at the end of the day he decided to round up all the Cajun's and make them work on his farm without him havin' to know anything else 'bout it. He figured one way or another he would have one of those Acadian beauties."

Suddenly Mérite-Lajoie's lips trembled. Her eyes seemed to swell and to take on a woebegone look.

"Y'all know the Cajun sometimes had to work for the Badjo or do sharecroppin', no?" added Mamere.

But Mérite-Lajoie was holding on to her narrative. It was hard to know if hers was the expression of a worn-out soul ready to complain to anyone who would listen, or that part of a storyteller's gift adorned by the reminiscence of personal tragedies. No one paid any attention to Harper who leaned over and pulled a strand of hair away from Emmy's face before kissing her on the cheek. The adults were all drinking and listening to Mérite-Lajoie's tale. The storyteller sustained, "This part of my narrative is not gay. The

291

overseers were cruel and they made all of the Cajuns—young and old alike—cut cane from dawn to dusk. At the end of the day, the rich man had a teacher come in and force them all to repeat lessons from a book. He thought in this way, he could make them all speak English like him, then they could keep no secrets from him."

Mérite-Lajoie shook her head and continued, "After a while he had one of the men brought to his house and he asked him what he thought about such or such he'd been taught. The Acadian said, 'I ain't thought much about it.' The man sent him away. The next day he got another Vieux brought over to the house. The poor *garçon* was all worn out from the lack of music and too much work. The rich man asked him his mind and the Cajun told him, 'it's the same as it always was.'"

Mérite-Lajoie took another draft of diluted whiskey and started up again, her large hands now deploying Mar's Field. "The rich man interrogated every Cajun in the camp. Every single one gave different answer, but none of them changed his ways for the Badjo."

Mamere exclaimed, "Papere is hoistin' up his eyebrows!" She glanced at Emmy, who laughed, enjoying her grandmother's additions even as Harper inched closer.

Mérite-Lajoie shook her head, "The man began to rip and rave and said he would have them all whipped at dawn. But that night came a terrible storm. The barn caught on fire and the horses were goin' mad. One of his best mares had kicked an overseer, scattering his candles all over the fresh straw. The horses were blind with fear and couldn't find their way out. The man howled and swelled up his chest, but the horses jest became more afeared."

"Now y'all know the Cajuns always had a way with horses," started in Papere. But Mérite-Lajoie wasn't ready to let her tale go. Papere nodded his head as if in agreement and squinting his eyes, energetically knocked over a bucket.

Mérite-Lajoie went on as though not entirely ignoring the spirit's presence, "A couple of them heard the noise and saw the flames. They came a runnin' up to the barn door. They told the man to let them in. The rich man was now reduced to tears. His horses were about to be roasted alive."

Papere pressed his hands on the sides of his face, clinched a fist, and shed a tear, prompting the story on. I could almost see him myself, remembering how he had acted the year before. Mérite-Lajoie's voice now trembling, "The man, now without words, could only wave his arms and cry desperately to the Almighty. Les *vieux* entered the burnin' shed. One of them got real close to the terrified mare and whispered somethin' in her ear. The Cajun's voice was gentle and from an old language the rich man had never learned, but the horse recognized it right off. The mare got quiet, and the Cajun took her out safely. Once she was out of harm's way, the other vieux was able to lead the other horses out without any trouble. The rich man cried this time with tears of joy. He thanked the Acadian family and promised to release them from their servitude. But he first wanted to know somethin' else."

Here the children all began to cry out excitedly different versions of the legend most of them had already heard, "he wanted to know how to talk to horses?" "He wanted to uncover their secret language." Emmy was listening to her mother again, but Harper kept vying for her attention; poking her in the ribs, touching her on her shoulder, and putting his hand on her bare knee. For the most part, I listened too, but couldn't help, but turn my eyes toward my friend from time to time. I don't know why I didn't go closer. I don't think they would have chased me off. I must have been somewhat afraid of Harper, or worried that they might all be angry with me for the tattoo that Skizzum had drawn on Emmy's back. I stood, petrified, under the trees, watching a drama I could not prevent as it began to unfold before my eyes.

Mérite-Lajoie continued, now assured the audience was hers until the end, "Mes *petiots*, there is yet misfortune left to tell. The old papere came up and said to the man, 'If you want to have my secrets you have to take my heart out, skin me, and tan my hide (this time his own skin).' Now the Badjo was not a murderin' man even if he was an imbecile and a scallywag. He knows by now he can't know the mind or reason of a Cajun and for that he can't chain him down for long. He was also genuinely grateful to the Cajun clan for savin' his horses. He said, 'Mon petit Vieux, I gotta allow you and your family's got more courage than most. And after all, I always thought your crafts and your hides were the finest. I's decided to give you my best wagons and some horses in exchange for your moonshine and fortunes from time to time.' And to this day his family marks the respect and gives presents to the Cajun to keep their kindred and their traditions alive."

Between the drafts of moonshine, a new legend was being spun. Now it was Dufrene Dufrene's turn. He relinquished his fantasies for a while; glad they had furnished an issue from Harper's whiskey-possum grin. As they turned their regard away from the ugly mask, they didn't see the flush in Emmy's face. Had she been drinking moonshine too?

"Vanity of vanities, all is vanity! What was, will be, what's done, will be done. There is nothin' new under the sun. Thus said the great King Salomon. In the hard days, the Cajun wanted to eat a cicada he found out on a tree, but the insect suddenly spoke up when the Cajun was about to throw him in the skillet: *'Mon vieux*, please, *je t'implore*, I beg you, don't kill me so thoughtlessly. I harmed no rice field and did you neither insult nor injury. By singing my rhythms, I'll teach your family to dance. You'll find no melody as beautiful as mine. Turn to the marsh to find the crawfish. He will better fill your dish and you'll preserve many other creatures he feeds on as well as your levees'. And so, the Cajun let the cicada join in with the other musicians and create new sounds for them all to dance to. Thanks to the cicadae, the Cajun discovered the crawfish that fills our plates from February to November, as well as a new instrument added to their family repertoire."

Thibodaux began, the same, "Vanity of vanities, all is vanity!" The story was clumsy in the making. Thibodaux kept forgetting, recollecting, rebeginning, knitting a half-forgotten tale about the half man, half wolf, the rougarou. When he had finished, his listeners almost collapsed from fatigue rather than fear. Mérite-Lajoie cried out, trying to preserve a more festive atmosphere, "Vite (Quick) Mamere! I've got it by the tail. Grab that skillet and make a roux!" Everyone laughed.

Then she came up with another tale. "Vanity of vanities, all is vanity! This is a story of Boudreaux's funeral. That's the sad part. Well, you all know how Boudreaux always said he wanted to be buried with his brass horn, but no one paid any mind to his request. So, after the funeral in the church, the family took his body off to the cemetery at the edge of town. Each one was havin' trouble fightin' back the tears. Everyone loved Boudreaux for his simple spirit. They lowered his coffin into the hole, but because of the ground water, and his body, bloated from too much whiskey, the casket kept floatin' back up out of the grave."

"His brother, T-Bob, suddenly cried, 'wait, wait, why don't we cremate him.' They all discussed this idea and figured they had to do somethin' soon because the heat would cause the body to corrupt before the water went down and they didn't have enough money to build a mausoleum. So, they built a small fire. All the same, T-Bob was worried he would be haunted by Boudreaux. He then remembered his brother's request. 'He'll forgive us for the fire if he's buried with his horn. I know'd it. Boudreaux always said he wanted to play one last time, but we never gave him the chance.' The priest agreed that God wouldn't mind either. They proceeded to open up the casket and put in the horn, but the Cajun was so swollen up around his chest that they couldn't fit the instrument in beside him. Somebody had the idea of puttin' part of it in his mouth. The priest said the dead ain't inconvenienced by such details. So, they tried pryin' his mouth open."

"As surprisin' as that was for Boudreaux, it was clammed shut. 'Come what may, he wanted to be buried with that horn. We gotta honor at least this part of his wishes even if we have to change the coffin,' declared T-Bob. One of his friends suggested puttin' the horn in the other end. So, they all agreed, as long as he'd take care of it, him bein' a friend and all. The horn was put into place and the lid closed." Dufrene Dufrene started to snicker and Mérite-Lajoie raised her hand to indicate she had not finished.

"They put the casket on the flames and sat down on a bench next to it and started to tune their instruments. Low and behold if the fire didn't begin to take hold. Blue gas flames were comin' out from inside the coffin. All at once, the horn started tootin' and tuned up to play a genuine jazz concert. His brother stopped cryin' and, in spite of the ruckus, explained to the others. 'I forgot to tell you folks somethin' you probably didn't know about my brother; Boudreaux played in the Whiskey Point Brass Band where the musicians were paid in whiskey. The thing is; he never could get much sound out of that horn before now. Before each gig, the other members of his band rightly thwarted him, thinkin' he was about to make fools of them once again and told him he wouldn't get a drop if he didn't shape up. Boudreaux showed up with his horn all the same, and before the concert, drank the entire proceeds before the others could stop him. He passed directly afterwards.' So said T-Bob to explain the observed phenomena."

"Full of whiskey, with the fire all around him and the horn tucked into his fundaments, Boudreaux finally made enough wind to get the notes right. The other pallbearers joined in to make the first funeral with music where the deceased played in the *second line* and, once his body was cut loose, played "When the Saints Come Marchin' In", in time with the others. Before the priest could protest, someone rallied up a coon and laid it out to roast next to the coffin. They all knew Boudreaux would be happy to supply his family and friends with at least three days of campfire, laughter, music, and a *coon's ass* as tender as a baby Jesus *dans une coulotte de velours*." Mérite-Lajoie's family roared. Cajuns like to laugh at themselves as much as they do at death, especially when they've had a few whiskeys.

Foreboding Spirits

Mamere was jolted from her nostalgia when from over the treetops and across the lake came the ripple of a distinct musical whisper, blending the color of a careless maid with a hint of a rose's lost perfume. Mamere made the sign of the cross.

"What does it mean?" asked Emmy.

Harper cried out with a forebodingly joyful excitement, generated from the situation his clan had the talent for diverting. "Hear their spirits", and started to tap on the side of the wooden box that he was sitting on.

Dufrene Dufrene started over to the trailer to get his fiddle or his guitar where he had left it.

But the *Aies* and *Olés* had already transmitted their riddle. Even if the fortune-teller's trade or the musician's art remained mysterious; in a family of tribal proportions, the quest for personal intimacy is about as vain as the Badjo's research. The day a young bride would lose her virginity, with or without three roses, everyone in the clan would know – and even those beyond—in unison.

What I, who was listening again from the diaphanous shadows of the trees, watching out for an obstreperous animal or even Grits, (in case he had been set loose) couldn't figure out is why everything else in the world was mysterious to everyone except what was the most enigmatic to me. "Weren't all young girls inevitably imprudent? Didn't all flowers wilt and fade? Could the voices they picked up on really be coming from spirits?" I thought this insensible substitution of public in place of private might have had its beginnings in the announcement made to Mary. Everyone who mattered knew that I was still a virgin. Emmy was too. She said she had seen a painting about it once. The haloed ones all agreed. All the same, even if my neighbors didn't believe in the sacred order and supernatural beings, at least I knew the truth about this: never in my life had I heard of any spirits, holy or not, who swore when they broke a guitar string. There was another clan somewhere out there. And they weren't the neighbors across the woods.

From where I was standing, I could account for most of the Robichaux-Dufrene-Harpers I knew. There was Mamere, or Esperanza, Mérite-Lajoie's mother, Emmy, her daughter. Then there was Harper, his wife, Leona, who was Mérite-Lajoie's cousin, and their four sons, whose names I don't remember. These boys were scattered all over the place. There was also Thibodaux, Mamere's second son and his son, Poochoo. Lena, his estranged wife, would show up from time to time to see her son, but Thibodaux was always angry with her, so she didn't stay long. Nevertheless, she was there for the evening, sitting with their son.

Next to Poochoo, there was Dufrene Dufrene, Mérite-Lajoie's youngest brother, who everyone called by both his first and last name, so we wouldn't get him mixed up with everyone else. He was born after Mérite-Lajoie's defunct sister, was the first to be born in a hospital, and was the first to have an official birth certificate. For these reasons, he had no chosen name the day he was brought home. Esperanza and Bienvenu, upon seeing his birth certificate, where the only name was Dufrene, had not come up with anything else by the time he was to be baptized. His father called him just "Petiot" and Dufrene Dufrene became official when he started to school. But he did have another name, something like Felix or Gaspard, or some other name that he felt too precious or aristocratic. Dufrene Dufrene wasn't married yet, but he had a girlfriend who would come over weekends from Natchez. She was Suzy's younger sister, Mary. Suzy wasn't in the family and she didn't come for the Mardi Gras festival.

There were other people more loosely connected with the clan, but who came to the party because they lived in the trailer park or in Helena Addition. Thibodaux was fond of one of the younger women there, Glenda I believe her name was. She sat across from her brother, Leroy, and their parents, the Bretchers. Leroy was in our class at school. They were of French dissent, but had been an ordinary protestant family, until they fell in with Harper's cult. Dufrene Dufrene was attracted to Glenda too, sometimes even more than he was to Mary. The fights the brothers had about music probably had more to do with her than the music, falling glasses, or anything else. During the Mardi Gras dinner, they both kept their distances. There were enough people for the conversations to go around, and unless they were called upon to mix, they could ignore much of what each other was doing.

These Beans Have Too Much Salt

The younger boys wrestled for the *petitfer* and other small instruments that needed very little mastering. Poochoo, the youngest able to participate, was satisfied for the moment with lilting the voice of a tall grass flute that he had found. He carefully turned up the edges with his fingers to form a reed and blew over the end without touching it with his mouth. *Weewou. Weewouuu.* He had a little cage containing crickets. These little creatures spontaneously joined in, on occasion, adding their chirps for measure, with their pure toned syllables. An older youth took out a zither his father had brought home from Europe. Leroy, wanted to play his father's fiddle, but he didn't dare make a sound without permission from Harper. He gently uncovered the rosewood instrument and caressed the catgut strings.

The concert might seem to bystanders, had there been any, as being of an untamed sort: drenched in syncopated music within half lay, half spiritual limits, exhaling tobacco and whiskey as well as more puritanical aromas. Even without the Romani triple harp, the ear was constantly tickled by some new sound. This golden maiden, after having made her debuts before dusk, now sought protection from further outrage, and crouched, hidden under an old sheet. Not that her cousins or her brothers were rude, but she had not yet been convinced by their traditional resonances, and was avoiding any possible reproach. An unruly fiddle or an occasional false note was not any worse than the electric outbursts that would twang at the Grand Ole Opera House at other epochs.

These Beans Have Too Much Salt

Thibodaux picked up the tune of one of his brothers. Ever since he was a mere child would squawk at the beginning of each operative passage with his father's accordion. Even with a third of its metal reeds broken, it made enough noise to be heard all the way to Arkansas. It probably seemed to him he didn't have enough hands to play the thing. But then, as now, these onomatopoeias were an exception and, in spite of a sometime unruly beat, new accords were coming alive. "Was born in a river of music…Spent my life swimmin' way from de blues…"

Most of the Dufrenes could play the guitar. Harper could also play the fiddle and about anything with strings. Bienvenu had so often kept his instruments to himself that none of his children really knew how to play them now. Of course, Papere had always insisted this shortcoming was from lack of the necessary discipline needed to play the *biniou,* a French bagpipe, rather than his jealous custody of the wind, which he reminded no one could tie down. All of his children laughingly agreed their revere for their father was enough to keep them from developing any air hot enough to make the honeyed-hive sound.

Mouth organ and tin whistles were distributed to the younger boys who had not already found bones or spoons to tap with. Emmy grabbed the washboard. The other girls started to dance. Mamere, trying to chase away her melancholy, insisted on giving the mandolin a try. She caught a glimpse of her husband again, who, the year before, had caught a hold of Poochoo and, putting his hand and his little arm up to reach the keys, he had put his own hand and arm underneath. He didn't have the heart to play his bagpipe alone one last time, but he held his grandson next to him in hopes that his love of the instrument would somehow continue on after him. Mamere missed him. She forgave his *peccadilloes*. Wrapped up in the night's soft wind, she followed what appeared of him back to the trailer.

Like the wind in the biniou, maybe life was a lot of noisy hot air, I ventured to myself. I listened to the music and thought about how even the insects seemed to participate almost like in the summer months, sometimes velvety like a mandolin, sometimes whining like a dobro, with intervening chirps and trills. Now came a shrill cry. Sometimes a caramel sound made my mouth water before bringing to my mind things I wasn't supposed to think about at my age. What Emmy was doing in the middle of the group continued to puzzle me, but mostly my body warmed to the inexperienced rhythms and commingled tones I thought at first coming from the music alone. Crzzzzzzzzhh Chrzzzzzaahhh. *Tshtke-Ehhhh-ou. Tshtke-Ehhhh-ou. Insequitur clamorque virum volant stridorque rudentum.* The roar of the men and the grating of the strings followed. In a chorus of overlapping beats, the insects of the forest began to buzz, swish, chirp and whoosh in flamboyant melodies under the early spring moon. Sounds came even from beyond the great water. Were those tree frog trumpets I noticed nearby? Had the *ouaouaron* (bullfrogs) learned some kind of flamenco rock or rumba? *Oum-pah, pah, pah, Oum-pah, pah, pah, to-oot, to-oot, to-oot...*

These Beans Have Too Much Salt

For a short while, I was able to forget the relentless mosquitoes already flying about and thought of the buzzing as something that had its beginnings in Louisiana. "God how I want to be able to play that! The music starts here and goes up the Mississippi River, passing Arkansas, buzzing by Vicksburg, Mississippi on to Tennessee. It zings in Memphis, and then spreads out like a base jest like the river does up there, all the way to its source in Lake Itasca. Maybe it goes further, but no one ever talks about singing in Nova Scotia. All the Cajuns are here now, and so are the mosquitoes, most of the time." It was such a night that you could see the Milky Way and count a million stars. I looked out over the lake and into the night sky and thought, "God must be sort of a fence post. If it weren't for that, for the music, we would get lost out there and so would all the noise." Tired, already as droopy as the moss on the trees, as lonely as a squirrel's nest in the summer, it was past midnight, and I was ready to go home. My mother was probably already at the house, back from her evening job, and Papou, in bed since after dinner.

I usually would have been more preoccupied by getting home to read one of *Nancy Drew Mysteries* at this hour than worried about what was going on at that festival. But yet, there was something I saw before me, or almost saw, like when the players come onto stage in a play you have already read and you wait for the next line, or gesture, and it doesn't come. Either the actor forgot it or it happened behind the scene, or perhaps you had read it wrong in the first place and it was yet to come. I kept watching out for it, as if it would finally come, as if anticipating nervously could have stopped a crime in the world's theater. I didn't want it to happen on my watch, and waited for Emmy to go inside Mamere's trailer; at least that is how I remembered this scene, until time caught up with me. I stood up and walked around under the trees. No one was paying attention now. They were laughing and playing music. What could I do? What did I perceive about those things?

The Mardi Gras-Pattern festival continued until the early morning hours. The last song I heard Harper sing was the "St. James Infirmary Dirge[1]". The ending floated out in the dark like a premonition; but then, everyone dies.

« Put a twenty-dollar gold piece on my watch chain
So, the boys will know that I died standin' pat. »

The music began to mellow out, and most of the members had gone home. Harper inquired about the situation of Emmy's mother. Now that she was gone, and Mamere had fallen asleep in her rocking chair, Harper was creeping in on Emmy. Was that what I was worried about? Could I be hoping for something bad to happen to my friend? I saw the predator slide closer, wind his arm around her, and even put his hand under her dress. She pushed his hand away, but didn't run or say anything. Was she under a spell? Were the others too busy playing music or too drunk to notice? I watched him take Emmy by the hand and lead her to the church. She

---

[1] This folk song of unknown origin is sometimes attributed to Joe Primrose. A 1928 recording by Louis Armstrong rendered it famous.

followed. I knew he was up to no good. She knew too. She had to know. What could I do to stop him? If I could have only seen my image in the water, I felt I would have known what to do, but it was too dark and too late for that. I couldn't see inside the church from where I was either. I didn't think he was taking her there for Bible studies. When a grown man takes a little girl somewhere off alone, something bad might come of it. Exactly what, I couldn't say. Nothing had happened to me at the gin.

A mixture of anger, fear, and curiosity drove me closer. I didn't think to call another adult. What would I tell them? Grits was chained up there near the back door. He barred and clashed his teeth at me, but didn't bark. I thought he remembered me teasing him in the truck. Knowing his master so close at hand, he kept quiet, but wouldn't let me come near. Never had I so regretted having been ugly to an animal or to a person.

The empty church was bright with candles. I looked around for something to throw at the dog. I could hear Emmy whimpering or crying softly. If Emmy had a scream, why didn't it yell out? In the complicit penumbra, Harper was surely doing something he shouldn't, and Emmy didn't know how to fight back like I did. One day when we were playing dolls alone together in the Sunday school classroom, he showed up in the doorframe, buck naked with his penis as a flag bearer. He grabbed me, pulling me down to the floor, and yanked my panties down, grabbing my buttocks, reaching for my snatch. Emmy just stood there and stared. I gave him one hard kick with my knee, there where it hurts, and jumped up. Grabbing Emmy's hand, I tore her away, leaving him on the floor with our dolls. We never got them back. We weren't supposed to play in the church or the Sunday school classroom, so we never told anyone and didn't even talk about it between ourselves. I think he expected us to come back for the dolls and he didn't expect us to tattle. We didn't know the difference between playing the police in our families and reporting a real crime. There may have been gestures before that we didn't know how to interpret. A tickle in the ribs, a dress pulled up, a dirty joke, all of these seemed like tiny insignificant ploys, especially when accompanied with laughter and a smile. Some of the boys did things like this at school and they never got into much trouble. We felt then like we had been the ones who had gotten away with something. However, even as we laughed, I never felt very comfortable around Harper and wondered if that was what he was now up to with Emmy.

There next to the church, I wished, and I wished, and I wished, and the wishing didn't stop wishing, didn't stop wishing that I had not encouraged Skizzum or been so mad at Emmy for telling on us about the tattoo, or been so curious about what was going on without me. The wishing would surely bring all the shooting stars out of the sky to crash down on my head. Our lives might have been different if I had told my grandfather about Harper the day he had bothered us, or gone to fetch another adult as I saw him take Emmy by the hand. If I'd only taken my wishes by their tails and tied them to the falling stars.

These Beans Have Too Much Salt

That night, as the preacher forced himself on my docile, yet terrified friend, he whispered these words I could hear through the thin walls of the building, but that she could no longer bear: "And there appeared unto the angels, cloven tongues like as of fire. And it sat upon each of them. They were filled each one with the Holy Spirit. And the spirit was finally reunited, re-welded and rejuvenated by the flame." Emmy gasped and sobbed.

Desperate, I found an old can near a trashcan and threw it at Grits. Even though I don't think it hit him, he found his voice when he saw me throw it. Leona heard and came fast across the yard carrying something. I wish I could say that I stayed, and we'd set Emmy free together, but I scampered away. Meteors are good for wishes, but not for supplying courage. Instead of a hero, I stood helpless at the edge of the woods again, not realizing how diverse reactions people can have to a child's cry for help. Skizzum had warned me of Leona's wrath. I ran home, glad to be safe. From afar, I heard the dog yelp once, its howl gashed and choking.

Cinders

"In the early morning hours when the sun began to rise, a haggard and wilted rose appeared near my mother's trailer porch. Emmy found her seated in her rockin' chair. A blackened stream of liquid tricked down from the corners of her mouth. We would have made fun of my great-grandmother, Mam, for dippin' snuff and not bein' very tidy about it, but Emmy only stared at her, empty eyed."

"'Ashes were flowin' out of her mouth and nose?' That was the only thing she told me that day, repeatin' a line from one of my tales. The church was beginnin' to blaze." Mérite-Lajoie's face contorted with what I thought was an unexplainable disgust.

Esperanza was dreaming as the fire flickered and even as her granddaughter was molested.

"One day I came up on her. She was still half-asleep and sort of confused with her dream: 'I was raped by some yonks. They are a pimp's grin. Should I file a complaint? I'm a witch's gin.' These words spoke of what sounded like a distant crime; one you read about or hear of on the radio or television, except they rhymed like in a song. She often wondered if her parents had loved one another, even for a night, wonderin' if she was the product of a crime or the victim of cruelty of an act or a lie? Untold deeds don't turn their backs. They come dancin' forth in dreams, more alive than in a memory and you'd best take them into account, but not repeat them to just anyone. She repeated her dreams and memories to me, tryin'

310

to make sense of what happened. She insisted on sharin' these clishmaclavers with all of us, along with her dreams, almost as if in absence of her mother she had not learned that some things mothers jest don't tell their daughters."

"'Allons; danse Esperanza.' She whispered, songlike, while rockin' in her chair. Then she told me she had been dreamin' she was at a dance. She was Gypsy on her mother's side, or so Mam said. My grandmother may have been Black, Mexican, or Redbone, but I don't know. This is a secret no one has ever completely uncovered. Mam was my mother's grandmother and one of my father's aunts. My mother only remembered the features of her mother's face, and her *duende* in dreams."

"It seems like history keeps repeatin' itself. Lena left Thibodaux like Carmen had abandoned my grandfather, or so Mam said. She raised my mother, just like my mother raised poor little Poochoo. One thing is for sure; on that side of the family, we were part regular Cajun, but had a part from somewhere else, somewhere that liked to go wanderin'."

"That night, in her rockin' chair, my mother went on dreamin' of a mother who was never there, and of a love that was forbidden before it came into bein' and fathered a child. She mourned like that whenever she drank heavily."

"Even the song that ran through her mind was her mother's. The pastel voice came back over and over, mixin' Andalusia's words and Cajun sounds. *Decir el cante, dire le chant,* whisperin' the song, like a confession or prayer we heard sometimes across the water. All this she told me as if tellin' it would erase the deed, and the distress that followed the crime, from one generation to the next."

"She chanted, 'warm dark skin, toned down sin,' wonderin' why her poems rhymed with skin or sin."

"These thoughts would make her laugh as she slept in her chair, an eye half open, cruisin' on her snuff. Where they came from, we both questioned, thinkin' perhaps from *au-delà,* the heavens. We wondered about our connection with the departed and wondered if they carried the truth."

"My grandmother had an earthy singin' voice, probably inherited from her own mother. My mother looked for her until I came to prison, sometimes just about distinguishin' her *contralto,* she said, slow, soothin', and almost lethal. This tiny thread of substance, combination of singin' hands and kneadin' voice, allowed Mamere to be the daughter of an absent mother. How she held on to these bits and pieces without the body to fit them in, I'll never know. What will Emmy remember about me…my stories, my songs? Bein' an artist or a healer don't make you no better. When our last puff is spent, we'll disappear like the rest. Blown away, ashes in the wind."

These Beans Have Too Much Salt

Mérite-Lajoie then whispered this song her mother had sung for her.

"Madre, cuando yo me muera
Que no me entierren mi cuerpo
Que me quemen en llamas vivas
Y den mis cenizas al viento
Que se la lleve el viento."[2]

"Before she died, my great grandmother, Mam, always had somethin' to say that made my tears tremble. She made my mother run too." Mérite-Lajoie looked away. "When she came to live with us, because she was my father's aunt as well, and she found herself alone in years when no woman should be alone; she said things to my mother she shouldn't have said. But she acted like it was all right to say those things. She was a fortune-teller for some, an artist for others. For my mother, Esperanza, Mam had been both her inspiration and her nightmare's terror.

"This woman didn't despise her granddaughter, but she had deeply regretted her son's love, which was like a wanderin' southern wind

---

[2]*Traditional Flamenco song,* translated by the author.
 Mother, when I die
Don't bury my body,
Burn me in hot flames
Give my ashes to the wind
And let it carry me away.

or tropical storm. Instead of him, she made her granddaughter pay for his insouciance."

"Many people wove in and out of our lives with their trips to the South. They found protection among the Cajuns in those days, and with security, celebration and exchange of musical and other traditions. But sometimes, I'm sorry to say; these reunions were not filled with joy. My mother was the fruit of an undesired relationship between my grandfather, Mam's son, and my mother's mother."

"Now that I'm much older and a grandmother, at least in name, I think of myself as a troll—a big, pale crone, scaly and wrinkled from too much sun and lack of sleep. It gives me character here. Mam aged quickly too. But my grandmother, at probably the age of fifty, was still a legend. She was remembered as a sort of *femme fatale*. This talk pricked my mother's nerves when my father was clumsy enough to stare at a woman that perhaps looked like her mother at those rare moments when the clans would find themselves in the same town. My mother could never remember what Mam had said against him. The night of the fire, my mother's response flowed back into her throat and crashed against her chest before it could become words, wakin' her with a start. Perhaps it was a far-off church's flames that ignited her dreams, or the music across the lake; her memories fused with the present events."

"She told me later that mornin', shaking her head, 'I came into this world like a torpedo. Plungin' through life, my eyes, wide open, and often lost tryin' to follow my loves far and wide. My hands have been the best part of me. Now they are gnarled and withered, more like a *boscoyo* (cypress knee) or a branch than a tool. I was once as tall and strong as a man too, made of solid muscle. My head is now like a cork on the water, floatin' around unanchored. Parkinson's disease the doctor called it. I guess if you live long enough, you always end up like this, or worse. Feet danglin' off a pier, waitin' to be nibbled down to stubs, your ears are the first to go. I didn't hear anything at all until Emmy showed up early at my door.'"

A Rude Awakening

"My mother told me how the sunlight shinin' through the trees had showed the willowy body of my daughter through her translucent cotton dress standin' in front of her. She reflected as she described the scene, wipin' her nose and mouth with her handkerchief, relatin' to me sometime after the fact, her conversation that mornin' with Emmy, all the while tremblin' with fear, not of anticipation, or of disease, but of learnin' the unharnessed truth. 'You're like a forest sprig that's lost betwixt the trees. What on earth do you want now at this hour? Couldn't you sleep late this once?'"

"'My tooth told me about my sister in the back on my throat, said Emmy.'"

"'God Almighty, now I've got one with a talkin' tooth,' thought my mother, all the while wonderin' where she came up with such an idea."

"'He touched her in my mouth.' Emmy was shaking so her teeth chattered. 'I didn't want him to, but he kept goin' at it hard. He said it was for the Almighty. He said that is how the Angels were sisters and the spirits united.'"

"Mamere tried to suppress the feelin' that she knew what Emmy was talkin' about. She questioned Emmy about who touched her, and if it was God."

"But Emmy just repeated nonsense. She said her tooth told her it was her sister who had been touched by the flame from the Antichrist and not the spirits. She said she had not seen him, but he burned the church."

"'My mother tried to get Emmy to say who the Antichrist was. She asked if he was the one Harper is always talking about, the man by the gin, Jim Taylor. She thought Jim had hurt Emmy and asked as much. My mother brought up Jim Taylor because of the hearsay. She didn't want to think what was formulatin' in her mouth."

"But Emmy only stared out beyond the last star of the mornin', askin' if they would help her. 'Can you ask the stars? She questioned. 'Is the Antichrist coming?'"

"My mother told her she didn't think so, but said he should be punished if he hurt her."

"But Emmy said she was okay. 'He didn't hurt me', she said, but added, as if it was someone's concern, that Grits was dead."

"My mother wondered if Emmy had a fever. In spite of her religious convictions, she decided she wasn't makin' much sense. Mamere decided to call me. She couldn't allow her mind to grasp what her imagination already held in a tight fist."

"'But according to my mother, Emmy pleaded with her not to call me. I could make nothing of that, and still cain't. Do you? She said I couldn't stop him and that only Heaven could help her now."

"Mamere led Emmy to her room and told her lie down on her bed in the trailer and rest. Her hair was tangled, and her dress was a mess, covered with filth and smut!"

"There had been some signs, my mother said. First, there was that one solitary Waxwing in the old pecan tree, when flocks usually fly in groups, twirlin' and pivotin' in unison and restin' in food trees. Then, there was the Banshee cry three nights in a row. Durin' the festival, after that terrible thunderstorm, there was the most important omen of all. A flash of millions of lightnin' bugs across the sky lit up for an instant the banner applaudin' over the trailers. The weather was much too warm for early March. She kept talkin' about omens and bad luck." Mérite-Lajoie drifted off in her thoughts.

These signs may have gone unnoticed by the clan, and yet even a grandmother with a talent for reading them may have a hard time seeing what is obvious. *Usus est magister optimus.* Practice is the best teacher. So, they say. And Esperanza apparently didn't want to discover the truth. Was it the blindness to the past that made her go unseeing as to the conspicuous? Anything as blatant as a preacher flirting with a child should be self-evident to any parent, with or without experience. What was she so reluctant to believe? Had her religious conversion veiled her conscious, stamped out her reasoning, closed her mind? Had she stepped into her grandmother's shoes, keeping an eye on but not protecting, watching without recognizing, forbidding without intervening, counting on her unique presence to foil off any danger? Had she so often interfered in her daughter's life that she would run off, refusing to see the danger as it rose into position and prepared to strike her granddaughter? What sort of hiss or prattle stopped her in her tracks when she went to intercede this time?

If you ever find a rattlesnake on your path you will ordinarily immediately know it's there without ever being told so and without it even biting. Whether you see it or not, whether you know from instinct or lessons learned in school or at home, whether you fight or fly, or mostly just freeze; you make sure that you and yours are no longer a person of interest for the creature at hand, or underfoot, for very long. They may be wise in experience, but grandmothers are like everyone else: unable to recognize the poison flowing inside their own veins. Paralyzed by a single drop of unedited memory, you can't act when the danger shows its ugly fangs a second time around, or a third time or a fourth. In fact, no matter how many times the same danger comes, it just gets worse. If the undiluted poison is still there, you might as well roll up your pants-leg and shake your ankle in front of it when the snake comes around. Because it won't be biting anyone else. Such is the true and veritable nature of luck.

"Emmy sat on the bed rockin' herself and repeatin' in a stream the verses of the *Rose of Sharon*, accordin' to my mother."

These Beans Have Too Much Salt

"'Like a peach tree among the trees of the forest is my beloved among the young men. I delight to sit in his shade, and his fruit is sweet to my taste. Let him lead me to the banquet hall, and let his banner over me be love. Like a peach tree among the trees of the forest is my beloved among young …' Tears fell down her cheeks and she rocked herself, tryin' to close off the confusion and the shame."

"Mamere bathed her and put her to bed. She then came across the Lake Road to find me."

"As I listened, I looked at the ground. I couldn't imagine Jim Taylor botherin' Emmy. I didn't have any idea how she could have even crossed his path these past weeks, much less, alone on Mardi Gras day while we were all together. I looked across the Lake Road and saw the smoke. My mother had not mentioned the fire. Emmy's situation would have to wait."

"By the time I arrived, the fire department was there, puttin' out what was left of the fire. The Sheriff was drivin' up. He had his deputy block the area off after assurin' no one was inside." In fact, almost all of Helena Addition had come over.

"'*Comment ça plume?* How is everyone doin'.' The sheriff didn't actually speak Cajun, but he often used a few expressions to make people comfortable. He figured it was a way of askin' how everyone was, collectively speakin', but didn't realize his question was usually reserved for everyday relaxed conversation and not for catastrophes.”

“Thibodaux had done a head count and spoke up sayin’ everybody was all right; the fire was stopped in time.”

“‘It’s the old chapel. We just use it as a storage room now.’ Harper was the first one to respond.”

“‘Uh, huh. Well, how do you suppose the fire started?’” Lookin’ around at everyone, the sheriff took out a small notebook from his shirt pocket and a pencil from behind his ear. Thinkin’ ‘bout it now, I think he had suspicions as soon as Harper stepped up.”

“‘Honestly, Sheriff, we don’t know. I figure it was a couple of kids playin’ with fire. Last night was the Patterns, a religious festival of course.” He had all the answers of course.

It was easy for Harper to lie. So many times, he was the orchestra’s director leading the musicians in his own direction, a smooth-talker, a swindler playing out his deck now before the sheriff, if not his deputy. By that time, practically all of Helena Addition was hanging around.

“A fireman came over and I overheard him whisperin’ in the sheriff’s ear, ‘Deputy Slaughter here tells me that it looks like there were some candles around the oratory. The flame probably caught on somethin', a box maybe, and started the fire. We are going to have to wait until the heat drops before we can get in there.'"

The sheriff looked worried, puzzled even. He wrote something down in his notebook. Just outside the back door, he found Grits, still chained-up, its skull cracked open with a heavy object. He asked, "Who would kill a chained-up hound? And why?"

At this point in my conversation with Mérite-Lajoie, my mind started drifting back to the scene where I had left Grits. Guilt swarmed in and stung me on my back like red wasps or yellow jackets do when you pass too close to their nest. The first one burrows its sting under your skin before you ever see it coming. The others pursue you with their harpoons while you try to run away from the awful scene of remembrance. I recalled the sheriff's words and could have told Mérite-Lajoie that day what I had seen, but I was worried, and worried she would sense that something was wrong. I remembered thinking I might be telling on Emmy if I sought out her mother with the truth. My sense of loyalty was bothered and distressed. I didn't think I'd killed the hound with the old, empty can. I thought I remembered him barking before I ran off. I began to wonder if guilt could distort your memory such that you didn't remember your act being yours. I thought about what Mérite-Lajoie had said about the condemned not admitting their crimes, and her wondering if you could feel guilty for a crime before you even knew you would commit it.

Mérite-Lajoie continued, "when the temperature dropped, he went inside the charred building with Deputy Slaughter and took some pictures. Another deputy stood outside the door to prevent anyone from enterin'.'"

He came out, more or less whispering something I partially overheard again. Adults pay such little attention to children as they unfold secrets in public. I listened attentively and have since put back together almost everything I heard that day. Slaughter said, "The back of the building's completely charred. But around the oratory! That beats me. I've never seen anything like it. That's sure enough a turd there, and it ain't been made by no dog. And it looks like semen there too. It looks like there were two fires. Maybe it's some kind of wacky rite. I never heard of these Cajun's doin' any voodoo. The Creole's maybe prax it. That old lady wears rattles on her arm, but even so. This is weird. I think that you are gonna have to do some questionin', Sheriff. Somebody's got to know somethin'. It ain't no kid that did this. The fire was started intentionally. Looks like they tried to burn that shit. Maybe they wanted to get rid of evidence. But it make neither rhyme nor reason. Why do it in the first place if you are just gonna have to git rid of it? Apparently, they didn't put enough toilet paper to hide it, or whatever that is anyway." The fireman pointed to something inside the building, but in the back, there wasn't much left to see.

"I'll get my man in here. We'll clean this up. Keep this down, will you? I want to get to the bottom of this without stirrin' these folks up. It takes all kinds, I swear. People never cease to amaze me!"

These Beans Have Too Much Salt

The sheriff was a professional man, but everyone has his limits. His turned around segregation.

I hadn't put two and two together yet. I hadn't seen Emmy, and I never imagined what I heard (or thought I heard, but didn't want to hear), was as tenebrous as it turned out to be. Yet, I noticed something about the sheriff. In addition to his exclamation of disgust, there was something shaken about him.

The church fire was a notorious enough event to be all over the local papers, but still nothing was said about Emmy. The causes were said to be unknown, and the embarrassing elements left out of the first reports. However, every time anyone would leave the neighborhood to do some shopping, rumors were overheard. Mérite-Lajoie told me her clients practically stopped coming and even Dufrene Dufrene was insulted when he called about his appointment for an audition in Monroe. Something wasn't right in the trailer park. The fire had not purged the crime any more than it had purified the scene.

Holy Thursday

A few weeks later, the sheriff drove up to Mérite-Lajoie's house. He questioned her about her past illegal postal activities, about her operating without a medical license, about the moonshine, about the fire, and about Emmy.

"'About my postal activities and medical ones, I'm certain you have records; about the still, you can ask anyone, but about my girl, I'll tell you what happened the day of the fire. I woke up to learn about it when my mother came over to tell me that somethin' wasn't right about my daughter who was then in her trailer. Later that day, I took Emmy to the hospital here in Concordia Parish. They drove her in an ambulance over to the mental hospital in Pineville.' She will have to go back there from time to time, I suppose. We didn't know exactly what had happened. The doctors never told us, if they even knew. 'Mamere woke up to find her tremblin' and talkin' such nonsense on the porch of her trailer.' I told the sheriff. 'She was dressed, but soiled and in such a state that we couldn't make anything out of it. She talked about what some call the Antichrist. You know around here; a lot of people believe the Antichrist is a person. She said she wasn't hurt and kept talkin' about her sister. She doesn't have a sister; you know that, of course. She just didn't make any sense. I was afraid she had been raped, but the doctor said she had not been deflowered. I don't know to this day if I believe him. Maybe even worse things happened.'"

These Beans Have Too Much Salt

"I told the sheriff, 'My Mama thought she was talkin' about Jim Taylor, on account of the gossip. Around the town there were rumors about how he had *ruined* her. But I just don't see how they could have been in contact; otherwise, I would have set after him. Sheriff, how 'bout you tell me what I need to know? Has my daughter been the victim of a crime? Do you think she started that fire? Was the fire enough to shake her up like that?'"

"The sheriff had tried to reassure me, askin' me to retain my composure enough to explain the circumstances of my absence. 'Mrs. Robichaux,' he said, 'I think you'd better sit down. We are still tryin' to put things together. We have listened to several witnesses. One says that Mr. Harper enquired about your whereabouts that Tuesday night. At that time, Emmy was still playin' music with her uncles. Apparently, you were no longer chaperonin' your daughter. So where were you around three AM that night? You are not a suspect in the arson, so you don't have to worry about what you reveal. That is, unless you are the one who started the fire? I'm lookin' for witnesses. Can you give me any information you might think relevant? As for Emmy, what we don't know is if she was in the church when the fire started. Her clothes and hands were smudged. We don't know if she started it or if she saw someone. We don't know if she ran into someone outside who frightened her. We know she was there around that time. We have a specialist in Pineville who will be questionin' her, but we need your permission.'"

These Beans Have Too Much Salt

Mérite-Lajoie again cursed herself for leaving the festival without her daughter. She had been a witness to the whispers concerning Skizzum. She knew we had spent some time near the old gin.

"'Sheriff, I'm 'shamed to say I went home around one AM,' I said. 'My mother was there, or very close by. She'd have stayed on her porch as long as they played. Emmy sleeps over at her trailer when there are special church events. All the kids stay out late when it isn't cold. Very late. Of course, I can tell you 'bout the noises and tell you 'bout a few things that happened with the congregation of late. My daughter came home from the Leblanc's before the fire with a nasty lookin', ballpoint tattoo on her back that week.' Forgive me, Bee; I don't want to upset you with these memories, you probably don't remember, you bein' a child at the time. You were so much a part of our lives in those years. So, then I told the sheriff, 'I took her to see our pastor, Dr. Harper, for advice. Emmy sings in the choir you know. She had been saved, you know, sanctified after confessin' to her sins. You know, I never had much faith in those services, but Emmy seemed fine after that and busy with the church. 'The Leblanc children are another matter,' I told him. 'I don't know what is goin' on in that family. I hear that the oldest girl is pregnant and about to give birth. She is only 'bout fifteen or sixteen, I believe. And Bee, she's a friend of Emmy's. She's always traipsin' about all by herself. The kids go to that old gin up the road. That's part of why there's tales bout Jim Taylor. He is the watchman there and apparently has never courted any girls since his wife died.'"

"The sheriff took some notes before respondin'. 'Yeah, we've called Jim in for questionin'. He seemed embarrassed about you and Skizzum.' The sheriff admitted sayin' they didn't have anythin' they could pin on Taylor. No police record. He had a clean slate. He even had an alibi for Tuesday night. Even though they hadn't checked it out yet, not one of the members of our families said they noticed him loafin' around the church or the trailer park. The sheriff said that if he was with Emmy, either they left in his car, or she went to him once everyone else was in bed. He asked me to keep quiet about all that. I was about to get nervous about Jim, so he told me he had asked for a search warrant just to be sure. Then he said, 'But, uh, I wanted to ask you this. Have you ever noticed in the trailer park, uh, well, this is embarrassin' for me even to ask you. Have you ever noticed that someone would do his business outside on the ground? You know, just lyin' around like that, or smeared. Disgustin'. I'm sorry to ask you this, but there was somethin' unnatural about what we found in the church, or too natural, dependin' on your perspective. Someone left his or her excrements, like on display, as an offerin' or somethin'.'"

"I began to feel queasy. The body knows before the mind apprehends. My head pounded at the temples. I gnawed on my fingernails. Something in me cracked apart. I felt *je pourrais rejeter* (I could throw up). The more the sheriff talked, the more a face came into my sight. I was certain Harper was to blame. I was certain because of disgustin' things he had told Deux Ours years before, things that singled him out as a man, and because Emmy's dress had been soiled. She wouldn't have done that to herself. Now I

328

knew what my mother hadn't said. Suddenly visions about gettin' my gun and finishin' what I thought I should've never prevented clouded my eyes. I wondered if intervenin' on destiny was what had caused our downfall. The military, the hand press, the printed catalog, the projects that were lost, torn apart, sequestered, overturned and abandoned... No matter how hard I tried, everything I did, turned into a fiasco, for one reason or another. They came flashin' back to me all at once in a fury. I still don't know why."

"When the sheriff left, I stumbled, reelin' around, then hurried to my office to get my gun. On my way back to the door, the room didn't look the same. It was like another room, another desk, another season. My desk was the same desk, as were my shelves, my chair, my cupboard with the remedies and other paraphernalia I'd put there. It was the same, yet it was different. It was if suddenly I took them into account, not as a chair or as desk, but as if there was something behind the chair or desk, as if the chair or desk was just there to hide the verity. All I could think of was that horrible kiss, and Deux Ours foldin' and fallin' on his knees on the steps of the church. But I didn't see the truth, and I couldn't have heard the voice of Deux Ours if he had tried to stop me. I was always ruminatin' on what I should've done before doin' the wrong thing, too late. For once, I resolved to carry out my plan to its end. I should've thought that the truth behind it all, was that I was about to give up everything else."

These Beans Have Too Much Salt

Mérite-Lajoie told me how she screamed at the absent figure lighting up her internal gaze as she loaded her gun: "How could you do this to us? I allowed you in my house, took you into my family, found you a wife, and you destroy my child to thank me!" She told me how in an instant she was worried about the *on dits à venir* (the anonymous gossip to come, the kind from which her family had so much suffered). In her frenzy, all of the files she had so tediously prepared and stored with each animal's record, all of the written analyses of her apothecary, all of her lists, notes, sharpened pencils and unachieved projects, wrapped in uncertainty and disappointment, all of these toppled down on her desk like a stack of Tarot cards on Destiny's table. Again, it was her own she had sealed. Life Up-the-Bayou would never be the same again for her, nor for any of us.

"As I neared the church, I could smell the suffocatin' odor of death. No one had buried the dog. Flies were emergin' from the swollen, putrid belly, the maggots flowin' out like a thick warm rice puddin'. The dried brains spillin' over the cracked skull had been partially eaten by rats. I put my hand over my mouth and nose. I doubted if I could ever eat Louisiana rice again. The whole world seemed at once torn inside out, rockin' me, sweepin' me away in a torrent."

"Further over in the trailer park where the smell had not yet aired, Minister Harper-Swaily slapped his hand on his thigh, visibly enjoying tellin' about how he had chopped off his son's dog's tail that very mornin'. Without a pause to let someone else intervene, he pursued tellin' of other dogs, of cats and kittens, of ant-beds and gasoline, leadin' from one horrific element to another, in a chronicle about how he came to this part of Central Louisiana. The other men of the clan listened, hypnotized by the prestidigitator puttin' on another show. They were cleanin' up the site before church service, according to my brother Thibodaux."

"As I approached, I heard part of what he was jokin' bout. Harper said he had only a vague memory of a Cajun's wagon, or even several wagons, one day in front of his family's car near Wallace, where some of them attended to blackjack gumbo farmland. His paternal honked the horn, yellin' he was after some skins while a poor-looking coonass (like they called us then) jumped out holdin' a gun, threatenin' to shoot his Vieux. He said that he didn't try to figure out what the man with the angry beard wanted from his old man, nor what his father might do or had planned to do. His father had told him to be ready and to expect trouble."

"He leaped from the family car while it was still rollin', tryin' to go round the caravan. 'That day I grew up fast,' said Harper. 'Havin' seen the gun before the man, I ran into the cane field. From there I heard the gunshots, people screamin' 'bout a dead baby, and angry Cajun curses. I couldn't find my father in town, so I went into the woods and stayed in a shack there 'til I met up with some Irish Gypsies and followed them 'til I was old enough to go to work on a boat. Then I came up river to Natchez. I never saw my old man again. To this day, I don't recall him saying why he was so hard on those particular coonasses, or why he burned their wagon even after he paid himself back for his losses. But the day I was born and

331

under what name are all behind me now. I lost track of how long I'd been in those woods. And since I was shot, I have yet to find my name in the obituary columns and don't even recall readin' about my old man.' Harper punctuated his story with a sharp almost incessant viperous laugh, hissin' between syllables.'"

"His statements brought out surprised laughter from the men. Although a few secretly thought Harper was probably lyin' about his amnesia, about him havin' a father with a car; and some didn't appreciate his jokin' around about fellow Cajuns, there was somethin' strange about this newly declared deficiency. Not only was his memory selective about his past, he also seemed to believe it was possible to read his name as if not in the final breathin' moment, but still attached to his body, and his eyes, still able to read his name in an obituary column. Editorial mistakes do happen and sometimes bodies are poorly identified. And I have heard that sometimes in a flood, bodies will even change tombs. Yet Harper seemed to think his written civil status or an article in his honor, were the only things that could vouch for his undoin'. And he presumed he would still be around, as with in his other forgeries, to read about it in the local paper."

"Nevertheless, the laughter of his audience all at once irritated Harper. He had neither a sense of humor nor tenderness for his fellowmen. He didn't have a clue what empathy was. He interpreted the Cajuns' laughter as a sign of disbelief. He knew better than to respond, and held their misgivins to be evidence of their ignorance about scientific phenomenon. He looked as though he suddenly felt oppressed by this circle of men that he thought he knew well. We all probably looked alike to him with our ragged kakis and worn faces. My brothers were leanin' on one another, putting tobacco wads under their lips, yet listenin' to each word."

"I showed up, feelin' the angry blood flowin' through my veins and allowed Harper to remain with his deceptions for a few instants; hopin', perhaps willin', that these reflections would subdue his attention. Maybe at that point I still hoped that Destiny would intervene to stop me. For some of the members of my family, this laughter wasn't that of mockery, but of pleasure. Perhaps the divine opportunity to be born with knowledge concernin' such things was given to some people, and not to others, and this, along with the rest, could be taken away. Such a favor was to be enjoyed while it lasted. They stood there. They all nodded their heads, saying *Inoc you* to Harper, even though they all knew, and probably preferred, *Que Dieu soit avec vous*, or even the ordinary English sanctification, *Bless you*."

"In that second, hearin' this blessin', foreign, an obstacle to my own faith and a picture of everythin' I'd come to despise, I realized what I wanted, what I wished, what I cared for and desired above all, was in all finality, in an entirely different realm from what would be. Part of me liquefied and flowed back to the years of my youth, in much the same way as when I ran back through my office after getting' my gun. Lookin' back, the truth I saw was more of the same grime, disgracin' the face of our flag even in my childhood. When had I changed? When had the words of others become encumberin' restraints? No family should have to undergo the barefaced indignities that my family has suffered. I couldn't put up with this any longer."

"It didn't seem like any of the members our community made the connection between what Harper was sayin' about his father and about the day when the man and his son practically drove our caravan into a ravine, honkin' his horn and openin' up the throttle of his Ford. We commemorated the day, when my little sister, my mother's last child, suffocated in the commotion of birth in a wayward bullet riddled wagon, strangled upon delivery by the umbilical cord, and buried in the Evergreen Cemetery. But we never talked about the causes. It was not the first time we had been harassed."

Remembrance

Almost none of them envied the man who near well ended their lives. Almost none of them remembered the boy who jumped from the assailant's car. Almost none of them recalled the explosion of the bullet from the gun of the slowed-down-speeding driver. Although many of them had begrudged giving up their muskrat pelages, Mérite-Lajoie, nine or ten at the time, riding eagle that day, high on one of the wagons, who warned her father to get the gun, as soon as she saw the dust of the car in the distance, remembered more.

"Even then, I didn't yet take into account what I was seein'. My mother's agony shattered even my efforts to speak in the followin' days."

As her tide ebbed, retreating over the same rocks she had passed over for a generation, she overturned one, recollecting the speed with which the man and his son appeared. She saw them now, as if they were before her.

"Their heads bobbed about like corks on a red river of road dust. One, suddenly detached from its anchor, rolled over to the edge and disappeared in a cornfield or a canebrake. The flash and the loud zing of one of the bullets impacted a tin pan hangin' on the side of the wagon. It ricocheted inside a second pan, and it finished its path, jinglin' down the curve of a steel trap. It was still hot from the blast when I picked it up off the ground."

335

"Maybe I did wish that day my father had been the owner of such a car and that my mother had been in greater comfort to deliver. It might have changed the course of my life as well."

The truth is, in those days; the Dufrenes were often obliged to leave camp quickly, threatened by one sheriff, or another. Mérite-Lajoie was old enough to notice. Whenever her family had a bit too many muskrats, (Hudson Seals, the Badjo called them in his hoarse voice) her family would soon have to move on. Sometimes they would even leave in the middle of the night packing up their pestilential skins under the silver moon. It is truthful to say the pelages smelled the high heaven. The landlords who once paid the Cajuns for trapping the animal suspected of tunneling through the levees and eating their crops, now wanted part of the money the Cajuns obtained for selling their furs. This envy left families sometimes liable for aggressions from locals, who deemed, besides the damage, the skins smelled up their communities. The Cajun was becoming an outlaw, in place of the suspected (but innocent) animal.

"In an instant, Harper reminded me of all this, givin' me another reason to hate him. I suddenly knew that neither pardon nor vengeance was possible."

From the carcass of the burnt church, I watched the group grow closer. Looking through the front sight of my grandfather's twenty-two propped up on what was left of a windowsill, I was thinking about doing away with the preacher too. My head was pounding. I vaguely got the feeling my hate only hurt myself. What good was it to ponder on Harper's or whatever-his-name-was, acts? He couldn't care less. I could wish him all the world's bad luck, lay down cards, wager on an accident. Swaily prevailed, even though he deserved retribution for all he had done. Mérite-Lajoie was there with her gun, but I no longer believed she would shoot. An eye for an eye, a tooth for a tooth. Give him back what he had given. Wouldn't that be justice? Mérite-Lajoie didn't hate Swaily for his own good; she hated him because he was loathsome. I savored it a moment; my own hate tasted like the muskrat smelled, and even worse; I couldn't spit it out. Harper-Swaily had committed a heinous crime. I was waiting to get a clear shot. The crowd was standing between Harper and the church.

"I then remembered, I then brought to fruition the idea; I then grasped what motivated Aimee Semple McPherson. Her radio message was clear-cut; that car had had temptation for a pilot, sin as the engine and the Devil as a passenger." Mérite-Lajoie's eyes sparkled again. "I thought I would speed this last one back to Hell."

The realization that this man, could also kill an infant, her own sister, or corrupt her daughter as easily as he could chop off a dog's tail, for the sole purpose of public acknowledgement, lifted her head out of the ethereal mist.

"Seein' me in the crowd, Swaily started up again tossin' out Bible verses with obscenities as if they were Mardi gras beads of different colors. His voice was more often than not, soothin' as cream. Suddenly a distant, but increasingly closer, roll of yelps carried it over the crowd. He slivered and shuffled, barked, like someone tryin' to shake off an entanglement of briars around his feet, when they were growin' down his throat."

"'And I, I saw three foul..uh..ghosts... like, like fro-ogs, comin' from the, the mouth of the drag...on... from the mouth of the beast, and from the mouth of the, the false...the false prophet.' Harper coughed as if a frog was stuck in his throat, then continued his tirade, 'These are demonic wraiths, preformin' signs, who go abroad to the kings of the whole world, to, to, to...assemble them for battle on the great day of God Almighty.'"

"Tyrone Swaily (Harper's true name) started to move backward towards his trailer, beginnin' to yell and grit his teeth. The other men stared at me in confusion. 'Why had Mérite-Lajoie brought a gun amongst them,' I heard them ask. Harper let loose a fountain of insults in my direction, pointin' his finger, callin' me, as well as the local priest, the mayor, and anyone else present; whores and sodomites."

His words came out so unexpectedly and without any foreseeable cause that the men gazed from one to the other, without moving, holding on to their rakes and shovels, waiting for what would happen. It was not like Harper to lose his composure if that was what was happening. His list evolved like all other diatribes, but grasping, under God's name, humanity's cesspool. It was in fact only seemingly aimed at the new arrival in the crowd, because the timing of her appearance. Other than its inappropriate use, its lack of pronominal guidance could have recommended the catalog to anyone; but with this indiscriminate shortcoming, the outburst was more like an index made by a preadolescent wanting to impress his friends of a newly acquired proficiency.

Just about as abruptly, Tyrone seized one of the rakes and began a sort of confession, all while defending himself from the approach of the men following him now towards his trailer; expecting them to suddenly attack, not knowing from where the call to lynch would come. Because he assuredly felt there would be the signal, like the one made by a bird, which all at once flies away without knowing neither where the enemy is, nor which of his flock first flew. But Harper could not fly, and neither could this small mob. Like the stuff of the effigy, eventually interwoven into the surrounding weft, he could only face the crowd and absorb what he had always absorbed: the fear, the surprise, the exasperation of others. This time he was without words, he sucked these in with his breath, swelling with new straw, more confident than the scarecrow he ultimately was. Then he started anew.

Prepared to fit into the enemy's slot, he declared he wasn't fit to live, but he didn't want to be put to death by any man. He avowed he was the author of many crimes, some involving juveniles. Making a new spectacle of himself as the other men approached. He conceded profaning a statue of the Virgin Mary and using a cross to ravish himself. He blurted out he was the Devil's plaything, on ears that asked to hear nothing of the sort. Yet the men stood there, captive, hesitating, fascinated by Harper's harangue, waiting for the signal.

"'Oh, parents! I dearly, tenderly implore you to teach your children to honor God! Make good examples of yourself and be righteous in his light! Ask to be forgiven for wanderin' out of God's will. Lawlessness is already at work.' I couldn't believe he was sayin' all this, but he jest kept on and on. 'Chas-tise those that stumble so they will not fall into the trap I've fallen in to. The lawless one will be revealed. Lord Jesus will destroy him. Satan uses mysteries. He uses every kind of wicked deception for those who refuse to be saved.'"

Out poured the Bible verses with tears of counterfeit remorse dosed out with detailed images of rape and defecation. Point after point, technicality after technicality, sequence after sequence. As a radio journalist describing a sporting event or procession, Harper had found his public again. They dangled on his lips while he whined out his shame, winced his humiliation and whipped in his regrets all wrapped in effusive laughter and religious enlightenment. They could not refuse to listen; it was impossible not to listen as the naked reality of Harper's rage poured down upon their ears. The bewildered spectators clenched to every word. They soaked up his purple voice, then coarse, now velour, pleasant yet paradoxical. The men had become speechless, horrified, petrified, disgusted, and yet thoroughly fascinated by the performance of this all at once appalling and smooth-talking barghest. While the blue vein on his right temple throbbed, and his neck grew crimson, Harper's eyes flickered with fluorescent disdain while a slight smirk of satisfaction slowly spread over his cunningly pursed lips. A metallic twinkle with black steel redirected its aim and dug right into Mérite-Lajoie's pupils.

"'I am the workings of Mephistopheles,' he said. 'I defiled innocent, pure children! I could do more, much more…. Emmy, oh sweet Emmy, what you offered to me was beyond charnel delight,' hissed Swaily, miming his grip on her neck or body, all while watchin' me move through the crowd."

"He wasn't talkin' about enjoyin' some sort of wacky kinks. He was talkin' about rapin' my daughter!"

"'Let me reveal to you the unadulterated ecstasy of pulchritude,' he bellowed. 'I have looked deep into the body and suffered much, but let me announce to you that I have found the fountainhead. Just as Jesus will Rapture all true believers out of this world, this child was offered to me to serve as my tribulation. Jesus will defeat the Antichrist wherever he may be, vanquish evil and then establish a new kingdom.'"

With unleashed enthusiasm and newly aroused passion, Swaily exulted, unfolding the details of his orgasmic struggle with Satan. Instead of shame, there was a kind of foul jubilation, obscene festivity and blackened joy suggested by his agitation and laughter as he told of his despicable barbarity and of the thrill he gathered from the testimony of terror and dishonor of an eleven-year-old girl.

"'There was the chapel, the candlelight, the sweet perfume of her delicate, silk flesh, her lips, pale pink moisture, her velvet tongue, the voice, a mysterious caress, the lily white…the absolute purity of her skin, the exquisite aroma of her pearly girl substance, the source of the soul…her breath, ambrosia, floating about her face, her neck; it is a gift for God. I was tempted to take it,' he said, 'to inhale its flame or to choke it out. Such beauty is not made for mankind. I wanted to honor her, make her a gift, but she led me with her innocence to my debauch. As I poised over her with carnal delectation, pourin' out my sacred libations, God told me to befoul her with my excrements. No one should be equal to his son. No, only Jesus should Rapture the true believers.'" Mérite-Lajoie had tears in her eyes as she spoke, but the anger seemed now somewhat appeased.

"I had not come to the trailer park to heed to the details of Harper's delusional religious bestiality (no animal would willingly take part in such filth)."

I hadn't come there for this either. But Harper's final tirade was an accusing finger pointed at Mérite-Lajoie, conjuring her into a hero's action. These exchanges took only one or two minutes, maybe three. I hadn't expected Harper to confess. I had no need for his explanations, but I was unaware of Mérite-Lajoie's plan.

These Beans Have Too Much Salt

"Who would avenge my husband and my child if not myself?"

Emmy's mother had appointed herself judge and jury and was no longer taking requests from the defense. She emptied her shotgun there where she certainly had not, five years before, in the same ubiety, the precise whereabouts, as aforesaid. "I fired knowin', havin' always known, that the *sirop et les biscuits cassent pas égale*." Syrup and biscuits never come out even. The world was not a fair place. These differences would never end for her. "But I still thought that I could save my daughter, and perhaps even the rest of the clan." Was there any way to light a muddy sky?

The blast sent me reeling out what was left of the church's door and on the path to the woods. It wasn't as if the seeds of doubt tossed upon the ground had ever taken root. Heresy, as well as Gospel, may flourish on fertile soil. The clan woke up to a bloom of unexplained insults, finding themselves unwilling humus for Harper's confession. This plot was no Garden of Eden where the men would be witnesses to the reunion of Terrestrial friendships. From penitents, they had become oglers. Without seeing, they involuntarily saw. Without inhaling, they strangled on Hell's effluviums. Without thinking, impure thoughts found their way into their minds through underground paths.

If there was such a place of total damnation, and Mérite-Lajoie actually wished for the nether world; she wanted to go there herself; to become one of Swaily's eternal tormenters; to make sure he was poked, probed, raped, frightened and disgraced. She would be executioner to this criminal, this madman, this *bourreau d'enfant*.

The Dufrenes (not Mérite-Lajoie, but her brothers) would not leave her to necromancy's pandemonium. Had she afflicted injury upon a dead man, she would forever be condemned to wrangle with his shadow. When they saw their sister raise the ax, her eyes glittering, they brought Mérite-Lajoie to the ground, struggling, wailing, half-blind with the insanity of sheer unrequited wrath. No one could kill a dead man. Would his grave be displaced, overturned, and forgotten; his conscious could no longer endure earthly vengeance. Violate his corpse would only cause suffering to his family and condemn Mérite-Lajoie's soul as surely as the delusional Confederate had doomed his own. No, it was better to save her from that.

Noticing the ruckus a few minutes before, Leona looked out the window and turned back to Suzy and the Tupperware woman, unloading a box of plastic containers, not interrupting her chatter, all while listening to an Evangelist choir sing on the radio.

She continued to address her visitors. "Now, I have some more spicy news for you! You know, the little goat's gone. He didn't make it through the night. Esperanza said T-Leblanc died just hours after his birth and would be buried next week in Evergreen. But there ain't gonna be no service. Not for a creature made from sin. That's for sure…That damned little bitch Skizzum never liked me anyway, she's a whore you know…T-Leblanc wasn't even his, and she knew I knew that…Yeah, it's true. I mean the baby didn't even have Harper's eyes. Thank God my boys all have Harper's eyes! Someone even said he was sprouted by one of those boys from the quarters. And I am still so mad I want our baby crib back from Old Leblanc or Gautier, whatever-his-name-is, before he croaks. Can you imagine? He just drove up one day, looked in the shed, threw the bed in his truck and rode off yellin' it was in honor of service to the church! If I'd been a man, I would have grabbed that wooden leg of his and used it to beat the tar out of him. They's just gotten might uppity here lately."

She turned back to peer outside, having heard the detonation, or having noticed the following unfiltered silence, and saw her husband lying on the ground in front of the same shed. The arena of death's theater was unreal. There was no visitor; not even one bent down beside the body. Harper was alone, stripped of his priorities, crumpled and face down in a pool of blood, his head blown open, like what could have been the flipside of *Bohemian Rhapsody*.[3] Leona thought of his dog, Grits.

Many footprints covered the muddy ground, but the other men had vacated the premises. Leona couldn't find the words to say to her friend, who had come over to help set up the Home Party that afternoon with the Tupperware woman, who was also one of my mother's cousins from Natchez. Her voice abandoned her. So did her rumor. Had she felt triumphant one minute, on the wave of some

---

[3] Author: Freddy Mercury, with Queen

These Beans Have Too Much Salt

obscure knowledge of her neighbor's plight, handing the spoon, with the gossip, over to her guest, and the next, completely undone? Suzy looked up from the stove and said, stirring the pot of steaming red beans, "These beans have too much salt."

Vendredi Saint (Holy Friday)

Mérite-Lajoie was tired, shifted in her bed, but plowed on. "The rain began again in the early hours of Friday morning. After several hours, the Mississippi had left its bed. In another day, or two, the trailer park, the neighborhood called Chocolate Quarters (at least by the Whites), and a large part of Helena Addition, as well as the rest of Ferriday, would wake up in the morning to find it under their own, with at least a foot of water in our homes. For now, it only rained, and the little community was soaked, but mostly in fear. There wasn't gonna be any Hallelujah Chorus. There wasn't gonna be any crawfish boil." In the morning, the Robichauxs, the Leblancs, the other Helena Addition families; together with what was left of the Dufrene-Harper-Swailys, would realize, would remember, would come to grips with, who they were, even without the Bible verses. The cemetery was still there to remind us all, with or without their names in the obituary column. But for now, it just rained.

Mérite-Lajoie was restless. Again, she could not find sleep. She recalled rising from her makeshift bed in her treehouse hunting camp, the morning after the shooting, moving towards the window, looking out at the rain, and returning to lie down. "If I slept at all, it was only for a few minutes. I kept askin' myself an absurd question, 'what was buried in Justice's grave?' I compiled a lot of evidence in my mind, details of Swaily's crimes. In half-dreams, I relived the scene of my own. There was no particular point upon which I could hang my attention; Swaily's movements, all in a

347

frenzy, swirled around mine. I saw the reptilian eyes aimed in my direction, gliding over my body, stopping at my gun. I watched the stiff, angular face suddenly recoiling, peeled-back lips spitting out horrendous verses, words strung together, dropping bluntly on my shoulders, heavy like wet dung. I tried to dodge it, to brush it off, to scrape it away, but it kept falling around me, like greenish yellow repugnance, stickin' to my shirt."

"That mornin', light ripped open my eyes, and I awoke with a start, still unrested. My heart wasn't at ease. My body ached with distress and loneliness. I thought I had been just, that I had served a noble cause. I began to realize I had lied to myself, adoptin' a posture of honor to serve the purpose of my hatred. Why hadn't we expelled Swaily from our community before all this? Had I nourished this loathin' until it had become an irascible passion? I wasn't a belligerent drunk like my father. When had this rage overcome me? When had I started lyin' to myself?" Full of despair, she had thought of putting an end to her life. What would become of her daughter? She covered her face with her hands and sobbed until she felt the brine tasting mucus fill her mouth and throat. She cried until her eyelids were swollen before falling back into a deep sleep.

"That Friday, and for the next few days, Mamere worried, about the flood, but mostly worried about Emmy. I hadn't come home. The telephone was out of order. She didn't know where I had gone after the shootin'. The trailers needed to be moved, fast. Bienvenu stood there accusingly, his eyes glassy, as water covered his bare feet. Before the flood, he had disappeared too. Now, he was everywhere.

These Beans Have Too Much Salt

A constant reminder of all the lost traditions, the change of language, the unsupervised children, the undoin' of the family, he stood there again, more cantankerous than ever, the water ripplin' higher and higher. Mamere gathered the instruments (the ones that weren't lost in the fire), the family photos, her clothes and sheets, and dumped them all in the car. The consequences of Ty Swaily's acts were not so simply disposed of as the man himself. Perhaps it could have been otherwise, but with a storm, not even a levee could always hold back a flood."

Mamere had followed a dazed Emmy to the hospital in Pineville. She held her granddaughter's limp hand and tried desperately to get her interested in conversation. She chatted on, spoke about the weather, the full waiting room, her new shoes, seemingly forgetting Emmy's trauma. She talked about the lovely church service the preceding Sunday, before the fire. She consigned the fire to oblivion, failing to remember her daughter had gone missing, obliterating the raw fear, the ruined dress, the sullied skin, and the talking tooth. Had she caught the news of Harper's death, of her daughter's hesitations, of the flood, she would have probably spoken as if these events had not occurred either.

"The new church will be better. Maybe Harper should put the altar on the other side of the buildin'. Then we could have a real choir, with an organ. These days there are many revival services. Some Evangelists are goin' on the road with big tents like in the thirties. Would you like to go on the road with Harper? I understood he was talkin' about buyin' a bus. About going on TV. Can you imagine?

These Beans Have Too Much Salt

He already has preached on the radio, and he has a camper of course."

Emmy's eyes were still empty when the doctor called her. Had she taken note of her grandmother's chatter? Had her grandmother even heard herself suggest she continue to ride with that man? Sometimes a shock will put a person's thinking out of commission and send them reeling back to before the shock, always already before.

It was hard to know if Esperenza's reaction was a dismissal of the facts. Was she was trying desperately to find and to look on the bright side of events in spite of massive evidence to the contrary? Was she so much under the effect of indoctrination she could not admit this man had harmed her grandchild? Was she somehow trying to preserve some personal advantage? Perhaps simply, she wanted to move backward to a time before Emmy had been violated, a time before when she was a small child. Shouldn't she have taken her home with her? She should have. Shouldn't she have supervised her meetings with him? She should have. Shouldn't she have watched over the other girls? She should have.

The *should haves*, but *didn'ts* went back so far that she couldn't see. They formed a veil over the present. She continued to jabber helplessly to her senseless child, and now to a concerned doctor. She wondered why her parents gave her the name of Esperanza. She had so little hope. There wasn't anything she could do to change the past or her name. There it was, as thick as mud. If she had only thought of her granddaughter, her daughter, and even her husband…The list of the *if onlys* were added to the account of the should haves. They added up to be more than anyone would want to pay. It is a pity, tenses like these can ruin a conscientious life.

"Time will tell all, but only time will not put food on the table. God will provide, but someone has to pay the bills; someone has to wash the shirts," said Leona to the neighbors, desperately trying to hold on to something material, as palpable as food or clothing, but letting slip by what one could perceive in a nonce.

She didn't know what to do. She wandered about with anxious, lusterless eyes, wringing her hands, hanging the shirts out in the rain, washing off the burnt church's steps, forgetting to make breakfast for her youngest son, but not for the dead maggot filled dog. Like a haggard Lady Macbeth who counted out stains as she hung out the shirts, mumbling under her breath: "Out damned spot! Out I say! Salt…stains…beans, oh, let me get that can! Yet who would have thought the old dog had so much blood in him. Or so many brains."

These Beans Have Too Much Salt

Samedi (Saturday)

This *baille a couru sa course*. This stretch has run out. At six o'clock in the morning, Deputy Slaughter and two other officers from the Sheriff's Department made their way through the rising water and kicked down gossip's door. With their pistols in their hands, they assured Jim Taylor was unarmed, and no one else was on the premises. They presented him with a search warrant. It wasn't long before they found Emmy's skirt, the same dirty torn outfit I had pleaded for and worn, still under his bathroom sink. Eyeing each other as if they already knew the truth, they rounded up material for starting a fire, his wife's old clothes, as well as the pornographic magazines I had seen, an ax, and started shaking Jim down.

"You git your hairy Black ass over here…boy and you sit down in this chair." The deputy didn't wait for Jim to come. He grabbed his arms, pulled him over, forced him to sit down, and put the handcuffs on the passive yet astounded man.

"You tell me what kind of a man shits on a little girl? Is that the kind of crap that gets you off? What are you doin' with all them girl's clothes?"

Deputy Slaughter shook one of Connie Taylor's dresses in front of Jim's face.

He was a caustic, brutal man, well over six feet tall and weighing more than two hundred pounds. He was a *righter* of perceived wrongs, suspected later by many of belonging to the Silver Dollar group of the Ku Klux Klan, and the following year, of orchestrating an arson in town, which left one Black man dead. If he had a criminal, he was going to make sure the fellow had his due. Without batting an eye, Slaughter was heard to say, "if you wanna live, don't yell."

"We'll get him out of jail later boys", he said to one of his colleagues, with a hand still on Jim's neck. "We'll take him to the woods with a rope and make sure he won't get away. Look at all this junk. What on earth do you need these tools for, and these machine parts? Do you use them in you project with little girls, too? And look at this photo album will y'all. There are a bunch of girls in 'em all right."

When Jim opened his mouth to say something, perhaps in his defense, Deputy Slaughter yelled, "You don't open your fat mouth 'til I say so." Jim didn't.

When Sheriff Ray-Byrd Riley heard about the arrest, he was not happy with Slaughter's report. He felt he knew people well and could not figure a perverse Jim Taylor. Still, the evidence was there, and rumor had led the way. He would have to question him, himself. Now, he had to get over to the courthouse fast enough.

These Beans Have Too Much Salt

In the car one of the deputies, a man who had dated my mother briefly, sat next to Jim and reported later that Jim said nothing for most of the trip. He was thunderstruck. Slaughter had slapped him several times in the face and hit him in the stomach. Trembling lips and sweat rolling down his face gave him the look of a condemned man on his last walk down death row. Later he confided that he had cried. He asked himself many questions. Had he been alone so long he had become blind to his actions, had rolled over in his heart, and had lost his mind? Was he guilty of abusing a child? The memory of a pubescent girl's long eyelashes and charming *Noli me tangere* jabbed him in the heart. Panic blew out his reasoning as he tried to remember what happened after he had found me in the gin, perhaps confusing my name with Emmy's. Gossip squeezed out its hard lemon drop of litigation.

"It's my fault. I'm guilty! I'm bad luck to all girls crossin' my path. Did you see her body? Oh Lord!"

He put his head in his hands and began sobbing. His voice was broken as he choked on his emotion, reliving the accident with his wife some years before. At the courthouse he tried to jump out a first-floor window, and then cuffed to the desk, he confessed to possessing the pornographic magazines. Besides a solitary pleasure, with a quivering mouth he tearfully proclaimed he hadn't had relations with anyone since his wife had been killed. The photo album could have been anyone else's family album, but it was Connie's, and the young girls: her mother and her aunts. He didn't have to explain about the tools. Sheriff Riley knew sometimes men confessed to crimes they didn't commit, but he never understood exactly why. Thought of as a compassionate man, he put his hand on Jim's arm and looked into his eyes. He gazed at him a minute and squeezed his arm then went out of the room. He had been on duty when a truck had hit the Taylor's car.

When he came back, Jim recovered enough of his composure to tell of his encounter with me during the storm earlier in the month. He explained how he frequently had to oust the neighborhood children out of the gin. He said he had no other contact with either of us. The sheriff led him to the jail cell and told him to remain there while he checked out his alibis. For some of the deputies, it was hard to let a Black suspect go, especially if he was accused of molesting a child. They wanted to harass him if they couldn't beat his brains out. They had already threatened him with their plans, showing him photos of other lynchings, called him a pussy for crying, and carried out any other misery they could come up with on short notice. "You know what a pussy is, don't you? Not the kind yore used to lookin' at, unless you look in the mirror, but I guess a wimp like you spends a lot of time in front of his." Deputy Slaughter looked around the room, miming what he thought to be an ape's walk and cries. He used florid, racist language, the kind I often heard at St. Gabriel's. The other deputies laughed and nodded their heads in agreement, gawking at their prisoner through the bars. Jim tried not to pay any attention. He sniffed his nose and blew it on a handkerchief. Another officer remained at the office to insure order among the men. He told them to cool off and find something else to do. Sheriff

These Beans Have Too Much Salt

Riley had received an anonymous call about a shooting several days before at the trailer park and he left immediately.

He drove his car through the water and left one of his deputies to restrict the area where the body had been located. He also called one of the men he knew from Hiram's area, the Black neighborhood, before driving over to our house and to speak with my grandfather. Leblanc was my absent father's name, but many people mistakenly kept calling Papou by my mother's married name. He felt the forgery kept him out of other people's conversations and protected his daughter's reputation as well. Thus, he never corrected anyone guilty of this misstep. In spite of this local obscurity, the sheriff was one to take care in using the correct name, especially for a man who had lost his leg on the field of honor.

"Mr. Gautier, you got a minute? Step out here will you. Now I don't want to bother you, but I need to talk to your girls. There has been some trouble over at the trailer park. I think you found out about the church burnin'? Now your girls are not suspects, but I need to check out a few things."

Papou didn't much like being bothered or even named by a law enforcer. It was hard enough to put up with it when our mother dated one, and he didn't want any coming to our home for any other reason either. He figured as long as he steered clear of their likes, our family would be okay. It wasn't good going against an officer of the law, however; he thought for a second Leona Harper had called him in for taking the crib. He yelled:

"Bee, come out here on the porch." Turning to the sheriff. "Skizzum is still in the hospital after a bad time deliverin'."

He gave a harsh look at me as I passed through the door.
"Do you know why Sheriff Riley has come to our doorstep?"

I looked down on my bare feet.

"Is it 'bout the church?" Full of my mystery stories, I was excited to participate in a police inquest, but what I thought I knew was weighing heavily on my heart.

"What do you think?"

"I don't know who did it, Sheriff. I wouldn't get near there anyway without Emmy, cause of Grits. He's one mean dog. But I don't know why anyone would burn it. It was a pretty church and all. The whole congregation likes to sing and pray. People come from everywhere to hear the choir. Even Skizzum used to sing in it."

"What about Skizzum? Was she mad at Dr. Harper?"

"Well Sheriff, you'll have to ask her. But, I don't reckon I know. She don't sing there no more. The Robichauxs might be mad at

Skizzum for drawin' a dirty tattoo on Emmy's back. She didn't mean no harm. We were just foolin' around."

"What about you, Bee. I hear you have been playin' in the gin again?"

I could feel my face redden. "Did he tell you that? I was just tryin' to get out of the rain. But…I didn't break anythin'. Besides…"

I thought about Jim sayin' he would write a report and remembered I didn't give him my real name.

"Besides what Bee?"
The sheriff took my arm.
"I didn't give him my real name. How did you know I was there?"

"Bee, I want you to think real hard about Jim Taylor's attitude when he found you in the gin. Did he punish you, or hurt you in any way?"

I was suddenly frightened. He was talking about something serious that had happened, not to me, not to Skizzum. He was talking about Emmy, but he didn't have the story right.

"Hon. Tell me exactly what happened when he found you in the gin."

I retraced my anecdote about the gin, moving away from Harper. I told about drinking the Coke and joking around with Jim, leaving out the part about finding the dirty magazines and about changing clothes.

After a while, the sheriff asked Papou if he could see me alone. We both sat out on the porch with a glass of lemonade. I began fidgeting and twisting my hair around a nervous finger.

"Bee, do you remember what you wore that day?"

Although the problem with clothes was by then far from my mind, I remembered all at once having worn Emmy's skirt, about tearing it in the briars, about soiling it in the gin and about changing it for one of Connie Taylor's skirts. I wondered if wearing a dead woman's skirt was bad luck, or if tearing and abandoning Emmy's skirt was cause for some trouble for my friend. These small make-believe moments kept me from dwelling on the greater problems I was facing. I wondered what would happen to me if anyone learned I had been at the trailer park with Papou's gun. I didn't want to get into trouble, not even for stealing, when Emmy knew all along. While I concentrated on childlike issues, I blurted out a great deal of what the perceptive Sheriff Riley was hoping to discover.

"Sheriff, I'm sorry for wearin' other people's clothes. I just like to, I guess. But I don't mean nothin' by it, now I see what come of it. Emmy and I wear the same size, and Harper buys her a lot of pretty stuff. Mrs. Robichaux doesn't like it much. Harper buys her more than he ever did for Skizzum. But…But I'm not an Angel so I don't get any of his presents and Skizzum won't let me wear hers. It was white with a petticoat. I pretended I was a princess in it. And when I tore it, and got it dirty, I was a vagabond! I was goin' to give it back before, but she ran off to church when Skizzum drew the naked woman tattoo on her back. I couldn't give it back like that. Jim gave me one of his wife's skirts so I wouldn't have to go home in a mess. She was small as I am, and for a grown woman! My Mama, who works at the funeral home, told us. But…But I didn't mind. I mean, wearin' Jim's wife's skirt even after the accident. It wasn't as fancy, but I thought I looked better in it. Was that okay? Besides, I never liked Harper anyway. He was a bad man. Is Emmy still mad at me? Is she okay?"

Sheriff Riley had not asked any questions about Emmy, or about Harper. I had no real comprehension of the relation between my friend and the bogus pastor. Although I was aware he had made her cry, I thought perhaps he might have exposed his nude body, made some inappropriate gestures, and perhaps forced her to the ground, or even touched her in inappropriate places, before Leona had showed up. Yet somewhere in my subconscious reality were the pictures I had seen at Jim's, and I put everything together. The events of that day bobbed up together as if a turtle or gar had all at once swallowed the hook and freed the line. All strung and stuck together on the same string of logic, the officer had only to snatch it quickly out of the surge: my meeting with Jim, the abandoned skirt, the change of clothes, the privilege of the Angels, who was who and why was why. These were not idle speculations, but neon signs flashing the way. The sheriff never suspected me. I had learned much from playing poker with Skizzum.

Now that the Sheriff had the clues, he had to gather up the rest of evidence. More than a church fire, he was investigating a full-blown inferno.

He rode again over to the trailer park where the men began attaching their trailers or evacuating to their houseboats. Some of the trailers were already flooded. The men looked at the Sheriff as he rounded them up. They had no desire to speak.

"Now I know you folks know somethin'. A man just doesn't get shot at home practically in front of his wife without someone knowin' somethin'. She told me there was a group of men a few minutes before he got shot. Don't you think I have some names? He was y'alls pastor and a respected man here. Are you just gonna let him be shot and not do anything about it? And that church didn't burn up by itself. Do you think this crime is linked with the fire? What about that dog? He wouldn't have let a stranger near there, especially at night. That animal wasn't put down by just anyone. He knew his aggressor. He wasn't shot. He was taken by surprise and bludgeoned to death."

"I need some answers here. I'm gonna to start linin' you boys up and one after another you're gonna bring your guns to the deputy here. We are gonna git to the bottom of this. Now someone has said Mr. Harper had another name. If any of you have information on that one, I need to know it. Harper was perhaps a little bit too flamboyant for a preacher. His wife is gonna choose his headstone, but he's goin' into the obituary column and in any other articles, journalistic or not, with his real name, as soon as I find it out. It will help my investigation."

Harper's body had been left out all day and all night in the rain for at least two or three days before the anonymous call. At present, it floated around, under a trailer. The sheriff tried to hire some of the men from the neighborhood across the woods to fish him out, but they all refused. They could have used the money, but on account of the fact it was a White man's body, or perhaps because it was floating around with the sewage, they wouldn't touch it.

Finally, the next day, a Louisiana wildlife agent came over with a trawling motor and scuba-diving outfit. He swam up under the trailer, hooked the body and trawled it out. I was told it was already a terrible sight: swollen, eyes bulging, brains spilling out the back of the head. Catfish or turtles had already started nibbling on these, unraveling them in the overflowed cesspool. "Thibodaux told me that the wildlife agent, who had a hard time reelin' in all the chitlins, left immediately afterward for a decontamination treatment. The sheriff figured, speakin' out-loud to himself: 'Ain't that somethin'. God put the pieces back together as they should be.'"

"Whatever God's deal was, as a forensic scene, it was incredibly chaotic. At least the sheriff knew where he was goin'. He recognized shit when he saw it, even without a DNA kit."

362

These Beans Have Too Much Salt

Most of the men had been present during Harper's speech. There seemed to be no mystery as to who was the avenger. The sheriff knew too, or thought he did. They all shared enough of the same values to know a man does not buy clothes for a little girl who is not his own, any more than a parent doesn't let anyone harm his child if he can do something about it. Protecting one of our own seemed like the natural order of things and not one of the men was willing to denounce the assassin. No, not one. They all thought it could have been their daughters, like it could have been their wagon, their furs, themselves. Even Swaily's oldest son, who had been in the crowd, would not talk. Perhaps one of his nebulous desires had found another issue. Someone had nevertheless, made the call to the Sheriff's office.

Once the body was packed up in the ambulance, the families housed temporarily in the high school gym, (or on the way out of there) and Leona sent to a psychiatric hospital in Jackson, the sheriff collected the guns and headed back to the courthouse.

At the end of the day, Jim was out of jail and had his bag packed for somewhere farther north where there were just as many rumors, but these had to do with someone else.

Mamere hadn't spoken with Mérite-Lajoie. She shook her head thinking of what her Mam had said and took her pipe out of her bag, "You can't git used to things anymore when you git too many words behind you."

These Beans Have Too Much Salt

That evening, for the families not yet flooded out, the familiar order of life seemed to settle back into place. On Saturdays, our mother and grandfather never missed *The Lawrence Welk Show*. Our family sat hypnotized watching in front of a black and white image as the television stars danced across the screen through the Champagne bubbles. I criticized what everyone was wearing, how they were made up, and imitated Germanic Welk's accent and English mistakes. A million summers before, in a parallel showing next to the television, I had dressed up like a Red Skelton hobo clown, had pretend conversations with Lawrence Welk, in contrasted apparel. Using temporarily someone else's clothes was something like pretending to be them. Making my sister and brothers laugh was fun, but I also liked to get something of the feel of what other lives were like. How could two people be so close, yet so unlike one another? I was thinking of Emmy.

"A one and a two… Now for the Lawrence Welk Show although I (Red Skelton) notice Lawrence looks very silly today in that pink coat. How can he get away with wearing his pajamas on TV? And just look at Norma Zimmer! She is too old for that red dress. And Tanya, she should put on more lipstick if she wants to marry Junior. Now for your accordion solo, either Myron or myself, can join you?"

I usually got out my grandfather's accordion and started to play. Papou was smiling proud, but my mother only had eyes for Lawrence. I think now that my imitations of Welk's accent were sort of an eye-opener for Papou who couldn't bring himself to respect anything German at that time. He laughed at me, but seemed like he became irritated all the sudden. Skizzum squealed with laughter at my improvised performances until she said she was going to pee in her pants. Once she even did. That day, Papou got up from his chair with disgust and left the room only to come back a minute later with beer, and a towel.

The Saturday after the flood began in our neighborhood, our family sat together in the living room and looked through our family albums, gazing dismally at the place reserved for little T-Leblanc. The accordion put away, Papou began to talk to our mother about the friendship between Welk and Governor Jimmie Davis. He told us to change the channel, calling both men inglorious names. We then watched Mr. Magoo. My mother went out on the porch to smoke a cigarette and watch the rain. I held the album on my knees and glued in a picture of a once well-loved lost kitten whose name no one could remember. In case Skizzum wanted to look at the photos, I didn't want her to see the empty space and to think what life might have been, had he survived. Under the photograph I sadly wrote: "Kitty Leblanc, our lost baby."

It is hard to say at this point if this disinformation was born from a white lie or a dirty one. Most all lies are dirty, except people, who aren't all dirty liars, don't realize it at first. In the days before her delivery, Skizzum went to see a fortuneteller, an old Creole woman in the quarters, who read cards. Hiram had helped to find the way at dusk and sat on the front steps waiting. The Tarot reader spoke

French, but hesitated. Skizzum tried to decipher her face. Was that fear she saw, some kind of mockery or ironic satisfaction? "Calme-toi," said the woman. "Der's mo' for laughin' 'bout in life dan a White girl in trouble wit' a Black boy. Nobody here be lookin' fo' vengeance bout dat neither. Der gotta be some kind of satisfyin' solution in de cards." She put her hand on Skizzum's shoulder trying to comfort her before taking place in a chair in front of a small table. Skizzum didn't want to give up her baby for adoption, but at the same time, she recognized she was too young to be a mother and she couldn't raise her child alone. Everyone said so, without even being aware of half the problem. Her impasse was mostly secret. "Idiot," Mama had yelled. Skizzum didn't respond. She knew she thought Harper was the father and figured, as a mother, she had some responsibility in the affair. Now she shunted the burden of being a parent with the insult she threw at my sister. "What are we goin' to do now?" she asked her, knowing she would not allow Skizzum to make the decision. She finally decided she would raise the baby as her own.

As the nurse placed her newborn daughter in her arms, she felt almost an instinct to run away to an unknown location taking the baby with her. But no one was forcing her to make a decision. She told me later her anxiety came from an inner charlatan as much as from our mother's announcement of a new sibling. A rabbit thinks experience costs too much if you get it from a trap and Skizzum was now at bay with her uncertainty, as much as with what she thought she knew. She had already given her child her best gift: her solid body. She had survived the difficult delivery with forceps and would without a doubt be fit for the life thrown in her direction. "I jest can't let my family know I let you go. I feel ashamed, not for what I did with Hiram, but for not holdin' on to you. I'm sorry to let you down so soon," she whispered in the infant's ear, holding back her tears as best as she could. "I won't know what happens to you after you go away with the lady. I feel bad because I know even if my family would love you once they got to know you, it would be impossible for us to stay in our neighborhood. Mama's idea wouldn't change anything. She don't control those men in the white sheets any more than the nosey neighbors. She cain't raise you like my sister, even if I could get over it. We would have to leave the state.

Skizzum cried for more than an hour when the services came and took her tiny girl to another floor. There another mother, a Colored-Cajun woman, was waiting to adopt. She had lost her baby at birth in the weeks before and the Mighty Arranger apparently lived in the Black neighborhood and knew of Skizzum's choice. On her daughter's birth certificate there was no name, only the mention: "still born". The doctor made sure no one would open the coffin and the funeral would be private, in the town of Evergreen where a child would be buried alongside the Robichauxs and other Cajuns who had lost their way to the family plot in New Orleans. Skizzum decided then that she would leave home at the end of the school year. I had so much grief that I couldn't get over it for years to come. Every time I walked by a cemetery, I thought of the Kitty who wasn't a cat and thought of her abandoned in a cemetery where people no longer had names. I was a grown woman when Skizzum told me the truth and felt all the gloomier because she couldn't tell me before then. As bleak as her situation was, she had needed this pregnancy to contemplate her submission to Harper and finally cast it aside. Pride was enough to reproach him for his betrayal, but not enough to realize he was incapable of loving or of cherishing another human. Without having her heart broken by this sacrifice, she wouldn't have been able to get on with her life, and even then, she chose a hard one.

Easter

All Mérite-Lajoie's life she had been waiting for one miracle after another. A miracle never came. In a country where self-made men are worshiped as heroes, she struggled to make a living and made one, although with a certain amount of derision. "I ain't a hero. I ain't even a man. Most of the time, that don't bother me. I never have been one of these women who could put an activity far ahead of herself, argue through each point, as planned, and stuff out any opposition, as soon as murmurs begin. Anticipation they called it. A slew of lies, mostly." Whatever the case, Mérite-Lajoie took care of her unpleasant trifles. One after another, she plowed through. "Since the passin' of Deux Ours, I prepared for complications, these were darn near always out of my hands, even before they came about."

As soon as the noise started, it would gather up into an uproar and get so loud she had to run off to keep from getting an earful. When she came back (she always did), there was more of it. An accumulation of dilemmas was nearly impossible for her to sort out and left her feeling powerless and depressed. On good days, her mind might clear. Suddenly she would be overcome with the feeling some new realm was about to open up and had come within her reach. Her affairs would seem at once orderly and submit to her understanding. She was about to see. Then, about as quickly, this vision would escape her, just like the goat or the worm. Again, she would be left empty-handed and would sometimes sink into whiskey.

Of forthright intelligence, though dispirited, Mérite-Lajoie now lacked the lighthearted imagination some had, and would no longer have understood my solutions to religious quandaries. At least they got me out of the thick and into a place I could fathom. While Mérite-Lajoie thought she was different from the likes of Harper-Swaily, who tied up his quagmires in a sack and threw them off the bridge, or chopped them up to pieces, abruptly, with her impulsivity, she realized she had done somewhat the same. Did she have any idea how much we all could have reacted in the same way?

"Was I a hater with a chip on my shoulder?" she asked, motioning for the glass of water. Her daughter was no block of wood serving on occasion for a shipwright to challenge her Master's authority, and Mérite-Lajoie had made no dare. "Did I not deliberately seek out Swaily to provoke him into battle?" questioned Mérite-Lajoie, as if pushing forth in a guitar solo, contemplating the weight of her crime. "I killed an unarmed man."

She had wondered if she should throw herself into the flames of justice. "Was what that man did to my daughter for a mother to bear witness to, or for God? Was the sin of that man greater than my own for killin' the culprit?" The Bible spoke of murder and revenge. "I allowed retribution to become my captain and bloodshed my command." Over and over these questions turned in her mind. She could not allow a man to desecrate her child and do nothing. But there had been no peace in doing it. I tried to interrupt her and at last tell her the truth.

"It was there. It flowed in my veins. I killed an unarmed man." Had there been any law against the outrages engendered by Swaily, why hadn't they prevented him from accomplishing his purpose?

"I obeyed the law. Why didn't I go to the sheriff before I loaded my shotgun?"

She hated her act. She wasn't a murderer. She wasn't even an ornery woman. How was it the noxious venom of one had infected the honest dignity of the other?

"I killed an unarmed man." What separated her from me if not her feelings of remorse? Didn't guilt make her as human as her passions? Was feeling guilty a virtue, or a disease? Hadn't I been the one to kill Harper? Although Mérite-Lajoie's long confinement abhorred me, for some reason I couldn't explain, I felt no longer so guilty. She had taken all the blame in every sense of the word.

That day, as she left the treehouse, Mérite-Lajoie felt her insides slosh from one side to the other, and her heart moved to her throat. On the side of the road, she heaved, ejecting the foul effrontery that had fallen upon her unwilling ears. Somber G minor sounds on timpani, and tenebrous, syncopated clouds as in a "March to the

Scaffold"[4], began to gather near her. On high ground, she parked her pickup on the edge of the woods and walked with a crate and a rope in hand. "We hang our criminals, be they our kin," she murmured. "I killed an unarmed man. I deserve to die." She made a slipknot and threw the rope over the tree limb and sank onto the ground soft with humus. "I was always against the death penalty. But I killed an unarmed man. Ain't I already dead?" The leaf rot moved under her, waiting; its mycelium singing out with its thin white low arms, willingly integrating any fallen newcomer.

"I killed an unarmed man. Justice would have me put to death. Where is my courage now? Where is the guiding light? Emptiness haunts me. I am worse than I ever believed. There is nothin'. No new hope. No new alliance. I lost myself. I killed an unarmed man. My soul has drowned, is bloated, and infested with disease." She was agitated now, tossing and turning in imperfect cadence. "Oh God, why won't you take me out! Give me to the muskrats and let them digest the filth that has entered my heart. I deserve no better. I killed an unarmed man." Mérite-Lajoie wove in and out of time on her deathbed. The loud drumroll and fanfare, she was hearing, came to a halt. In moments of perfect lucidity, she explained how her fugacity had come to an end.

In a moment of elation, she had called the sheriff's office. She had wanted to vouch for the shooting. Killing Harper had not felt like a crime. Not yet. She almost felt like a hero, although one who acted

---

[4] Berlioz, *Symphonie Fantastique,* Fourth Movement. 1830.

out of incontinence and rage. Once the anger had passed, she felt not quite proud when she drove up to the courthouse building and got out of her pickup. As a still determined woman, she had walked to the steps. With her ascension, with each step, she had found it harder and harder to move. Her legs had felt like lead. Midway, it was impossible to proceed. It was impossible for her to put one foot in front of the other. She had felt as if she was falling down an endless stairway, slipping on each step, unable to catch herself. Trembling in the warm rain, holding on to the stair rail as if she was groping around in the dark, Mérite-Lajoie had managed to turn in the opposite direction.

She didn't know why she had floundered. The weight of what she didn't know or understand made her knees feel weak. At what point could she have modified the course of history? Was she too, a fraud, believing to be a hero?

One of her customers, a farmer who raised rodeo horses on the side, had tipped his Stetson under his army poncho then stopped on the way up the steps. "You look like you've been rode hard and put up wet. Are you okay?" he asked. Mérite-Lajoie put her hand on her chest as if to indicate some weakness, managing a feeble smile. She took a step downward to avoid talking, nodding, unable to open her mouth. The man replied for her, comforting Mérite-Lajoie's agony without knowing, "a hard night birthing? Get some rest." He would have patted Mérite-Lajoie's shoulder, but the horse healer was already too far. The farmer continued towards the courthouse, like someone who wanted to file his land claim (the deed, not the goods) as an insurance against the flood. He did not know this time; the indifferent river would leave his foundations, with its soil, if not intact, at least on his property.

Caught in a mudslide, slipping with notes of an E-minor pentatonic scale, Mérite-Lajoie was now detached from these ordinary concerns. Her teeth had cemented. If with the blues, words were growing in her mind, and her mouth was filling with these, her soul remained petrified, and she could not articulate a sound.

The sheriff drove up and parked about thirty feet away. He got out of his car and started over towards Mérite-Lajoie, but noticed she had already put her truck into gear and was starting to back up. If Mérite-Lajoie saw him, she pretended not to see, pretended to hurry, trying to look unhurried. She turned onto the highway and drove this time to a landing near the river. She was unaware of the sheriff's thoughts; "She'll turn herself in when she's ready."

Hounded by an unconscious cause, her father's voice came to mind. After having disavowed him for not reacting to Swaily's misconduct, the memory of her Vieux putting his gun away, even while the Badjo took their furs, even while her sister strangled in the wagon, even while the rascal fled, came to her mind. Mérite-Lajoie put her face in her hands and her elbows on her knees and again, cried.

The morning light played through the wavering branches. The rain had paused, a hungry cloud refilling its paunch before spilling itself again on the lonely hunter. Mérite-Lajoie thought she saw her father, now camouflaged, without his shotgun, armed, not with reproof, but with concern, walking among the trees. The wind blew the budding limbs and shook water down on her uncovered head. She had forgotten her hat in the treehouse. Usually silent when he confronted his children with some misdemeanor, Bienvenu's reprobating gaze had been enough to procure the tears of confession. This look was absent now though Mérite-Lajoie remembered it and perceived, or thought she distinguished, her father's voice whispering through the breeze, echoing from ear to ear.

"You killed that scoundrel. *Tu l'as tué, c'est vrai. Il est mort.* The scoundrel's dead and won't bother you no more. You forgot about somethin', though. I am now under the oath of Heaven and I can tell you, you ain't finished with him yet. You thought you could arrange things yourself? You thought a man's life depended on you? A step more and you'd think you were a martyr! You can't take back what you've done!"

Harper was a fool; like the possum in the woods, in the end he delivered an ambiguous message. Once his alibi was made public, he acted as imprudently as the animal, boasting about his own destruction. But he had not killed. He had not wished for death, although he had perhaps wished for, longed for, even hoped for the theater of his own funeral. Wallowing in the wake of some obscure perfidy, finding pleasure in other men's confusion, undressing a child's innocent worship, he was doomed to prompt admonishment.

He had cherished this girl in a dark perverted way. He believed the source of the soul was enclosed in her body. Fearing the child would replace God in his heart, he could not act on his decision, and lost his mind. His death had not been the final act he had so aspired for, and he did not shine in its light. He would have preferred the realm of courtroom drama even with another prison term at hand. At least he would have had the occasion to unreel once more a tragi-comic delusional scene before a multitude of unknown spectators.

Mérite-Lajoie, alone that day with her thoughts, her lips trembling while facing her demons, her mouth still frozen, tried to speak in her defense. "I stopped him," she cried out, her voice full of tears. "He hurt her; he hurt us all with his filthy corruption. I have done some good. At least I saved our family." Was this an inkling of the bleeding of others, or was she trying to stop her heart from hemorrhaging? The more she rationalized, the more she bled. It was as if her own bodily substance was pouring out on the ground, leaving her weak, bringing her back again, encore and encore, to the smiling possum. "I had a revelation." Mérite-Lajoie began to reconstruct her meeting with Harper, and the dreams that followed.

"You still believe that? You can keep it for the court of men. But it don't do me no good. Why have I strived for most of my life to teach you *petiote* if it's to see you die on the scaffolds like my brother? You are better than he was. You are my daughter, my first born, and the best of us. Harper's atrocity wasn't about you. It never was. What was it I forgot to teach you?"

The wind spoke these words without hate. Her father would have been horrified by the violence of the scene between the two. Bienvenu had never sought revenge, despite all the wrongs. He had known unruly barroom brawls, (especially when called a bastard or a coonass), heated quarrels with his sons, desperate disputes with his wife, and the grievance of the death of a child, his child, dying at birth for lack of assistance. However, in spite of a nose that had become as crooked as a mountain road, he had always sought to escape unabashed cruelty or acrimonious ways. He even had a hard time killing an animal to feed his family, much less a man for all his sinister barbarisms. Once a fourteen-point buck stared at him for more than a minute before finally slipping into the protection of the trees. Bienvenu could not fire. As a soldier, he had seen too many deaths. He had been the cause of a few. There would be no trophy in killing. Bienvenu understood this fact in any language. One man could not deal out destiny like a deck of cards.

Why did Mérite-Lajoie come here to this place in these woods, near the flooded river, in the same spot her ancestors had debarked Up-the-Bayou after the hurricane had taken their homes? Did she come to persecute them with her questions, to transfer the burden of her guilt? Could she kill them now that they were already dead and prevent them from hearing of her demise? She could not answer, not even to herself. Death had seemed a solution to many of the problems she carried around with her. She had only thought of suicide but realized now, at least for an instant, she had been the unwilling scapegoat of those she had unconsciously wished dead.

Perhaps she could have found an answer, early on, before, before she had killed. Now her whole body was shaking, in fits. She tried, but could not stand up. She wavered, crashed against a tree before falling again, on her knees. She thought how fortunate the native Americans had been to find a world with predators capable to speed them to death when the time had come, when they were tired of living, or were guilty of crimes to themselves, to their forefathers and even to their enemies.

Mérite-Lajoie cried out, her self-blame turning into self-pity: "Why have you forsaken me." Was it blasphemous to speak to her father in this way? She did not want to be disrespectful. Perhaps she wasn't absorbed in her troubles; the kind soaked in pride. Her heart was drenched in tears. She listened, but there was no response.

From Shadow to Light

Once again, the branches shook water onto Mérite-Lajoie's bare head. The floodwaters were moving in on this last remaining dry ground. She found some solace as she watched a possum with several babies on its back as it struggled to climb a tree. This animal was so common in the Louisiana landscape; she could not kill them all or accuse them for what happened, although a shift in blame somehow makes one feel better. How many would survive the insensitivity of the flood? Could she find atonement in the endurance of other creatures? She couldn't know. She never would. She felt she had been contaminated by evil and would now have to accept the justice of her fellowmen.

In the filtered light between the trees, had she finally killed her hatred? She would have had to allow her child to suffer injustice before she could know. Could she admit her enmity for Harper-Swaily was an animosity for her fellowmen, for her Vieux, for God even? "Sometimes you just can't git used to what you've done," she cried out loud to her deceased father. She felt no longer so lost to herself, but could not find it in her soul to pardon Swaily. Even with a kind of divine injustice or imbalance, the mother possum's scramble for life encouraged her to fight for her own. The possum wouldn't pretend to be dead with the younger generation's lives at stake. Mérite-Lajoie could live with that. She could assume responsibility, but she wasn't ready to accept all of the guilt. With the storm, cruelty swayed away from its center of balance. The moral sentiment of local society was offended and would seek condemnation to meet *Newton's Third Law* and call it Justice. Harper had been a respected man for those who had not known him intimately.

In the late morning hours, Mérite-Lajoie came back to Helena Addition. She looked out at the rusted farm equipment that now littered the grounds behind the gin. Mérite-Lajoie had noticed once proud International Harvesters that had been replaced not so very long ago. These cotton pickers (the machines, not the people), looked like huge rust-red insects with partially deployed wings creeping out of weed cocoons. Thick brambles covered the tractors. They were now parked over the other cotton pickers, all former slaves. The few tombstones there were cracked and sunken. The equipment had been abandoned there, as the tombs had been. The new Farm Outlet had to make room for its new machines, and the cemetery was taken for an empty parking lot.

Here, it was said the profaned workers were not happy with their resting place and could be heard, and sometimes seen, at night protesting outside the gin guardian's door. The watchman stayed on. These crimes of neglect had been committed long before he was stationed there. Mérite-Lajoie considered the ghosts of the enslaved Blacks once again: "They're wasting their time. No one listened to them around here while they were alive. Now they be dead and buried, how could they protect their graves from desecration?"

She pondered that even a cemetery could reflect such changes in the workforce, and even more, of the devilish schemes of men.

Sinister measures of piercing supernatural sounds lured Mérite-Lajoie towards the vandalized and forgotten tombs. "Flesh! Flesh!" cried the *ignis fatuus* chorus behind the Southern utopian's ghost whose shadow loomed still heavily over the graves. "You cannot slumber here! This paradise was never yours!" wailed the once enslaved. A roving, quivering wind echoed over exhaust pipes and empty oil bassoons. "Money! Money! Lots of dough! Lots of dough! *Crème de cacao*! We will not let you go!" Howled sardonically the Beelzebub of the rusted industrialized laborers. Mérite-Lajoie thought she saw eyes flickering among their metal skeletons. A bolt of lightning crashed down on the gin making her start and she was convinced she heard the monster chuckling, "Money! Laugh at me! You've got no soul to free! Make her pay! Make her pay! You'll dance for us this day!" Mérite-Lajoie wheeled away, wondering if the bodies of these machines would ever find rest under the alien sky where they would be taken apart and reused. The enslaved people had not. Their souls chanted, while a lot of McCormick Deering scythes and clamps remained suspended and chained together, repeating burlesque rhythmic movements in the wind. The snickering horn continued. Mérite-Lajoie trembled now with fear. She began sloshing through the water as fast as she could; thinking she heard the chorus screaming, "Let us go! Let us go!" -- mixed with a familiar, haunting, pounding litany of "Laisser les bons temps rouler[5]," deformed now in a mi B-flat whistling through the gin's cracks.

---

[5] Acadian expression: « Let the good times roll. »

A frenetic whirlwind blasted through the abandoned farm equipment causing Mérite-Lajoie to lose her balance and fall headlong into the greasy water. Wrestling this time with an invisible catfish, she almost could not tell if the hammering sound she heard, came from inside her chest or from the murk, where incandescent chemical residues gleamed at her like the *silure's* eyes. Her heart throbbing, she forced herself to her feet and thought she perceived a funeral bell ring out solemnly in the dark, when suddenly, a *senza stringendo* of white clashing sounds resonated grotesquely through the gin siding. The familiar horror, whose presence she had often felt in moments of solitude, found its name at last. And as the orchestra screamed, sounding like a demoniac musical movement, the Prince of Darkness cachinnated perversely, "But we will not you go!"

Did she deserve this torture? Did she cherish her terror and rely on it in some remote way? I tried several times to explain how I hid in the church and had fired my rifle that day. She nodded then shook her head. "Don't go there, Bee. This is mine. I killed Harper." She knew all along I had been there. She managed to glare at me then shifted halfway on her side to indicate a scar on her arm. I had missed Harper, but my bullet had grazed her instead! My relief came with conflicting colors.

Then, she plunged on, pushing away decisively any accumulating commotion. Chasing her fear, Mérite-Lajoie hung her mind once more on the descendants of the first occupants of the layered cemetery. They had not deserved the hell that would be brought upon them. Beyond the neighborhoods, across the lake, and beyond the forest, the Mississippi rolled on proudly. Its thick prevailing deep waters were as indifferent to the struggling endeavors of the people in the ghettos as it was to the animals in the nearby forests.

Mérite-Lajoie waded through the water to her home. A large percolating cinnamon-colored roux was floating near her front steps. Looking closer, because it was a relief to think of something other than murder or rusting cemetery ghouls, she found the conglomerate to be an army of fire ants crawling over one another in what appeared to be an angry pursuit of survival, similar to the one that founded this country and left so many stranded on islands of retribution. Their community could float about for weeks on their own until they found dry ground. She pushed them away with a branch. Seeing her horses nod in their pasture, she winced at the thought that the ants might happen upon the trapped animals before the floodwaters receded. She left the gate open to allow them to escape to higher ground. They wouldn't go far. Gautier would tend to them until her brothers returned.

She heaved open her front door and walked in, sending water curling over her couch and the relax-armchair where Deux Ours had so often napped. It was soaked. Beside it on a small table was a framed photo of her family standing with Harper at Emmy's birthday picnic party. The phone service was still out of order and she could not reach the hospital. Her church, Saint Martin de Tours, came to mind. They would be having Easter Mass now. Still looking at the photo, and chasing its memory, she remembered a

Sunday of long ago, with her parents and brothers together on the family pew. Feeling as if she had crossed the tenebrous floods of undocumented crime, she made the decision to turn herself in to the sheriff. She picked up the photo. Remembering her question about the Confederate's flags, she decided souvenirs are precious after all. Instead of helping you remember, they make you forget. They send you off on a well-chartered path of familiar tales instead of leaving you dangling, stranded like after a hurricane, without words, startled, and naked between the branches of a cypress tree.

Without further elaboration, she put the framed memory into her pocket. Preoccupied by the future of her family in a changing world, she had not thought about the penitentiary; yet she was on her feet. She waded back to her 1952 Chevy Pickup, bought new when Emmy was born. It had been a good year without many disillusions. Thinking of her daughter and remembering her out-stretched arms, in her mind, she lifted her and helped her over the flood. She would be spared, at least for now. She would find the strength to do what had to be done; to do what she thought was best for the rest of the community, come what would for her. Opening her armoire, she found her only dress, almost unworn and still dry, and she felt comfort in the idea that she would be presentable to her judges.

Before starting up the motor for her last drive, she joined her hands in silent prayer, shutting off the remaining grief reeling around her and imagining again for an instant she had found the truth; she forgot once more that people must satisfy themselves with what they can never completely know. Her restlessness gave way to new tranquility. A slight smile moved across her face. There is always a calm after a storm.

Mérite-Lajoie rummaged in her pocket and took the photo back into her hands, looked at it, and without asking herself why, flung it into the flood. The flattened ship turned around, stalling, caught by a small eddy; the frozen glass flickering over its would-be captain's eyes. Before it sank into the muck, Harper's smile seemed to recompose an instant into a crooked grin, almost a sneer. Mérite-Lajoie imagined a faint expression of anxiety on his face, as he turned yellow and capsized with another's family.

With these torn sentiments she drudged again through the muddy water of her past to tell me these last details of her story. Her one true enemy had been herself. Without words her language could speak, she prayed in unanswered questions. "How was it so many preachers, and even possums, spoke of death and damnation? All I wanted was life. To go on with what was left of my own, I forgot to try to set things straight. I forgot to forgive him. I couldn't at the time. I just couldn't. I spent more time and effort hatin' him than takin care of my daughter."

"Maybe Harper needed God more than the rest of us? Maybe he thought he could justify everything he did in the name of God?" With her questions unresolved, and within her fleeting mind, the old Cajun woman back-paddled her pirogue, and hearing a far-off guitar riff kick in, she turned around, and traveled Up-the-River, then on to Ferriday. In her inner ear, a piercing voice mounting in a sinister crescendo reminded her she must complete her journey. She found the graveyard where Harper was buried and went to the Funeral Home. "There are a couple more favors I need to ask of you, Bee. Damn that Harper. Nobody bought him a headstone! He's been comin' back to haunt me all these years cause he ain't tied up good and tight with the identity he wanted. There's only a rottin' nameplate with the name of that scoundrel, Swaily, and all that it meant to him on it, all that he had tried to escape!"

Mérite-Lajoie asked me to take some money out of her meager account and set things right for her. This small tribute was a lot for her. It was her way of asking for forgiveness, even absolving the scoundrel Swaily evidently had been, and for her own neglect, which she now felt, had contributed to the attack on her daughter. When we were done, she knew she had at last completed her task.

Thinking of the old salt covered animal she laughed at herself as she prepared for her last voyage. She shook her head. "What a con artist! What a weird sacrificial lamb! Maybe he didn't die after all and it was he who was insultin' me from the briars all these years. I'll tell you what though; I should have gone fishin' instead."

After Mérite-Lajoie's funeral, I called Emmy and told her I would be coming by with a letter from her mother. She lived in another house, but had never moved on. Before going to her home, I drove to the outskirts of Ferriday, at the piece of the swamp where her parents had founded their trailer park. The families had all moved after the shooting, when the flood began. In their place, there was a new Sportsman's Campground where people would come, fish, and have fun from the piers on weekends, ignorant of the plight of the Cajuns who had lived there years before.

I wandered around a minute or two before I saw the crawfish-praying-rhythm-flapping flag, still feebly flying overhead. The only letters left of the once bold green lettered motto, *AUSSI INENEBRANLABLE QUE L'ECREVISE,* read: E…N…V…I…E, (*en vie* as in ALIVE or *envie,* as in DESIRE, depending on how the wind blew, yet both coherent in French). Translated into English, the spelling would not work; the banderol would show its disreputable character, forgetful of its pride; envy is probably what constitutes the fundament of any flag. Like people, they usually hide their ambiguous nature, flaunting only their culture or cuisine, until their threads are made bare and their souls, unmade.

Mérite-Lajoie had feared talk more than she had heard of it. What she thought went on behind the curtains, but had disdained to act upon, boiled over into her distinctively decorated living room when the sheriff only hinted of the crime. Neither a rebel, nor faithful to her God, she had suffered much from her incomprehension of the chains of the past. In the end, her greatest desire was to deliver her community from the throes of passion as well as from the successive waves of moral hesitation she felt had been the cause of her downfall. "I didn't want to be forgiven for killin' Harper." Mérite-Lajoie looked at me with the sadness and resolve of admission. "I just wanted to be rid of him and go home. I had forgotten I robbed not only his life, but also his freedom to amend for his ways." Locked behind the bars of presumption and vindication, I realized, I, too, had been a prisoner of my own hatred and jealousy.

After having exposed the awfulness and the pain on all parts, we could both have a glance of the truth. Mérite-Lajoie's soulful guitar took off one last time in a riff I could not hear as she issued her last requests. "Let my family be freed", she chanted as she strummed over a loud accordion pattern that was drumming away in her mind. "I had that stuff about honor and justice all wrong. It only led to violence and murder, instead of courage and deliverance." In addition to this composition, she asked that I dispose of the emblem to which they had all pledged.

Back-paddling deeper and deeper into Mérite-Lajoie's muddled bog, I found that harsh judgment of others is soaked with personal guilt and gossip's alliances. In such circumstances, it doesn't take long for one to outbid the other, forgetting that the severity of one's judgments is more of a reflection on the judge than it is of the criminal. In the long run, each one is condemned to suffer. I thought about Mérite-Lajoie, my grandfather, my parents, and all the other Cajuns on whom the storm had taken its toll. Although I fear, while I remember its gusts turning us into playthings, I realize with this memory how precious life is. As I lowered the flag and fumbled the banner I took into my hands, the remaining textile crumbled, and the weave fell apart. A salty tear of relief rolled down my cheek while my heart followed the cantankerous crawfish, skedaddling free in a backward two-step to its home in the bayou.

I don't know if I'm done; in fact, you never stop doing and undoing; but if you live without praise or disgrace, without standing for your cause, your dreams will unravel and yourself might, as well. I got in my car and dropped off the package at Emmy's, thinking it might somehow help her make peace with the past. She might not want to open it alone. I remembered suddenly, that she is still the girl who could charm snakes. Surely, she can look into these pages? Before taking a seat behind the wheel I noticed a forgotten scrap of paper that twirled to the ground like a maple whirly-bird startled from its rest. On it I had scribbled a wrinkled song, singing of my new resolve.

"I sense sometimes the bits and pieces of me that have fluttered away,
Like pages torn from a well-loved book, thrown out among the waves. Like small children's boats they struggle, hurdling over mass and muddle,
Until a larger swell SOGS[6] them, stepping over dusk and dell.
Yet these odd bits of fleeting fantasies become sometimes-vain mysteries, Cladding themselves with deformed mirrors,
Reflecting both opinion and shame.

---

[6] SOGS, a nautical term, acronym for *Speed Over Ground*, plural in order to create a neologism or verb/play on words. The children or *Sons of God*, create waves for their small boats, as if they were gods themselves.

These Beans Have Too Much Salt

These waltzes cannot last forever; some hold on, some sail away."

While honoring my promise to Mérite-Lajoie I have become aware of the sort of madness that encumbered Harper. A swaggering braggart, always ready to run or to take a beating, he wasn't less mean for all his peculiarities. His blood ran cold, and mine with it. My shot came close to causing the death a loved one. But, had it not been for Mérite-Lajoie, someone else would have shot him, again. That day, it could have been me. And yet, now I wonder if killing him to extract some sort of vengeance was not kind of like hanging Mary the Elephant for crushing her trainer's head in the ring performance by the *Spark's World-Famous Circus Show* one September evening in 1916. Witnesses said this hired hobo had prodded her, without knowing much about Mary's disposition. There is no grace in killing, whatever the reason.

Mérite-Lajoie and I no longer exclude Harper from humanity for his part of blame, although we decided that his place was the one we had unhappily occupied for so long. This is what happens when you take justice into your own hands. You exchange costumes with those who have harmed you and you adopt their ways. You wind up looking like them too, and smile with their ugly face. You forget about the others, and you take to old cheap tricks, pretending you have reasons, pretending they are sick.

Emmy was the first concerned and we had forgotten all about her. Harper committed a crime, perhaps many crimes, but finally, we all pulled the trigger and we all contributed to the ensuing violence.

These Beans Have Too Much Salt

We came to this understanding even while we grieved; and in grieving; we made our peace with him, and with ourselves. We issued our complaints, then together, a constant lulling sound. A rhythm, a rock; these can make melodies if thrown out into the ebb and flow. Perhaps lapidating our stagnant righteous waters with this song will help our families to abandon our desires for retribution and allow us to reconcile our past. Harper believed he could achieve perfection and truth, if he only could find the source. He felt he didn't need the assistance of another soul. Broken templates, crippled incantations---only edges of real beings filled his existence, blocking out every single living light other than his own. Oh, how we need each other to remain human!

Driving back through town, I ran over a water moccasin, migrating from one-water hole to the next. Like Mérite-Lajoie, like most of us Cajuns, I suppose, I backed up the car and looked out the window, watching it unwind and recoil; its metallic luster swiftly waning, its dazzling bronze eyes all-at-once dull, poisoned with its own venom. Yet, it was only a snake. After having taken one last look at the creature, and at Ferriday, I drove out of town and to St. Gabriel, resignation in hand.

The End
Barbara Bonneau
May 2015

Acknowledgements

First and foremost, I want to thank my family for their precious encouragements and patience over the years, and in particular, Cindy Bonneau Middleton and Alison McMillin. My heartfelt thanks equally to Mathilde Halcomb, Michelle McMillin, Keith Ott, Blanca Valbuena, Jackie Mitchell, Rob Keuhnle, and Louis Bourgeois for their patient reading, encouragements and/or advice in preparing this novel. Thanks to Jill Harp, for her research about Louisiana prison conditions. Applauses to Bashar Lulua for his musical expertise and advise on finding and using classical music in writing. A special tribute to my friend, Alain Lacombe, who has recently left this informal reading circle for higher realms, but provided his reassuring advice for French translations. Thanks to many Louisiana Cajuns, and Acadians everywhere, who, with their story-telling talents, have provided me with a life of memorable tales to share. Thanks to Elodie Pritchartt for her *Watermelon Possum Song*. All mistakes must be attributed to me.

About the author

Barbara Bonneau has published professional articles and two books about body image and language. *These Beans Have Too Much Salt* is her first completed novel.

Barbara Bonneau spent most of her youth in Ferriday, Louisiana and attended both Louisiana State University and The University of Texas. She obtained a doctorate degree in psychopathology from the Université de Paris Cité in 2001, and practices today as a psychologist for children with special needs. She currently shares her time between France and Austin, Texas.

About the novel

These Beans Have Too Much Salt was created in 2005 under another name: *Sweetbriar*, then *Sweetbriar Cajun*, focalizing especially on the question of identity for displaced peoples. This idea collided with another when I started working on the question of destructive cults. The cult leader in my story was inspired by cults active today as well as loosely inspired by Jim Jones of the "People's Temple". The subtropical climate of Louisiana provides a similar backdrop for this cult where nine hundred people committed mass suicide at the command of their cult leader. I wondered what would happen if someone had said "no", well before the fatal day, but also thought about the consequences of any radical act engaged by a desperate person, acting alone.

The crimes committed by the cult are real in the sense that crimes of this nature occur, both in, and outside of cults.

Much of what I learned about brainwashing and thought reform came from the books of Robert Lifton, Janja Lalich, and Steven Hassan, but also conferences and readings of books and articles by Matthew Feldman, Chip Berlet, Dennis King and Yves Messer. Another part came from the personal experience of trying to help a cult member.

These Beans Have Too Much Salt

The name: *These Beans Have Too Much Salt*, is inspired by a common Cajun dish, "Red beans and rice", an expression about telling the truth: "spill the beans", and a 1930's song: "Ces Haricots sont pas sales," with the pronunciation of "ces haricots" much like the name for a branch of Cajun or Creole music now known as *Zydeco*. "Ces Haricots sont pas sales," translated in English would be: "These Beans Have No Salt", meaning locally, I have no spicy news for you. *These Beans Have Too Much Salt* is, on the other hand, takes into account what happens there is too much gossip. Victims tend to isolate themselves within their community, in other words when the beans are saturated with salt, or the dish isn't edible at all.

These Beans Have Too Much Salt was first shared among friends, transferred from one person to another for correction, from July 2015. Parts were posted on a professional Facebook page in May 2016. During this period, the principal characters and the text were modified. The novel was posted online. A trace remains of this publication in the form of photos of the first chapter. During part of this period, the narration changed and the location of the chapters were changed. One of the main characters became a woman and changed names. Others were recombined. The decision was made to use the genuine names of some of the places and institutions, instead of fictious ones. Songs have been added/ or modified.

The cover is an original enhanced photo of a common Louisiana animal, the possum, stranded in the middle of a flood.

These Beans Have Too Much Salt

These Beans Have Too Much Salt is an entire work of fiction. It was not enhanced by any artificial means. Any references to real people, living or dead, real events, businesses, organizations, political movements, churches, and localities are intended only to give the fiction a sense of reality and authenticity. All names, characters and incidents are either the product of the author's imagination or are used fictitiously, and their resemblance, if any, to real-life counterparts is entirely coincidental.

The work here is entirely fictive, however, it was essential for me to understand, as an adult, how evangelistic style preaching and music, with a charismatic speaker, could federate an audience. This talent, as well as many others, could be used in the closed environment of a cult, to gain control over every aspect of the member's lives. Real life Evangelist preachers and political figures were viewed to this effect. Sermons were taken out of context and deformed for this work of fiction, which is about a destructive cult involving families with children, and not about a particular religion. To add a touch of reality to the novel, extracts of Evangelist style preaching from Ferriday's own Jimmy Swaggart were used. Examples of Mr. Swaggart's talents can be easily viewed on Youtube. and read about in: *Swaggart, The Unauthorized Biography*, by Ann Rowe Seaman. Aimee Semple McPherson, a 1930's female Pentecostal radio and Evangelist preacher, equally inspired some of the sermons. All of these religious services were taken out of context and deformed for the novel, and not intended to be offensive to anyone from either of these congregations.

These Beans Have Too Much Salt

Ebook Edition September 2016© Barbara Bonneau 2016
978-0-9884598-1-6
Words in the Eye
Paperback
978-0-9884598-2-3

www.ingramcontent.com/pod-product-compliance
Lightning Source LLC
Chambersburg PA
CBHW060221030726
47499CB00004B/1133